An Invitation to Seduction

LORRAINE HEATH

AN INVITATION TO SEDUCTION

AVON BOOKS
An Imprint of HarperCollinsPublishers

AVON BOOKS
An Imprint of HarperCollins*Publishers*
10 East 53rd Street
New York, New York 10022-5299

Copyright © 2004 by Jan Nowasky
ISBN: 0-7394-4331-3

Avon Trademark Reg. U.S. Pat. Off. and in Other Countries, Marca Registrada, Hecho en U.S.A.
HarperCollins® is a registered trademark of HarperCollins Publishers Inc.

Printed in the U.S.A.

It is the nature and folly of youth not to fully appreciate the gifts we're given until it is often too late to appropriately thank the giver.

To the teachers who once taught English, Creative Writing, and journalism at Angleton Senior High School, who gave me an appreciation for the written word, who inspired and encouraged me to reach beyond the limits of my small world, to explore endless possibilities, and to believe in my dreams, I owe a debt that I can never truly repay.

With my sincerest gratitude,
I dedicate this book to:

Marie Adamson
Mrs. Gene Meier
Dan Chaney
Sarah Kelso
Merle Wilson
Linda Winder

Chapter 1

The Cornish Coast
May 1881

He had the look of danger about him.

Kitty Robertson recognized it the moment she spotted him, standing alone on the rocky shore, gazing out to sea, toward the horizon, as though he were daring the sun to rise.

Or perhaps he was commanding it not to.

Because its brightness would surely reveal what the dawn shadows were presently hiding, what had immediately captured her breath and her attention when she'd clambered over the rocks, hoping for a bit of isolated seashore: his perfect, naked form standing proud as though he had been carved from the very boulders on which he stood.

He was truly magnificent. It took every bit of willpower she possessed to stay rooted exactly where she was when she desperately wanted to cross the short distance that separated them and touch him. Trail her fingers over those sculpted muscles that were burning bronze as the sun pushed back the last remnants of night.

She'd never seen anything so glorious—except in that secret, dark corner of her mind where lustful thoughts tempted her with wickedness, shamed her with their clarity. She knew a lady of her upbringing shouldn't harbor such vivid, carnal images—much less crave the sight of them. And yet she did. Whenever her mind had occasion to drift, it was lured toward perilous thoughts that threatened her purity.

And that was the very reason that this man was so extremely dangerous. Because he embodied every sinful fantasy that she'd ever dared to dream.

As the morning's light faded from gray, she could see that the thick, black strands of his hair were too heavy with dampness to move much with the breeze that wafted in across the sea. He'd been swimming no doubt, and she marveled that he wasn't shivering. The waters off the coast of England were cold, not nearly as welcoming as the warm currents that washed in off the Texas coast in summer.

She'd often swum in the Gulf of Mexico, had actually been contemplating a quick dip into these chilly waters.

Until she'd happened upon Poseidon here. The man did truly resemble a god. From the top of his head, along the entire length of his long torso and longer legs, down to his rounded heels. As unacceptable as it was, she wished he'd turn so she might glimpse a full view of him.

A decent woman would have averted her gaze immediately upon spying him; she wouldn't have ducked back and prayed that she wouldn't be sighted while she leisurely took her fill of him, cataloging each dip and curve and flat plane that had come together to create such perfection.

Unexpectedly, he twisted and crouched, to retrieve his clothing she realized at the exact moment that his gaze fell on her, holding her captive as easily as his lean body had only moments before. He seemed slightly startled, not overly alarmed, more curious than anything else. And she realized the sun that had so clearly revealed him was now also exposing her.

She spun on her heel, lifted her skirts, and darted back the way she'd come, scampering over the rocks until they gave way to the pebble-and-sand shore. She broke into a full run, the wind whipping her hair in her face, pressing her skirt against her legs. She ran until she reached the path she'd followed to the shore. Ran until she reached a less desolate area, where her passing would no longer be marked. When the brush thickened, she found a place where she could lie on the cool grass unobserved. She curled into a tight ball, wrapped her arms closely around herself, and wept.

Wept because she was as wicked as the woman who had given birth to her without the benefit of marriage. Wept because no matter how hard she tried, she never was as pure as the woman who had raised her.

Wept because her body was hot with lust, and she feared a time would come when the lust would consume her.

Richard Stanbury, the sixth Duke of Weddington, pressed a light kiss to the papery-thin cheek the duchess had turned up toward him as soon as he'd entered the dining room. "Good morning, Mother. You're up early."

"Not nearly as early as you apparently."

Deigning to ignore the tone of chastisement in her voice, he walked to the sideboard and exhibited unparalleled interest in loading his plate with the varied offerings. He was always starving after an early-morning swim. Starving and invigorated.

He was especially invigorated this morning after catching sight of the siren who'd been watching him from behind a massive boulder. He'd wanted to follow her, but he'd hardly been in a state to do so, and by the time he'd thrown on his clothes, she'd disappeared. Not that his damp and rumpled appearance would have impressed her or caused her not to fear him. Still, it might have been worth the effort and the risk. He was trying to determine whether he should be embarrassed, intrigued, or merely amused by the fact he'd been caught— quite unawares and obviously naked—by the young woman.

He sat at his place at the head of the table, set down his plate, and took a sip of the tea that the footman had already prepared and sweetened to his liking.

"I'm not quite certain it's seemly for you to be going out at dawn," his mother said.

"It would be more unseemly should I be arriving home at dawn, I should think."

His mother harrumphed. Deducing that he'd expertly put an end to that avenue of conversation, he enjoyed his first bite of poached egg before opening *The Times,* which his butler had dutifully ironed and set at Richard's place before his arrival—exactly as it had been prepared for his father when he was alive. More than sixteen years had passed since Richard had easily, albeit guiltily, stepped into his father's shoes and inherited the daily rituals and traditions as well as the titles.

"Anne and I shall be leaving for London at the end of the week," his mother said.

"Jolly good for you," he responded distractedly, more interested in the country's news than the social gossip. He couldn't invest wisely if he didn't keep abreast of the latest inventions and industrial progress.

"You should join us in making the social rounds this year."

"I have far too many other important matters to attend to."

"Nothing can be more important than providing an heir to your titles."

Tightening his jaw, he lifted his gaze and met the challenge in his mother's eyes. "I am well aware of my responsibilities, Mother."

She seemed to shrink before him. "Oh, Richard, I'm sorry. I know you are. You've always been such a good lad—except in this one area. You are all of four-and-thirty. It's high time you took a wife." She leaned forward slightly, hope in her blue eyes. "Don't you think?"

Ah, the shrewd manipulator. She'd learned long ago that if she told him what to do, his stubborn nature would insist he stand strong in his defiance against her. Ask him politely, and he caved in like a castle built of sand when the waves washed over it.

"I shall consider it—"

"Splendid!"

"—next Season."

She pursed her lips in annoyance. "And whatever is wrong with considering it *this* Season?"

"I am not in the mood for the hunt."

"The hunt? Dear God, Richard, there will be no hunting to be done. The unmarried women will flock to you like sheep in need of a shepherd."

"And I daresay that I shall not find a single one of them suitable. I have devised a standard of specific amenable behaviors that I shall expect my duchess to exhibit, and I assure you, Mother, that *flocking* is not one of them."

Her mouth twitched, and he knew she was fighting to hold back her smile. She couldn't properly chastise him if she was laughing.

"By flocking, I simply meant to imply enthusiasm. Surely you want a vibrant woman."

Vibrant? Most assuredly. He thought of the young lady he'd sighted that morning. She'd been dressed quite plainly, but her attire could have been due to the early hour. Surely she'd not expected to encounter anyone before dawn had welcomed the day.

Her hair had drawn his eyes to her: a brilliant red that rivaled the morning sun with its radiance. The sea breeze had toyed with it, whipping loose strands around her face and shoulders, and an image of her writhing on satin sheets had immediately filled his mind. His lower extremity had quickly hardened. Another reason—besides the lack of clothing—that he'd been unable to give chase. It had been a long while since he'd reacted so strongly to a woman, a reaction more mysterious because he'd been too far away to acquire a distinct impression of her features. A pity that.

He turned his gaze back to the newspaper, but his attention was not drawn to the words, rather it was still trying to make sense of his reaction to the woman. She was petite, slender of form, but he'd gained none of the details he usually required in order to start his blood to boiling. He didn't know if her breasts would fit snugly within the palm of his hands or overflow. Were her hips and waist as narrow as they appeared, or narrower still, disguised by the drab cut of her dress? Would her eyes draw a man in or hold him at bay? With titian hair and fair skin, would she be powdered with freckles or as unblemished as freshly fallen snow?

Freckles he decided. A ghastly abundance of them since she'd obviously intended to greet the day without benefit of a hat or parasol to shield her face from the sun. Again he thought it a pity. He was not overly fond of freckles, was of the opinion that a woman should take more care with her appearance. Decidedly any woman he took as his duchess would do so. The image one projected to the world held more importance than one's true self—particularly within the circles in which he walked.

"Good morning, all!" Anne sang out as she strolled into the room, her skirts swishing over the polished wood.

Richard lifted his gaze in time to see his sister bend down and kiss their mother's cheek much as he had only moments earlier. She'd come late into his parents' lives, when they'd all but given up hope that another child would grace their family. Anne took great care with her appearance, so she was always a pleasure to behold, a ray of sunshine on the dreariest of days. Her husband would be a fortunate man, a fortunate man indeed.

"You seem in high spirits this morning," their mother said.

"I have no reason not to be. We shall be off to London in a few days, and it promises to be an extremely interesting Season."

She fairly skipped over to the sideboard. Even knowing that incessant babbling would soon begin, Richard gave his attention back to his newspaper and the assortment of food on his plate.

"What have you heard?" his mother asked with obvious curiosity.

The two of them could spend hours discussing matters that bored Richard to distraction. While they spoke words, he generally heard only a distant humming. He focused more intently on the article he was reading, as Anne took her place at the table.

"Before I tell you, I have to confess to being terribly upset with Richard."

"My goodness, what's he done now?" his mother asked.

"He kept a secret from us. I can't believe you didn't tell me about Farthingham."

The humming gave way to clarity, the words on the page blurred, and Richard's heart beat with such ferocity he heard the pounding between his ears. He slowly lowered his newspaper and looked at his sister. "How did you hear about him?"

"I received a letter from Prissy yesterday, and she told me all."

Lady Priscilla Norwood, the Earl of Blythemoore's daughter, and one of Anne's sillier friends. She had a tendency to begin and end each sentence with a bout of giggling that preyed on the hardiest of men's nerves.

"Farthingham is your best friend," Anne continued. "I should have been the one to start the juicy rumors. I can't believe you didn't tell me."

He shook his head, unable and unwilling to believe the secret was out. "It wasn't my place to tell anyone anything."

Then anger took hold. Anger for what his friend would endure, and for the absolute pleasure his sister seemed to be taking in it. Was she so naive that she failed to understand the impact this knowledge would have on his friend's life? "Besides, gossip is the domain of silly girls who have nothing better to do with their time," he remonstrated.

"I'm not a silly girl! I'll have you know that I'm a young lady—"

"Then behave like one for God's sake!" he roared, coming to his feet. "Can you not comprehend how this knowledge spread throughout England without his consent will ruin his life?"

"Why? Because she's American?"

Everything within him calmed, his heart slowed, his blood settled. Good God. Was it possible Anne was referring to another secret, a secret Richard had been unaware of, *didn't* know?

Narrowing his eyes, he gave his throat a sound clearing and demanded of his sister, "What exactly did Lady Priscilla say?"

"That rumors abound that Farthingham will soon announce his betrothal to an American heiress. That's all really. But you've never liked Americans, have you? Is that the reason you kept this bit of news to yourself?"

He'd kept it to himself because he hadn't known about it. A part of him couldn't fathom the notion that Farthingham was taking a wife. Another part of him understood that his longtime friend, by virtue of his rank and birth, had no choice. Richard sat, trying to appear calm, fighting not to reveal exactly how upset he'd become.

He slid his gaze to his mother, who was studying him as though he'd suddenly sprouted a second head. He gave his attention back to his sister, who, at nineteen, had not yet achieved the maturity to be aware of such shifting undercurrents.

"I'm not particularly fond of them, no. The ladies appear to be interested only in securing themselves a title without the benefit of a heritage that can ensure they appreciate exactly what it is they are attaining."

"I find them fascinating. They are so confident. And so beautiful. Have you ever seen an American lady who wasn't beautiful?"

"Truthfully, Anne, I've paid them little notice."

"That's because you avoid the social scene. I have heard some of these ladies have as many as two hundred evening gowns. Can you imagine that? I have only four."

"Then have another sewn," Richard suggested as he again picked up his newspaper and strove to give the articles his undivided devotion.

"Richard, you're missing the point entirely."

"The point, Anne, is that they are spoiled. They live a life of excess. Why would any woman need two hundred gowns? She wouldn't. That's ridiculous. They're ridiculous."

"Apparently Farthingham doesn't think so. *If* the rumors are true, which I'm fairly certain they must be since Prissy has a reputation for spreading reliable gossip."

"I find it inherently troublesome that you're concerned about the integrity of her reputation for spreading gossip when that very gossip has the potential to damage others' reputations. Do you not see the irony in your thinking?"

"I see that you're in a foul mood this morning. You've yet to take delight in a single comment I've made. Is your back troubling you?"

"No," he answered succinctly. The pain his back sometimes gave him was a reminder of his weakness and failures. It was not something he wished to acknowledge or discuss. "The spreading of gossip troubles me."

Anne wrinkled her nose at him and turned to her mother. "What do you think, Mama?"

"I agree with Richard that gossip is troubling." Her eyes sparkling, she leaned toward Anne. "However, it can also be a great deal of fun when it isn't malicious—as is true in this case, I would say. If the rumors surrounding Lord Farthingham are indeed true, however, I suspect he is more interested in what the lady can bring to the family coffers than the number of evening gowns in her wardrobe. And we may be grateful our family is not in a position that would force Richard to marry an American in order to secure our future."

"Oh, I do hope you're wrong on that point and that money is not the reason he's marrying her," Anne lamented. "I believe one should marry for love and love alone."

"That's because you're young," Richard said.

"And you're cynical."

"I'm pragmatic."

"Do you suppose Mother's right? Do you think it's her money that has drawn him to her?"

"Probably," he said quietly.

She pinched off a bit of muffin and popped it into her mouth. "A shame that. I've always liked Farthingham. For a while I thought he might even have an interest in me."

"I thought you wanted to marry for love," Richard reminded her.

"I do. But I think I could have fallen in love with him." She laughed lightly. "He's such fun. You didn't have a quarrel, did you? He hardly comes around anymore."

"Of course, we didn't quarrel. If Lady Priscilla's rumors are true, then I suspect he has been busy hunting for a suitable heiress. Courtship is a rather troublesome and time-consuming affair."

"As if you would know. Honestly, Richard, the mamas only express an interest in me because they think I'll bring you along. You could have your pick of any woman in London."

"I was telling him much the same thing earlier, my dear, before you came down for breakfast," his mother said.

"Am I to assume you two will plot against me this Season?" he asked.

"We could have a double wedding," Anne said. "Wouldn't that be fun?"

"I think you should have a day devoted exclusively to you."

She sipped her tea before looking askance at him. "Were you serious? May I have a new gown?"

He laughed. "Of course, you may have a new gown. Order a hundred if it will make you happy."

"But not two hundred?"

"We wouldn't want anyone to confuse you with an American, now would we?"

"That'll never happen. I haven't their poise."

"You're extremely graceful. Lovely. Enchanting. Any peer in England would be fortunate to catch your fancy."

"I'd rather you say any *man* in England."

"Any man then. What's the difference?"

"Not all men are peers."

Ah, an undercurrent. The little brat might indeed understand how they worked, because he was certainly aware of one threatening to work itself into an undertow. "Any man you marry will be a peer," he stated succinctly.

"Why?"

"Because your father was a duke, your mother is a duchess, and by God, you are worthy of a man with a title. To consider a common man is absurd."

"But what if I cannot love a man with a title?"

"You will learn to love him."

She released a shriek that damn near pierced his eardrums. "Oh! You are so archaic. You cannot force love; you cannot make it happen. It simply comes upon you, enfolds you in its warmth."

She had tears brimming in her eyes.

"Don't be distressed, Anne. I won't force you to marry a man you care nothing for."

"But neither will you allow me to marry a man I love if he is not titled."

He shook his head in frustration. "This is ludicrous. Why do you argue for marrying a commoner when not more than ten minutes ago you were lamenting your inadequate selection of gowns?" He held up a hand. "Two hundred gowns." He held up the other hand. "Commoner." He made a great show of trying to press his palms together and never letting them get within an inch of each other. "Conflicting desires. You cannot have both."

"There is no guarantee I'll acquire the gowns by marrying a peer. What if he is an impoverished lord like Farthingham?"

"Then I shall make a settlement on you for a yearly sum that will ensure you have the gowns."

"If I'm to have such a generous settlement, then it matters not whether he is a peer or a commoner."

"Of course, it matters. Why do you persist in arguing for your right to marry a commoner?"

"I persist in arguing for my right to marry for love!"

"Why upset yourself by debating falling in love with a commoner when it will not happen?"

"Because it very well might have happened already."

She jumped up from her chair, nearly toppling it over, and rushed from the room. As a general rule, he was not slow-witted, yet he stared after her, unable to make any sense of her words or what exactly had transpired.

"Well, that didn't go well at all, did it?" his mother asked, pressing her napkin to each corner of her mouth.

"Tell me she has not fallen in love with a commoner."

"To tell you that would be to lie to you, and to the best of my recollection, I have never lied to you."

Richard slumped back in his chair. He had an irrational urge to return to the shoreline, find the vixen he'd sighted that morning, grab her, and toss them both off a cliff into the sea. If he was going to drown, he didn't wish to drown alone.

"How could it have happened?" Richard asked, absolutely dumbfounded. "No gentleman has been calling."

"Perhaps courtship is not as complicated as you presume."

He snorted. "If she has spent no time in this man's company, then she is no doubt only experiencing infatuation. Probably in love with the color of his eyes or some such unimportant drivel." An image of red hair flashed before him, unsettling him. "Still, it might be best if you leave for London a bit sooner than you'd originally planned. Introduce her around—"

"She's been seen by everyone."

"Then she'll be seen again. I shall make inquiries and find someone to take her mind off this *person*." He shook his head. "I suppose I'll need to be a bit more involved this year."

His mother's face brightened. "And in so doing, perhaps you'll find someone for yourself. I mean, if Farthingham is marrying, then surely it is time for you."

"As you said, Farthingham is in need of funds. I am not."

She sighed. "Like Anne, at one time I thought he might ask for her hand in marriage."

"Be grateful he did not. He would not have made Anne happy. I cannot imagine him making any woman happy. He would try. I'll grant Farthingham that much. But I seriously doubt he would succeed."

"Perhaps you underestimate him."

"I think it most unlikely. But if he must marry, an American is probably an ideal solution for him. For her sake, I pray it *is* only his title she is after."

Because he knew Nicholas Glenville, the Marquess of Farthingham, better than most. Well enough to be trusted with his secret, a secret Richard knew would doom any marriage before vows were ever exchanged.

Chapter 2

Crouched on a boulder near the top of the heap that storms and nature had delivered without care over the centuries, hidden by the night's waning shadows, Richard waited in tense anticipation to see if the woman would show. He couldn't explain his behavior. He'd never sighted her before yesterday and had no reason to believe she would miraculously reappear today.

And yet here he was contemplating the possibility that perhaps she was at the shore on holiday. Or more likely, her employers were here on holiday—considering the plainness of her attire. He was unaccustomed to seeing anyone within this cove. His family had laid claim to it generations before, and the locals were well aware that trespassing was not allowed—another reason he'd deduced the woman must be a visitor in the area.

The possibility also existed that she was demented, not right in her mind, wandering about without benefit of chaperone until she'd stumbled on him, obviously taking her fill of him. He wondered if she'd liked what she'd seen, then chastised himself for caring.

As a general rule, he was not vain. Mainly because he found little about himself that lent itself well to vanity. Without the proper attire of a gentleman, he could easily be mistaken for a dockside worker or a fisherman, a laborer of some sort. He simply did not possess fine patrician features. Rather he looked as though his face had been hewn from rock, chiseled with care to be sure, but never finely sanded into perfection.

So the possibility existed that the lady—on getting a clearer inspection of him when he'd twisted around yesterday morning—had run, not because she'd been spotted—as he'd presumed—but because she hadn't found his face nearly as interesting as she had his bare back, buttocks, and thighs. For all he knew, she might not have given him another thought once she'd dashed off.

While he had been burdened with the inability to cease thinking of her, of the fiery shade of her hair that had so mimicked the sun. He couldn't help but believe she would be equally bold, daring, and passionate. Surely God would not give such an alluring feature to a docile woman. It would be cruelty in the extreme, when she so easily captured a man's attention.

No, indeed. If Darwin's theory of evolution were to be believed, then women such as she would have no choice but to populate the world with titian goddesses, and men would be powerless to prevent it. Indeed, they would be overjoyed to ensure it.

The more he pondered what he knew of her, the more conclusions he drew regarding what he did *not* know. He thought it highly unlikely that her features would be unflattering or that he would find anything about her unwelcoming. Within his gut, he'd experienced a sharp primal attraction the instant his gaze had fallen on her. He couldn't explain it, and yet neither could he deny its existence.

It was the solitary reason he now waited with the uncharacteristic patience of a saint for her arrival when he had no way of knowing if she would even appear. Madness. He was engaged in absolute madness. He should take his morning swim, be done with it, and return home.

Instead he waited as though he did not have businesses to oversee, estate managers to meet with, and preparations to be made for the journey to London. He'd become responsible for all five of his family's holdings when he was a mere eighteen, and the sea had savagely stolen his father from him. Richard had taken control with a firm hand and a vision his father had argued against, a vision that would serve to catapult them into the next century.

Modern advances were moving forward too rapidly. A man either embraced them or drowned. His father had drowned. Literally.

Richard fought back the images threatening to overcome him. He did not wish to deal with them now, preferred never to deal with them, but they lurked in the corners of his mind, waiting until he lowered his guard, until he was weakest, to pounce. They were the reason he seldom imbibed alcohol and seldom lay down to sleep unless he was completely exhausted. Only a strong, determined will could beat back the memories. And *that* will he had inherited from his father tenfold.

He forced his thoughts back to the woman who had deprived him of his morning swim. Not that it was too late to take one, but fate would no doubt deliver her as soon as he was too far out to return to shore in time to approach her.

He truly couldn't understand the overpowering desire to see her again. It wasn't so much that he wanted a woman as much as it was that he wanted *this* particular woman. And it was this realization that baffled him.

It had been some months since he'd had a mistress. Having parted on good terms with his last one, he'd been in no hurry to replace her. One did not choose a mistress carelessly for fear one would end up paying more dearly than one anticipated. Richard had a well-planned budget he allowed for such things: a residence, servants, clothing, and appropriate jeweled gifts from time to time. He did not require spontaneity in his life, detested it actually. He expected a mistress to be available when he called, to be reading the same books as he so they could discuss them, to enjoy the same sorts of entertainments he did—in bed and out.

He had a feeling the little sea urchin he'd spotted the day before would not make a good mistress, and oddly, he was not even considering her for the role. Which begged the question: Why was he hiding behind rocks, his gaze trained so intensely on the spot where she'd disappeared as to give him a headache?

She was disrupting his morning routine. He should get on with it, settle for a quick swim, and return home for breakfast and his other morning rituals. But even as he contemplated the foolishness of his quest for the elusive siren, he spotted her silhouette clambering over the rocks that served as a natural barrier to that portion of the coast. His heart slammed against his ribs with a force similar to that of the waves crashing against the shore during the worst of storms.

From his perch, he could discern that she approached with wariness, as though she'd hoped he wouldn't be there more than she'd hoped that he would be. A pity.

She reached the narrow ribbon of shoreline, set what appeared to be a blanket on the rocks, and gazed out at the dark sea that the sun had yet to unveil. Richard was halfway to his feet, ready to make his presence known, when she suddenly reached down, grabbed the hem of her dress, and brought it up over her head, in what he was certain to her had been quick movements but in what seemed to him to have taken forever to accomplish.

His heart very nearly stopped on the spot.

She was still silhouetted shadows, but what an incredible shadow. Her bared legs were slender and appeared longer than he'd expected they would, considering she did not appear to be at all tall. The hem of her dress fluttered up over her bottom, revealing its perfect rounded shape, and he could well imagine splaying his fingers over each cheek and pressing her hips against his . . . or coming up behind her and trailing his fingers over her narrow back and the delicate slope of her shoulders, of running his hands up and down her arms, folding them in front of her, and leaning her against him until not even the wind whispered between their bodies.

Her outlined perfection cast her dress onto the shore, before she shook her head, freeing her hair to the gentle ocean-scented breeze. She was more shadow than light, difficult once again to see details, but he was fairly certain her hair stopped short of curling over her bottom. He very much wanted to test his theory, to make his presence known, and discover what possessed this woman to display herself with such wild abandon.

A woman with absolutely no inhibitions—the possibilities astounded him. She would be molten passion beneath his fingers, raging desire beneath his rocking body.

She did not test the water with caution, with the dip of a toe, the tap of a heel, but simply rushed into it, splashing droplets around her. Then she released a tiny screech and disappeared beneath the dark surface.

Merciful heavens! Kitty was taken off guard by the frigid water. She'd known if she didn't plunge under immediately, she'd retreat to shore before she'd taken two strokes.

Breaking through to the surface, gulping in a great draught of air, she felt invigorated and alive. She thrived in water, sensed its healing value, loved the way she could immerse herself and allow her mind to wander. She'd known returning to the same spot carried the risk of encountering Poseidon, so she'd approached with caution, scanning the rocks and water for any sign of him, as grateful as she was disappointed that he wasn't there.

She'd had a strange, unsettling dream of him—of them—in the water, without clothes, their bodies intertwined. Only the water was warm, like that off the Texas coast. No, not warm like that. Hotter. Much hotter.

Awaking damp and breathing heavily, she'd thrown back the covers, scrambled out of bed, and rushed to the chair by the window, where she'd brought her feet up and pressed her bent knees against her chest. Chairs somehow always seemed safer, a place where lurid dreams couldn't take hold.

She'd been unable to go back to sleep, but at least awake she had more control over the images, could prevent them from rushing headlong—

Suddenly tentacles wound around her. Screaming, she bumped against a rock-hard wall, the heat of its warmth in direct contrast to the coolness of the water surrounding her.

"Don't fight me," a deep, resonant voice commanded. "You'll only drown."

Drowning might be a preferable outcome when compared against what his intentions might involve. Where had he come from? Was it Poseidon? And if so, was he as dangerous as she'd first surmised?

Her heart pounded against her ribs, against the arm with which he'd secured her against his body. Her breath came in short pants, her limbs shaking, her skin tingling. She grew colder than she thought it possible to be while still living. Her mind was unexpectedly cluttered with fear and anger and dread.

She'd scouted the area, thought she was alone, and now she was being hauled to shore by a stranger, a man, a strong man. She stopped fighting because she needed to conserve her strength, to make a concerted effort to escape as soon as her feet touched land.

The water grew shallow and with a sudden ungainly lurch before her feet had an opportunity to touch land, she found herself nestled in his arms as he strode toward the boulders.

"What sort of foolish woman are you?" he asked with a voice devoid of threat and more accurately reflecting true concern.

Before she could respond, he'd set her on a rock, wrapped her blanket around her, and was briskly rubbing her quaking body. Surely his weren't the actions of a man who intended harm.

And then he became even more dangerous, because she saw him more clearly now, the drenched strands of his dark hair falling across his brow. It *was* Poseidon.

He was still more shadow than light, the sun only just beginning to peer over the distant horizon. With a trembling hand, she touched his jaw. Bristly and rough. He'd not shaved recently.

He stilled, and with his hands no longer working to dry her, she was more frightened than ever. Not of him, but of herself, of her need to trail her fingers over his face, along his shoulders, across his chest. To have the heat from his body sear her fingertips. To touch in life what she'd only ever touched in forbidden dreams.

She could not explain what drew her to him. She only knew it was wrong, incredibly wrong, the musings of a wicked girl who could not escape her heritage.

Then his mouth was on hers, hotter than she believed possible, shooting sparks through her entire body, sending bursts of fire through her limbs, curling her toes. She plowed her fingers through his hair until they became entangled in his thick strands. His kiss—decidedly carnal, absolutely feral in its intensity—terrified her as much as it drew her in.

She'd never experienced anything like it in her entire life. With each bold sweep of his tongue, he enticed her into contemplating the merits of lying beneath him, of allowing his naked body to serve as her blanket, to feel his velvety flesh in place of the soft cotton.

His guttural groan echoed between them, competed with the sounds of the surf, wind, and birds. His hands tightened their hold on her arms, and she instinctively knew it was not she whom he wished to hold in place, but himself, because her hands wanted to roam over his flesh, wanted to touch all of him—surely he wished to do the same with her.

He broke free, his breathing harsh and rapid. She heard it from a great distance, as though she held seashells against her ears, the constant roar of the ocean replaced with the heavy echo of shuddering breaths.

"Who are you?" he rasped.

A woman on the verge of committing an unpardonable sin. Shaking her head vehemently, she drew the blanket more closely around herself and scooted back.

Slowly he got to his feet, walked to where she'd tossed her dress earlier, and picked it up. She watched as he made his way back toward her. She snatched the dress from him, and when he turned his back to her, she worked the simple clothing over her head, shoulders, and body as quickly as possible. Once again, she brought the blanket around her, because she suddenly felt in need of more adequate protection.

As though sensing her stillness, he turned and extended his hand. He wore no shirt, and she wondered if he'd discarded it before coming into the water. His wet trousers were tight, stretching across his thighs. His feet were bare, making it easier to walk over the rocks and sand, the intimacy of the discovery compounded by the fact that hers were as well.

She knew she was courting disaster, enticing ruin, but she could not deny his invitation any more than she could prevent her lungs from drawing in air. With a deep, shuddering sigh, she placed her hand in his, welcoming the slow curl of his long fingers over hers.

He pulled her up and led her to a spot where they were hidden from everything except the vast expanse of the sea that lay before them and the majesty of the rising sun glinting off the water. With her gaze on the horizon, she allowed her hand to remain in his, nestled between their bodies as though it belonged there, although she knew undoubtedly that it did not.

She sensed his watching her, and it was all she could do not to look at him, not to risk being ensnared by his gaze. He was dark and forbidden—which made him enticingly alluring.

"Why did you return here today?" he asked quietly.

Without the huskiness in his voice that had followed their kiss, he sounded cultured, refined. Nobility maybe. Or a servant in a wealthy household. No, she could not envision her sea king as answering to anyone other than himself. A businessman, perhaps. Like her father. An educated man. A man of wealth who had time for the leisurely pursuits of vacationing at the seaside.

Turning her head, she held his gaze and answered truthfully. "I don't know."

In the last remnants of dawn's shadows, she saw a corner of his mouth curl up.

"You're American," he stated, as though the notion had been inconceivable to him only moments before and was now somehow humorous.

Or perhaps he was simply confounded by the fact that they'd shared a searing kiss, and yet he knew none of the little details of her life—or even the important aspects for that matter.

"Texas," she offered softly with fond memories.

"I might have guessed. I detect a slight drawl."

A drawl which the finest tutors, abundant traveling, and her vigilant practicing had managed to all but erase. The woman who'd given birth to her was the daughter of a saloon keeper. She spoke with a voice that mimicked that of many cowboys: smoky and drawn-out, the endings of words cut off as though the slow pattern of her speech forced her to make up for it somehow. Her manner of talking had stood her in good stead when dealing with drunken cowboys or when she'd boldly trailed cattle north. But as in all things, Kitty wanted to be associated with the woman who had raised her, not the one who had borne her.

Madeline Robertson was genteel in nature and in actions. She always spoke and acted as a lady should, and Kitty strived to attain her perfection.

Only now she more closely resembled a hoyden, not a woman who had spent countless hours with a book balanced on top of her head while walking, sitting, rising, bending, and bowing. She'd curtsied before royalty, waltzed with a prince. Twice a year she visited Paris so Charles Worth could design her latest wardrobe, each piece always an exquisite work of art designed exclusively for her delicate frame, which he'd called a work of art in itself. He would be appalled to see the dress that hung on her damp body, a servant's castoff that Kitty had hoarded away and wore on occasions when she needed to escape from the demands of being a wealthy American's daughter.

"I thought you were drowning," he said. "I was coming to your rescue."

How ironic. In the water, she'd not needed rescuing, and now she did. She felt as though she were wading into uncharted oceans, that at any moment she'd have to acknowledge that she was out of her depth, in danger of drowning.

"I'm a strong swimmer," she said inanely. "I've swum the world over."

"Indeed. Where exactly?"

She angled her head. "Wherever I wanted."

"Alone and undetected?"

She smiled slightly. "Until today."

"Then I am grateful for today."

Holding her gaze, he lifted her hand and pressed a kiss to each of her knuckles, although *kiss* was too tame a word for his exploration. His lips enveloped, while his tongue stroked and tasted, sending dizzying sensations swirling through her. His gaze was as hot as his mouth.

"I shouldn't be here," she whispered, surprised by how breathless she sounded.

"Who are you?" he asked again.

Shaking her head, she averted her eyes, focusing on the horizon, stunned to see how much of the night the sun had pushed back.

Gently he angled her hand until her wrist was exposed, and he continued his subtle seduction. Her eyelids fluttered closed, and she imagined him taking this leisurely journey along the length of her entire body. Was this how the woman who had given birth to her had been lured into a scoundrel's arms: slowly, tenderly, with only a hint of passion revealed?

She drew her hand free of his hold and folded it up against her body, beneath her tingling breasts. He stirred to life sensations she'd never before felt.

Odd. When she'd danced with dozens of men, spoken with them, flirted with them, batted her eyelashes, and smiled becomingly. She'd done none of that with him, and yet there she was, drawn to him as the tide was drawn to the shore.

As he tucked strands of her hair behind her ear, a shiver shimmied through her, and she turned her attention back to him, realizing too late that he was closer than he'd been before, closer and more dangerous.

The sun had worked its magic, revealing him as one might an expensive gift, slowly, savoring the discovery. His eyes were darker than his hair, almost black, and she thought their shade had little to do with the remaining shadows. His lashes were long, spiked. On closer inspection, she saw tiny lines within his face, lines that marked him as a man who spent a great deal of time outdoors. She thought it unlikely he was an aristocrat. He was a laborer of some sort then. A fisherman perhaps. A sea captain. A man who was accustomed to taking women into his berth, then leaving them ashore.

That would explain his unanticipated kiss. As for her response—it rose from the uncivilized part of her that she fought daily to control. With him she was in danger of losing the battle.

And she cared not—which frightened her more. To have no regard for where this moment might lead was blatant folly, recklessness.

He touched his lips to hers, a tentative exploration this time, like a butterfly testing the welcome of a budding flower. Yet there was nothing fragile or dainty about him or the desire she recognized smoldering within his eyes. He threaded his fingers through her hair, bracketing his palms on either side of her face, and pressed his luscious mouth against hers.

With his tongue, he stroked the outer edges of her lips, the seam that separated them, coaxing her mouth to open, bidding her to allow entry. Then he was exploring more deeply, more intimately, slowly, leisurely, as though the sun would cease to rise farther, as though the day would not give way to the night.

She knew nothing about him except that she shouldn't be there with him. She'd worked her entire life to be good, to be above reproach, to be the perfect lady, and here she was casting it all aside because of a man who drew her to him with little more than his existence.

She returned his kiss, anxious to know the feel of his lips, the varying textures of his mouth, her tongue darting again and again, frightened by her boldness, disappointed in her cowardice.

With his deep, feral groan, the nature of the kiss changed: It deepened, demanding that doubts be cast aside, and that desire triumph. She lost herself in the searing kiss that seemed to encompass more than simply her mouth. It was as though her entire body participated, savoring each thrust of his tongue, feeling a tension build that cried out for release.

Her body felt as though it needed to be anchored to something, to him. Her hands were grappling, striving to find something substantial with which she could secure herself, while his hands stroked her back, her shoulders, her sides, her rounded backside.

She broke free of the kiss, suddenly realizing that she was straddling him like a wanton woman, her nerve endings humming, her skin sensitive to each whisper of the wind. Her breaths coming in short panting gasps, she was intensely aware of the hardness of his body, of the press of his hips against the hollow of hers.

"Oh, dear God," she whispered. She scrambled off him, ashamed and mortified. How close she'd come to devouring him, how close she'd come to giving in to the carnal creature living inside her.

She huddled away from him, her shoulders hunched, her chest aching, fighting for control. She heard his harsh breathing echoing around her. He laid a hand on her shoulder, and she jerked away. "Don't. Please."

"There is something between us," he said quietly, his voice a deep and resonating timbre that touched the chords deep within her heart.

She shook her head forcefully. "There can be nothing between us."

"At least tell me your name."

Even as she rose to her feet to escape him, she heard her answer wafting on the breeze. "Kitty."

"Where can I find you?"

"You can't. I'm leaving for London today, for the Season."

"I'll go to London then. I want to see you."

She looked back at him, to memorize quickly the sight of him on the rocks, to sever the bond between them that should have never existed. "You can't see me. I'm soon to be married."

Then she scrambled over the rocks, tears blurring her vision. She did not want to be with this man who called out to the wildness in her. She wanted Nicky. Safe, dependable Nicky.

Her haven from the storm of desire and lust. With him, she would be happy. With him, she could be the lady she'd worked so diligently to become.

Richard swam until the sun had cleared the horizon, until he saw its blinding rays glinting off the water—long, strong, sure strokes that carried him out to sea and returned him to shore. Again and again until his limbs grew heavy, until he collapsed on the ribbon of sand where she'd stood.

He was breathing as quickly and as heavily as he'd been while kissing her. Had he ever tasted anyone as sweet? He thought not. If he had, he had no memory of her or her taste.

His lady of the sea had erased all others from his mind, until she alone remained, taunting him with what she'd given him, teasing him with what she'd withheld.

With his cheek pressed against the sand, he reached out a tired arm and touched the edge of one of the footprints she'd left behind, evidence that she was indeed flesh and not mere fantasy.

I'm soon to be married.

The words seemed to be carried on the wind. He circled the outline of her footprint. He wanted her. He was not a man who denied himself the things he wanted.

He would have her. One way or another. He would go to London. He would find her. And he would do whatever it took to possess her.

Chapter 3

Gazing through her bedroom window into the splendid garden of the London town house her parents had begun leasing four years earlier, Kitty tried to find comfort in the familiarity, sought to place herself back on an even keel. It had been three days since they'd arrived in London. Her gentleman by the sea should have become a distant memory, seldom thought about. Instead he haunted her every waking moment, frequented her nightly dreams.

She didn't know how to purge her memories of him, and yet she knew she must. He wasn't safe. He made her feel things she didn't want to feel, caused her to experience sensations forbidden to a decent woman.

Kitty was certain that only lust had driven her actions by the sea. Hers and his. Entwining themselves around each other without conceivable thought, they'd imitated animals on the verge of mating, with their actions based on instinct, not true love or affection. Nearly bared bodies unable to resist temptation.

Their deplorable display of impropriety was the very reason people in a civilized society wore as much clothing as they did—to provide a shield against the body's instinctual inclination to mate. Inherently disgusting behavior when not controlled. Thank goodness, she'd never again see her gentleman from the sea.

"Are you afraid to get married, Kitty?"

Turning away from the window, Kitty smiled softly at her ten-year-old sister, who was stretched on her stomach on the bed, raised on her elbows, her latest book spread out before her. She was a voracious reader. "No, of course not. Why ever would you think that?"

Emily furrowed her dark brow. "Because you look so worried."

"I'm not worried. I have no patience when it comes to waiting. It's worsened by the fact that I haven't seen Lord Farthingham in weeks."

"When do you think you'll get married?" Emily asked.

"I'm not sure. Lord Farthingham and Papa are still working out the settlement. Until the lawyers and Papa are happy with everything, we won't make an official announcement. Then I want to wait an entire year before we actually get married." She intended to have a leisurely betrothal, to leave no doubt in anyone's mind that she was chaste. She wanted no scandal associated with herself or her marriage.

"I wish Nicky would hurry up and get here," Emily lamented.

Pursing her lips, Kitty gave Emily a hard stare. Emily simply rolled her eyes and her shoulders. "I know, I know. I'm supposed to call him Lord Farthingham." She giggled. "But he's so much fun. He seems more like a Nicky than a Lord Farthingham."

Kitty laughed. "Yes, he is fun, isn't he?"

"Why didn't he meet us in Cornwall?"

"Because he had business he needed to attend to in London. A lot of responsibility comes with his title. Some people don't realize that."

"You'll help him when you get married."

"Of course." She'd prepared her entire life to take on the role of the wife of a prominent man.

"You love him, don't you, Kitty?"

"Very much so. He makes me feel safe."

"So, he's a hero of sorts."

"He's my hero," she readily admitted. He had been since the first moment that they'd met.

She'd been sixteen. Her family had been in London visiting the Earl of Ravenleigh and his family. Longtime friends, her father and the earl had several mutual business ventures. Too young to attend balls, she'd been standing in the garden, looking in on the grandeur, when Lord Farthingham had passed by her, suddenly stopped, looked back at her, and smiled his devil-may-care smile.

She'd often suspected that he'd been on his way to meet with someone, but whoever it was had been forgotten. He'd danced with her then, there in the garden with her in her plain dress and he in his evening attire, but she'd never felt more beautiful. She'd only recently begun to show an interest in men, and he'd given her a sense of security that had made the strange yearnings fluttering around inside her seem not quite so frightening. With him beside her, she could tamp them down.

From that one fleeting encounter, a friendship had developed and love blossomed. He'd proposed to her this last April, she'd accepted, and then as tradition dictated, he'd approached her father to ask for his blessing and to discuss the settlement. She knew the settlement was a necessary and wise part of the betrothal process, but she thought it might be nice if people simply got married and trusted each other to do the right thing.

But the world wasn't perfect, and men were known to be scoundrels. Her existence was living proof.

"I'm going to miss you, Kitty." Emily's sweet face was caught up in a frown. "You won't be sailing with us anymore."

"Sometimes I will. Farthingham likes yachting as well."

"Remember when we were on the ocean, and late at night, we'd sneak up to the deck and watch the stars?" Emily asked.

The last time they'd done it had been not more than ten days earlier. "Of course, I remember."

"Out on the ocean, the sky always seems so big, and I always feel so small. Who'll lie on the deck of the ship and watch the stars with me after you get married?"

Kitty crossed the room and sat on the edge of the bed, wrapped her hand around Emily's, and squeezed. "I will."

"But you won't be with me."

"I won't be beside you like I am now," Kitty said softly, "but I'll always be with you, Em. Every night, I'll go into the garden and gaze at the stars and think of you."

"But you can't see the stars in London. There's too much fog."

"I'll see them, Em, because I'll be looking with my heart, not my eyes. And I'll always see you, too."

"Promise?"

"I promise."

Leaning over, she pressed a kiss to her sister's hair.

She did wish Farthingham would arrive. Without him to distract her, her thoughts kept returning to the man by the sea, how hard his body was, how hot. How dangerous it had felt to have his strong arms banded around her. She knew his scent, his taste, the softness of his lips, the roughness of his jaw.

Taking a deep breath, she wondered where he was at this moment, where he spent his nights. Did he sleep on board a yacht? Did he sleep with a tavern girl?

She almost laughed aloud. For all she knew, he was married, had ten children, and swam at dawn seeking peace from a hectic household.

Only she didn't think he was married, didn't think he had anyone. A loneliness she couldn't explain had emanated from him—something that went deeper than solitary swims.

It was the way he stood on the shore—a defiance that had been born out of something she couldn't identify.

A knock sounded, snatching her from her dangerous thoughts. "Come in."

Her bedroom door opened slightly, and a young woman wearing a white cap, a dark dress, and a frilly white apron peered into the room with a smile. "Lord Farthingham is here."

"Thank you, Nancy."

Emily squealed and bounded off the bed.

Closing her eyes, Kitty breathed a sigh of relief, issued up a prayer of thanksgiving. Farthingham was exactly what she needed to set her world back on its axis. Because he'd not called since she'd arrived in London, she'd begun to worry that he'd somehow discovered that she'd been led astray, that her doubts had surfaced, and that she'd been harboring impure thoughts.

Following in Emily's wake, she hurried out of her room to the stairs. The stairway's landing was a balcony joining two sides of the house, meeting at its center to flow down into a sweeping marble staircase. While Kitty halted at the top to gaze down on her suitor, Emily continued on, rushing down the stairs, skidding across the floor, and coming to a halt in front of Farthingham.

"Lord Farthingham!" Her voice, riddled with excitement and joy, echoed up toward the frescoed domed ceiling.

"Hello, Moppet." With a gloved hand, he tweaked her nose.

"Did you bring me a surprise?"

"Of course, I did. You're my second-best girl, don't you know?" He held out a package wrapped in brown paper.

Taking it, Emily gushed her gratitude before saying, "Kitty's been waiting forever for you to arrive."

"Has she now?"

Then he shifted his attention to the top of the stairway, and Kitty felt all her doubts and worries melt away as though they'd never existed. His blond hair had grown a bit longer than she remembered from when she'd last seen him, his side whiskers a tad bushier. But he was as handsome as ever, his blue eyes dancing with mirth.

Walking down the stairs with all the dignity a young lady should exhibit, she dearly wanted to rush down them in the same excitable manner that Emily had only moments before. She approached her suitor and curtsied. "Lord Farthingham."

He bowed. "Miss Robertson, you are a welcome sight for a lonely heart."

"As are you, my lord."

He took both her hands and pressed a kiss to her knuckles. "I have missed you terribly, my sweet."

"I missed you, too."

"Kitty, look! It's a book. *Hans Christian Andersen's Fairy Tales.*"

"With colored illustrations," Farthingham said, still holding one of Kitty's hands and squeezing it. "Colored illustrations are becoming quite popular and readily affordable with these newfangled printing techniques they've developed."

"Thank you," Emily said. "I'll start reading it tonight. Did you bring a gift for Kitty?"

"Emily!" Kitty scolded.

Ignoring Kitty, Emily grinned. "You did, didn't you?"

"Of course, I did." He reached into his pocket and brought out a small box wrapped in white paper.

"You shouldn't have," Kitty said as she took it and slowly peeled back the paper.

"I know, but I couldn't resist."

Opening the box, she smiled at the delicate cameo. "Oh, Nicky, it's lovely."

"Not as lovely as you."

"You flatter me, my lord."

"Not as much as I intend to once we are married."

"Mother and Father are out for the afternoon. Would you like to join me for some tea on the terrace?"

"I'd rather have a stroll in the garden if Miss Emily will serve as chaperone."

Before Kitty could announce that she didn't think they needed a chaperone, Emily had already proclaimed her willingness to take on the role.

With Emily walking ten paces behind them, Kitty walked through the garden with her arm wound around Farthingham's. She'd grown up with little chaperoning. It simply wasn't as prevalent in America as it was in England. She'd spent more time alone with her gentleman by the sea in two days than she had with Lord Farthingham in all the years she'd known him.

Guilt swamped her with that admission. If she was to be alone with anyone, it should be with the man she intended to marry. If she needed a chaperone, it was when she was with any man other than Farthingham.

"How was Paris?" he asked.

"Lovely."

"How many new gowns?" he asked.

"Enough to see me through the Season."

"You're not comfortable with your father's wealth," he speculated quietly.

"He worked hard to build his empire, without any help from me. I simply don't see the need to brag on it."

"We're close to agreeing on the settlement."

Patting his arm reassuringly, she looked away. "Good."

"You know you mean a great deal more to me than money, my sweet."

She returned her gaze to his. "I know. This whole settlement business . . . I understand it's necessary for both our sakes. It just"— she lifted a shoulder—"I don't know. It makes our marriage seem more like a business arrangement. I find the whole process hardly romantic."

"Hence the very reason I brought you a gift."

Which he probably shouldn't have. An expensive piece of jewelry—no matter how lovely—when she had so much already. He could use the money for other more important purchases. But she kept her thoughts to herself, because she knew him well enough to know he had an abundance of pride.

"A lovely gift," she said. "I'll wear it to Ravenleigh's ball next week."

"Ah, is that the one we'll attend?"

"Of course. Ravenleigh and father have been friends for as long as I can remember."

They walked along in companionable silence for several moments before he asked, "How was your holiday in Cornwall?"

She almost tripped over her feet, with the unexpected change in topic. "I was ready to come to London straightaway, but Papa likes to spend a few days getting his land legs back after traveling on the yacht."

"After all the adventures you've been on, I fear you'll find life with me exceedingly dull."

She smiled warmly at him. "Never."

Reaching up, he stroked his gloved thumb across her cheek. "I will make you happy, Kitty, and you'll never regret marrying me. I swear it."

"I'm happy now, Nicky."

He kissed her forehead. "I'm the luckiest of men to have such a devoted lady by my side."

She averted her gaze, not wanting him to see that she'd not been as devoted as she should have been. She made a silent vow to resist all temptation in the future, to be the loyal, dedicated wife he deserved, so that he might never have regrets. Because she did love him. Her future resided with him, and together they would find happiness.

From that moment, she would never again think of her gentleman by the sea.

From the credenza in the entry hallway, Richard picked up the silver tray brimming with invitations. Since his mother and Anne had arrived in London, they'd been busy making the rounds, and he was the grateful beneficiary of their concerted efforts.

He strode into the morning room, where his mother was busily engaged in delicate needlework that required she wear spectacles to do a proper job. She looked up at him with owl-like eyes that made her seem lonely, and he was hit with a pang of guilt. His father should still be with her, offering companionship and love. Although their marriage had been arranged, they'd always doted on each other, and he knew his mother dearly missed his father.

"Finished with all your business matters so early?" she asked.

"Hardly, but I thought to take a few moments to attend to another urgent matter." He set the tray on a table beside her. "I require your assistance."

She removed her spectacles and offered her undivided attention. "Of course, dear."

He sat in a nearby chair, leaned forward with earnestness, and held her gaze. "Those are various invitations to an assortment of dinners and balls."

"Yes, dear. I'm well acquainted with invitations."

She wasn't going to make this easy for him.

"And I am *well acquainted* with the gentlemen of London. I am also well aware that it is their wives who yield the real power when it comes to the social scene."

His mother smiled. "I always knew you were a smart lad."

"Not so smart. I need help in determining which of those I should accept."

"Splendid. As you can well imagine, I am only too eager to offer my assistance." She placed her spectacles back on the bridge of her nose and reached for an invitation. "I shall determine which parties shall be attended by the ladies who will make the best selection of a wife."

He wasn't searching for a wife but revealing that would no doubt dim her enthusiasm. He cleared his throat. "I am only interested in balls and dinners which are hosted by people who are most likely to entertain Americans."

She stared at him, her large, round eyes blinking rapidly behind her spectacles. "Pardon?"

"Which parties would an American lady most likely attend? *That* is what I do not know, what I need your assistance in ascertaining."

Leaning back in her chair, his mother held the invitation with one hand while flicking its corner with fingers from the other hand. "Would you care to explain your reasoning?"

"Not particularly."

"Has this anything at all to do with Farthingham?"

Now it was his turn to stare. "Farthingham? Why ever would you think that?"

"You two have always been most competitive, and not only when it came to sports and games. Since he's apparently decided to take an American as a wife, I thought perhaps you'd decided to outdo him by finding one who has more beauty and wealth at her disposal."

"My request has nothing at all to do with Farthingham. And I care little about her beauty and absolutely nothing about her wealth."

"Then why have you developed a sudden keen interest in Americans? It seems most odd when you were listing all their unattractive points to Anne only last week."

"I'm not interested in *Americans*. Rather *an* American. One lady."

"So you already have a particular lady in mind? This revelation is most interesting. If you were to tell me her name, I could make inquiries."

"I'm not exactly certain by what name she might be known." And he wasn't going to admit that he knew so little about her that he only knew her as Kitty. "Besides, I prefer to be subtle in my endeavors to locate her."

"Subtle? Men are subtle when searching for a mistress."

He heaved an impatient sigh. "Mother, all I need to know is to which balls she is most likely to have received an invitation."

"I had so hoped you'd finally decided to search for a wife."

"Well, I haven't. And I'm not entirely certain that I'm searching for a mistress either." Frustrated by the direction taken by their conversation, he came to his feet, strode to the window, and gazed out.

From that vantage point, he saw his greenhouse, already displaying riotous colors in bloom. He had a man who saw to the flowers when Richard wasn't in London, but when he was in residence, he preferred to tend to the delicate plants himself, many gathered from different parts of the world.

When it came to women, he'd always remained true to England, never desired the exotic. He pressed a hand to the window casing and bowed his head. "I only know that it is imperative that I find her." He glanced over his shoulder. "Will you help me?"

Something of his desperation must have shown on his face because his mother suddenly looked as lost as he felt.

"Yes, of course." She placed the tray on her lap and began quickly to look over each invitation.

He returned to the chair, unable to reconcile his tension over so simple a matter or this driving need he had to find Kitty. He thought of her day and night, relived their fiery kisses, and heard the constant echo of her parting words. He wasn't even certain what he would do once he found her—but find her he would. He was not one to give up the chase simply because the quarry had no wish to be found.

"I should think Ravenleigh's ball would be a good place to start," his mother said, holding up a gilded invitation. "His wife is American, you know."

"Yes, I believe I do recall hearing that."

"They have developed the habit of opening their home to any and all Americans, particularly those from Texas."

"Texas," he repeated. He thought of her slow drawl, the way she'd not been content simply to be known as an American, but had felt a need to be more specific, to identify her precise origins. *Texas.*

His mother nodded. "Ravenleigh's wife comes from somewhere in the state. Her accent is most grating on the ears, but other than that she is most likable."

"I'll start there then, but if you'd recommend a few other parties where I can make an appearance if the lady doesn't attend Ravenleigh's, I would be most grateful."

"You're quite determined to find her, aren't you?"

His answer was succinctly given, leaving no doubt as to his intent or his determination. "Yes."

Not only to finding her but to possessing her as well.

Chapter 4

She drew his attention the moment she glided through the doorway at the top of the stairway. She looked as though she not only belonged, but as though she owned the ballroom and every heart within it.

Even from his place on the opposite side of the room, near the French doors that led on to the terrace, Richard could see the sparkle in her green eyes—although the shade was but a memory—and the soft smile she bestowed on her host and hostess, the Earl and Countess of Ravenleigh.

Her upswept hair was wreathed with pale pink roses. He would have thought the color would have clashed with her red hair, but she had the ability to appear at home in whatever she wore—even when it was nothing except that in which she'd been born.

The sight of her caused him to wonder if Anne's babblings about love might contain a thread of truth, because he swore his chest expanded with Kitty's radiance.

And just as quickly it collapsed.

I'm soon to be married, she'd said.

Yet, he'd read no announcement of her betrothal in *The Times*. Not for a Miss Kitty anything.

Although the announcement could have been made months before he was searching for her name, months before he knew she existed, before she'd stumbled into his life. He'd taken a chance coming to London, hoping if she was an American there for the Season that she would travel in the same social circles as he. And he was probably a fool for holding out any hope at all that he could entice her away from her betrothed—whoever he might be.

A man and woman, both elegantly dressed, walked behind her. An older couple. His initial thought at their proximity to her was that they were her parents, but although both were turning silver, it was obvious that at one point their hair had been dark. They seemed to belong with Kitty, so he supposed it was possible that Kitty's coloring could have come from a relation a generation or so back. Certainly not unheard of.

Evidently of good breeding, she would make an outstanding duchess. His mother would be tremendously pleased. Anne as well. Perhaps she could borrow some of Kitty's gowns—if she did indeed have two hundred stuffed in her wardrobe.

Not that any of the qualities he'd touched upon just then truly mattered to him. He'd decided by the seashore that he would have her. Had he not seen her at this affair, he would have prowled every soiree in London. As Anne had mentioned, he was one of England's most eligible bachelors, and that status provided him with invitations into every home of prominence.

Gracefully, Kitty strolled away from her hostess and began to make the rounds. It quickly became obvious to him that she was known to a good many people, that she was not new to the social scene. He cursed himself for tacitly avoiding his social obligations as long as he had. It was quite likely that he could have claimed her before another had captured her fancy.

I'm soon to be married.

How soon? To whom? And what would it take to undo it?

Two years had passed since Farrer Herschell had introduced a resolution in the House of Commons to abolish lawsuits involving breaches of promise regarding marriage. The exception being where money was involved. Richard had yet to hear of a marriage between an American and an aristocrat that did not involve money, a complication that would make his pressing his suit that much more difficult. But then he'd never been one to turn away from a challenge. Truth be told, he preferred it when winning was not too easy, because he tended to appreciate the victory that much more.

"Good God! Weddington, is that you?"

With a great deal of reluctance at the intrusion to his thoughts, Richard turned his attention from his quarry and presented a broad, glad smile to his friend of many years. "Farthingham. How have you been?"

"Well. Very well indeed. I can't quite reconcile the idea of your being here. I suppose your mother must be quite beside herself with hope that you'll take a wife this Season."

Richard gave a slight shrug. "If she has hope, it is only because she's heard the rumor that you are to marry."

Farthingham gave a devilish grin. "I daresay it is not rumor but fact." His smile evolved into one reflecting pride. "She's lovely, Weddington. I have to confess to considering myself quite fortunate that she favors me. She could have her choice of gentlemen, don't you know."

"So, it is not money alone that draws you to her?"

Farthingham grimaced. "I hope that rumors regarding my financial straits aren't going about as well."

"Does she not know?"

"Of course she knows. She's not only lovely beyond belief, but damned smart. Her father made his wealth in railroads and banking. Our solicitors have been hammering away at the settlement for close to a month now."

"I'll admit to being surprised to hear you were to wed."

Farthingham averted his gaze, seeming to take great interest in all the goings-on surrounding them. "I have the regrettable misfortune of being the firstborn son. What choice do I have, except to take a wife? The family coffers are empty. It is my duty to see after the welfare of my family and provide an heir. My only hope of avoiding my obligations is to die and allow my younger brother to inherit."

"And that alternative has certain disadvantages."

"Decidedly so." Farthingham's face suddenly lit up. "Here comes my salvation now. I do believe you'll find her to your liking."

Richard turned, and everything within him stilled at the exact moment that the joy in Kitty's eyes transformed from actuality to pretence. All the poise seemed to drain out of her.

"Kitty, my sweet," said Farthingham. "Don't let my friend's stern visage put you off. He's not nearly as frightening as he appears."

Richard was suddenly conscious of the fact that he did not have Farthingham's aristocratic features and blond coloring. Richard was as dark as a storm, his face weathered by the sea and regret.

"Kitty, allow me to introduce His Grace, Richard Stanbury, the sixth Duke of Weddington. And, Weddington, it is with even greater pleasure that I introduce to you Miss Mary Ellen Robertson. Her dearest friends call her Kitty."

Mary Ellen. He could have easily overlooked her announcement in the newspaper. He bowed. "Miss Robertson."

"Your Grace." She curtsied, a rosy hue working its way up her face.

"I believe I've mentioned the duke on occasion, haven't I?" Farthingham asked.

Her gaze darted between Richard and Farthingham. Had he never seen her smile at dawn, he might not have realized how forced her smile was now.

"Yes"—she nodded quickly—"you mentioned him."

"I hope he was not too unflattering," Richard replied.

"On the contrary, Your Grace, Nicky thinks most highly of you."

Nicky. She'd wrapped a wealth of warmth around the name. A name Richard had never heard applied to Farthingham, not even in his most intimate circles. No doubt her pet name for him.

"I can understand now why he considers himself a man of fortune," Richard said.

A fire sparked within her eyes. "If one does not measure fortune by its weight in gold."

"Which I assure you I do not," Farthingham interjected.

"I meant no offense," Richard assured her. "Perhaps you'd honor me with a dance later in the evening."

She angled her head triumphantly. "I fear, Your Grace, that my dance card is already filled."

Sharp disappointment rammed into him, while Farthingham laughed, the resounding chuckle ringing with gratification.

"It seems I am not the only one who is won over by Kitty's charms. Surely one dance is available," Farthingham said.

She shifted her gaze to Farthingham. "I'm afraid not."

"Then scratch someone's name off your dance card, my sweet, someone of a lesser rank."

"That would be rude. I won't make another gentleman feel less worthy by casting him aside."

"No one will be offended, no feelings will be hurt," Farthingham assured her. "Weddington is a duke—"

"Which means nothing in Texas and absolutely nothing to me."

That sentiment was a complete surprise, but then Richard was coming to realize she was a constant source of astonishments.

"Miss Robertson, do you mean to imply that your interest in marrying Farthingham is not dependent on his title?"

Her delicate nostrils flared, and he saw the fury ignite her lovely green eyes. "I would marry Nicky if he were a pauper."

"I *am* a pauper, my sweet."

Regret washed over her features, as she touched Farthingham's shoulder with slender gloved fingers. She smiled softly. "Not to me."

He grinned. "Do you see why I adore her?"

"Indeed I do," Richard said quietly.

"Allow Weddington to have my first dance, Kitty."

She released a delicate bubble of laughter, an echo of incredulous disbelief. "Don't be absurd, Nicky. Rumors abound that we are only days away from announcing our betrothal. People will expect my first dance to be with you."

"When have you ever cared what people expected?"

"I have always cared a great deal."

Farthingham winked and gave her a gentle nudge. "It's more important that I dance the final dance with you. Be a sport. Weddington is a close friend. He'll no doubt serve as my best man once I get around to asking him. I want you to get to know him, and he you. Now come along. Your dancing with him will please me greatly."

With perfect timing, the orchestra filled the ballroom with the strains of a waltz. The gentlemanly part of Richard knew he should make an excuse and tactfully retreat. The baser side that sought to control the sea held out his gloved hand. "Miss Robertson, if you'll grant me the honor of a dance."

She gave Farthingham a brittle smile before placing her hand in Richard's. He was surprised to find it trembling as though she'd only just emerged from the cold waters off the Cornish coast.

He led her onto the dance floor, grateful when he reached its center that he could at last take her into his arms. When he looked down on her, fury met his gaze.

"You did not tell me you were a duke."

"You did not ask."

She scoffed. "I've never met a man of rank who did not wrap himself in it like a shroud."

"You sound as though you disapprove of the nobility."

"I disapprove of you—pretending to be what you are not."

Within her eyes, he saw hurt mingling with the fury, battling and winning.

"I never pretended," he assured her. "I might have omitted some facts—which I believe I am within my right to point out that you did the same . . . until the moment you dashed away, I was not aware that you were already spoken for."

He heard his own fury lashing through his voice.

"I did not expect to see you again. I did not *want* to see you again."

Again, the sharp prick of disappointment that he did not mean to her what she had come to mean to him. "Smile. Farthingham is watching, and he is too clever by half. I would not want him to wonder why you look as though you are on the verge of weeping."

It was an amazing transformation to watch, as though she buried every emotion she currently felt and replaced it with the fine veneer of civilization. He was so incredibly aware of her: the warmth that seeped through her gloves, her sweet flowery perfume that wafted between them, the rapid beat of her pulse at her throat. She was graceful gliding across the dance floor within his arms, and he was loath to think of her lying in Farthingham's bed. While she'd angled her head and was smiling as though she was glad to be with him, her gaze failed to meet his, but seemed to have settled on his chin.

"Why didn't you tell Lord Farthingham that you'd already met me?" she asked quietly.

"Why didn't you?"

She lifted her gaze to his, her smile faltering. "I didn't wish to hurt him. As you said, he's clever. He would have asked questions that I have no desire to answer."

"Farthingham and I have been friends for a long time. I have an enormous amount of respect for him, and I know him extremely well. He is not the man for you, Kitty."

Although she stiffened, she continued to waltz with grace, but fire had returned to the green depths of her eyes. "Of all the arrogant . . . to presume to know who is and who isn't right for me—"

"I do not who is. I only know that he is not."

"You insufferable lout. You call yourself his friend, and here you are questioning his judgment—"

"Not his. Yours."

She made a motion to move away from him, and he tightened his hold on her, keeping her in place. "You and I need to go someplace where we can talk in privacy."

She shook her head. "No, we don't. You're right to question my judgment, but not where Farthingham is concerned. Rather where you are concerned. I showed extremely bad judgment in returning to that cove where I'd spotted you the morning before, worse in remaining once I realized you were there. Our time on the rocky coast is best forgotten. Farthingham is my future."

Unfortunately for him, the final strains of the waltz drifted on the air, shimmered through the room, ending any opportunity he might have had to argue in his defense, leaving him with no excuse to continue holding her. As a gentleman, he had no choice except to release her and step back.

Because too much remained to be said, neither spoke as he escorted her back to Farthingham, who was grinning as though he'd recently won the America's Cup.

"By Jove, you two hardly stopped chattering. Bodes well for a friendship developing, I should think," Farthingham said.

"The duke and I have little in common," she said softly, her attention on Farthingham.

"On the contrary. You should see his yacht. Kitty loves sailing, don't you, my sweet?"

"I'll love being your wife more."

Farthingham beamed at her response, and Richard could hardly blame the man. Her devotion was quite convincing, and a part of him feared that it might also be quite honest and true.

"If you'll excuse me," Richard said, "I need to make the rounds."

"Quite so," Farthingham said. "It was good to see you again, Weddington."

"And you." He bowed slightly. "And it was my absolute pleasure to meet you, Miss Robertson. Thank you for honoring me with a dance."

"I believe you owe your appreciation to Nicky."

It didn't escape his notice that she neither thanked him nor admitted it was a pleasure to have waltzed with him.

He made his excuses again and wended his way through the crowd, barely acknowledging those who acknowledged him, making certain not to make any motion toward anyone that would serve as an invitation to begin conversing with him.

He hardly knew the woman who had danced in his arms, who proclaimed her love for Nicholas Glenville, the Marquess of Farthingham. What a fool he was to have thought she was of a passionate nature. Elegant and lovely, but as were all American ladies, she was in want of a title. Willing to lie and pretend favor in order to achieve one.

Surely she would not have sought him out that morning by the sea if she truly loved Farthingham. But if she did not love him, why settle for him?

Perhaps because she did not know that she could marry Richard and become his duchess. He imagined her at his side forever.

It was where he wanted her. He had little doubt that she would be his easiest conquest yet. And beyond any doubt, she would be his most rewarding.

Chapter 5

With the draperies drawn so none of the glow from distant streetlights could enter, Kitty sat curled in a chair beside the window in the darkness of her bedroom, contemplating her wedding.

Her wedding to Farthingham. In whose arms she felt safe. Gazing into his blue eyes did not start a slow melting of her bones. His fingers closing over hers did not create a sensation of butterflies fluttering beneath her ribs. Waltzing with him did not cause her knees to weaken or her mind to wander toward forbidden thoughts of unclothed bodies writhing on satin sheets alternately cooled by the night and heated by passion.

Tightly wrapping her arms around herself, she fought to stem the trembling that she'd somehow managed to keep contained throughout the evening until she'd returned home, until she'd prepared for bed, until she'd dismissed her maid. And then she'd been engulfed by violent tremors that threatened to loosen her teeth.

Her gentleman from the sea. She'd thought, hoped, prayed that she'd never set eyes on him again. He tempted her with the forbidden, and it took all her strength of character not to give in to the temptation. She knew at the center of her being lurked a dark core lured by sin, a part of her that craved a man's touch, that enjoyed the sight of the bared human form. Primal. Uncivilized. Uncultured.

A part of her that she'd inherited from the woman who'd given birth to her. A woman who had dared to fornicate without the benefit of marriage. A woman who had been alone when she'd given birth to Kitty, alone with no family standing beside her, no husband worrying over her. Without benefit of funds or a husband, she'd given her daughter up for adoption only hours after she was born rather than

suffer the shame and humiliation associated with her own unacceptable behavior.

Kitty had been forced on several occasions to tolerate the
woman's presence. Jessye Bainbridge. Now married. With three
daughters who did not have to endure the embarrassment of having
been born out of wedlock. Illegitimate, ill-conceived, suspicious origins. Bastard. Kitty had spent years scouring the dictionary, trying to
find a word that didn't hurt like a knife being stabbed through her
heart, a term that could give a favorable slant to a terribly unfavorable start in life.

No such word existed, and nothing had the power to alter her
perception of her beginnings. Not even Madeline Robertson—Kitty's
true mother, the woman who had nurtured her and sheltered her and
taught her right from wrong. A woman who Kitty was certain had
gone to her marital bed on her wedding night untouched.

Kitty had always been determined to follow Madeline's example.
To be purer of heart, purer of body, purer of soul.

The warmth of a heated memory embraced her, shattering what
little peace remained to her. How close she'd come to sharing her
flesh with a man without the sanctity of marriage vows. On the
coast, without shelter, without locked doors. With nothing except the
sun, the wind, and a man, and she'd barely been aware of the sun and
the wind.

Always believing Jessye to be weak, without morals, Kitty suddenly felt her foundation shaken to its core and in danger of crum-
bling. She'd thought herself superior, stronger of will, capable of
resisting temptations of the flesh. Now she feared she might have
inherited Jessye's propensity toward wanton behavior. Kitty's train-
ing and preparations to become an exemplary wife would all be for
nothing if she slipped into the quagmire of lust as the woman who'd
given birth to her had.

Thank God for Farthingham. Farthingham whom she loved. Farthingham who never stirred to life such unwanted passions. Farthingham with whom she was always comfortable.

He would make an excellent, upstanding husband, ensuring that
she made an excellent, upstanding wife.

She would share his bed, his kisses, his body, while burying the
baser instincts that yearned for what she might have experienced that
morning by the sea. She would lie beneath him, welcome his body
into hers—without gasps, writhing, and moans. With him, she
wouldn't lose her way, she wouldn't journey toward forbidden
desires.

So buried within her thoughts had she become that she barely stirred when she heard the knock. "Come in."

Her bedroom door opened slightly, and her lady's maid peeked into the room. "Are you feeling poorly, miss?"

"No, Nancy, I'm fine, thank you." But she didn't think her voice reflected her answer.

Nancy entered, carrying a silver tray. "Mr. Robbins instructed me to bring this up to you. You have a gentleman caller."

"At this time of night?"

"It's well into the day, miss. Long past noon."

Startled by that revelation, Kitty slipped her fingers between the heavy draperies and sunlight sliced inside. "My goodness, I had no idea."

She rose to her feet, unable to believe she'd sat there with her thoughts throughout the early hours of the morning and into the afternoon. Taking the card from the tray, she asked, "Will you please open the draperies?"

Almost blinding light spilled into the room, revealing the identity of her caller, written in elegant script: the Duke of Weddington. She considered refusing him, contemplated feigning illness. Instead she squared her shoulders.

"Will you please see if my mother is agreeable to having tea on the terrace and inform the duke that I'll walk with him through the garden? Then please return to help me with my toilette."

After Nancy left, Kitty collapsed on the bed. What could he possibly want? Had she not made her intentions and feelings toward Farthingham clear?

Part of her wanted to see the duke, and part of her dreaded the meeting. She didn't know why she'd feel safer in the garden. Perhaps because under her mother's watchful gaze, she knew she'd have more success at remaining a lady and keeping her wanton side under control.

All doubts that had surfaced within Richard's mind regarding Kitty's bloodlines evaporated the moment Madeline Robertson strolled into the parlor and introduced herself. Then she had invited him to join her on the terrace, an invitation that clearly indicated acceptance of the offer was preordained if he wished to meet with her daughter for even the shortest of time.

So he sat across from her, the small, round, lace-covered table between them decorated with a vase of freshly cut flowers and a tea service gilded in gold. He'd been greeted by a butler, they'd been served by a housemaid, the gardens were expertly kept. To a keen observer, which he prided himself on being, it was obvious that the Robertsons lacked for nothing. Yet neither did they exhibit the crass American habit of flaunting their wealth. Subtle and refined. They were comfortable with what they'd attained and sought to make others comfortable around them.

Little wonder Farthingham had been drawn to them—not only for their wealth, but for their elegant mien. He could so clearly see Kitty reflected in the manner in which Madeline Robertson held herself. Obviously Kitty had taken her poise and grace from her mother. Her smile. Her ability to make a man feel as though he held her complete attention, as though nothing would distract her from her purpose of pleasing him.

"I understand attending balls is quite unusual for you, Your Grace," Madeline Robertson said.

"I must confess that I have made a point to avoid them in the past, Mrs. Robertson."

"You gave many mothers hope that your presence last night indicated that you'd decided to take a wife." She poured his tea. "Sugar?"

"Yes, please. Four and a half helpings."

She arched her brows and smiled softly. "You possess a sweet tooth."

"Several of them, in fact. I fear sweets are my weakness." As was her daughter, although he suspected she might not appreciate hearing that bit of information. Some matters were best revealed later.

Handing him his cup of tea, she glanced toward the French doors. "Kitty should be down any moment. I can't imagine what's keeping her."

It occurred to him that perhaps she had no wish to meet her caller—or perhaps she was taking the time to make herself particularly presentable. Having seen her at dawn and at midnight, he imagined that at any moment of any hour, she was beyond comparison.

"Farthingham indicated that her Christian name was Mary Ellen," Richard said.

Mrs. Robertson's smile warmed considerably as though she were touched by a tender memory. "She's always had a fondness for cats, kittens especially. Whenever my husband was trying to find her, he'd simply call out, 'Here, Kitty, Kitty.' And whenever a cat answered his call, our daughter was not far behind. I can't remember exactly when he started calling her Kitty exclusively, but as she grew into a young lady, it seemed to suit her."

He agreed wholeheartedly. The name reflected a lightness that seemed to capture her spirit. He couldn't imagine her as Mary Ellen. The name was too common, and she was incredibly uncommon.

"Am I to understand, then, that you and Farthingham are friends?" his hostess asked.

"Yes. We've known each other for many years. Attended the same schools." The same clubs, the same brothels, the same gaming hells. But again, he didn't think she'd appreciate knowing the entire truth.

"Strange that our paths haven't crossed before now," she said with a hint of suspicion and protectiveness.

Strange indeed. "You've known him for a while then?" Richard asked.

"Over the years, we'd see him from time to time when we came to visit the Earl of Ravenleigh and his family. The earl and my husband have some joint business ventures that require they meet occasionally. Kitty has always had a soft spot for Farthingham. I think they make a lovely couple."

Was that a bit of warning he heard in her voice? *Don't interfere. Don't poke your nose where it doesn't belong.*

"He seems quite smitten."

"I'm sure he is. My daughter has many admirable qualities."

"I doubt that not for a moment."

The door clicked open, and Richard was grateful that his reason for coming had finally made her appearance, and he thought the wait was quite worth every second. The lines of her pale lilac dress were elegantly cut, enhancing her perfect form so it resembled a work of art. Lace at her throat revealed a hint of skin, but other than that, she was dressed almost as completely as a nun. And yet still, desire speared him, hot and unrelenting. He couldn't explain it. He only knew he experienced it each time his gaze fell on her.

Shoving back his chair, he came to his feet.

"Your Grace," she greeted, before he could speak.

Her speech was stilted, carried a hint of disapproval that made him want to smile, a reaction he could not have explained had his life depended on it. "Miss Robertson."

"Shall we take a turn about the garden?" she suggested.

"I would be honored."

She glided past him. He quickly excused himself from her mother's presence and joined Kitty where row upon row of red, pink, and orange blossoms added fragrance to the air.

"I thought I made it clear that you were not to call," she said, as soon as he was within hearing distance and her mother was not.

"You did."

"Then why are you here?"

"I couldn't stay away."

"Am I to deduce, then, that you are a man who possesses absolutely no willpower and lacks complete self-control?"

He smiled at her tartly delivered assessment of him, certain her intent had been to insult him with her sharp barb. "Apparently, that is indeed the case where you're concerned."

Her gaze darted over to him for only a heartbeat before she looked away. "Truly, why are you here?"

"I believe I understood you to say last evening that you and Farthingham have made no formal announcement regarding your betrothal."

"Indeed, we have not. Farthingham, Father, and the lawyers only recently finished haggling over the settlements."

"Then I am here to ask you to marry me."

She came to an abrupt halt and faced him, abject horror clearly etched over her lovely features. He supposed he shouldn't have continued, but he'd gone too far to stop. From his pocket, he withdrew an envelope that was sealed with wax embossed with his ducal crest and held it toward her. "My formal request. I know it should have been delivered before I voiced my intentions, but time seems to be of the essence."

"Are you mad?"

"Probably. I am not a man who acts impulsively, Miss Robertson. But neither am I a man who easily gives up what he has determined that he wants."

The horror transformed into disbelief. "And you've decided that I am what you want?"

"Precisely."

Her lips curling slightly as though she were suddenly amused, she shook her head and began to walk again. "We are not well suited."

"I disagree."

"You may disagree all you want. I assure you, we are not well suited."

"Give me this Season to prove otherwise."

She stopped again, her eyes traveling over his face as though she sought to memorize each facet of his appearance. "I have loved Farthingham from the moment I met him."

"Then why did you seek me out at dawn?"

Tears welling in her eyes, she averted her gaze. "It had nothing to do with love."

"Is it possible that it could?"

She looked back at him, holding his gaze, honesty and regret in her eyes. "I could never love you. And I won't hurt Farthingham or risk damaging what he and I have by even entertaining the notion that you are more suited to me than he."

"And if Farthingham loved another?"

She smiled with absolute certainty. "He doesn't."

She turned back to their walk. "It was wrong of me to meet you by the sea. I hope you'll forgive me for any false hope I might have given you that anything more than a passing moment could exist between us."

He was damned near tempted to take her in his arms, there within the garden, and prove to her that considerably more existed between them. A wise woman to insist that they walk where her mother could keep a watchful eye on them, where a man of his rank wouldn't behave badly.

"So you will not consider me?"

"No, Your Grace, I will not."

"I am not in need of funds, Miss Robertson."

She hesitated, but did not cease her walking. "It doesn't matter."

"You would be a duchess."

"It is not rank that I seek, but love."

"I would have thought you could have found that in Texas."

She spun around, anger in her eyes. "I have been brought up to be a lady, to manage a household of immense size, to stand beside a man of tremendous influence. That I have fallen in love with an Englishman suits me, and I suit him. We'll be happy. I won't settle for less. Like you, Your Grace, I'm accustomed to gaining what I desire. I made a grave error in judgment in seeking you out, and I do not intend to pay for it for the remainder of my life. It was a mistake, but no harm came of it. You profess to be Farthingham's friend, and here you are striving to steal me away from him. What sort of friend would do such a despicable thing? Is he aware that you're here?"

"No."

"Can you conceive of him approaching a woman who holds your regard and asking her to turn away from you?"

He slowly shook his head. "No, I cannot."

"Would he betray you?"

He released a low sigh. "No, he would not."

"And yet here you are, striving to betray him. *That*, Your Grace, is only one of the many, many reasons why I am absolutely positive that I could never love you. I value loyalty." She quickly held up a finger. "And before you chastise me or remind me of our prior meeting, I am well aware that I strayed, and I've vowed to dedicate myself to forgetting that encounter and ensuring I never again do anything similar."

"A harsh punishment for so innocent an act."

"Not a punishment. I'm simply recognizing a failing on my part. It won't happen again."

Strange how he found himself more enamored of her than before. He desperately wanted her loyalty bestowed on him, wanted her dedication, and her heart.

"Will you at least postpone your betrothal announcement until the end of the Season?"

She released a laugh that floated toward him as light as the breeze. "Have you not listened to a single word I've said?"

"I've heard every word, and I assure you that I shall not forget a single one. But I am also a proud man. To read your announcement would be to rub salt in the wound of your rejection."

Her brow furrowed. "When you came here, did you honestly think that I would turn away from Farthingham?"

"I'd hoped. Apparently I vastly misjudged the affection you hold toward him."

"Apparently so."

"He is a most fortunate man. I shall envy him until the day I draw my final breath."

She shook her head. "No. Be happy for us, for what we'll have. You'll find someone else and easily forget me."

"Now it is *you* who have misjudged *my* affection for you." He bowed slightly. "I bid you good day."

He strode from the garden, more determined than ever to possess her, to make her his wife, his duchess, his mate.

Breakfast was becoming a terribly glum affair, Richard thought, as the only sound in the dining room was the consistent tapping and sliding of forks, knives, and spoons against china. He'd always longed for quiet while he'd read his newspaper, always tolerated the constant chattering of his mother and sister, turned a deaf ear, so to speak, yet constantly aware of them.

Their continual silence these days, however, was driving him to madness!

Precisely their goal, he was certain, and the very reason that he refused to acknowledge it. How could silence be so incredibly distracting and utterly annoying? And yet he found it was, beyond belief.

He imagined Kitty greeting him each morning with a smile and a kiss and enlightening conversation. He hadn't yet determined the best way to proceed where she was concerned. He'd considered speaking with Farthingham, but it seemed a bit presumptuous on his part to urge his friend to give up his claim to the Texas lady. He preferred a more subtle approach, perhaps to win the lady over first. Farthingham, as a gentleman, would surely step aside with the realization that he'd fallen out of favor, and Richard was more than willing to generously compensate his friend for his loss.

On second thought, perhaps monetary compensation was the best way to go from the outset. Simply offer Farthingham far more funds than whatever settlement he'd obtain from marriage. He recognized, however, that funds would do little to satisfy the burdensome need for an heir. He cursed the duties that fell to a peer and forced obligations on him.

But then he couldn't deny that being a peer also brought with it a considerable number of benefits. Especially if one's predecessors had the foresight to move beyond agriculture—as his had.

The butler entered and presented a silver tray bearing a card to Richard. Richard took the card, read the name, and smiled. "Send him in, Watkins."

Richard came to his feet.

"Who is it, Richard?" his mother asked.

"Farthingham."

"Oh!" Anne popped up from her chair, her face suddenly animated.

Farthingham strode into the room, bowing before his mother, taking her hand, and pressing a kiss to her fingers. "Duchess, I do believe you grow more lovely with each passing day."

"Oh, bosh, I do not grow lovelier. I simply grow older. But I see you are still a charmer, Farthingham."

"Dear lady, my charm is always only equal to the beauty before me. If it pleases you, it is only because the sight of you pleases me."

His mother laughed and waved her hand. "Off with you now! Take your charm elsewhere."

Smiling grandly, Farthingham approached Anne and held out his arms. "Lady Anne."

With a delightful and very unladylike squeal, she flung herself into his arms. "Oh, Farthingham, it's so terribly good to see you."

He set her aside and made a big production of studying her. "I did not think it possible, but I do believe you are more beautiful than ever." He touched the back of his knuckles to the dark hair at her temple. "My God, how you've grown."

She patted his shoulders. "Don't be silly. I saw you at Christmas. Now gather up some food and join us. We have much catching up to do."

"Gossip, you mean?"

"Of course! Now come on. Hurry."

Farthingham finally looked Richard's way. "Weddington, I hope you will forgive my intrusion."

"I would never consider your presence an intrusion." He gestured toward the sideboard. "Anne is correct. We have an abundance of offerings here. You are more than welcome to join us."

"I believe I shall then."

Richard and Anne took their seats, waiting patiently while Farthingham heaped food on his plate. The marquess took his place at the table, looking like a man who had conquered the world. "I hope you'll not think me greedy, but I left home this morning before Cook had prepared breakfast."

Richard thought it more likely that Farthingham was not having breakfast prepared. He knew the man's financial situation was in dire straits, and one could pretend for only so long before the creditors began knocking on one's door.

"Eat all you want," his mother urged. "We have plenty."

"You are too generous, Duchess." He savored his first bite of pheasant by closing his eyes and purring. "Excellent." His eyes popped open. "I do believe you have the best cooks in all of London. Now on to the gossip."

Anne fidgeted in her chair and leaned toward him, her eyes opened wide. "Is it true you plan to marry an American?"

"Indeed it is, Lady Anne. Why were you not at Ravenleigh's ball? I would have introduced you to the lovely lady."

"I wasn't feeling well," she replied meekly.

Richard narrowed his eyes. "She thinks I am being unfair to insist she marry a man of rank. She has decided to hide away this Season, which means I'll have to select a husband for her without knowing if she favors him."

"You wouldn't!" she snapped.

"What choice do you give me?"

"Why would you not wish to marry a peer?" Farthingham asked. She turned her attention back to him. "I believe I've fallen in love.

It's truly a wondrous thing. My world is brightened by his presence, and he is a good man, but he is not a peer, and Richard disapproves."

"As well he should, my sweet."

"Oh!" She released a tiny shriek. "I thought you, at least, would be on my side."

"It is not a matter of taking sides, Lady Anne. One simply does not marry beneath one's standing."

Her mouth dropped open. "And what of you, marrying an American? Richard would argue that you're marrying beneath your standing. He can barely tolerate Americans."

"Indeed? It appeared to me that he was tolerating Kitty rather well when he waltzed with her at Ravenleigh's."

Anne glared at Richard. "You've met her, and you said nothing?"

"Since we left Drummond Manor you've acted as though I do not exist," he reminded her. "You've not spoken one word to me. I assumed you had no desire to talk with me, and I had no wish to make you unhappy by forcing you to endure my conversation."

"He's quite right, my dear," his mother said. "You've been most unpleasant in a pleasant sort of way. So let's move on to more pressing matters. Farthingham, tell me all about your lady."

"With pleasure, Your Grace. Kitty is a delight. Her father made his fortune in railroads and banking and other wise investments. Her mother is a lady of the highest regard . . ."

As Farthingham continued on, touting Kitty's illustrious pedigree, Richard was amazed by how differently two men could view the same woman. Ask him his opinion of her, and he would have painted a portrait of a woman who burned with passion, who believed in loyalty. A woman who sneaked out at dawn to enjoy the sunrise. A woman who swam nude in the waters of the world. A woman who had given him brief memories and left him the better for them. A woman he would forever remember, even if he never set eyes on her again. A woman with a smile that took his breath, haunted eyes that made him want to serve as her protector, and a strong enough will to stand firm against him.

His sister's tart voice snapped him out of his reverie. He turned his attention to her, certain her question had been directed at him, but unsure as to what she'd been asking. "Pardon?"

"I asked if you agree with Farthingham. Is she beautiful?"

"Beautiful?" He thought of her flaming red hair touched by the sun, the smattering of light freckles across her cheeks and nose revealed by the arriving dawn, the sea-green shade of her eyes, the fine arch of her eyebrows, the way her lashes landed on her high cheekbones as she closed her eyes to receive his kiss.

"I consider her to be the loveliest woman I've ever had the pleasure of meeting."

"Oh, I would so love to meet her," Anne lamented. "I shall definitely plan to attend the next ball. Which one are you going to, Farthingham?"

"Haven't a clue, my sweet. Whichever one Kitty decides is the one she wants to attend. However, I am equally anxious for you to make her acquaintance. Which is the very reason that I popped by this morning. I have plans to join Kitty for a bit of lawn tennis this afternoon. I thought you and your brother might care to join us."

Anne's face lit up. "Splendid. Oh, Richard, do say yes."

"Yes," he responded without hesitation, unable to believe his good fortune.

Anne smiled at him as she hadn't in days. He had an uneasy feeling that Miss Robertson wouldn't.

Chapter 6

Kitty was restless, desperate to prowl. She felt as though she needed to crawl out of her skin and just . . . do *something*!

Using her racket, she smashed the ball against the side of the house.

Bam!

She needed an ocean in which to swim—

Bam!

—a meadow to run through—

Bam!

—a mountain to climb.

Bam!

Something physical that required a great deal of exertion.

Frustrated by her limitations, she snatched the ball as it bounced toward her. Her lawn tennis dress with its trimmed skirt restricted her movements—which she recognized as a good thing. Otherwise, she might be bounding all over the court like a harridan. Right then she longed for something that would tax her strength, leave her weak and gasping for breath . . . not unlike how she gasped after Weddington kissed her.

She still couldn't believe that he'd had the audacity to come to call. To ask her to cast Farthingham aside like so much rubbish. She didn't know what she'd do if he ever decided to tell Farthingham about the wanton behavior she'd displayed at the seaside. Little wonder Weddington thought so little of her as to believe she could be easily swayed into giving up the man she loved for a man she desired.

Turning, she leaned against the wall, her knees suddenly weak. She didn't want to desire Weddington, didn't want to think of him at all. Yet every time she closed her eyes, he filled her vision. Every moment when she had nothing to occupy her thoughts, he taunted her with promises. Even now she thought of him wrapping his arms around her and pressing her close—the very reason she wanted to crawl out of her skin. So she'd no longer be tempted with the memories of his touch.

Voices, a deep timbre mingling with a softer cadence, alerted her to the arrival of Farthingham, who'd obviously brought others with him. She often thought of him as a traveling party, bringing guests and festivities wherever he went.

Kitty headed round to the back of the house, where the voices were originating. Beyond the gardens were the facilities for playing lawn tennis. With an audience, perhaps she'd have more luck at getting Farthingham to at least give her a worthy match.

She turned the corner and froze. The voices had keyed her in to that fact that he wasn't alone. Still, she hadn't expected to come face-to-face with Weddington.

Seeing him again, standing beside Farthingham, was like comparing night to day. Farthingham of the fair features and the easy smile. Farthingham who thought all of life was a game to be enjoyed. Who made her laugh and teased her when she was melancholy. Dear, sweet Farthingham, who made her feel safe.

Weddington, on the other hand, was as dark as her fears. If eyes were the windows to the soul, the obsidian depths of his served as frightening barriers. They hinted at an overpowering darkness she didn't wish to uncover. He possessed a sensuality that lured her when she didn't wish to be tempted, an attraction that she didn't want to acknowledge.

He was not for her and she was not for him. She knew that as surely as she knew her name.

Nervously, she patted her hair beneath her hat, fearful that the brim was not wide enough to shade her eyes, to hide all the raw emotions she was feeling.

"I brought you some worthy competition, my sweet," Farthingham said, beaming as he took her gloved hand and bussed a quick kiss on her cheek. "You remember Weddington from Ravenleigh's ball?"

Nodding, she forced her lips to form a smile. "Yes, of course."

Weddington tipped his head slightly. "Miss Robertson, it's my pleasure to have the opportunity to see you again."

"And the lovely lady standing beside him is Lady Anne, his sister."

Kitty was incredibly embarrassed that she'd not noticed the lady before—that her world had narrowed down until she was only vaguely aware of Farthingham and intensely conscious of Weddington's presence. She broadened her smile. "Lady Anne, it is my pleasure to make your acquaintance."

"I'm so frightfully glad that Farthingham invited us," Lady Anne gushed. "I've been dying to meet the lady who stole his heart."

"Only after he stole mine," Kitty said easily.

"Oh, splendid!" Lady Anne squealed. With her racket, she tapped Weddington on the shoulder. "There you see? I told you it was true love." She turned her attention back to Kitty. "Richard, the beast, said your marriage was based on—"

"Anne!" Weddington's voice rumbled with authority, hissed with warning. "That's quite enough."

Lady Anne pressed her mouth into a tight line until her lips were almost invisible, her cheeks blossoming into a shade that rivaled the pink petals of some of the roses in the garden.

Kitty angled her chin defiantly. "Now my curiosity is piqued, Your Grace. Upon *what* exactly did you think our marriage would be based?"

He narrowed his dark eyes, and she saw the tightening of his jaw. A remarkable jaw, really. Unlike Farthingham's, which looked as though it would crumble like week-old bread with a single punch, Weddington's gave the impression that he could use it to drive nails into fence posts.

"I thought that, like most American ladies who seek out the aristocracy, you were lured by the title rather than the man who holds it."

He'd surprised her by answering, and she was beginning to understand why he'd sounded disappointed the first morning that she'd spoken to him. "You don't seem to have a very high opinion of Americans."

"Oh, he despises them," Lady Anne confirmed.

"Anne!" Weddington barked.

The irony made Kitty smile, until she read in his eyes that he, too, was struck by the paradox of his attraction for her. And she could not help but recognize that he was drawn to her, enough so that he had proposed marriage when they knew almost absolutely nothing about each other, at least nothing of any importance.

"Perhaps you despise these American ladies because you view them as being as narrow-minded as you are, Your Grace. Judging a woman based on her country of birth and upbringing rather than on her true self."

He angled his head and smiled. "I have indeed developed a bias where American ladies are concerned. Perhaps time spent in your company will show me the error of my ways."

You scoundrel, she thought. *Setting yourself up so Farthingham might take no offense at your seeking me out.* "I am not the only American in London."

"But you are the only one with whom I am familiar."

Familiar fairly purred out of his mouth, hinting at intimacy, reminding her that he was dangerous on so many different levels.

"I would seek to remedy that by introducing you around, but I find myself much too busy this Season. However, you strike me as a man of considerable resourcefulness and I trust you can make do without my assistance." She turned to Farthingham, desperately hoping that Weddington understood that her answer encompassed just as many levels. "Are we going to play?"

"Kitty is lovely, isn't she?" Farthingham asked.

Standing to the side of the area marked for the tennis court, Richard watched Kitty and his sister play. He thought they were well matched in skill. But Anne did not have the drive for victory that seemed to fuel each of Kitty's moves. For Anne—as it was for most ladies—tennis was merely a way in which to pass the time, perhaps engage in a bit of flirting with a gentleman opponent. For Kitty, it seemed defeat was not an option.

"Indeed she is," Richard finally answered.

"I was unaware that you had such an unfavorable opinion of American ladies."

Richard shrugged. "A great deal depends on their motives."

"Interesting. I was under the impression during breakfast that you are insisting Anne marry a man of rank. How does that differ from American ladies seeking out a gentleman for a similar reason? A man is his rank."

"Anne's situation is different."

"How so?"

"It is her *right* to marry a man of rank. Her duty if you will. To keep the bloodlines pure. There is an indisputable difference between those born into the aristocracy and those who seek to enter it through marriage."

"You're a snob."

"Damned right."

Richard took his gaze off the players and looked at Farthingham. "Our world is changing. The differences between those who hold titles and those who don't are narrowing. I fear a day will come when even a king will settle for marrying an American. And then where will England be? They cast us off a hundred years ago, and now they want us back . . . on their terms."

"So? We take them back on ours." Farthingham grinned. "Our future is not as dire as you predict. Besides, I find Americans fascinating. Their ladies are so very different from our own. You can see it right there, watching Kitty and Anne play. Kitty possesses a competitiveness completely lacking in Anne."

"If money were not a factor, would you marry her?"

"Yes. I need an heir, and Kitty stirs me as few women do."

"Will that be enough for her?"

"I shall devote myself to her and ensure that she is constantly happy. What more could any woman want?"

Richard could think of a good deal more that a woman should not only want, but deserved to receive.

"Game!" Kitty suddenly cried. Her triumphant laughter echoed around them as she marched to the net, hand extended. "Good game, Lady Anne."

"Hardly."

The ladies walked toward them, chattering away as though they were the best of friends. It seemed that Kitty was comfortable with everyone except him, although she'd certainly taken comfort in his arms by the sea.

It did not occur to Richard until the pair reached them that he stood on Kitty's side of the net, Farthingham on Anne's so that it was left to him to greet the winner, to Farthingham to greet the loser.

Farthingham took Anne's hand and patted it gently. "I thought you played splendidly."

Anne rolled her eyes. "I gave Miss Robertson no competition whatsoever. Hopefully, you'll prove more of a challenge."

"I doubt it. I've yet to beat her."

"A pity Richard doesn't play."

Kitty arched a brow that seemed to say she wasn't at all surprised that he couldn't master a game that required physical skill and cunning. She touched her racket to Richard's chest. "Yes, a pity. Shall we retire for tea?"

The others had begun to move away from the court when Richard's pride spoke up. "I accept the challenge."

Anne spun around. "I was only teasing. You know you shouldn't—"

Silencing her with a hard look that spoke volumes between brother and sister, he held out his hand. "Lend me your racket."

"You are too stubborn by half." She handed it over to him and walked to the side of the court.

"Let's make this interesting, shall we?" Farthingham asked. "The best of five. Kitty has an interest in opera that I've been unable to satisfy. If she bests you, she and I will have use of your box at the Royal Italian Opera House for the Season."

"And if I win?"

"She'll accompany you to one performance."

"Nicky, no!" Kitty urged, panic in her voice. "You're being ridiculous even to consider such a wager."

Farthingham spun around, took her face between his gloved hands, and kissed her forehead. "I have absolute faith in you, my sweet. You'll beat him, I've no doubt at all. Then you and I shall enjoy the opera while he sits at home brooding over his low opinion of Americans."

"Or I shall spend the evening at the opera with Miss Robertson while you stay at home and brood over your misplaced faith," Richard said drolly.

Bless her! It took all his strength of will not to smile with satisfaction as a mutinous gleam came into her eyes. He'd known she had too much of a competitive streak within her to accept a taunting of her skills meekly.

Her chin came up in what he was coming to recognize as her show of defiance. "Would you like to take a few practice swings, Your Grace, in order to warm up? I don't want to be seen as having an unfair advantage that would cause you to cry foul."

"I assure you, Miss Robertson, I would never claim unfair advantage on your part, and I'm quite ready to accept the challenge whenever you are."

"Very well." Reaching up, she unpinned her hat, removed it from her head, and handed it off to Farthingham. "I find hats to be bothersome," she explained. "Shall we spin our rackets in order to determine who should serve first?"

"I should say not. As a gentleman, I'll allow you to begin."

She turned to Farthingham. "A kiss for luck?"

He bussed her cheek. "Now off with you and win us a season at the opera."

Richard went to take his place on the court, passing Anne along the way.

"Do take care, Richard," she said, concern etched in her voice.

He glanced over at her and winked reassuringly. "It's a genteel sport, Anne."

"Not the way she plays. You'd think she thought we were playing at Wimbledon."

He had a fondness for all sports and had taken Anne to the first amateur event held four years earlier. "As you'll recall, women don't play at Wimbledon."

"They should," she snapped.

Perhaps, but it wasn't an argument he wished to pursue at this moment. He had other prizes to win, other areas where he needed to place his efforts.

He walked to his end of the court and took up his position, balancing lightly on the balls of his feet so he could respond quickly if need be. He watched as Kitty tossed the ball down. When it bounced back into the air, she lobbed it over the net.

He had to move quickly, but only because he'd been mesmerized by her graceful movements, almost forgetting that he was not an observer, but a player who intended to win. He sprinted across the short area and hit the ball harder than he'd meant to. It sailed over the net and out of bounds.

His competitor smiled. "Are you certain you wouldn't like to take a few practice swings, Your Grace? The game isn't as easy to play as it appears from the sidelines."

"I am well aware of that, Miss Robertson. Continue on with the game, and I shall strive to pay closer attention."

"As you wish, Your Grace. Fifteen–love."

Fifteen–love. Love. It suddenly occurred to him that he wouldn't mind her applying love toward him in a conversation that would take place away from the tennis court. He'd first thought he felt only desire for her, but he was no longer sure. What was it about her that called to him so?

The ball was back in his court before he'd expected it, but he volleyed it across to her side with less force. She scampered across, gracefully swung her racket, and returned the ball to him. They volleyed back and forth. If she were Anne, he would have kept the volleying going, but she wasn't, and he didn't. He waited until the timing was right, until his previous swings had carried the ball and her farther back on the court, and then he lightly tapped the ball, giving it only enough momentum to clear the net.

She scrambled for the ball, but only succeeded in knocking it into the net. Picking the ball up off the lawn, she glared at him. "You seem to be a natural, Your Grace."

He tilted his head slightly and grinned. "I merely follow your example."

He enjoyed watching her play. Her graceful movements belied her determination to win; but the set of her jaw, the firm line of her mouth, the concentration in her eyes all spoke more loudly than any words might have. She won the first game and seemed quite proud of herself.

As well she should have been. He'd not allowed her to win. She'd earned the victory, and he suspected if he didn't try a little harder, she'd earn his box at the opera.

He held up his hand, his fingers curled slightly. "Toss me the ball, and we shall see if you have any better luck returning my serves than I did returning yours."

She was more skilled than he'd realized and made him work for every point. He was not hampered by a skirt or corset. A gentleman would have made allowances for that handicap, but, as in all things, he played to win. Defeat was not an option. He controlled the game, the victory.

The second game went to him. The third to her. Luck was with him for the fourth. The fifth was especially hard fought, hard won, and the winning point cost him dearly. He'd misjudged the velocity of the ball, its arc, had thought it was going to go out of bounds, realized too late that it wasn't and had to make a mad dash, fairly flying through the air to make contact with it, twisting his body, hearing Anne screech, swinging the racket . . .

Thump!

The ball flew back toward her, and before he hit the ground, he saw her miss. Victory at last!

She was a worthy opponent. By God, she would make a worthy duchess.

"Richard, are you all right?" Anne asked, scampering to his side.

"I'm fine, Anne." Actually, he was almost wonderful, even if his body did protest his rising to his feet. He walked a bit stiffly toward the net to receive his congratulatory handshake. Kitty met him there, breathing heavily, her features set with determination.

"By Jove, Weddington, I'd forgotten how well you played," Farthingham said.

Kitty's eyes hardened. "You said you couldn't play."

"No. Anne said that I *didn't* play, meaning that I played once and no longer play."

"Then you had a disadvantage over me because I thought you were a novice."

"Are you implying that you went easy on me?"

The familiar hiking of her chin. "No. I played for all I was worth."

"And you are worth a great deal, Miss Robertson."

It pleased him to watch a blush blossom on her cheeks, to imagine the shade deepening with passion.

He extended his hand. "Do you only shake your opponent's hand when you win?"

"Of course not." She put her gloved hand within his. Her touch was brief, stiff, and obviously resentfully given.

"As fate would have it, there is a performance at the theater this evening. To the victor go the spoils. I'll be by for you later."

Ah, he saw the anger flare in her eyes, the rebuke hovering on her tongue. He watched the delicate motion of her throat as she swallowed, and once again the angling of her chin. "All you've won is my presence in your box."

"Had I indicated that I expected more than that?"

"Kitty, whatever is wrong with you?" Farthingham asked. "This wager was quite clever on my part, if I do say so myself. Whether you won or lost, you'd have the opportunity to attend the opera as you've wanted to do for some time now."

"I'm simply not accustomed to losing," she pointed out.

"Neither am I, Miss Robertson," Richard said. Nor was he usually one to gloat over his victories. "Anne, we need to go before we overstay our welcome."

"Of course. Miss Robertson, you played a splendid game."

"Thank you, Lady Anne. I hope you'll return so we might play another game sometime."

"I'd be delighted."

"Did you want us to drop you off at your home, Farthingham?" Richard asked.

"Yes, please, if you don't mind." He reached out and squeezed Kitty's hand. "Enjoy yourself this evening. I'll see you tomorrow, and you can tell me all about it."

"I'll fill you in on every detail."

Richard thought he detected a note of warning in her voice, a subtle command that he should behave, because she would go beyond discussing the finer points of the operatic performance and include all the details of the night.

He was quite looking forward to the evening.

Chapter 7

She was dreading the evening.

Kitty still found it impossible to believe that Farthingham had placed her in the awkward position of attending the opera with Weddington.

"I don't know what you're worried about," he'd said before he left that afternoon. "He's a gentleman and a good friend. You'll enjoy yourself immensely."

A good friend. She'd been incredibly tempted to send that notion to hell by revealing Weddington's visit earlier in the week, but to do so would no doubt leave the door open to Weddington's revealing how he and she had originally met, which would only lead to further inquiry and discoveries. With the truth of her exploits exposed, what would Farthingham think of her?

She cared for him so much. Briefly she'd lost her way for a few days at the coast. Farthingham's presence served as her anchor, and when he'd not been there, she'd flirted with danger, danger in the form of a man.

And tonight she would attend the opera with that very man. She loathed the passing of each moment that brought her nearer to being in his presence.

Her parents had already left for the evening, to attend dinner with friends. Kitty hadn't bothered to tell them about her plans, because she'd known that they'd be appalled to learn of Farthingham's wager and more disturbed to hear of its outcome. Besides, they trusted her completely, expected her to have a swirling social season, and didn't require that she inform them of every outing she intended to make.

American ladies were much more liberated, seldom chaperoned—

which probably accounted in large part for the reason that many English lords sought them out. The gentlemen could get away with much more when with an American lady. Among Kitty's American friends it was often commented that an English lady went to her wedding bed without ever having the skin at her elbow touched by a gentleman.

Kitty had come to realize that the English way might be a good habit to follow, especially when she took into account how she reacted whenever Weddington was near. Despite Farthingham's protests to the contrary, she fully believed that Weddington might seek to take advantage of his time with her that evening, might attempt to touch a good deal more than her elbow. Best to dress with that possibility in mind. A woman's clothing could serve as protective armor when need be. That night it needed to be.

Kitty spent an inordinate amount of time trying to decide what to wear. She couldn't dress as drably as she would have preferred because she would be in public, and although Farthingham wouldn't be in attendance, many of his friends and acquaintances would be. For his sake, she had to make a favorable impression, because word would no doubt travel about London that she'd been at the opera without him. At the same time, she didn't want her clothing to give the impression that she was seeking to impress Weddington.

She cursed Farthingham for the hundredth time since that afternoon, then for good measure cursed Weddington for the thousandth.

After carefully considering every evening gown at her disposal, she chose one of pale blue silk and satin. The sleeves were gracefully gathered right below her elbow. Wearing her gloves left none of the skin on her arms exposed. She didn't know why that detail should make her feel safe.

Lace gathered around the gown's square neck kept the exposure of her throat modest. In her hair, she wore a wreath of jasmine flowers and forget-me-nots woven together with a pale blue ribbon, its loops graced with heron feathers of the same color. All in all, she thought she appeared exceedingly elegant, yet quite unapproachable.

She had no plans nor desire to encourage Weddington's attentions in the least. If forced to converse, she would discuss the weather, fauna, flora, and her intention to become an excellent wife to Farthingham. She smiled triumphantly at her reflection in the mirror. Yes, indeed, she would mention Farthingham and the affection she held for him at every conceivable opportunity.

The rapid knock on her door set her heart to racing with trepidation and her confidence plummeting. She took a deep breath to shore it back up. "Enter."

With her dark hair flowing down her back, a red ribbon tied into a perfect bow keeping it from her face, Emily bounded into the room. "The Duke of Weddington is here. Why are you going out with him instead of Lord Farthingham?"

"Because Farthingham lost the wager."

"He bet on you?"

Turning away from the mirror, she tweaked Emily's nose. "As is Farthingham's way, he thought he was doing me a favor, giving me something that I wanted."

"You wanted Weddington?"

She forced herself to laugh lightly while her heart was pounding furiously. "No, silly girl. I wanted to attend the opera."

"Papa could take you to the opera anytime you wanted."

"I know, but I think sometimes Lord Farthingham is bothered by the fact that he can't give more to me himself, that he's reliant on Papa's generous nature for so much."

"I don't understand."

"You don't have to." She sighed, considered inviting Emily along to serve as a buffer between her and Weddington, discounted it as inappropriate, and strolled out of the room.

It was from the balcony that she first spotted Weddington, standing within the entry hallway. His black trousers were tightly fitting, and she imagined that if she looked closely enough, she would discover they revealed the finely defined muscles of his thighs. She did not wish to look that closely, but her mind apparently already had because even though her gaze had moved on to his black, swallowtail coat, she continued to see muscles. She gave herself a firm mental shake. Holding his top hat in the hand that also balanced a walking stick against the floor, he appeared darkly dashing, and she cursed him yet again, certain she would reach two thousand before the evening was finished.

He must have felt her uneasy perusal, because he slowly lifted his gaze, capturing hers with a startling intensity and accuracy. He'd not had to glance around, but had homed in on her like an arrow aimed for the center of its target.

As though butterflies had taken flight below her ribs, she experienced an unsettling yet pleasant fluttering.

"Why does he look so angry?" Emily asked, crossing her arms on top of the railing and leaning over to place her chin on her hands.

"I don't think he's angry. He's simply deadly serious. Not nearly as much fun as Lord Farthingham." She patted her sister's back, finding comfort in the contact and Emily's innocence. "I'll tell you all about the opera tomorrow."

"I could wait up, and you could tell me about it tonight."

"Best not. I shall be very late, I'm sure. Besides, I'd have to take it up with your governess first, and I really don't have time. Be a good girl and do as she says."

Emily made a comical face that at any other time would have caused Kitty to burst out in laughter, but she was too anxious about the coming evening to do anything more than offer her sister a winsome smile.

Then she began her descent down the stairs into what would surely be hell—an evening spent in the company of Weddington.

Damnation! As she neared, she saw approval in his eyes and wished she'd chosen to wear something a little less flattering. A potato sack, perhaps. Anything that might make it appear she'd not gone to great lengths to prepare herself for her evening with him.

He bestowed on her a devastatingly handsome smile. "Each time I see you, I am amazed to discover how my memory of your beauty pales when compared with the reality."

"I am very close to being officially engaged, Your Grace. I think we should keep that in mind as we go out this evening."

His smile dimmed. "Believe me, Miss Robertson, when I say that particular thought is never far from my mind."

He settled his hat on his head and extended his bent arm. "Shall we go?"

The challenge in his eyes forced her to place her hand on his arm as though being so close to him mattered not at all. The butler opened the door.

"Have an enjoyable evening, miss."

"Thank you, Robbins," Kitty said, surprised the dryness of her mouth allowed her to speak at all while she walked through the doorway as though she were being escorted to her own execution.

The black coach with the duke's family crest emblazoned on the door loomed before her. While the vehicle was grand, it suddenly seemed too small to hold both of them. She thought of being enclosed within its dark interior with his scent wafting around her, suffocating her, his presence pressing in on her. Within the confines of the coach, she would find no escape from his powerful masculinity.

A footman dressed in full livery opened the door, and the black abyss yawned wide and threatening. She thought if she fell into it, she might never escape. It was only when her fingers started to ache that she realized how tightly she was gripping the duke's arm. Avoiding his gaze, she snatched her hand free, placed it in the hand of the waiting footman, lifted her skirt, stepped up, leaned into the coach, and froze.

"Good evening, Miss Robertson," Lady Anne announced, sitting in the shadowy corner, her smile bright enough to dim the darkness.

"Lady Anne, what an unexpected pleasure."

"Surely you didn't expect me to risk tarnishing your reputation by taking you to the opera without some semblance of a chaperone?" Weddington asked near her ear, his breath skimming along the sensitive skin at her neck, the collar of her gown suddenly seeming not nearly high enough.

She jerked her gaze around to glare at him, to offer him a smile of appreciation for his thoughtfulness, to chastise him for confusing her, to thank him for his consideration. "I wasn't certain what to expect."

"I assure you that I have no wish to cause you any unhappiness, Miss Robertson."

"You have a strange way of accomplishing that goal."

"If you will recall, I was not the one who suggested the wager. I also firmly believe you would have been more angry at me had I purposely lost."

She couldn't stop herself from truly smiling then. "You are quite right, Your Grace."

"Then let us make the best of the evening."

She wasn't exactly sure how to interpret that comment, but decided that she'd been reading much too much into his actions. He was behaving perfectly gentlemanly, and she couldn't determine why she didn't trust him or his behavior.

She clambered into the coach and took her place on the seat beside Lady Anne while Weddington climbed inside and sat opposite her. With his walking stick, he rapped the ceiling of the coach, and the conveyance lurched forward.

"I'm so pleased you're joining us this evening," Lady Anne said. "I do so love the opera."

"Then you shall miss it when you marry your commoner," Weddington said.

Kitty smiled although she doubted it was visible within the shadowy confines of the coach now that the door had been closed, effectively cutting off most of the light, except for that which sneaked in through the windows. "Are you engaged, Lady Anne?"

"Hardly. Although I am quite taken with a gentleman."

"Only taken with him?" Weddington asked. "The last I heard he'd captured your heart for all eternity."

"Don't be difficult, Richard."

Kitty was amazed by the obvious affection in Weddington's voice as he verbally sparred with his sister, the affection in hers as she parried back. She didn't know what possessed her to cast herself into the fray. "Do you not believe in love, Your Grace?"

"I believe in it wholeheartedly, if you'll forgive my pun. I am also of the conviction that women give it away far too easily, before they've considered all the ramifications."

"So you believe one should shop for love as one might consider a new evening gown?"

"More along the lines of purchasing a new pair of gloves, I should think, where the *snug fit* is as important as the appearance."

"Perhaps it has failed your notice, but the bodice of an evening gown may fit just as snuggly."

"I promise you, Miss Robertson, the snug fit of your bodice did not fail to garner my notice. However, you did not specify the bodice, but rather the entire gown. It is the skirt which I believe completely fails your analogy."

"On the contrary, Your Grace, it allows freedom, which I believe is essential to the success of love. Gloves can be quite confining; my fingers often become numb before the evening is done. I should hardly welcome your concept of love, and I fear you will have little luck in securing a woman who does."

His laughter rumbled through the coach, a sonorous echo that pleased her for reasons she couldn't begin to fathom. It was a sound much deeper, much richer than any laughter Farthingham had ever engaged in. As though Weddington saved his for special moments, which made it so much more precious, while Farthingham shared his with casual abandon.

Lady Anne had begun to clap. "That was marvelous, Miss Robertson. I do believe you've met your match, Richard."

"I doubt that not for a moment, Anne."

Lady Anne placed her hand on Kitty's arm. "Most women say very little to Richard for fear in opening their mouths and wagging their tongues, they'll lose favor."

Losing his favor was exactly what Kitty had hoped to accomplish, but she was left with the impression that she'd failed miserably. "I take it, then, that you've never held a woman's heart, Your Grace."

"What would it take to hold yours, Miss Robertson?"

His question hardly served to answer hers, and she wondered why she'd thought Lady Anne's presence would protect her. His voice shimmered with memories that united and divided them. If she claimed that Lord Farthingham held her heart, would Weddington then ask why she'd met him at dawn? What would he reveal in front of his sister, what would he keep secret?

"That is a complicated question, Your Grace, not easily answered. I don't have a list of attributes that I can check off to ensure that a gentleman gains my favor."

"And what of you, Anne?"

Although he'd asked the question of his sister, Kitty could feel his gaze riveted on her.

"It's intangible, more of a sensation of belonging together, I should think. I can't describe it, Richard. I believe that is both the beauty and the frustration of love. That each person must experience it in his own way, and, therefore, should never advise another on it."

She wanted to cheer Lady Anne's sentiments. *Mind your own business, Weddington*, she thought, yet even as she thought it, she was left with the distinct impression that perhaps he was.

The Royal Italian Opera had at one time been known as the Covent Garden Theatre. Kitty sat beside Lady Anne at the front of the balcony box while Weddington sat directly behind Kitty. She was acutely aware of each breath he took. The tangy lemony scent that was such a part of him, and had enveloped her in the coach, continued to wrap around her in the balcony.

As the curtains opened, Lady Anne leaned forward slightly and placed a tiny pair of silver binoculars to her eyes. Kitty had not brought hers, but they were truly not needed. The duke's box was close enough to the stage that every performer and set scenery was clearly visible, the details remarkably viewed. Even her father never acquired seats so perfectly located for the optimum enjoyment of the performance.

Her mastery of Italian had come at an early age, along with French. Her father's success had allowed her to move in circles that she knew few ladies did, and she'd been determined to make the most of the opportunities he provided and always to make him proud. She'd applied herself to her studies with the same fervor she applied herself to all things. So for her, the opera was an experience she truly appreciated and relished, and as she became caught up in the performance, her awareness of Weddington gradually began to recede.

Until his warm breath fluttered against the nape of her neck.

"Hold still," he murmured so quietly as to almost be unheard, his lips so close as to almost be felt. "Your maid failed to properly secure a button."

With his gloved finger, he slowly stroked her spine from the base of her skull to the top of her shoulders. Down and up. A small circle. Down. A tiny circle. Up. Over and over. So incredibly leisurely. So incredibly sensuously. The warmth of his flesh seeped through the cloth that separated his skin from hers. She was aware of the slow turning of his hand, the pressing of his palm against the side of her neck, his knuckles coming to rest beneath her chin, the tip of his finger taking an unhurried journey along her collarbone until it dipped into the hollow at her throat.

She breathed shallowly, swallowed hard, certain he could feel the movement of her throat against his finger.

Heat swirled around her, through her until it settled in the most unexpected of places: at the apex between her thighs. It was all she could do not to shift within her chair, not to seek the pressure that her body instinctively cried out for.

As though he had all the time in the world, as though the curtain would never be drawn closed and the performance would never end, he trailed his finger back up along her collarbone, then up the side of her neck, tucking his finger against the sensitive spot right behind her ear. She was conscious of her breasts swelling against the fabric of her gown, her nipples hardening, and she wondered how so simple a touch could feel as though it caressed every sensitive inch of her body.

Biting back a moan, she fought to ignore his attentions, but it was not a battle she had any chance of winning. Her vision blurred and darkened, and she realized that her eyelids had fluttered closed. Then his thumb joined the game, stroking her earlobe, outlining the delicate shell of her ear. She thought in her weakening state that she might simply slip off the padded velvet cushion of the chair. How did he manage to so thoroughly distract her with so simple a maneuver?

His hand slipped around back, and she felt movement indicating that he was at long last slipping the errant button through its loop.

"There," he whispered, his lips skimming against her ear. "All has been put to rights."

His withdrawal was hard felt, almost brutal with the longing it left in its wake. She shivered, not from cold, but rather from her detestable desire to abandon her chair, climb onto his lap, and beg him to find more buttons that needed his remarkable attention.

Richard settled uncomfortably in his chair, his swollen manhood aching almost as much as his lower back. He'd been a damned fool to taunt her, because in so doing, he taunted himself. One touch was not nearly enough, but then he knew if he touched her for each star in the infinite heavens he would still be far from satisfied, would still not consider it enough.

By God, he'd even been wearing gloves, snug ones at that. It was as though his fingertips remembered the silkiness of her skin from the moments he'd held her, touched her, and caressed her by the sea. He longed to trail his lips over the same path that his finger had just taken, but Anne would likely notice. He knew he'd taken a chance that her absorption in the performance would prevent her from noticing little else. The result had been worth the risk, but he dared not go any further, because his own restraint was likely to break, and he might give in to the temptation to lift her out of the chair and onto his lap.

His touch had affected Kitty as well. He'd felt it in the tiny shimmers noticeable beneath his hand, her quiet swallowing, the stillness of her breathing. He was incredibly aware of every aspect of her being.

Did Farthingham heat her up as Richard did? Would she be as quick to flare under Richard's ministrations if Farthingham did ignite her so? Or did her quick, sharp reaction indicate her body was in want of pleasure? Did Farthingham grant her gratification, or did he withhold it?

And what could Richard do about it, if anything? Her loyalty to Farthingham was commendable, and caused him to admire her all the more. She would stick with Farthingham through thick and thin, in spite of the fact that he might not be the right man for her, because she believed in Farthingham, believed in them as a couple.

She'd made her bed and was determined to lie in it, even if it was rumpled and unkempt.

He'd witnessed Farthingham kissing her cheek and her forehead, taking her hand. And yet, Richard had not taken notice of her heating up as she seemed to whenever he touched her—even with something as innocent as a gloved finger. Although his intentions had been anything but innocent. He'd purposely sought to unsettle her, to make her wonder what it might be like to experience his touch in its entirety. He'd only given her a hint of what he had to offer, and, in the offering, he'd caused his own suffering.

He shifted in his chair, grateful that it was only his back that nagged at him. He'd resurrected an old injury when he'd made his mad dash for the tennis ball and subsequently landed inelegantly on the ground. It was the reason that tonight he sported a walking stick: to help relieve some of the pain he suffered when he walked.

The injury usually flared only in the cold and the damp or when he didn't take care to hold it at bay, when he was exhausted. Anne had expressed concern at his intention to play lawn tennis because she was well aware that it took little to make the muscles in his back revolt. He should have heeded her concern, but he was determined to win what Kitty was so reluctant to give.

He couldn't reconcile his fascination with her. If he set his mind to it, he could have any woman in all of England, probably any woman in all of America. While he might not possess the angelic face that Farthingham did, Richard thought his features were not too disagreeable. He possessed five prestigious titles, wealth, five grand estates, two residences in London—one to become the dower house once he took a wife—yachts, carriages, a fine stable of horses, the list of his possessions was endless, required five managers working tirelessly to keep track of everything. A woman married to him would never want for a single item.

So why did the woman sitting in front of him not cast Farthingham aside and rush into Richard's arms after Richard had made it undeniably clear that he would welcome her there? Was it possible that she did indeed love Farthingham? Was love so powerful, so important that it mattered more than all the material possessions and advantages that Richard could provide?

And if he added love to all he had to offer?

He shook his head. While he believed in love, it was not an emotion he had any interest in experiencing firsthand. Oh, he loved his mother, he loved Anne, and he had loved his father. But a woman to whom he was not related?

Never. Love of that sort robbed one of control. Anne was a perfect example, spouting off about some commoner and realizing all she would give up if she took this man as a husband.

Or perhaps she recognized that Richard would see that she did not do without, that he would give her an ample dowry and lift her husband up rather than letting him drag her down.

Once again, he shifted in his chair. He should have postponed this outing, given his back time to recover. Swimming helped. He wasn't sure why. Perhaps the buoyancy took all the weight off his body, cocooned him. He thought being cocooned by Miss Robertson might help as well. He imagined her delicate hands rubbing linseed oil over his back, taking the time to massage each muscle, to leave no bit of flesh untouched. Yes, he rather enjoyed the image those thoughts conjured up.

And with the image, more than his back began to ache again.

Incredible. He was no novice when it came to women, and yet he could not recall reacting so quickly nor so intensely to ponderings about even one female who had ever caught his fancy. He had but to let a solitary thought of Kitty flit through his mind, and his body was ready to give chase. For a man of his years, he should behave with a bit more decorum.

He'd brought Anne to the opera so Kitty would be more at ease around him. He'd also spoken true. He had no wish to tarnish her reputation—particularly if he were to succeed in convincing her that he was the one she should marry and not Farthingham. He wanted his duchess to be above reproach, free of scandal.

Several eyebrows had of course been raised when he'd walked in with Kitty at his side. To the right ears he'd delivered a few words of explanation—he'd brought her as a favor to Farthingham, who'd had an unexpected engagement. By the next afternoon all of London would know he'd not brought Kitty without Farthingham's knowledge, consent, and blessing. Not that it was truly anyone's business except his and Farthingham's.

But he was too familiar with the damage that unkind rumors could cause. He'd suffered through enough of them when his father had died. It hadn't been bad enough that the doctors had doubted whether or not Richard would survive and if he did, whether he would ever again walk without a limp. Oh, no. Gossipmongers had a field day, upsetting his mother no end, speculating as to what had really happened between him and his father out on the sea.

He turned his attention back to Kitty. He'd much rather contemplate her than his past. He thought he could spend all night simply watching her. He wondered what he could offer Farthingham that would make him consider giving her up.

Chapter 8

During the journey home, Kitty stared at her gloved hands, stared out the window, stared at the shadows inside, doing all she could to avoid looking at Weddington. She'd thought she was aware of him before. Now it was as though he actually inhabited her skin. She was aware each time he shifted on the seat, each time he released the tiniest of sighs, each movement of his hands, and the intensity with which he continually watched her.

She considered taking him to task for the liberties he'd exhibited when he'd touched her, but she simply wanted to forget it had happened. Although she thought it unlikely that she ever would. It was as though he'd branded a circle around her throat, a velvet collar that drew her to him.

These feelings, these sensations were completely wrong, went against all of her upbringing. She'd worked diligently to bury the faintest hint that they existed, and all it took from Weddington was a light touch, a gentle caress, and she was burning with forbidden desires and lacked the wherewithal to squelch the flames.

She longed for Farthingham's comforting embrace, a place to hide away from the sensations and lurid thoughts that tormented her. She felt incredibly on edge, and feared the slightest touch from Weddington would catapult her into an arena she had no wish to enter.

"Did you not enjoy the opera, Miss Robertson?" Weddington asked.

Startled by his voice, she fought to regain control of her emotions. He'd unsettled her earlier, and she had no wish for him to know it. "I enjoyed it very much, Your Grace, thank you."

"Anne and I attend performances quite often. You are more than welcome to join us at any time."

She gave up the battle of not looking at him. "I appreciate your generosity, but honestly, I spent much of tonight thinking of Lord Farthingham and missing him."

"Bring him along next time, then."

His offer surprised her. Did he think Farthingham wouldn't notice Weddington's finger trailing along her neck, beneath the laced, raised collar of her gown?

"I'll let him know you've extended an invitation."

"It would be jolly good fun having Lord Farthingham along," Lady Anne said. "I always enjoy his company."

"I think he's gifted at ensuring everyone around him has fun," Kitty admitted. "He has a way of putting people at ease. I've always felt very comfortable around him."

"You strike me as a woman who would prefer risk over comfort," Weddington said.

"I'll admit that in my youth I possessed a streak of wildness. I've worked very hard to tame it."

"A pity. I prefer a woman who has a bit of wildness in her nature."

"Gentlemen might prefer her, but they do not marry her."

"You say that as though you speak from experience," he said.

The familiar pain and loathing burned her stomach. "I know a woman who was once extremely wild. She paid a high price for her actions."

"So you have taken your lessons from her mistakes?"

"Yes."

"And are you happy with your choices?"

"Very much so. And a good deal happier than you, I would think." Rather pleased with that volley, she turned her attention back to the window.

"Upon what do you make your assessment regarding my happiness?" he asked.

"You seldom smile, and I've only once heard you laugh."

"She has you there, Richard. You are quite glum at times," Lady Anne said.

"Thank you, dear sister. I'll keep that in mind the next time you request a new gown."

Kitty was surprised to note that his voice still carried no offense, but genuine affection. She wondered if Lady Anne could ever truly garner his wrath.

"I thought you believed a woman should speak her mind," Lady Anne said.

"Most certainly, that is my belief—as long as her mind is of the same persuasion as mine."

Kitty snapped to attention at his ridiculous remark. "You can't be serious."

"Did you not just say that I was *always* serious?"

Was that a hint of teasing in his voice? How she wished the coach contained enough light that she'd be able to look in his eyes and determine if he was indeed mocking her. The notion of his teasing was so contrary to what she knew of him . . . she didn't want to consider that he might possess a lighter side. To her he was and would always be dark and dangerous, a man who tempted her with feelings best left unfound.

As the coach rocked to a stop, Kitty couldn't have been more grateful with the timing and the fact that the journey had come to an end. She turned to the woman sitting beside her. "Lady Anne, I thoroughly enjoyed your company. Thank you so much for making it an unforgettable evening."

"You're most welcome, Miss Robertson. And I do hope you'll accept Richard's invitation to join us another time. Truly, neither of us will object to Lord Farthingham coming along."

"Thank you. I do hope to see you again."

She twisted slightly and before she could offer her thanks to Weddington, he said, "I'll see you to the door."

"That's not necessary."

"I must insist."

Of course. He was a man determined to have his way in all matters. As if on cue, the door opened, the steps dropped down, and the footman extended a gloved hand inside.

Kitty made her way out of the coach and waited impatiently while the duke did the same. As they walked toward the door, she was acutely aware of the tapping of his walking stick and the tread of his feet, one obviously heavier and more labored than the other. At the opera house, the slowness of his movements had irritated her because she'd thought he'd purposely prolonged their reaching his box so that everyone would take notice of her accompanying him.

But now no reason remained for him to lag behind, nothing his slowness would accomplish. She faced him, and in the dim light cast by the gas lamps illuminating the front of the house, she saw a hardness to the set of his mouth, a tautness at the corners of his eyes, and a stiffness to the way he held his body. He was not moving with the fluid motions that had characterized him that afternoon nor on the rocks where she'd first sighted him.

"Are you in pain?" she suddenly surprised herself by asking.

Surprised him as well if the astonished expression on his face was any indication.

"My back is troubling me, but I thought I was disguising my discomfort quite well," he said.

"You were . . . you are." She shook her head. "I was rude to ask. Forgive me."

"I would forgive you anything, Miss Robertson."

"Why do you do that?"

"Do what?"

"Speak to me as though I mean more to you than I ever could."

"If you think that, then you fail to realize the full extent of my esteemed regard for you."

"I intend to marry Lord Farthingham."

"The best intentions sometimes go astray."

"Is that hope or warning in your voice?" she asked.

The tightness at his mouth eased, and he smiled. "A little of both, I should think. I am not a man who gives up easily when he wants something."

"I think you want me because you cannot have me. Forbidden fruit is perceived as being much sweeter."

He took a step closer, his smile fading. "What do you know of forbidden fruit?"

What she knew of it, she had no wish to discuss, so she decided to ignore the question and distract him with a warning. "Your sister can see you from the coach."

"So she can." He tucked a gloved finger up beneath her chin. "I could make you happy."

"I love Lord Farthingham. He makes me happy."

"I would make you happier."

Laughing lightly, she stepped back, freeing her chin from his claim to it. "You are too arrogant."

"Only if my claims are proven false."

"Why didn't you tell me that you were in pain?" she asked, determined to change the course of his thoughts.

"Would you have offered to rub where I ache?"

"No, but we could have postponed our night at the opera until you were feeling better."

"The discomfort is tolerable. Not spending the evening with you wasn't."

She shook her head, amazed that he had the ability to turn everything to his advantage. It was past time to take her leave. "Thank you, Your Grace, for the evening."

"What? Will you not describe it as you did for Anne? Enjoyable? Memorable? Unforgettable?"

"Where you're concerned—irritating, bothersome, infuriating—might be more appropriate. This evening you took liberties to which you had no right." There. She'd said it. It was out in the open.

"I didn't notice you objecting."

"What recourse did I have except to endure it? Slap your hand and draw Lady Anne's attention to where you'd placed it?"

The scoundrel had the audacity to hitch up one corner of his mouth in the semblance of a smile. "Endure it? Miss Robertson, I strongly believe you relished it."

The crack of her palm hitting his cheek echoed between them, as tears stung her eyes because she had indeed savored every caress. "I don't like you, Your Grace. I don't like you at all."

Spinning on her heel, she shoved open the door and escaped inside before she could humiliate herself further.

The astonished butler snapped to attention immediately. "Miss Robertson—"

"Please, send my maid up so she can help me prepare for bed and instruct her to bring a bottle of my father's finest whiskey."

She admired the man for not showing surprise at her request. She trudged up the stairs, each step harder to climb than the one before it. She wished she'd never taken a walk along the seashore, wished she'd never spotted Poseidon.

She endured Nancy's help in undressing and preparing for bed only because removing her gown and undergarments was impossible to accomplish alone. Why couldn't women have clothing that was constructed as simply as a man's?

She avoided her reflection in the mirror while Nancy combed out and plaited her hair. Why couldn't women wear their hair as short as a man's? Not that she really had any desire to chop off her hair, but at times when she was anxious for solitude, it was an inconvenience she'd prefer not to be bothered with.

After Nancy left, Kitty poured the whiskey into a large glass and went to sit in her favorite chair beside the window. Downing the whiskey as though it were water, she coughed, relishing the burning to her throat, the watering of her eyes. Whiskey was her secret sin—if she did not count encounters with Weddington. She suspected her father knew of her drinking, but he'd never confronted her when a bottle disappeared. But sometimes indulging simply seemed the quickest way to obtain oblivion.

Tonight, however, rather than dull her senses, it seemed to sharpen them. Closing her eyes, she trailed her finger along her collarbone. She could still feel Weddington's touch as though he'd left behind a part of himself.

Damn him, damn him, damn him for making her want to experience his caress again. And damn her own traitorous body for wishing he were there now to inflame the fires still burning within her.

She awoke in hell. Her head pounded with the erratic rhythm of a drummer who'd yet to learn a consistent cadence. A dry fuzziness tickled her mouth as though she'd swallowed a cat's tail. Her eyes ached, her temples throbbed, and her stomach roiled.

A heavy price to pay for deciding each tear shed should be followed with a drop of whiskey. She didn't even want to contemplate how she'd explain the missing bottle to her parents should they deign to ask her about it. Her father kept inventory of his liquor the way she kept inventory of her jewelry. Hopefully, he'd overlook the short count as he had in the past when she'd sneaked a bottle.

She cringed as the pounding in her head grew in intensity and loudness.

"Miss Robertson?"

She squinted into the darkness. "What?"

Her voice sounded like the mating call of a bullfrog, not the delicate soft voice of a lady. *Oh, dear God, spare me.* She'd reverted to her origins. The saloonkeeper's granddaughter. She thought she might be ill.

She was a snob . . . exactly as Weddington appeared to be, spouting all his nonsense about commoners. She detested having anything in common with that man.

The door squeaked open, and her skull threatened to split in two at the sound.

"Oh, Miss Robertson, they are the loveliest!"

She heard a thump, and then the awful rasp of draperies being drawn aside, and the unforgiving sunlight crashing against her eyes. With a moan, she threw the covers over her head and buried herself deep within the feather mattress. With any luck she could hide here forever.

"Miss Robertson, you are the luckiest of ladies. Will you not at least read Lord Farthingham's note?"

She moved the blanket down until she could peer over the thick coverlet. "What?"

"The flowers, miss."

Kitty became aware then of the subtle fragrance wafting toward her: a lovely blend of orchids and roses. She opened her eyes farther and saw Nancy holding a missive toward her. And beyond Nancy was a vase in which had been arranged the most beautiful and abundant collection of flowers Kitty had ever seen.

Her headache forgotten, she forced herself to sit up. "Are they from Lord Farthingham?"

"We assumed so, miss."

She thought the brightness of her smile might make her jaw ache. No doubt he'd missed her last night as much as she'd missed him. She took the note from Nancy, unfolded it . . . and her headache returned in full force. Not from Farthingham.

My dear Miss Robertson,

A thousand apologies for what you were forced to endure while in my company evening last. You and Lord Farthingham may have exclusive use of my box at the Royal Italian Opera House for as long as you are in London.

Yours most devotedly,
The Duke of Weddington

"Whatever's wrong, miss?" Nancy asked.

Kitty shook her head, regretting the movement as soon as she began it. "They aren't a gift from Farthingham. They're an apology from Weddington."

"All of them?"

Kitty scoffed. "No, only the roses. I've no earthly idea who the orchids are from." She scowled. "Of course, *all* of them are from the duke. Why would you think otherwise?"

"Because he sent so many, miss."

Kitty scrambled out of bed for a closer look. Without counting, she thought it looked as though at least two dozen flowers filled the vase. Each one exquisite, each one a blossom to be admired. But she found it difficult to appreciate them knowing from whom they'd come.

"Why don't you take them down to the parlor so everyone can enjoy them?"

"I don't know that there's room, miss."

Why must inefficiency run rampant on this of all mornings—when she was in no condition to deal with it properly?

"I realize it's a large arrangement, Nancy, but then again, the parlor *is* a large room."

"Yes, miss, but the other flowers are taking up almost the entire space in the parlor and the drawing room."

"What other flowers?" she asked, a sense of apprehension filling her, as Nancy's earlier exuberance about the flowers began to take root.

"All the others he sent. There must be close to a thousand, I should think. They've been arriving for the past hour, and we can hardly locate enough vases to arrange them all properly."

Kitty snatched her robe off a nearby chair, shoved her arms into it, tightened the sash, and hastened out of the room. Down the sweeping stairs she dashed, halfway expecting to see Weddington waiting at the foot of them.

She came to a stuttering halt at the entry to the parlor. Every type of flower in every imaginable color filled the room. Some in vases, most simply bound together with ribbon. *A thousand flowers. A thousand apologies.*

"Kitty, what on earth is going on?" her mother asked, holding a large bouquet as though she was at a loss as to what to do with it.

Kitty shook her head. How could she even begin to explain without revealing all?

"Your father will not be at all pleased to see that Farthingham goes to such excess and extravagance—"

"Not Farthingham. Weddington."

Her mother looked as though Kitty had drawn a pistol on her. "The duke?"

Kitty nodded.

"Why would he send—"

"To apologize."

"What does he need to apologize for?"

Kitty couldn't decide whether to laugh or cry. "He has an interest in me, Mama. And I have none in him."

"He's apologizing for having an interest?"

"It's complicated."

"Appears so."

Shaking her head, Kitty walked to one of the vases and touched a velvety petal. "How typical of a man to think he can win a lady over simply by spending money on her."

"He doesn't know you well at all if he thinks you can be lured by objects."

Kitty sighed. "You're absolutely right. He knows nothing about me."

And if she kept to her original intentions, he never would.

Kitty's headache started anew when she received word that the Duchess of Weddington and her daughter had come to call. Of all the afternoons for them to make an appearance—when she wasn't feeling quite herself. Still, she dressed appropriately, pinched her cheeks and bit her lips to get a little color into them, and went down to the parlor to greet her guests.

A petite silver-haired woman was wandering through the room admiring all the fresh flowers. Lady Anne sat on a sofa, her hands folded on her lap. She rose to her feet as soon as she saw Kitty.

"Miss Robertson."

"Lady Anne."

The older woman turned, and Lady Anne beamed. "Mother, I would like to introduce Miss Kitty Robertson."

The duchess smiled warmly. "Miss Robertson, it is indeed a pleasure."

"Your Grace, I'm so honored that you would pay me a visit. Please, sit." Twisting slightly, Kitty signaled to the waiting servant to bring tea.

The duchess sat beside her daughter on the sofa, and Kitty took her place in a chair sitting opposite them.

"The flowers are absolutely lovely," the duchess said.

"Thank you, Your Grace, but I can take no credit for their beauty."

"I am well aware of that, dear girl. Anne says that I'm mistaken, but I do believe these are Richard's flowers. Too many resemble the ones that filled his greenhouse until this morning. I daresay, he must have been up all night preparing them for delivery here."

Kitty barely noticed the servant placing the tea tray on the table in front of her as she stared at the duchess. "You don't believe these came from a flower shop or vendor?"

"I hardly think so. His conservatory was filled yesterday, and when I sent my girl out this morning to gather a few fresh flowers for my room, she reported the place was practically barren of blossoms." She waved her hand. "And here they seem to be."

Kitty felt somewhat better that he hadn't gone to great expense on her behalf. "Your gardener is to be applauded—"

"No, no, no, dear girl. Not our gardener. Richard. They are his flowers. He allows no one to touch them when we are in London, which is the very reason that I must send my girl out at the crack of dawn if I want any. To sneak a few out without his knowing. She said this morning that he was instructing servants to load them into carriages."

"Are you saying that your son grew these flowers?"

"If they are indeed his, which I have no reason to believe otherwise." The duchess arched a finely shaped brow. "Are they?"

Kitty shifted her gaze between the duchess and Lady Anne. She felt the heat climbing up her face. "The note that accompanied them was from the Duke of Weddington."

"Whatever did you do to gain such favor from him?"

The lid clattered as Kitty picked up the teapot, because her hands were trembling so badly. "I really can't say," she said, hoping the manner in which she emphasized the words gave the impression that she didn't have a clue rather than that she wouldn't say. *I kissed him at dawn and set our blood to boiling. Apparently, he's having no more luck forgetting it than I am.*

"Orchids are a hobby of his, although I don't think he's as obsessed as Joseph Chamberlain is reported to be. I believe Richard finds solace in his conservatory. There and on the sea."

Kitty handed the cups and saucers to her guests. "I'm fond of the sea as well."

"You must visit us at Drummond Manor sometime," Lady Anne said. "We would make you feel most welcome, wouldn't we, Mother?"

"Yes, of course."

"Richard could take you out on one of his yachts."

"I really don't see where I'll have time, with all the plans I need to make with Lord Farthingham."

"Of course, but still it's a pity. I was telling Mother how very much I've enjoyed your company since meeting you," Lady Anne said. "We do hope you will come to call."

"I'd be most pleased to do so."

"Splendid," the duchess said. "Now, we must be off. We have other calls to make this afternoon."

After the duchess and Lady Anne left, Kitty sat in the parlor, surrounded by the sweet fragrance, her gaze lighting on each flower. She would have preferred that he'd purchased the blasted things. She didn't like the idea of his giving her something he'd nurtured and coaxed into blooming—didn't like the idea of him alone all night standing in a greenhouse with plants, standing alone on a rocky shoreline gazing out to sea.

She'd had three Seasons and not once had she met him. How could such an impossible loner be friends with Farthingham, who constantly gathered people around himself as though he needed them in order to breathe?

And why, oh why, could she not tear her thoughts away from Weddington?

Chapter 9

Richard heard the deep laughter echoing into the hallway long before the butler escorted him into the library.

"Weddington! So glad you came by," Farthingham said, coming to his feet and greeting him as soon as he entered the room. "You've had the honor of meeting Frederick Montague, haven't you?"

"Yes, we were introduced a few years ago."

"I thought so."

"I managed to catch your performance in a play that Farthingham recommended to me," Richard said to Montague. "I was impressed with your acting talent."

Montague was young, but his gray eyes reflected intelligence and perhaps a bit of seeing more of the world than he would have liked. He bowed slightly and smiled. "Your Grace, I am honored that you would be impressed by any of my humble efforts."

"As well you should be, Freddie. Weddington, would you care for some port?"

"I believe I will." Richard sat in a plush chair, one of four that sat around an octagonal table.

Farthingham lifted the decanter and pointed it toward Montague. "Freddie has recently left the stage, however, to work behind it—as a playwright. I was just reading his latest work. It's fantastic."

"Based on the laughter I heard before I came in, I presume it's a comedy."

"Quite so," Farthingham said, handing Richard a goblet. "It's the story of a man who commits murder in order to gain a woman's affections."

"I've never considered murder to be humorous."

"Admit it, Weddington, you consider very little in life to be humorous. But Freddie's play is brilliant. I predict it would make even you chuckle a time or two. Perhaps he'll let you read it."

"Oh, no," Montague interjected. He blushed, his gaze darting between Richard and Farthingham. "It's only a first write. I still need to polish it a bit more."

"When you're comfortable with it, then, I'd like to read it," Richard said. "I trust Farthingham's opinion."

"Thank you, Your Grace. I will be incredibly honored to have your opinion of my work."

Richard sipped his port.

Smiling, Farthingham took a seat, lounged back, and crossed his legs. "So what brings you to my door?"

Richard shrugged. "I thought a visit was in order."

Farthingham's smile faded. "You can speak candidly in front of Freddie."

"Very well. I wanted to speak with you about Miss Robertson."

"My goodness," Montague piped up. "I'd forgotten that I have an appointment. I must be off." He came to his feet. "It was a pleasure to see you again, Your Grace."

"I was serious about reading your play once you're comfortable allowing me to see it."

The man looked inordinately pleased. "Thank you, Your Grace. I shall be certain to get a copy to you."

"He'll stay up all night writing it out himself," Farthingham said.

Montague laughed self-deprecatingly. "I am but a poor playwright."

"I understand that even Shakespeare died a pauper," Richard said.

Montague's eyes widened. "I would not dare compare myself to so great and gifted a man."

"Freddie is planning to move to America before the year is out," Farthingham explained. "He thinks he might have more success selling his plays in New York."

"I wish you the best in your endeavors then."

"Thank you, Your Grace. Now if you'll excuse me, I really must be off."

As Frederick Montague disappeared through the door, Farthingham shook his head. "I do not envy those who seek to make a living through creative endeavors. It seems a terribly difficult road to travel, and yet I have the utmost respect for those who possess that gift. If I had the means, I'd serve as patron for every writer, artist, and musician in London."

Farthingham downed his wine, got up, and poured himself another glass before returning to his chair. "I assume you're here to tell me that your night at the opera went splendidly."

"I'm here to ask you to consider not marrying Miss Robertson."

"After spending a harrowing month with the solicitors and her father working on the settlement, I think the possibility of not marrying her is extremely remote." Leaning forward, planting his elbows on his thighs, Farthingham studied the liquid within the goblet he held between his hands. "Although I'm pleased you enjoyed her company, I must admit to being quite fond of her myself."

"Fondness is not love. You'll destroy her, Farthingham."

Farthingham's head came up abruptly. "Don't be so melodramatic."

"She is a passionate woman who needs a man who can love her passionately."

Farthingham dropped back, extended his legs, and cradled his chin in his palm. "You deduced all this from a single waltz, a game of lawn tennis, and one night at the opera?"

Richard's friendship with Farthingham had weathered many storms, so Richard did not hesitate to confess, "Before all that, our paths crossed near Drummond Manor."

"I should have guessed. I thought I detected a definite undercurrent at Ravenleigh's ball. Did she ask you to speak with me?"

"No. She wants nothing to do with me."

Farthingham laughed. "Oh, that's rich. Still, you've decided to save her from me."

"I truly don't believe you can make her happy."

"And I truly believe that I can." Farthingham came to his feet, walked to the window, and gazed out on the garden. "As I said, I'm very fond of Kitty. I would never harm her. I enjoy her company and take great pleasure in spending time with her. I find her beautiful. I will remain faithful and never give her any cause to doubt my devotion."

"I do not doubt your willingness, but rather your ability to carry through on your plans. A man's past often speaks loudly of his future."

Farthingham turned and held Richard's gaze, his face deadly serious. "And yet there comes a time when a man must set his past aside and embrace his future whether he wishes to or not. As a firstborn son, you know as well as I that our lives belong to England, that we have a duty to those who came before us and to those who will come after—to provide a good financial foundation and an heir, to be honorable, to put our wants and needs last. Whatever my life has been, once I take Kitty as my wife—" he shook his head as though he needed time to regain control of his commitment—"I will dedicate myself to her and her happiness."

Richard came to his feet. "Farthingham, I have always admired and respected you. I know you possess a profound sense of duty and an understanding of obligation that exceeds most men's grasp, but I beg of you, do not take Kitty as your wife. She deserves so much more than a marriage based on duty and obligation. You cannot bring to your marriage the passion for her that I could."

Farthingham shook his head slowly, his smile one of sadness and—Richard dared not acknowledge—pity as well. "Still have a driving need to control everything, Weddington, to believe you and you alone know what is best for everyone? You're not God, man. You can't *know* what one's life will hold."

"I don't profess to have some omniscient power or gift, but I feel strongly that she is not the one for you, nor you the one for her."

"Do you love her?"

Richard lowered his gaze. "You know I don't."

"You speak of passion when you cannot love. Not even yourself. You hold yourself responsible for your father's death, and you've never forgiven yourself for it. I can think of a thousand reasons why marriage to you would make Kitty unhappy. I, on the other hand, love myself and everyone who surrounds me. I shall make her laugh, I shall bring her joy."

"If I ever determine that she is not the happiest woman in all of England, I'll do everything in my power to free her of you."

"You've never been one to do things in half measures. I'm surprised you're not doing everything now."

Richard grinned. "Who's to say I'm not?"

Farthingham laughed. "Who indeed! I suppose now is not the most opportune moment to ask you to stand as my best man when I exchange my vows with Kitty."

Richard decided he was a glutton for punishment. "Now is as good a time as any."

"Because the answer is no."

"Because the answer is yes. We have been friends far too long for me not to feel honored by the request."

Farthingham swirled the wine in his glass. "You hold within your grasp the power to very easily turn her away from me."

Richard made a move to leave. "I don't wish to turn her affections away from you, Farthingham. I merely wish to turn them toward me."

* * *

Kitty loved the intimacy of small, friendly gatherings, preferred them actually. Although she adored balls and elaborate dinner parties, she also found them extremely taxing. To always have to worry about how one was presented and perceived. Within Farthingham's home, a home that would soon be hers, she usually felt comfortable and safe.

Tonight, however, sitting at the dining table with Farthingham to her left and Weddington directly across from her, she was acutely conscious of Weddington's stiffness and formality. She could hardly blame him. She'd not sent a written thank-you acknowledging receipt of his lovely flowers. On his arrival with his sister, she'd done nothing except awkwardly greet him.

Lady Anne sat beside her brother and across from Freddie Montague. Kitty had read a few of his plays. She thought they were well done, but she was always surprised by the hard edge she detected in his work. He had such a boyish face that she expected his writings to reflect what she knew of him: youthfulness, charm, innocence. But his biting humor made her often wonder if perhaps he wanted to strike out at a world that he thought unfair. Surely a writer's words reflected some part of him.

"If America is so wonderful, then why are so many ladies seeking out our lords?" Lady Priscilla asked.

Apparently one of Lady Anne's dearest friends, she sat on the other side of Freddie and obviously thought he was the most fascinating of men. Since her arrival she'd hardly taken her eyes off him. She was clearly not happy with Freddie's announcement that he was planning to move to America.

"Good question," Farthingham said. "Why do you think that is, my sweet?"

"America is wonderful," Kitty admitted, her gaze darting around the table, staying the briefest amount of time on Weddington. "But I think it's only now beginning to achieve the refinement England has held for so long. It takes a while to recover from a civil war. I would have thought your own history would have taught you that."

"She has you there, Prissy!" Farthingham crowed.

"Oh, bugger off."

Farthingham laughed. "Such unladylike talk for the daughter of an earl."

"I think we all get tired of being on show," Lady Priscilla said. "Don't you think, Freddie?"

"As the fifth son of a viscount, I've hardly ever been on show."

"I didn't know your father was a viscount," Kitty said.

Freddie blushed, and Farthingham provided, "He's rather the black sheep of the family, my sweet. A man trying to *earn* his keep in the world—as a playwright, no less—is hardly behavior befitting of an aristocrat's son."

"Your family doesn't approve?" Kitty asked.

"They don't approve of a great many things about me."

Kitty wondered if it was that disappointment that she saw reflected in his writings. "It's their loss, Freddie."

"You are too kind, Miss Robertson."

"Come, come," Farthingham said with a generous wave of his hand. "No formalities tonight. We are friends among friends, free to be ourselves. Why do you think I did not make us sit according to *Debrett's*?"

"Quite honestly, Farthingham, I assumed it was because you did not yet have a wife to sort it all out for you. By the by, when are you going to make a formal declaration? People are beginning to doubt the integrity of my gossip," Lady Priscilla said.

"Kitty has asked me to wait until the end of the Season to announce our betrothal," Farthingham said.

Kitty lifted her eyes to Weddington for only a heartbeat, but it was long enough to recognize that he wondered if perhaps her desire to wait had anything to do with his request that she delay the announcement. She lowered her gaze to where Farthingham had wrapped his hand around hers, watched as he lifted it and kissed the back of her hand.

"I am more than willing to do whatever my lady desires in order to keep her happy."

"Hear, hear," Freddie said. "Allow me to offer a toast for happiness to the both of you."

The toast was acknowledged by all present, glasses lifted, sips taken. Kitty felt as though her stomach were tightening into a knot. She had no doubt she would be happy with Farthingham. Yet she could not seem to ignore the presence of the man sitting across from her. While everyone else seemed to be on the fringes of her world, he seemed to be ensconced directly in the middle of it. She found that acknowledgment extremely unsettling.

She wished he'd say something. Anything. He'd spoken so little since his arrival that she was beginning to wonder why he'd bothered to come at all, and even as she thought it, she knew, because he'd known he'd find her there.

He wasn't using a walking stick, but neither did he move with the fluidity she'd seen on the rocks. She somehow sensed that he was still experiencing discomfort, but fighting to mask it.

"How is your back, Your Grace?" she asked quietly.

His jaw tightened. "Much improved, Miss Robertson. Thank you for your concern."

"My God, Weddington, must you be so formal?" Farthingham asked.

"Unlike you, Farthingham, I have no desire to imitate the masses."

Farthingham chuckled. "Then you'll absolutely adore what I have in mind for entertainment later."

"Whatever is wrong with your back, Your Grace?" Lady Priscilla asked.

"He injured it while trying to beat Kitty at a game of lawn tennis," Farthingham said before Weddington could respond.

"I did not *try*, I succeeded in winning," Weddington said tartly.

"How unsporting," Lady Priscilla said. "What sort of gentleman are you, Weddington, not to allow a lady to win?"

"A gentleman who—" Kitty and Weddington began at the same time, stopped simultaneously, and looked at each other.

Weddington angled his head. "Who recognizes a worthy opponent," he finished.

She'd been on brink of saying he was a gentleman who disliked losing a wager. Kitty felt the heat warm her face under his perusal, and she hardly knew what to do with her confusing thoughts. She studied him. "What if there had been no wager, Your Grace?"

"I would have fought just as hard to win, Miss Robertson."

"Fought?" Farthingham asked. "Good God, Weddington, you weren't at war."

"I disagree, Farthingham," Weddington said, holding Kitty's gaze. "It was a battle of skill. One does not dishonor one's opponent by retreating before the decisive blow is delivered."

"It's little wonder you've yet to marry," Farthingham said. "I, for one, recognize that a woman is a delicate creature and must be handled as such. I would not deign to hurt her fragile feelings by actually striving to beat her at lawn tennis."

"Instead you insult her," Kitty said.

Farthingham jerked his head around, his blond brows raised in shock. "Pardon?"

"When we play, you never try to win."

"Of course, I don't strive to win, my sweet. I want you to have the honor of winning."

"But it isn't *winning* if *you* didn't try. Nor is it an honor. Rather it's a hollow victory."

"I should think that would be better than no victory at all."

"You wouldn't beat her," Weddington said.

She did not need his endorsement or his support, and yet she found herself warmed by both. Although she'd lost to him, she'd savored the game like none she'd ever won previously.

Farthingham blinked and released a strangled laugh. "I jolly well would if I set my mind to it."

"I'll wager you won't win," Weddington said.

"What will you wager?" Farthingham asked.

"What do you want?"

Farthingham leaned back with a triumphant smile. "*The Fair Lady.*"

"Done."

"And if Miss Robertson wins?" Lady Anne asked.

"She won't," Farthingham said with confidence.

"She will," Weddington said. "Then you must pay a forfeit. Whatever I choose, at the time of my choosing."

"I accept."

"Farthingham, don't be a fool," Freddie warned. "You don't accept a wager without knowing exactly what is at stake and when it will be paid."

"Whatever he desires is a moot issue, Freddie, because I will win, without a doubt."

Stunned, Kitty had watched the exchange as though she was of no consequence, a mere ball played on a court she didn't understand, lobbed back and forth without care. "Have I no say on the matter?"

"None whatsoever," Farthingham said, beaming. "You wanted me to play you to win. Now I shall."

But she didn't want her victory to result in Weddington gaining anything, and she saw by the way he was studying her that he knew it. Now it might be she who wouldn't play for all she was worth. But honor would dictate that she must. What an unconscionable position to find herself in.

She opened her mouth to insist she wouldn't partake in a game when such a ludicrous wager was at stake, saw the gleam of triumph in Weddington's eyes, and snapped her mouth closed. They were battling on another level: she and he. He was challenging her to accept, expecting her to retreat.

She squared her shoulders. "What is the fair lady?"

"One of his yachts," Farthingham said. "She's a beauty. I know how much you like to sail, my sweet. This wager will give me the opportunity to take you out on the seas in my own vessel. Not your father's."

Dear God, she wanted to weep. Because Farthingham did resent taking what he so desperately needed from her father. Because Weddington placed such faith in her ability to win that he was willing to risk losing something of such immense value.

"It's a game of lawn tennis, gentlemen. Wager something a bit more reasonable," she urged.

"I'm content with the wager as it stands," Weddington announced.

"As am I," Farthingham said.

"You are both insane."

"Don't fret so, my sweet," Farthingham said. "Weddington can well afford to replace it."

"That's not the point, Nicky."

"If you're so concerned about his giving up his yacht, don't lose." He grinned and leaned toward her. "But don't experience a single moment of guilt when you do."

"You truly believe you play tennis with more skill than I do?"

He nodded quickly. "Afraid so, my sweet. I'm really quite good."

He'd certainly never even given a hint of any talent at all when they played. That knowledge angered her almost as much as the thought that Weddington would benefit *should* she win. Would pride insist she win? Or would dislike for the man sitting across from her force her to lose? Not knowing what would influence the way she played was almost as challenging a dilemma as playing Weddington had been.

She shrugged nonchalantly as though she couldn't have cared less when in fact she couldn't have cared more. A part of her was bothered that Farthingham had never considered her a worthy enough opponent to apply himself wholeheartedly toward beating her. "All right. If you insist, I'll play you."

"Splendid! The challenge is made, the wagers accepted. Tomorrow afternoon our skills will be put to the test," Farthingham announced.

She glanced toward Weddington, discovered his gaze riveted on her. He lifted his wine goblet and offered a silent salute.

Dear God, she found herself praying for a torrential rain.

Chapter 10

Charades. Richard found it ironic that Farthingham was so fond of the game when it seemed his entire life *was* little more than an elaborate charade.

Trust Farthingham to bend the rules until they were unrecognizable. No teams, no competition really. Everyone simply striving to guess the answer so one might have a turn at standing before the others and making a fool of oneself. Amazing really that everyone tried so hard to accomplish just that feat.

Richard sat on one end of a sofa with Lady Priscilla bouncing beside him, as though she thought jiggling would stir up her thought processes to the point that she could determine the title of the serialization that Anne was miming.

Pickwick Papers.

Kitty was in the chair beside the sofa, her brows deeply furrowed in concentration. He admired her ability to focus so intensely when those around her were shrieking like the inmates at Bedlam. Even Farthingham and Montague were quite beside themselves, fidgeting as though they suddenly found themselves covered in fleas.

"*Pickwick Papers*," Kitty said.

"Yes!" Anne cried, before shaking a finger at Richard. "You knew what it was long before she announced it, didn't you?"

He shrugged nonchalantly.

"If he knew the answer, he would have spoken up," Farthingham said.

"Why give the answer when the reward is to have to stand in front of everyone and behave like a jackanapes?" Richard asked.

"The reward, my dear fellow, is to beat the others with your sharp wit."

Richard grinned. "I did."

"So you say," Kitty said.

"Are you questioning my word, Miss Robertson?"

She blushed prettily. "No, Your Grace. It is simply that I would have thought your competitive nature would force you into demonstrating your superiority."

"So you acknowledge that I am superior?"

Her eyes flashed fury. "No, I acknowledge only that you believe you are."

"I have an idea," Farthingham said. "Another wager."

Kitty laughed lightly, causing his heart to rejoice in the sound.

"I think you have enough wagers going, Nicky," she said with obvious amusement and affection.

Farthingham raised a finger. "Hear me out. I believe everyone will agree that of all of us with the courage to test the answer aloud, Kitty is the most skilled at guessing correctly."

Anne, Lady Priscilla, and Montague bobbed their heads.

"Excellent! Here is what I propose. The four of us"—he pointed to Anne, Lady Priscilla, and Montague—"shall each perform one pantomime. Kitty and Weddington will be the only two eligible to guess the answer. Should Kitty guess correctly more often than Weddington, he shall have to stand before us and perform a pantomime to the best of his ability—which I fear is sadly lacking and is the true reason for his hesitation to call out the answer."

"And if I give more correct answers than Miss Robertson does?" Richard asked.

"Kitty shall take a turn about the garden with you, allowing you to be spared our theatrics while we continue to play and are relieved of your sour disposition."

"I accept."

"No!" Kitty cried. She twisted around to face Farthingham. "You can't make a wager that requires me to do something if you lose."

"But I won't lose, my sweet. I have absolute confidence in your ability to beat that rapscallion. He claims he always knows the answer, and yet we've seen no proof."

She looked quickly at Richard before turning back to Farthingham. "It would be entirely inappropriate for me to take a walk with him in the dark garden when you and I are so close to announcing our betrothal."

"If he makes any untoward advances, you have but to scream. I shall come to your rescue."

"You're making light of my concerns."

"Of course, I am. Weddington is a gentleman and my friend. I trust him completely. The garden is lit by gas lamps. You will be perfectly safe. Although, honestly, I don't believe I will lose the wager. Trust me, my sweet, and have as much confidence in your abilities as I do."

Richard felt the competitor within him unfurling as her chin came up a notch. She slid her gaze over to him, challenge mirrored in the sea green of her eyes.

"I do trust you, Nicky. With all my heart. Let the games begin," she said.

With a mere bowing of his head, Richard acknowledged the gauntlet tossed. He wondered how she would feel if he informed her that her trust was misplaced. The irony of trust was that it worked on many different levels. She trusted Farthingham, Farthingham trusted Richard.

Unfortunately, Farthingham's was not a trust Richard was willing to breach, which meant he played the larger, more important game with an unfair disadvantage.

Kitty trusted Farthingham. She truly did, but obviously he shouldn't have trusted her. Or at least he shouldn't have trusted her skills at charades. Fighting not to press her arms across her chest and bunch them up beneath her breasts, she slowly walked through the garden alongside Weddington.

She simply couldn't believe he'd won by calmly revealing the answer—sometimes only a mere syllable before she did—as though he found the entire exercise tiresome. He'd been at a decided disadvantage because everyone had cheered for her to win, had played to her, had encouraged her to shout out the answer before Weddington could.

While he'd delivered each answer in an infuriatingly subdued, arrogant tone. Damn, but she hated losing; she especially despised losing to him. Regrettably, she realized that her attitude was going to make it even more difficult to play honorably the following day. She truly had no desire for him to benefit from her skills, but for her to lose purposely . . . once again she cursed Farthingham for placing her in such a deplorable position.

"Aren't you afraid that I'll play poorly tomorrow so Lord Farthingham will receive your yacht?" she finally asked into the silence.

"The possibility of your playing poorly had not entered my mind, Miss Robertson."

"You have my permission to call me Kitty."

"Only if you will call me Richard."

She glanced over at him, in the shadows of the night. It seemed most of their intimate encounters took place when neither was clearly visible. She couldn't decide if that placed her at an advantage or a disadvantage. "I was under the impression that most aristocrats went by some nickname derived from their titles. But neither you nor Farthingham seem to have adopted that tradition."

"My father was known as Weddy by his intimates. I had no desire to inherit his nickname when I inherited his title."

"Because you disliked him?" she asked speculatively. As competitive as he was, she could well imagine him displaying the same sort of competitiveness toward his father.

"Because I loved him. I respected him, admired him, and would have preferred never to have had occasion to inherit his titles."

An impossibility unless his father had outlived him. Having recognized a tinge of sorrow and regret in his voice, she wondered if he would have indeed preferred that outcome: his father outliving him. "How did he die?"

"Arrogantly."

His hands were clutched behind his back, and she considered that perhaps he held them to prevent himself from touching her. "You can't leave me with such a simple answer."

"I can if I so choose. However, no harm would come from your knowing." He sighed as though something inside him needed to be released, a gate opened or a wall torn down. "We'd taken a yacht out with a crew of six. A storm came up, but we did not turn back to shore. We thought we could control the sea, he and I. But the sea cannot be tamed. He died. The ship sank. The crew and I made it to shore."

He recounted his tale as though he'd memorized the details and facts, one after another, to be delivered on command, like the poems she'd had to recite in school.

"The first morning I spotted you, standing on the shore, facing the sea, I thought you appeared defiant," she said quietly.

"The sea terrifies me."

She almost stumbled over her feet. His words were the last she'd ever expected him to utter. She couldn't imagine this strong, virile man being frightened by anything. But with his statement, she now comprehended why he was so willing to wager a yacht, and she found a bit of her discomfort with the wager slipping away. "Then it seems you won't mind losing a yacht to Farthingham."

"On the contrary, I mind a great deal. Should he manage to win the wager, I shall simply replace my yacht with another."

"But why? If the sea terrifies you—"

"*Because* it terrifies me. It is the very reason that I swim in it each morning when I am in residence near the shore. It is the very reason that I take my boats out on the water. I refuse to allow my fears to control me."

She heard the passion shimmering through his voice, so different from the telling of his father's death. He captured her attention, her interest in ways that he shouldn't. Even at that moment, she found it difficult to remember that Farthingham was inside the house, in the parlor, playing games with his friends.

Weddington cleared his throat. "I have never shared my fears with anyone. I trust you to be discreet with the knowledge."

"I won't tell a soul."

"So you are not like Lady Priscilla, prone to passing gossip around with the ease that one might a calling card?"

"I've never cared for gossip."

"An admirable quality in a woman."

They strolled along, the silence easing between them. She was always amazed that Farthingham, who had so little wealth, still managed to give the appearance of a man with money at his disposal. He continued to employ gardeners and servants. Not as many as some in his position, but enough to run his household with efficiency. And the fragrance that was fading with the night reminded her of what she'd not done.

"I've been neglectful in properly thanking you for the lovely flowers you sent," she finally managed to say.

"They were my pleasure to send."

She gnawed on her lower lip. "And your penance? Your mother thought they came from your greenhouse."

"She has always been far too wise. She was quite impressed with you, Miss Robertson."

"Kitty."

"I have decided the informality would not be wise."

It seemed that mother and son were equally wise. And it was time that she must be so as well. "On another matter, I must decline your kind offer of the use of your box—"

"The offer has already been made, and Farthingham has accepted."

"You told Farthingham?"

"Of course."

"And how did you explain your offer?"

"I told him that I'd never seen a woman enjoy the opera more."

"You're amazing. You deliver lies when they suit you."

"I spoke true. I have never seen a woman enjoy the opera more, not even Anne. I did not say it was the reason I was offering my box. My offer merely followed my comment. Should he conclude that my comment was the reason for my offer, so be it."

Laughing, she stopped walking, not at all surprised that he did the same and faced her. "You are weaving a tangled web, Your Grace."

"I am well aware of that, Miss Robertson, in ways that you cannot even begin to imagine."

"What would happen if you released your hold on your hands?"

"I would take you in my arms. Why did you tell Farthingham to delay your announcement until the end of the Season?"

"I'm self-centered. The newspapers contain too much gossipy news right now. Our announcement would not receive the attention it rightly deserves."

"Now who weaves a tangled web?" he asked.

She had to fight to draw in every breath, to stand her ground, not to run. "You terrify me."

"I would never harm you."

"You make me feel things . . ." She lowered her gaze.

Then his gloved hand was below her chin, lifting her gaze back to his. "I have found it is better to face the things that terrify us, rather than retreat from them."

"I'm not retreating; I'm conquering—"

"By Jove, you two are the slowest people on earth," Farthingham called out.

Weddington quickly dropped his hand. Kitty heard Farthingham's footsteps on the path, his and others, and she wondered what they might have seen, what they might have thought.

Turning, she forced herself to smile. He was still far enough away to be more shadow than man, and she could only hope that she and Weddington appeared the same to him.

"Send me on a turn about the garden, and I could reach this spot and be back in far less time than it took the two of you to get here," Farthingham said.

"I was experiencing some discomfort in my back and had to slow my step to accommodate it," Weddington said.

If he was indeed one not to lie, then she realized that he was in pain, probably the reason for his stiffness.

"You really should use your walking stick more," Lady Anne said. "People who don't need them use them all the time; no one would think anything of it."

"You're quite right, Anne," Weddington said.

"Well, while you two were out here dallying around, Lady Anne had a scathingly brilliant idea," Farthingham said. "She has invited us all to spend a few days at Drummond Manor for a respite from the whirlwind of the Season. I, for one, am all for it. What do you think, my sweet?"

Drummond Manor. Lady Anne had mentioned her home the morning she'd visited with her mother. If Weddington's yachts were nearby, then it must be where he'd been in residence when she met him. A dangerous place, a very dangerous place indeed.

Kitty would have preferred to decline, but her mind seemed to have stopped functioning, and she couldn't think of a single plausible reason not to accept the offer. Since she'd be announcing her betrothal at the end of the Season, she couldn't very well say she needed to remain in London in order to meet a prospective husband.

Besides, she felt Weddington's gaze on her, almost sensed his unspoken challenge. "If it's what you wish," she finally forced out of her mouth.

"Splendid!" Farthingham exclaimed. "All right now. Everyone follow me back to the parlor. I have the rules to a new game I think we'll have some jolly good fun with."

He marched ahead with everyone following him. Kitty walked slowly behind the procession, Weddington at her side. She could have sworn she heard him grinding his teeth.

"You don't like parlor games," she speculated.

"Not particularly, no. Although I will admit that I was extraordinarily pleased with the results of charades."

"I wasn't. I was looking quite forward to seeing you behave like a jackanapes."

He chuckled low. "Perhaps the opportunity will present itself at Drummond Manor."

"I doubt it. You strike me as a man who guards himself extremely well. What forfeit will you ask of Farthingham if I win the match tomorrow?"

"I've not yet decided, but you may rest assured that whatever I choose will revolve around you."

Chapter 11

"You don't mind that I invited everyone to Drummond Manor, do you?" Anne asked.

"Of course not," Richard replied, gazing out the window as his coach rumbled along the cobblestone street. "It's your home as well."

"You and Miss Robertson walked for such a long time. What did you talk about?"

"She spent a good deal of time describing the two hundred gowns in her wardrobe."

"She did not!"

Smiling, he turned his attention to Anne. "No, she didn't. We actually spoke very little. I don't think she's at all comfortable with Farthingham's wager."

"He was rather bold to propose it."

"It is easy to be bold when you have nothing to lose and all to gain."

"Whatever will you ask him to forfeit?"

Richard looked back out the window. "Something he holds dear."

"Something as dear as *The Fair Lady* is to you?"

"The yacht is an object, Anne, easily replaced. I prefer to ask of him something a bit harder to come by."

"Which would be what exactly?"

"I haven't yet determined the exact nature of my request."

"You must have something in mind."

"Oh, yes, I definitely have something in mind."

"But you won't share."

"Afraid not."

"I don't know why you must be so secretive." She sighed. "Prissy and Freddie seem to get along quite well. Do you think he has more than a passing interest in her?"

"I wouldn't know."

"Her father would never approve of a match between them. A playwright. And an unsuccessful one at that."

He heard no censure in her voice. She could completely under-stand Lady Priscilla's father not approving of such a match, but she couldn't comprehend Richard's disapproval of her marrying a com-moner. Amazing how she could view things differently when they didn't apply to her. He wondered if Kitty was the same way.

"For an American, Miss Robertson is quite levelheaded, don't you think?" she asked.

"Quite."

"I think she and Farthingham make a splendid couple. They com-plement each other. Together they are quite elegant. She is always dressed to perfection. I feel quite dowdy beside her."

"You are hardly dowdy, Anne."

"You only think that because you're my brother. You can't imag-ine how difficult it is to try to garner a man's attention during the Sea-son. I find it rather demeaning actually. I really prefer the more intimate occasions—like this evening. And I fear you're not listening to a single word I'm saying."

"I'm listening, but there is little I can add to the conversation."

"Honestly, Richard, you're not nearly as much fun as Farthing-ham."

He snapped his head around. "Is that what a woman wants, Anne? A man who is *fun*? A man who prefers play to work, a man who would allow others to carry him through life rather than deter-mine how he can best carry himself?"

"I meant no offense," she responded rather tartly.

"None taken."

"You certainly didn't sound as though none were taken." Leaning toward him, she placed a comforting hand on his knee. "I realize the management of all our estates and holdings is quite a burden. I don't know how you manage to do it all, I truly don't. You will require a special woman to become your wife." She straightened and looked out the window, as though like him, she thought all the answers resided outside the coach somewhere.

"It's a shame Miss Robertson is taken," she finally commented.

Holding his tongue, he joined her in gazing out the window. A shame indeed. Although the forfeit he would require of Farthingham could very well alter Kitty's status in that regard.

Kitty had only recently finished eating a late breakfast and was on her way to change into her lawn tennis dress when the two dozen yellow roses arrived. Even without the note, she might have guessed who they were from.

My dear Miss Robertson,

Please accept my sincerest apologies, but pressing business concerns prevent me from attending the match between you and Lord Farthingham this afternoon. I have little doubt that you shall give him a sound thrashing, but should he prevail, rest assured that I will hold no ill will toward you. My yacht is insignificant when compared against your happiness. Still, I wish you good luck and a skillful hand.

Yours most devotedly,
The Duke of Weddington

Releasing a tiny growl, she spun away from the flowers. She wanted to give *him* a sound thrashing. His intended absence would add considerably to her dilemma—because he wouldn't be standing at one end of the court holding her to the moral high ground. She could purposely miss a ball, and his keen eyes wouldn't take note of the intentional blunder.

She wanted to shriek. Had he really been called away to business, or was his absence part of some grander game, bedeviling her with indecision? Or was he being considerate, not truly wanting to burden her with the loss of his yacht? Was he placing faith in her to win, or placing faith in her to try with all her might even if she couldn't win?

Or was he offering her an easy way to do neither? Did he think she had the ability to win, but fully expected her to lose?

She studied the flowers before reading the note again. It seemed simple and straightforward enough. He had more important matters to attend to. Fine. So did she.

She certainly had more important things to consider than his true motives. She had a tennis match to win.

As she headed toward the stairs, she cursed Farthingham for placing her in this unconscionable position. Then for good measure she cursed Weddington for being so damned understanding should she lose. Damnation! She'd show him. She'd win.

She staggered to a stop. He'd achieved his purpose. He'd made her angry enough that she wouldn't even consider losing.

Surely not. He couldn't be that clever, couldn't know her that well. Oh, he was the most infuriating man. She'd show him. She'd purposely lose. Yes, indeed. Let him sacrifice his yacht.

She started up the stairs and paused. No, no, no. He'd sent his letter, expecting her to lose and wanting to remove her guilt. She would have no guilt to suffer. She would win. Yes, that's what she'd do.

Two more steps, and she stopped again. Why in thunderation did he have to be so understanding and infuriating? If she won, what would he ask of Farthingham? Would it be something as simple as a dance at the next ball, her company at the theater, or a stroll through Hyde Park? Or would the forfeit concerning her involve much more?

It didn't matter. She had no intention of winning. There. The decision was made. The only forfeit that would take place that day was the giving up of a yacht.

With a lighter step, she headed up the stairs.

Richard had not planned to attend the tennis match. Indeed he had business matters that needed to be seen to, but more he'd wanted to relieve Kitty of the burden of being forced to put her best foot forward. In retrospect, he regretted accepting the wager, because he realized too late what a heavy obligation it had placed on her.

On the other hand, it pleased him immensely that she did not take lightly the possibility of his losing his yacht. He'd expected a woman with two hundred gowns in her wardrobe not truly to understand the value of money, the true worth of objects. But she was concerned with them, as well as with fairness and honor.

Another aspect to her which fascinated him. He so enjoyed discovering the little things about her that made her the person she was. He could spend the remainder of his life searching for the differing aspects of her character. She was not flighty or dull. When any other woman—particularly Anne—spoke, he tended to drift off into his own thoughts. With Kitty, he listened to every word, wishing he were better skilled at memorization and recall.

And so it was that as the time for the match had drawn near, he'd been unable to resist making his way to Kitty's garden, standing unnoticed off to the side, and observing the game that truly was quite well matched.

As most ladies tended to do, Kitty held her skirt with her left hand to prevent herself from tripping over it, and she batted the ball underhand. She was such a delight to watch, skipping over the lawn, elegantly enticing.

Anne stood at the net, while Montague and Lady Priscilla were at opposite corners, watching the lines in order to judge accurately when the shots went out of bounds. With so much at stake, it seemed no one was willing to take the game lightly.

And it really should have been simply a game, a bit of sport, a bit of fun. He was surprised that Farthingham had never revealed to Kitty the full extent of his sporting skills. Normally, he was a competitive sort—or at least he'd always been so with Richard.

Perhaps Richard was wrong to think that a woman would welcome competition as much as a man—although Kitty had certainly indicated that she appreciated his views on the matter. Not enough that she'd cast Farthingham aside, however.

What was Farthingham's appeal? Surely for the long haul, a woman desired more than laughter, fun, and parlor games.

Richard cut his musings short and focused more intently on the game. Kitty had but to score once more in order to win. It was a situation in which she'd frequently been since he'd been watching. It seemed each time victory was within her grasp, Farthingham snatched it away with a well-executed shot. She returned the favor the next go-round, so that it was making for a most exciting game.

Perhaps Anne was right. Perhaps women should be allowed to play at Wimbledon.

He considered moving closer to the court, so he could more readily cheer Kitty on. But he decided he would serve as a distraction rather than as anything positive. He was terribly pleased that she was putting forth such a tremendous effort to win . . . and he was left to wonder if it was because he'd indicated the forfeit would have something to do with her—and she was curious to determine what it might be—or if she simply played well for the thrill of the victory.

The ball traveled back and forth between the two: Kitty, Farthingham, Kitty, Farthingham, Kitty. Farthingham reached out, the ball tipped the edge of his racquet, and rather succinctly plopped to the ground as though suddenly weary.

One hand on his hip, Farthingham stared at the ball. Anne was the only one to release a jubilant shout of joy, then looked quite embarrassed for having done so. Hand extended, Kitty walked to the net as Richard imagined one might walk to the gallows.

"I'm terribly sorry," she said, her voice traveling softly to where Richard stood.

"No need to be, my sweet. It was a game well played. I shall find another means of acquiring a yacht. Lady Anne, I suppose you'll carry the good news to your brother and inform him that I shall pay the forfeit of his choosing at his convenience."

"Yes, of course," Anne said. "I'll relay the message. Don't look so incredibly sad, Miss Robertson. I'm certain my brother won't be too harsh with Lord Farthingham."

Richard turned on his heel and made his way back to where his coach waited. He wondered if Farthingham would have played with a good deal more determination to win had he realized that the forfeit would involve the relinquishing of his claim on Kitty.

Chapter 12

The Harrington ball had been lauded as *the* social event of the Season. Richard could certainly understand the reasoning behind the claim. The Harringtons' London residence had always been grand, equal to Richard's in size and stature, but now it possessed a gaiety that it had been lacking in it before. The newest anointed duke and his American bride of almost two years were quite adept at making people feel welcome. It was also equally obvious that they were madly in love, because they seldom took their eyes off each other—even when the width of a room separated them as it did just then.

"Are you certain you wouldn't like to pop upstairs and take another look?" Harrington asked.

Richard slanted his gaze toward Harrington. As the second son, Rhys Rhodes had thought it highly unlikely he'd ever inherit his father's titles. Some falling-out with his family years earlier had made him scarce in Richard's circles. As a result, Richard hardly knew the man, but he was pleased to discover that Rhys did not seem to have much in common with his older brother, who had drowned, leaving the way clear for the second son to become the heir.

Upon being introduced to the firstborn, Quentin, some years before, Richard had felt an immediate aversion to the fellow and had gone to great lengths to avoid him whenever possible. He couldn't explain exactly what it was about the duke's firstborn son that he'd disliked. Something in his eyes, however, had made Richard think the man would enjoy pulling the wings off flies and watching them struggle with their unexpected limitations.

"Your daughter is a beauty, but far too young for my tastes," Richard said.

"Good God, man, I wasn't suggesting you consider her for marriage. She is but a babe, still in the bassinet. I simply thought you might enjoy spending more time in the company of Lady Katherine. She has a way of lifting a man's spirit, filling his heart, and bringing a smile to his face. You seemed in need of all three."

"I apologize if I appear somewhat distracted. I've much on my mind these days. Tell me, how do you find it, being married to an American?"

Harrington grinned. "Much to my liking. Much to my liking, indeed."

"They seem somewhat more independent than many of our ladies."

"Indeed they are. Do you know I once had to rescue a chap from Lydia's scathing rebukes? She is magnificent in her fury. I think it might have been at that moment that I fell in love with her." Harrington finally shifted his attention away from his wife and looked at Richard. "Why the keen interest in how it is to be married to an American?"

"Not interest really. More like morbid curiosity." A curiosity that had been rekindled the moment he'd spotted Kitty arriving earlier with Farthingham, Montague, and Lady Priscilla. They were becoming quite the foursome. Anne was there as well—somewhere. He did wish he could find someone who interested her. "Your wife seems to fit in nicely with this crowd."

"She thrives in all this glitter." He glanced around, as though he sought to encompass not only the room but all of London. "She studied diligently to prepare herself for her dream of marrying an aristocrat. Her place is well earned, well deserved."

"If she was so set on gaining a title, do you ever doubt her sincerity in regard to you?"

"Never. She stood by my side when no one else would." His gaze homed back onto his wife as though he'd never lost sight of her to begin with. "I would do whatever necessary to keep her happy, regardless of the cost to myself."

Strange how Richard experienced the same strong determination where Kitty was concerned. He allowed his gaze to circle the dance floor until it settled on her, waltzing with Farthingham. He couldn't deny that they made an attractive pair: she the brightest star within the room; he wearing his aristocratic lineage as though it were still as powerful and respected as it once had been. Perhaps they possessed enough love between them to see them through, because she certainly appeared elated.

Was he arrogant to be so utterly convinced that he knew what was best for her? Was he being guided by his heart or his head? She was a worthy prize, and he was not a man who gave up easily. But more was at stake, so much more. He couldn't help but believe that marriage to Farthingham would eventually dim her smile and wither her joy.

The music drifted into silence, and Richard turned to his host. "If you'll excuse me, I have the next dance with Miss Robertson."

"Of course. I believe I'll run up and see that my daughter is sleeping peacefully."

Richard left him, surprised the man didn't bring the babe down and introduce her into the party. He'd never seen a more devoted father or one showing quite as much interest in his child—as though she were a miracle to be revered as though he thought no one else possessed children save he.

Then thoughts of Harrington and all else faded away. Kitty stood before him, and for the next few moments, she would be in his arms and none other's.

From the moment she'd arrived at the ball and dispensed with the social niceties of making the rounds, she'd danced. Every dance. The first one with Farthingham. The one before this one with Farthingham. And in between the two, a steady stream of men whose names were etched on her dance card had each taken a turn and guided her through the various dances.

But it wasn't until she waltzed within the circle of Weddington's arms that she truly felt as though she attended a ball. Farthingham gazed into her eyes, but Weddington held them captive. She couldn't have turned away had she wanted to.

Unfortunately, she had no desire even to contemplate doing so. With him, the music was a little sweeter to her ears, her step seemed a little lighter, her body hummed, her breasts tingled, her lungs craved more air, her blood thrummed between her temples . . . her nose was more sensitive to his scent, her fingers to his warmth.

It was as though all else faded away until only the two of them remained, their senses heightened and attuned only to each other. She was intensely aware of him: the way each strand of his hair stayed in place as though he would tolerate nothing less than complete obedience. The obsidian darkness of his eyes, which never strayed from hers. The chiseled features of his face, where wind, sun, and surf had each left its mark, forcing tiny furrows to appear at the corners of his eyes and mouth.

As aware of him as she was, she was more alert to her own body's reactions to his nearness. Not a weakness, really, but a melting. As though she might become fluid and pour herself into him. She could hardly believe the incredible sensations he invoked. Carnal images flashed through her mind, images that never teased her when any other man was near.

How did Weddington manage with nothing more than a touch or a searing look completely to undo her world and the respectability she'd tried so hard to obtain?

"You look remarkably lovely this evening," he said quietly.

"Are you implying that I do not always look remarkably lovely?"

His smile traveled from his lips to his eyes. "Sparring will not save you from me."

She almost remarked that she had no desire to be saved. Where he was concerned, her heart, body, and mind could not come into agreement. Confusion ruled, and the harder she tried to sort out her feelings, the more lost she became.

"Accept the compliment," he said, "and do not read more into it than I intended to deliver."

"Very well, Your Grace. Have you decided what forfeit you'll ask of Farthingham?" She was surprised he'd not gloated when he'd greeted them earlier. He'd not even mentioned the match, although she was certain Lady Anne had told him of its outcome.

He shook his head slightly. "I am in no hurry to claim it. I do, however, owe you for placing him in my debt."

How difficult it had been to accept the win, but despite all her earlier arguments with herself and her determined resolve to lose—honor had dictated that she not allow defeat if she was fully capable of winning.

Although Farthingham had played an excellent game, and his skills had matched hers better than he'd ever demonstrated in the past—which irritated her no end when she thought on it too long—the decisive points had gone to her. "I took absolutely no pleasure in scoring more points than he did."

"I never, for one moment, thought that you would. You are a remarkable woman, Miss Robertson, to have held on to your integrity when I believe everyone would have forgiven you for a moment's lapse."

"Would you have forgiven me?"

"Do you truly care?"

She found herself nodding, surprised by the depth of her feelings, of her need to know how he might have viewed her had she purposely lost. "Yes. Strangely enough, I find that I do care what your opinion on the matter would have been."

"I would have forgiven you."

Disappointment stabbed her. And she couldn't explain its origin, unless it was because she wanted him to value the win as much more than a means to gain a forfeit.

"Then I would have walked away," he continued, "and we wouldn't be dancing now."

"Because you would have lost your yacht?" she asked pointedly.

"Because I would have lost all respect for you."

She despised that his sentiments meant so much to her. Farthingham wouldn't have minded at all had she lost purposely. He would have relished the victory, no matter how he'd gained it. He didn't truly comprehend her competitive nature. He only wanted to have fun, and she so enjoyed having fun with him, but sometimes she recognized that more was at stake. All of life was not a game to be played at everyone's whim. Actions carried consequences, and sometimes more was to be lost than the stated wager.

"I didn't realize I could rid myself of your attentions so easily, Your Grace," she said. "You'd best take care before wagering against Farthingham in the future. Now that I understand what is truly at stake, I might find myself so incredibly tempted to lose that I might just accomplish that end."

"And what would truly be at stake?"

"My peace of mind and your complete absence in my life."

"Why do you resist the attraction that is so strong between us?"

"Because it is not lasting, and it will very quickly burn out."

"There is but one way to know for certain . . . give in to it."

The music came to a blessed end. Kitty stepped back. "Never. Just as it is not in my nature purposely to miss an opportunity to win, neither is it within me to give in to lust. While I will confess that where you are concerned, it seems to rear its ugly head, I find it decadent and unworthy of my consideration. I possess the wherewithal to ignore it, completely and absolutely."

"I think you protest too much—in an effort to convince yourself that the words you speak are true, when I know they are false."

"You assume too much, Your Grace, and know nothing."

With her head held high, when she would have preferred ducking and escaping, she allowed him the courtesy of escorting her back to Farthingham. The entire way, within her own mind, she strived to achieve exactly what he'd alluded to: convincing herself that her feelings toward him were of no consequence.

One dance was not nearly enough, but then Richard knew a thousand wouldn't be either. A few moments with Kitty nestled in his arms left him aching with need, desperate with desire. He'd never before experienced this overwhelming lack of control. It terrified him, almost as much as the sea with its unmerciful depths.

Perhaps Kitty's assumptions were true. Perhaps the fire that threatened to consume them would burn out. If she was correct in identifying the cause of their attraction, then so was he in offering the remedy. Give in to it, feed it, embrace it, let it flare, and die a quick, merciful death. Then they could both go on to other more pertinent matters. He could resume a life where his every waking moment and every nightly dream didn't include visions of her.

He almost laughed aloud. He didn't believe his silent argument any more than she did the words she'd uttered aloud.

Presently dancing with her host, she appeared to be gaily engaged in pleasant conversation. Richard couldn't recall her ever looking as at ease in his presence. But how could she when this damned hunger gnawed at them, demanding to be fed. When this acute awareness of him as a man and her as a woman existed? He was not so delicate that he could not put a name to it: lust was too tame, too meek a word. Carnal desire, pure and simple. Craving. Desperation. He wanted her, wanted to bury himself deep within her, hold on tightly, and carry them both into the realm of unadulterated ecstasy.

Out of the corner of his eye, he caught sight of Farthingham. Richard shifted his attention away from the dance floor in time to see the marquess glance around the room quickly before subtly escaping through the French doors and into the night. He had the look about him of a man who planned to engage in a secret assignation.

Then Richard noticed as another slipped out, and he knew his suspicions of a tryst in the making were justified. Farthingham might be fond of Kitty, but he did not love her. He would never love her. Her father's wealth was purchasing the attentions Farthingham showered on her, and she deserved so much more than to have her affections bartered.

She deserved a man whose blood boiled at the sight of her, a man who would drive himself into her until she was screaming his name while caught up in the throes of passion. Farthingham might believe he could cast aside the feelings he held for another and become the kind of husband Kitty warranted, but Richard thought it highly unlikely, exceedingly impossible.

Richard noticed Kitty wandering toward the French doors that led onto the terrace, Harrington nowhere to be seen. The man had probably excused himself to run up and look in on his daughter again, leaving Kitty unattended and available for mischief.

Since Kitty was glancing around with the obvious expression of someone not wanting to be seen rather than someone searching for someone, since she was nearing the door through which Farthingham had disappeared only moments earlier, Richard was quick to deduce that she'd no doubt seen Farthingham make his exit and thought he'd sneaked away with the possibility of meeting her in his mind. Jolly good. Her seeing Farthingham in a compromising position with another would no doubt have her running straight into Richard's arms.

The hell of it was, though, that he didn't want her to turn to him under those conditions, on those terms. Nor did he want her heart shattered, and the possibility existed that it would if she learned the naked truth. How many times had she professed her love of Farthingham, how diligently did she struggle against her desires where Richard was concerned? He did not want her to suffer a rude awakening. He did not want her to suffer at all.

Which was the very reason that as soon as she slipped outside, he quickly glanced around to make certain that no one was paying attention to the little drama unfolding, then followed in her wake.

Kitty had enjoyed her dance with the Duke of Harrington, an extremely handsome and proper gentleman, who obviously doted on his wife and daughter no end. During one of their turns, she'd spotted Farthingham standing near the French doors. He'd given her a passing glance, but it was enough for her to know—when she saw him slip outside—that he wished for her to follow.

She couldn't have been more grateful when the duke mentioned that he'd like to run up the stairs and see his daughter. She'd excused him from the waltz and headed onto the terrace and out into the garden.

She desperately longed to have some time alone with Nicky. He was such fun to be around that he drew people the way a magnet attracted metal shavings. She completely understood everyone's desire to be in his company. Possessing an uncanny ability to make people feel comfortable and at ease, he made them laugh and smile and enjoy the occasion so much more.

Although she was spending more and more time with Farthing-ham, they barely had any opportunities to be alone and scarcely had a chance to discuss the most private of matters. They had time for little more than a few whispered words and quick touches.

She knew the British etiquette of courtship wasn't nearly as informal as Texas customs. In Texas, her half sisters, when they were of a proper age, would no doubt attend dances and picnics without the benefit of chaperones. Kitty had done so herself on several occasions when her family wasn't in England.

But never with Farthingham. Not since their first clandestine waltz. Once his intentions had become clear, at his insistence, everything had become so irritatingly proper. His desire to be above reproach was only one of the many reasons why she loved him as deeply as she did. He'd never instigate her fall from grace. He walked the high moral ground, and she wanted to stroll right along with him.

But she realized that never having any time alone was probably as difficult for him as it was for her. Hence, the subtle message in his gaze and his disappearance from the ballroom.

Walking cautiously and peering through the shadows, she discovered that Harrington's garden was a maze of shrubbery and hedgerows. Not nearly enough light to guide her way, which was probably the reason Farthingham had determined it would be a perfect place for them to meet. She knew even if they were alone in the darkness, nothing untoward would happen. They would behave, but they would have a few moments of holding each other, whispering intimate thoughts, perhaps experiencing a kiss or two. Pleasant.

It would all be pleasant and away from prying eyes. But not wicked, never wicked. Farthingham never sought to tempt her into wickedness. It was not his way, and she couldn't have been more grateful for that aspect of his character, an aspect sadly lacking in Weddington.

She heard a quiet murmur, a muffled giggle—so Farthingham wasn't the only one with the notion of seeking some privacy. She did wish he'd alert her to his whereabouts. If she tarried much longer, they'd be missed, and she certainly didn't want to draw attention to the fact that she'd left the ballroom. While she didn't mind being a little bit naughty, was even excited by the prospect, she didn't want to sully her reputation.

A hand wrapped gently around her arm, drawing her off the path and behind a trellis of roses, deep into the shadows.

Nicky!

But the mouth that swooped down to cover hers, the tongue that parted her lips, didn't belong to the man she sought. Neither did the taste that filled her mouth nor the scent which teased her nostrils. Nor did the broad chest she was pressed against or the wide shoulders that she'd wrapped her arms around. Nor the thick strands of hair that were curling around her fingers as she scraped them along his scalp.

She knew she should withdraw, step away, return to the path, and escape back into the house. Her next dance partner would surely be looking for her soon. But she had no desire to leave.

She sank against Weddington as though she possessed no will of her own, as though he were a safe harbor when she knew he was anything but. He was the tempest, the storm that caused dizzying sensations to swirl through her. Changing the angle of the kiss, he settled his mouth more firmly against hers, his tongue darting and probing, enticing her to join him in playing the same game.

She clutched his hair, tugged on the strands, found herself wanting to crawl all over him. To know him completely, absolutely. His naked form was emblazoned on her mind, and she could envision him as he'd been on the rocks—without the confinement of clothing. Man at his most vulnerable, his most savage, his most primitive.

Raging desire surged through her. And suddenly nothing was enough. Not his touch, not his kiss, not their hips rubbing against the other. She alternately touched his cheek, ran her fingers through his hair, slipped her hand beneath his jacket, pressed her palm against his chest, and felt the hard pounding of his heart against her palm.

He glided his hand along her neck, throat, and collarbone, as he had at the opera—except no gloves protected her from the heat of his touch. She wondered when he'd removed them, because he'd been wearing them when they'd danced. She relished the strength she felt in his hands, the warmth pulsing between his flesh and hers. His mouth, damp and hotter than imaginable, replaced his fingers, skimming along her throat, his tongue swirling over her skin, his teeth nipping her flesh here and there.

Then he was peeling the bodice of her gown down, as though its low, revealing cut had been designed for exactly this purpose: to give him easy access to that which he desired. He closed his mouth around her turgid nipple, suckled hard, and she cried out.

"Shh, shh," he commanded as he returned his mouth to hers, his tongue delving inside while his fingers kneaded her breast. "Shh, shh." Another kiss. "You must"—a kiss—"remain quiet."

But how could she when she felt as though her entire body was erupting with intense sensations she'd never before experienced. She needed someplace to put them, because they were not of a nature to be kept tightly inside. They screamed for release, insisted on it. She didn't understand what her body was demanding of her, of him. She only knew he appeared to possess the remedy.

When his mouth began to journey along her flesh again, she moaned and dropped her head back, lost in the sensations he stirred to life. Shivering, yet burning, she dug her fingers into his shoulders, seeking purchase. This time when he took her nipple between his teeth, she swallowed back her cry, but couldn't prevent the escape of a whimper.

Her knees jelled and threatened to melt beneath her. "Richard."

Groaning low in his throat, he snaked an arm around her waist, brought her up against his hard body, and turned her, walking her backward two steps until her back met a stone wall, the hardness of which matched that of the man pressing his lower body against hers.

Peering through half-lowered eyelids, she studied him— immersed in shadows, moving silently, his motions only detected by the pleasure left in their wake. Oh, God, she thought she might die there and not care one whit. She felt as though her body were already ascending to heaven, carried on the wings of his unrelenting fervor.

With his head bent, he continued to play his lips and tongue over her bared breasts, giving attention to one, the valley between, then the other, suckling and stroking, caressing and nipping, while his free hand gathered up her skirt until it was bunched between them, held in place by two bodies pressed tightly together.

He skimmed his warm fingers up her thigh, trailed his fingers down, then back up. She shouldn't allow such liberties, but she didn't have it within her to protest because to deny him would deny her. Instinctually she realized that, and she'd become too lost in the sensations even to consider stopping the madness. The ability to control anything had moved rapidly beyond her realm of power and into his. From him she wanted to beg for deliverance, for an easing to what she couldn't name, for the rendering of a climax to a sensation that should have never been created, but having been started left no recourse except to be allowed to reach its full potential.

He skimmed his fingertips along the inside of her thigh, up, up, higher, higher, until he reached his destination: the heart of her womanhood. Squeezing her eyes shut more tightly, she clamped her hands around his shoulders. With a finger, he stroked intimately, with his thumb he rubbed provocatively. Her body jerked in response to his attentions before pressing against his palm, urging him on, all thought of retreat lost in the wicked sensations cascading through her, rippling over her flesh, curling toward her core.

The tender nub between her thighs was almost unbearably sensitive, and when he glided his thumb over it, she released a tiny whimper, a resounding plea. To stop, to continue. To carry her ever higher.

He returned his mouth to hers, deepening the kiss as his fingers increased their pressure. She bucked against his hand, like a wild thing, untamed, savage, desperately seeking what hovered unknown on the horizon.

And then she exploded into a thousand sparks of intense pleasure, every conceivable color shimmering behind her eyes, every glorious taste filling her mouth, every distant sound muted except for her frantic gasps and his harsh breathing.

She thought she might never again move a single muscle, that she would simply stand there forever, a wilted woman who had scaled the pinnacle of wanton pleasure and somehow managed to survive.

Breathing heavily, he slid his mouth close to her ear. "Farthingham will never make you feel like this," he rasped.

Her eyes flew open, her chest tightening as the knowledge of what she'd done slammed into her. Oh, God, oh dear God, she'd opened herself up to him, urged him on with moans, undulations, and writhing. Drawing him near, holding him close when she should have been pushing him away. Tears of mortification stung her eyes for what she'd allowed him to accomplish. Allowed? She'd relished it, encouraged it.

And well he knew it. As though needing to affirm his knowledge, he pressed his hot mouth to the side of her neck. "You were meant for this," he growled.

"No," she whispered, terrified by the implication of his words.

"There's more, Kitty, so much more, and I can give it all to you."

"No." She shoved against his chest until he staggered back. "No."

She quickly straightened her clothes, sickened by the dampness on her skin where his mouth had been and passion had flourished. She darted past him, around the trellis, stumbling toward the house. As she neared, she took refuge in the shadows near the terrace. She patted her hair, surprised to find it still in place. Her cheeks were burning, her swollen lips tingling from *his* kisses. Her skin was more sensitive, each whisper of the breeze a caress that reminded her of *his* touch.

"Kitty?"

She spun around. "Nicky."

"My sweet, whatever's wrong?"

"I couldn't find you. I saw you come outside . . . I couldn't find you."

"There, there, dear girl." He took her in his arms, and she felt him stiffen, before drawing her closer until her face was pressed within the nook of his shoulder. "You're trembling. What happened?"

She shook her head quickly. "I couldn't find you. I feel safe when I'm with you."

"Because you are safe with me. You'll always be safe with me. I promised you that long ago."

She leaned back until she could see his familiar, trusting blue eyes, the color obscured by the night, but she'd memorized it by sunlight and gaslight and candlelight. "Do you love me, Nicky?"

"Of course, I do."

"Then marry me."

He laughed softly, a quiet chuckle filled with affection. "I thought we agreed on that outcome months ago. No need to ask me."

She shook her head. "No, I mean marry me now."

"Now? This moment?"

"This year. As soon as the Season ends."

"I thought you wanted a proper period of waiting after the announcement—"

"I've changed my mind." Reaching up, she cradled his beloved face between her hands. "I'm so afraid I'll lose you."

"My sweet"—he pressed a kiss to her forehead—"you'll never lose me. I am yours until the end of time."

"Promise?"

"Promise." He held her close. "Are you certain nothing untoward happened?"

"I was simply feeling lost without you and not knowing where you were."

"Well, I'm here now, aren't I?"

She nodded, suddenly aware that her face was wet with tears. "I'm only safe with you. Will you please take me home now?"

"Of course, if that's what you wish. Let me escort you to the carriage, and then I'll find Freddie and Lady Priscilla and let them know that we're to leave."

"Do you have to get them?"

"Certainly I must. We brought them, did we not? I can't very well tell them that they have to hire a hansom. Has Lady Priscilla done something to upset you? I know she often speaks without thinking."

She shook her head briskly. "No, of course Lady Priscilla hasn't upset me. It's simply that you and I never seem to have any time alone."

"Time alone? That's an American courting ritual that we have yet to adopt over here. A gentleman does not put a lady in a compromising position where she might draw unwarranted gossip."

A gentleman might not, but Weddington certainly had no qualms about doing exactly that.

"But we never have any time together when it's only you and me," she told him.

"Tomorrow, we'll do something."

"Promise?"

"I promise. We'll take a stroll through Hyde Park or visit the zoological gardens."

His suggestions weren't what she had in mind. Surrounded by crowds, they still wouldn't be alone, but she was still reeling from her encounter with Weddington and hadn't the will to object. She would take what Farthingham offered and be glad for it.

"Let's go the back way round to the carriage," he suggested. "I'm not sure you want anyone to see you quite so upset."

"I don't. You're so kind, Nicky."

"Of course, I am."

With his arm around her, she allowed him to lead her around the house and toward the carriage. Everything would be all right now. Nicky would keep her safe. With him, she would always be safe.

Chapter 13

"**O**h, look, Farthingham went and did it!" Anne exclaimed.

Richard looked up from his breakfast and scowled at his sister where she sat at the far end of the table with *The Times* spread before her. His mother leaned toward Anne, as though striving to see what had captured her daughter's attention.

"Did what?" Richard asked curtly, still irritated that Anne had arrived at the table before him and claimed his newspaper. It put him out of sorts not to begin his day with *The Times* close at hand.

"Announced his betrothal to Miss Robertson."

Richard came up out of his chair with such force that it overturned—quite an accomplishment considering how heavy it was. He stormed to the other end of the table, barely noticing the widening of his sister's eyes as he snatched the paper from her grasp. He quickly scanned the words that confirmed his worst fears. "Damnation!"

"Richard!" His mother chastised. "Your language. Ladies are present."

"My profound apologies, Mother, Anne. Watkins!"

The butler suddenly appeared in the doorway. "Yes, Your Grace?"

"Alert my driver that I need a carriage immediately."

"Yes, Your Grace."

"Richard, whatever is wrong?" his mother asked.

"Nothing. I simply wish to visit Farthingham and offer him my congratulations regarding his announcement."

His mother blinked as though he'd lost his mind. He was beginning to think that perhaps he had.

"This is hardly an appropriate time of morning to be calling on anyone."

"I am well aware of that." Then he stalked out of the room, the paper still clutched in his white-knuckled grasp.

Richard burst through the door into Farthingham's parlor.

"My lord, I'm terribly sorry," the butler stammered behind him. "I tried to stop him."

"It's quite all right," Farthingham said as he sat up straighter and set his teacup on the table beside the sofa in which he lounged. "I was expecting the duke to call."

Richard stood his ground, silent and angry, until the door clicked closed behind him, leaving only him and Farthingham to square off.

"It appears you've seen the announcement," Farthingham said drolly.

"You said you'd wait until the end of the Season."

"She wanted the announcement made." Farthingham came to his feet, walked to the window, and gazed out on the street. "I gave you every opportunity to win her over."

"A game of charades, a walk in your—"

"She doesn't want you, man. Accept it. She is not a prize to be won."

Taking a threatening step forward, Richard experienced an unnatural urge to wrap his hands around Farthingham's aristocratic neck. "Not a prize? Are you daft? She is the *only* prize in this world worth winning."

"Then you shouldn't have followed her into Harrington's garden."

Shaking his head, Richard gazed down at the rumpled newspaper still clutched in his hand. "I was trying to protect her—"

"I know, and I'm grateful. I didn't realize she saw me slip out. I thought I was being so cleverly discreet." He shook his head as though the action would undo the damage he'd almost caused. "I owe you for diverting her attention away from her search for me."

Richard shook the paper at him. "You have a damned strange way of showing your appreciation."

"She *wanted* the announcement posted, was quite adamant about it," Farthingham repeated. "I told you before that I would do everything to see her happy."

"Why you? What does she see in you?"

"I'm charming, fun, witty, and have a wonderful sense of humor, which you do not possess even a hint of. You're surly, competitive, controlling."

"You'll destroy her."

"Once we are married, I'll dedicate my life to her. No more sneaking out at parties for a bit of tomfoolery. No more surrounding myself with others so she doesn't notice that she might not have my complete attention. As I've said before, Weddington, I'm extremely fond of Kitty. I can play the part of attentive husband."

Fond? He wanted to smash his fist into the man's face. "She deserves more than fondness and someone merely playing the part."

"Be that as it may, she doesn't want *you.* Even I can see from the manner in which she watches you that she's not comfortable around you. It's as though you terrify her."

Richard dropped heavily into a nearby chair. "I don't understand. I've never harmed her. What is there to fear?"

"Who can understand the workings of a woman's mind? This woman's especially. Kitty is unlike any woman I've ever known."

"When will you marry her?"

"At the end of the Season. Sometime in August, September perhaps. We've not yet set the exact date, but she no longer wishes to wait."

"Do you still plan to spend a few days at Drummond Manor?"

"Yes, of course. Unless you'd rather we didn't."

Richard stood, his mind reeling. He'd demonstrated only a few nights before what he could offer her. Why was she now intent on rushing to the altar? "We'd be most pleased to entertain you," he finally said, recognizing that Farthingham had fewer answers than he did.

With nothing more to say, he headed for the door.

"Weddington?"

Halting, Richard looked back over his shoulder. Morning light streamed through the window, giving Farthingham an angelic appearance.

"Has it ever occurred to you that perhaps *you* are the one who could destroy her?"

Without a word, Richard charged out of Farthingham's house. On the journey home, as the carriage swayed and clattered over the streets of London, he allowed the ominous chill to sweep through him as Farthingham's words echoed through his mind, words with which he was far too familiar, words that had haunted him from the first moment he'd spotted Kitty at the seashore—

That it was indeed *he* who would destroy her.

The flowers arrived an hour before Weddington did. A simple bouquet of yellow roses. No note this time, but Kitty didn't require one to know they were from him. She didn't know why the gesture touched her so, or why she joined him in the garden while her mother sipped tea on the terrace. Surely, it would have been wiser to feign a headache.

But wisdom seemed to elude her. She shored up her pride and did meet him, strolling beside him, unable to meet his eyes. She'd not seen him since the night of the Harringtons' ball, since their time in the garden there—and she hadn't truly seen him then. At least not with her eyes. Her body had certainly recognized him.

She wondered why he'd come when it was too late to undo what she'd insisted be done hastily. Her betrothal was now official. She no longer had the option of turning back, changing her mind or her course. Honor, duty, responsibility, all woven tightly together, impenetrable, because a few words printed in black ink changed a possibility into an obligation. She would marry the Marquess of Farthingham and never again be tempted with the forbidden desires offered by the Duke of Weddington.

She refused to be the daughter of the woman who'd given birth to her, refused to accept the lustful thoughts and stark images of nude, writhing bodies that haunted her. She would not give in to wicked temptation. She possessed a strong resolve, a will as unbending as the iron tracks her father had laid down for the railroads.

"We've been in the garden for all of a quarter of an hour, Your Grace, and you've not yet spoken, which makes it difficult to determine why you are here," she said, finally gathering up the courage to end the silence when she feared what might lie on the other side of it.

"I wanted to see you again."

"It's entirely inappropriate considering the fact that I am now officially betrothed to Lord Farthingham. And don't dare spout off about his making me unhappy when he has already proven your prediction false."

He chuckled low. "By God, but you are loyal. I wonder if he truly appreciates exactly how magnificent a catch you are. I would surrender my fortune for such loyalty."

"It cannot be purchased, Your Grace. My dedication to Lord Farthingham comes from my heart. It is pure"—she wanted to say as pure as she was, but he had the knowledge to refute that false claim since he was the one who lured her with impurity—"and will see us in good stead."

"I have no doubt of your devotion or how well it will serve you. I find myself envying a man whom I never thought to envy in the slightest."

"Other American ladies are in London for the Season."

"Ah, yes, but among all of them there is only one you."

"You flatter me, Your Grace."

"Obviously not enough, or you wouldn't have hastened with your announcement and sealed your fate."

"I don't know how to say this any more plainly: I do not feel for you what I feel for Farthingham."

"No, you feel much more for me, something deeper, more torrid—"

"You touch me in ways that I do not wish to be touched, and I'm not referring only to the physical liberties which you took the other night." Tears stung her eyes. "And don't you dare tell me that I enjoyed it."

She had, but dear God, she didn't want it acknowledged, especially by him.

"Passion is not something to hide from. I know I stir it within you, because I feel the same stirring."

Stopping abruptly and shoving her crossed arms beneath her breasts, she faced him and hissed, "I did *nothing* to make you feel as you made me feel."

"You need only breathe to stir the flames of my desire for you."

Shaking her head in frustration, she studied every line, curve, angle of his face, striving to find something that would explain what drew her to him when she had no wish to be drawn. "Why do you do this? Why do you persist in tormenting me?"

He looked as though she'd slapped him. "I don't understand why you see the gift of pleasure as torment."

"It is not your gift to give to me."

"Farthingham's gifts in that arena will pale when compared against mine."

"How can you be so certain? Are you some sort of voyeur? Have you watched him make love?"

"Of course not. But his reasons for marrying you—"

"I am well aware of the reasons he is marrying me. What you have failed to take into consideration is why I am marrying him!"

He seemed to come up short at that, as though totally taken aback by her words. "Why *are* you marrying him?"

"I like the way he makes me feel, I like the way that I am when I am with him."

"Without passion," he stated succinctly.

"Does everything with you come down to passion, and mating, and animalistic desires? What happened in Harrington's garden was uncivilized and barbaric. Yes, you possess the undeniable ability to make my body sing, but, Your Grace, I take no pleasure in the tune!"

She spun on her heel, striding quickly toward the house, leaving him standing where he was, apparently dumbfounded.

Her mother stood as she neared. "Is everything all right, Kitty?"

"Couldn't be lovelier. I've taken a sudden headache is all. I'm going to lie down."

But once she reached her room, she curled up in a chair, not the bed. She didn't want to sleep, didn't want to dream about Weddington. Every time she closed her eyes, he spawned dreams that left her hot, damp, and gasping for breath.

Only marriage to Farthingham would rid her of those shameful desires. She bit her knuckles while tears streamed down her face. Dear God, the marriage couldn't happen soon enough.

Chapter 14

"Is Weddington's home not absolutely magnificent?" Farthingham asked.

Standing within the entry hallway of Drummond Manor, waiting while the butler followed Farthingham's request that the family be alerted to the arrival of their guests, Kitty admitted that she was indeed impressed. "It's very grand, but I still prefer your ancestral home."

"Is she not a dear?" Farthingham asked looking at Freddie and Lady Priscilla before taking Kitty's gloved hand and pressing a kiss to its back. "With the help of your father's settlement, we shall restore Farthingham to its grandeur, but even then, I have serious doubts that it will rival this residence."

Lady Priscilla giggled. "And this isn't even Weddington's main residence. You should see those grounds. They and the house are incredible. Lady Anne would invite me to visit, and I might be there days before the duke would even notice that I'd arrived."

"I would always notice," Freddie said.

Lady Priscilla giggled again. "You are too sweet by half. I do wish you'd reconsider this silly plan of yours to go to America."

"Why? So that I might become your lover? You'd never marry me, Prissy, and well you know it. I am fifth in line, not likely to inherit, and even if I were, your tastes are too expensive."

"Your words are all too true. Still, we can have fun this last Season."

"Ah, you've arrived!" Lady Anne called out as she hurried down the sweeping staircase.

"Where's your brother?" Farthingham asked as he pressed a kiss to Lady Anne's hand.

"Richard got called away this morning to see to some problem with something or someone involved with the estate. I pay as much attention to him when he mentions business concerns as he does when I discuss gowns. Which is none at all. He'll return this evening. Meanwhile, I'm to entertain." She slipped her arm around Kitty's. "Come along, I'll show you to your rooms."

Kitty hesitated, suddenly uncomfortable with the notion of staying there. "If your brother has business concerns, maybe we shouldn't impose right now. We could return to London, perhaps visit another time."

"Oh, no, don't be silly," Lady Anne said. "Richard always has business concerns. If you waited until he didn't, you'd never visit. I honestly don't know how he manages all that he does. Mother swears he's not human."

Perhaps that would explain his hold on her. Otherworldly.

Arm in arm with Kitty, Lady Anne led her up the stairs, the others trailing in her wake.

"Speaking of your mother, is she about?" Farthingham asked.

"No, she stayed in London," Lady Anne said. "She prefers visiting with her friends to the loneliness of Drummond Manor."

"Why does she find it lonely?" Kitty asked. "There's a lovely town near here where my family stayed before we went on to London."

"It's too near the sea," Lady Anne said quietly. "It reminds her of Father and all that happened . . ." Her voice trailed off, before picking up with resounding enthusiasm. "You're all to make yourselves at home here. You may make use of the stables, the gardens, anything you wish."

"The duke's liquor cabinet?" Farthingham asked.

Laughing, Lady Anne glanced over her shoulder. "By all means! When has my brother ever denied you your liquor?"

"That's true. Weddington has always been a most generous host."

They reached the landing where sunlight streamed in through a wall of windows. The opposite wall had many doors.

"This bedchamber has been reserved for you, Miss Robertson," Lady Anne said, opening the door. "I'll have your bags brought up."

Kitty smiled. "Are the family's rooms on this hallway as well?"

"Oh, no. Our rooms are in other wings. I'll give you the grand tour once you've rested."

While Lady Anne escorted the others to their rooms, Kitty walked through hers, admiring the fine workmanship of the furniture, the detailed carvings in the dark wood, the comforter spread over the bed, and the heavy draperies that hung from the canopy. The comforter and draperies were lavishly decorated with the family crest. On a long table set along the foot of the bed were several books, atop one was a yellow rose, and beneath it a slip of folded paper.

Ignoring the letter, she walked to the window and gazed out on the beautiful Cornish countryside and the sea beyond. From here, she imagined she could see the path that Weddington would have walked to the spot where she'd first sighted him, where he took his daily swim, where she'd first realized the power of temptation.

She glanced over at the table, the rose, the books, the letter. *His* letter, she was certain. What had he written? Was he really away on business or was he waiting for her by the shore, hoping for a clandestine meeting? Was his letter a summons?

Had he accepted that she was now Farthingham's? Or would he continue his attempt at seduction here? To lure her away from the man she wanted to marry with promises of passion she had no wish to accept?

Even as she stood there, her body grew hot, her head light with dizziness. How could he hold such power over her when he wasn't even in the room? She wondered in which room Farthingham would sleep, if the gentlemen would even be in this wing of the house.

Probably not. Proper behavior dictated that the men be placed elsewhere, not within easy reach of ladies who were not properly chaperoned. She thought of Freddie's comment in the entryway. She wondered if he was going to America with the hopes that success might give him more to offer Lady Priscilla. Although truthfully, she thought the girl was a little too flighty for a man who possessed the tragic thoughts that were so characteristic of his plays.

Her gaze returned to the letter. Although she'd not looked at it, she knew, without any doubt that it came from Weddington. As did the yellow rose.

She cursed him as her curiosity got the better of her. She crossed back to the table, snatched up his letter, and unfolded it.

My dear Miss Robertson,

Regrettably I cannot be in attendance to welcome you the moment you arrive, but all members of my staff have been

*informed that your slightest wish is my command, to be fol-
lowed without hesitation or question.*

*Until I return this evening, it is my fervent hope that you
will enjoy the hospitality of Drummond Manor.*

*Yours most devotedly,
The Duke of Weddington*

She walked back to the window, suddenly feeling restless and
caged in by the extension of *his* hospitality. Why did he have to do
little things that made her feel special, and why did she not trust a single one of them?

As his guest, she would behave pleasantly and with the appropriate decorum. She wouldn't allow him to unsettle her.

Still, she needed to get out. Lady Anne had mentioned that the
stables were available. As soon as the servants brought up her lug-
gage, she'd send for a maid and get help changing into her riding
habit. She thought a jaunt across the moors was exactly what she
needed.

Richard spotted her the moment he cleared the rise. Dressed in
emerald green, she was the fairest creature he'd ever set eyes on.
Although he'd never before seen her on a horse, he'd known she'd sit
one perfectly. He wasn't surprised that it seemed she was riding alone.
His little independent Texan didn't seem to understand the concept of
a chaperone, giving him ample opportunity to take advantage.

Where she was concerned he was invariably weak in his restraint.
He urged his own horse forward, galloping over the land until he
caught up to her. She seemed neither surprised nor flattered by his
appearance, simply resolved to accepting his presence.

"Where are the others?" he asked without preamble.

"When I left the house, Lady Anne was having tea, Lady Priscilla
was napping, and the gentlemen were nowhere to be found. Lady
Anne speculated that they were out exploring caves."

"No doubt she's correct in her assumption. Farthingham has
always hoped to find buried treasure left unattended by smugglers."

"Would your ancestors have happened to have been those smugglers?"

He laughed deeply. "Legend would have one believe that is the
case."

"I always thought you looked like a pirate."

"I'm flattered that you gave any thought at all to how I looked."

"It won't work, you know."

"What won't work?"

"Bringing me here, reminding me of those mornings by the shore. My heart belongs to Farthingham. I've consented to marry him. We've made our announcement. You're too late, Your Grace."

"You're quite certain of that?"

"Absolutely."

"I shall keep your certainty in mind. However, if you will recall, it was Anne's suggestion that you all come here, not mine. Did she give you a tour of our home?"

"Yes. It's lovely."

"I can take no credit for it except to say that I chose my ancestors wisely."

She smiled. "I didn't know one could choose one's ancestors."

"A bit of attempted humor on my part. Farthingham claims you dislike me because I am not jolly."

"I don't dislike—"

She stopped abruptly, and Richard arched a brow. "Don't you? I was given to understand that you do dislike me."

"Not you personally. I'm simply not comfortable with certain aspects of your . . . your behavior."

"And if I could make you comfortable with them?"

"You can't! So cease and desist. Let me go. Let me find my happiness with Farthingham."

"I would if I were convinced that you would indeed be happy with him."

"I fail to understand why you believe that my happiness is any of your concern."

It was impossible to explain without appearing to be a fool. He wasn't even certain that he could put a name to his feelings.

"You have spoken before about how I touch you—not in the physical sense, but in other ways, in a manner that is beyond the flesh."

"Your Grace—"

"Allow me to finish. From that first dawn when I spotted you near the rocks, I have a felt a bond that I cannot explain."

"Lust."

"No." He shook his head in frustration. "I did not have a clear vision of you that morning, and I am not the type of man who desires every female he lays eyes on. I was drawn to you. Perhaps it was your boldness in watching me."

Her cheeks blushed pink, and she looked away.

He cursed his awkward tongue. "I apologize. I did not mean to embarrass you. I don't understand this attraction any more than you do. I only know that it grows each time I am with you."

She turned back to him, sadness in her eyes. "It must cease to grow, Your Grace, because I am soon to marry."

"You've closed your mind and your heart to the possibility of anything existing between us?"

"I have. I belong with Lord Farthingham."

"Very well. Then I wish you the very best." Although even he had to admit that his sentiments sounded surly, like a child telling another that he doesn't want something simply because he knows he has no hope of ever attaining it.

"It'll be dark soon. We should head back to the stables," he said.

She nodded, before sliding her gaze over to him slyly. "Why a yellow rose?"

"Pardon?"

She sighed. "The first time you sent me flowers, you sent them in abundance, in all colors, all varieties. Lately, it's always a yellow rose."

He grinned. "I'd once heard a song about the yellow rose of Texas. Not a flower, but a woman that a soldier was striving to find. I can't recall if he found her, but it seemed an appropriate flower to send you."

She smiled softly. "Thank you. They're actually my favorite."

He bowed his head slightly. "You are most welcome."

It was so seldom that she appreciated anything he did that he embraced her gratitude with open arms.

Kitty heard the light tapping on her door shortly after she'd heard a clock somewhere counting out the hour of midnight. Her first thought was that it was Weddington, come to torment her with caresses and kisses, but then she realized that he wouldn't have risked knocking and taking a chance on disturbing someone and being caught. She did have to give him credit for the care he took whenever he did approach her with naughty intentions in mind.

"Miss Robertson?" a soft voice called out before another round of tapping on her door commenced.

She slipped out of bed, walked to the door, opened it, and peered out. "Lady Anne?"

Dressed in their nightclothes, Lady Anne and Lady Priscilla nodded eagerly.

"We thought you might like to join us," Lady Priscilla whispered.

"Join you?"

Lady Anne bobbed her head. "We're going to the bathhouse."

"This time of night?" Kitty asked, astounded that they'd even consider it.

"Oh, yes, it's the best time really," Lady Anne said.

"It's a ritual that we began when we were younger," Lady Priscilla explained.

"I'll change—"

"Oh, no, that's part of the fun," Lady Priscilla said. "We'll simply dash to the bathhouse as we are. But do get a blanket so you can dry off and be warm afterward."

"Although the wine will warm us as well," Lady Anne said with a mischievous gleam in her eyes.

It was then that Kitty noticed the bag that Lady Anne was carrying and heard the slight clinking that occurred whenever Lady Anne moved.

"What of the gentlemen?" Kitty asked.

Lady Anne's eyes widened. "You Americans are exceedingly bold! I'd not thought to invite them."

"Oh, no," Kitty hastened to explain. "I didn't think we should invite them, but what if they see us scurrying about in our nightclothes?"

Lady Priscilla giggled. "Oh, they shan't. When last we checked, they were still in the billiard room smacking balls around."

"I daresay they'll be there all night," Lady Anne added. "They usually are. They'll take no notice of us."

"Hold on, then, and I'll grab a blanket," Kitty told them.

"Jolly good," Lady Priscilla said.

Kitty ducked back into the bedchamber, grabbed a blanket off the bed, and hurried into the dimly lit hallway. Lady Anne and Lady Priscilla were already waiting by the stairs.

"Are you certain we should do this?" Kitty asked.

"Oh, most assuredly we *shouldn't* do it," Lady Anne told her, laughing lightly.

"Which is the very reason that we do," Lady Priscilla said.

Both ladies hurried down the stairs, their bare feet slapping out a soft cadence. Quickly following after them, Kitty supposed three ladies going to the bathhouse at midnight was really quite innocent. It wasn't as though they intended to meet any gentlemen there.

Amidst whispers, shh's, and giggles, they made their way out of the manor. The chilly night air was brisk, and Kitty felt shivers erupt on her skin. With the ground cool beneath her bare soles, she thought they were rather silly not to have put on shoes.

The moon was out and it was a very different sky from what she saw in London. Thinking of Emily, she wondered if her sister was trying to identify the various constellations tonight.

Kitty stubbed her toe, tripped, stumbled, caught herself before she landed flat on her face, and hurried to catch up with her partners in mischief. Quite suddenly the large stone bathhouse loomed before her. She'd noticed the building late in the afternoon when she'd gone to the stables to fetch a horse, but she'd given it little attention, certainly hadn't realized its purpose.

Dashing up the steps between stone pillars, Lady Priscilla and Lady Anne giggled as they went, leaving Kitty to wonder how much wine the young ladies had sipped before deciding to fetch her.

"Come on," Lady Anne urged in a whisper, shoving on the wooden door. It moaned and squeaked in protest as though its hinges were rusty and seldom used. Once more filled with trepidation, Kitty glanced around, and when she looked back at the entrance, Lady Priscilla and Lady Anne had already disappeared inside the building.

Kitty slipped through the opening into a plain entryway. Gaslights flickered, causing shadows to waver over the stone walls, shaped in an oval, flush with the water except for the area where she stood. A wide flight of stone steps led down into the pool, steam hovering over the surface like a misty gray fog.

"The changing room is off to the side there," Lady Anne whispered, pointing behind Kitty. "But we don't usually bother with it. We'll trust you to close your eyes."

"Why are we whispering?" Kitty asked.

Lady Priscilla giggled. "I don't know, but we always do."

Even with the whispering, their voices echoed around the cavernous structure.

Kitty looked toward the pool. "How deep is it?"

"You'll go under," Lady Anne said. "It was actually a plunge bath a 150 years ago or so when everyone was convinced freezing cold baths were the way to good health. Insane really to jump in like that. I'm surprised our family line didn't cease to exist at the time. Anyway, hidden beneath the water is a smooth stone ledge around the side, which is where we sit. The water comes up only to our shoulders." She glanced around smiling. "Who wants to go first?"

"I will," Lady Priscilla said.

"Splendid." Lady Anne put her hands on Kitty's shoulders and turned her so she no longer faced the water. "Close your eyes."

"Why?"

"So Prissy can undress without embarrassment."

"We're going in nude?"

"Absolutely. But we can be trusted. We don't look when anyone goes in or out."

Kitty closed her eyes, wondering what she'd gotten herself into.

She'd gotten herself into heaven, she decided a few minutes later when her turn had come to enter the pool. She sat on the stone ledge, with the warm water enveloping her like a snuggly blanket on a chilly day. "This is absolutely lovely."

"Isn't it?" Lady Anne asked. Sitting near the steps, she poured wine into glasses and passed them around before easing toward the side away from the steps.

They formed a triangle in the pool, Kitty at one end, Lady Priscilla and Lady Anne on the sides. Kitty sipped the wine, thinking she really didn't need anything else to relax. Once she moved into Farthingham's ancestral home, she'd have to see about having a bath-house built. Although his home did have a bathing room, it didn't allow for swimming or for more than one person to take advantage of it at the same time as this bathhouse did.

"You said this pool used to be a plunge bath?" Kitty asked. "With cold water?"

"Yes, it was quite popular at the first part of the eighteenth century. Richard paid a fortune to have proper plumbing and hot water piping installed, but it was all well worth it. When his back is troubling him, he'll spend hours soaking in here."

Kitty glanced at the stairs, followed the railing up to the door. "Is there any chance he'll come here tonight?"

"I shouldn't think so," Lady Anne said.

Sipping more wine, Kitty couldn't help but wonder if the possibility of him and the other men arriving unexpectedly was the reason behind their whispering and giggling on their journey there. She was certain Lady Priscilla wouldn't mind if Freddie appeared.

"About his back," Kitty began. "I know it's an old injury. How did he hurt it?"

Lady Anne darted a glance at Lady Priscilla, who merely shrugged.

"I suppose there's no harm in telling her," Lady Priscilla said.

"I suppose not." Lady Anne finished off her wine. "You mustn't ever tell him that I told you. He's really quite private about it."

Kitty sat up straighter, the water rippling around her. "I promise. I'm quite good at keeping secrets."

"It's not a secret really. It's simply that he'd prefer to forget every-thing associated with his injury." Lady Anne took a deep breath. "It happened when our father died. I was only a child, so I don't actually remember the particulars except what I've been told or overheard when people thought I wasn't listening. Much whispering was going on immediately afterward and in the years since."

"How long ago did it happen then?" Kitty asked.

"My goodness, I've never been skilled at ciphering, but I know Richard was eighteen. I do remember that. He's thirty-four now—"

"Sixteen years," Kitty offered. "That's a long time to have discomfort."

"He doesn't always hurt. Not that he usually tells us when he does, but after a while you begin to notice the signs."

"Carry on with your tale," Kitty urged.

"Right. Well, one afternoon he and Father went sailing. They'd had an argument the day before, and from what Mother has told me, they were in the habit of sailing together whenever they fell out of sorts with each other. Apparently working together on the yacht helped to strengthen whatever bonds might have been weakened by their argument. While they were out, a storm came up. I don't know exactly how it came about, but the crew made it safely to shore in the lifeboat. I can't imagine how . . . because the storm sank the yacht. But there you have it. They did. Papa died, and Richard swam to shore dragging Papa along behind him. He refused to leave him to the sea."

She remembered his telling of the tale. He and the crew had made it to shore. He'd neglected to mention that they'd arrived separately.

"Why weren't your father and brother in the lifeboat with the crew?" Kitty asked.

"I really don't know. It seems most odd, but as I said, Richard won't talk about it. Sometime during the storm—I don't know if it's when he was on the yacht or in the water—he somehow twisted his back. From time to time, when he exerts himself too much, it pains him. He doesn't like to talk about it, and he doesn't like for people to know. His attitude is silly really, as though he thinks people will hold him responsible because he hurts."

Kitty leaned back against the slick wall. "That must have been very difficult for him, though, to have lost his father like that." She remembered his version of the story, the curt, unemotional telling of an event that had such a profound effect on his life.

"Extremely difficult. As I say, I was very young, but I remember he was in bed for the longest time afterward. Seemed like forever to me then. I remember mother fretting so. I would cry at night because I was afraid Richard was going to die, too, like Papa had."

The sea terrifies me. Kitty remembered Weddington's confession from their walk in Farthingham's garden. The first morning that she'd seen him, it wasn't the sun he'd been standing defiantly against, she realized now, but the sea.

"I'm surprised that he continues to yacht as much as he does," Lady Priscilla said. "If I ever got caught in a storm, I don't think I'd ever go out on the water again."

"I'd have the same feelings as you, Prissy," Lady Anne acknowledged. "But Richard possesses an incredible love of the sea. He has four yachts, and a smaller sailboat that a couple of men can manage. He loves to design, then hire men to build his boats."

Was it possible that Kitty was the only person he'd ever told about his fear of the sea? Or had he lied to her in order to gain her sympathies? No, she couldn't see him plying her with falsehoods. With her, he'd simply revealed a part of himself that he'd never exposed to anyone else. Although it really wasn't simple at all.

Draining her glass, she wondered if he was correct about the bond that seemed to draw her to him, him to her. Did it go beyond a heated look, a sensual caress? She'd so easily confessed that he frightened her, found she'd been able to mention sensual yearnings and lust . . .

She'd never so much as truly kissed Farthingham, and they'd certainly never discussed how their bodies felt when the other was near.

"More wine?"

Startled, Kitty almost lost her seating on the ledge. Lady Anne had the bottle poised for pouring.

"Yes, please." Watching the liquid cascade into the glass, Kitty remembered how she'd wanted to pour her body into Weddington.

"You are ever so lucky to have caught Farthingham," Lady Priscilla said.

"I quite agree," Kitty murmured, and sipped more of her wine.

"You're not having much luck with Freddie, are you?" Lady Anne asked.

Lady Priscilla shook her head. "Not really. He's lots of fun, but I gather he's not really interested in me."

"He's a fool if he's not," Lady Anne said, and Kitty heard the defense of her friend in her voice.

Kitty had friends, but she'd spent considerable time traveling the world, experiencing so many wonderful things that she'd never really taken time to develop any deep and lasting friendships. Except for Farthingham. She supposed that he was her one true friend. How truly fortunate she was that he would also be her husband.

"Miss Robertson, may I ask you a rather personal question?" Lady Priscilla asked.

Kitty laughed lightly. "If it's going to be personal, don't you think you should call me Kitty?"

Lady Priscilla giggled. "Yes, I suppose so."

"Here, drink some more wine," Lady Anne encouraged, leaving Kitty to wonder if they'd purposely brought her there to ask this "personal question."

Kitty drank and nodded. "Go on and ask."

"Well, we're all aware that American ladies aren't chaperoned quite as closely as we are over here."

"Not chaperoned at all usually," Kitty acknowledged.

Lady Priscilla and Lady Anne exchanged quick glances before they both focused all their attention on Kitty, making her decidedly uncomfortable.

Lady Priscilla took a deep breath. "Have you ever been kissed? I mean truly kissed?"

The heat suffused Kitty's face and traveled down to her toes. She nodded quickly.

"What was it like?" Lady Priscilla and Lady Anne asked at the same time.

Kitty released a small self-conscious laugh. "I don't know that I can describe it."

"Please, do try," Lady Priscilla pleaded.

Kitty released a deep breath. "Well . . . it was very much like being here. Warm. Misty. Like drinking too much wine—so the warmth travels outward as well as inward. It's like feeling lethargic and energetic at the same time." She closed her eyes, remembering Weddington's mouth moving provocatively over hers. It had made her want to touch forbidden places in forbidden ways. She opened her eyes. "It's enjoyable."

"I'm positively certain that it *was* enjoyable," Lady Priscilla said. "Farthingham makes everything enjoyable."

Kitty downed her wine as though it were water. Should she confess to these ladies that it wasn't Farthingham who had kissed her or allow them to believe it was? And if they said something to him . . .

"You won't mention what I said will you?" she asked.

"Absolutely not," Lady Anne said. "Everything said within these walls remains within these walls. Isn't that right, Prissy?"

"Oh, absolutely. Not a single word to anyone."

"More wine?" Lady Anne asked.

Kitty laughed. "Absolutely." She waited while Lady Anne opened another bottle and poured another generous amount into everyone's glass before posing her question. "Lady Anne, I recall a conversation in the coach on the way to the opera . . . something about a young man holding your heart. Has he never kissed you?"

"Oh!" Lady Anne pressed her hand to her mouth and her shoulders curled forward as she glanced shyly at Kitty. "I've never even spoken to him."

"Nor he to her," Lady Priscilla said.

"He does address me when our paths cross," Lady Anne said curtly.

"And yet he holds your heart?" Kitty asked.

"From afar," Lady Anne assured her.

"She doesn't even know his name," Lady Priscilla said.

Although the warm water had made everyone's face turn pink, Lady Anne's darkened into rose with embarrassment. "He is an assistant to one of Richard's solicitors. I see him from time to time when he delivers messages or papers."

Kitty contemplated the first morning she'd encountered Weddington and how she'd been drawn back to the same spot the next morning, her initial disappointment because she hadn't spotted him again, her conflicting feelings when he'd suddenly appeared. Did something indefinable but recognizable exist between people?

"Lady Anne—"

"You must call me Anne."

She smiled. "All right. Anne. This gentleman . . . if you've never engaged in conversation with him, why are you certain that he has the potential to hold your heart?"

She shook her head quickly. "I'm silly, aren't I? I don't know why I feel as though it's so. I'm sure Richard is right. I should be looking among the aristocracy for a husband. And perhaps if I got to know the fellow I would find him rather unsuitable, and yet something tells me that I wouldn't."

"He's your soul mate," Lady Priscilla said with a sigh. "So you recognize that part of him that speaks to you, even though he never actually speaks to you." She giggled. "That was a profound thought, wasn't it?"

Anne laughed. "No! It was silly. I think you've had far too much wine."

"Hardly. Pour me some more."

While Anne did the pouring, Kitty dared to ask, "Anne, why has your brother not taken a wife?"

"My mother has been asking him the same thing for years now.

She's quite beside herself with worry. After all, he has no brother to inherit the title should an accident befall Richard. It is a mystery as to why he has not yet shown any interest in getting married."

Only he had shown interest . . . to her. Proposing in her garden.

"Perhaps he is waiting for a woman to want to marry him," Lady Priscilla offered.

"I should think that wouldn't be a problem," Lady Anne said, clearly in defense of her brother.

"He's not what I'd call classically handsome," Lady Priscilla said.

"Well, no," Lady Anne reluctantly admitted.

"And he's not exactly . . . jovial."

"No, he's not," Lady Anne said.

"And he tends to be domineering."

Lady Anne nodded. "Indeed."

She appeared to be remarkably sad, then she brightened. "He dances well."

Kitty burst out laughing. She couldn't help herself. Perhaps she'd had too much wine, but she'd sat there listening to their inconsequential descriptions of the man. Abruptly she quieted under their direct stares.

"You don't think he dances well?" Lady Anne asked, clearly offended.

Kitty had to swallow another bubble of laughter. "I think he dances marvelously." She shook her head, her mind swirling. A combination of the wine and the warm water was loosening her tongue, and she seemed to have no power to hold back the words.

"You say he is not classically handsome, and I say that I have never seen a man who portrayed such"—she thought of him that first morning by the sea—"magnificence. A power that is evident the moment your gaze falls on him.

"You say he's not jovial, and I'll admit I've never heard him erupt with bold laughter, and yet I sense in him that he finds joy in ensuring that others enjoy life. The wagers with Farthingham . . . Farthingham's prize should he have won was always so much more valuable than what Weddington would have gained. And yet I think he was more inclined to accept the wager because Farthingham so enjoys wagering.

"As for his domineering attitude, would you truly want a man who couldn't exhibit power, influence, and control to inherit the family's titles? In many ways, he reminds me of my father. He possesses a determination to succeed. Call it competitiveness or the inability to settle for less than one deserves, but it's not a negative attribute. I find it incredibly appealing when a man will strive to achieve.

"I've found your brother to be thoughtful, considerate, and dependable. He does not play when responsibilities call him. He places his obligations first, and in so doing, he places his family above all else. I find him admirable."

With their eyes wide and their mouths agape, both ladies stared at her.

"My Lord," Lady Anne finally said. "If you have such flattering comments to say about my brother—with such conviction—I can well imagine that you've placed Farthingham, the man you intend to marry, on a golden pedestal."

Kitty suddenly felt ill. A result of too much wine, she was certain of it. Otherwise, she might have to admit that the roiling in her stomach was caused by her fear that they'd ask her to expound on Farthingham's virtues, and the only thing she could think to say was that he was fun, and he made her feel safe.

Chapter 15

⟨⟨ **I** do believe Cook has outdone herself this morning," Richard said as he began to cut into the slice of ham on his plate. "Everything smells incredibly delicious. Don't you agree, Anne?"

From her place at the table, his sister shook her head and pressed a hand to her mouth. All three ladies were a bit off-color that morning. Seaweed green. No doubt a result of their excursion to the bathhouse.

He'd been standing by the window in the billiard room, waiting for Farthingham to take a shot, when he'd heard the commotion outside. He'd excused himself and followed the whispering, giggling ladies to the bathhouse, then kept watch to make certain no one disturbed them.

They'd stayed so long he was surprised that they hadn't shriveled up into nothing.

"Miss Robertson, are you certain that I can't fetch you a helping of eggs? Cook seasons them with some sort of rare spice, so they have a most distinct flavoring that makes them a delightful gift to the palate."

She gave him a scathing glare that might have sliced a lesser man to ribbons. "No, thank you. The tea will suffice."

"Well, if you happen to change your mind, I'll be only too glad to fill a plate for you with all the varied offerings designed to make a person's mouth water."

Narrowing her eyes at him, she pressed her fingers to her temples.

"Whatever is wrong, my sweet? Did something you ate during dinner not agree with you last night?" Farthingham asked.

"I suspect something following dinner agreed too much," Richard said.

"You're enjoying this, aren't you?" Kitty asked.

"I don't enjoy that you're miserable, but I certainly don't mind goading you about your foolishness."

"I feel as though Freddie and I have been left out of something quite important," Farthingham said.

"I believe the ladies spent a bit of time at the bathhouse last night. How much wine, Anne? Two bottles, three?"

"Four, if you must know."

Scoffing, Richard shook his head in amazement.

"I suppose you've never drunk to excess," Kitty stated.

"Actually no. I prefer to keep my wits about me."

"But wine makes it easier to talk," Anne said.

"I've never noticed you having difficulty talking," Richard said. "Too much wine can loosen one's tongue, which is not the same as making it easier to converse."

"I disagree. I'm certain without the wine, Kitty never would have confessed that Farthingham is an amazing kisser," Lady Priscilla said.

"Prissy!" Kitty snapped.

Horror washed over Lady Priscilla's face. "Oops! That was supposed to remain our little secret, wasn't it? I'm dreadfully sorry. Truly I am. I simply forgot."

"I don't mind having my talents revealed," Farthingham said, placing his elbow on the table, his chin in his palm. "Not at all. I'm quite pleased to know, my sweet, that you take such pleasure in my wooing of you."

Kitty looked as though she wanted to die on the spot, and Richard was certain it wasn't simply from the ill effects of having finally gone to bed in the wee hours before dawn with too much alcohol in her blood. She pushed back her chair. "I'm going to lie down."

"Will you be up to going out on the yacht this afternoon?" Richard asked.

She nodded. "Yes."

As she walked from the room, Anne stood. "I think I shall return to bed as well."

"And I," Lady Priscilla said.

Once the ladies were out of earshot, the gentlemen passed glances among themselves, shaking their heads, and smiling.

"Perhaps we should postpone taking the yacht out," Farthingham suggested.

But Richard was anxious for Kitty to see his fine vessel. "We'll go after lunch. They should be all right by then."

"Four bottles of wine among the three of them? No telling what else they confessed," Farthingham speculated.

Richard wondered if Kitty had mentioned his kisses as well as Farthingham's, or had she found his to be easily forgotten? More importantly, was it Farthingham's *amazing* kisses that kept her tethered to him? It was a notion Weddington hadn't considered. Perhaps Farthingham did have the skills required to bring her passions to the surface. It wasn't a thought he much liked having.

The Fair Lady was moored in the harbor of the small port town where Kitty and her family had vacationed only a few weeks earlier.

Weddington had gone ahead of them to see to readying the vessel and had helped her and Farthingham board his yacht as soon as the small rowboat used to get them to the yacht had drawn up alongside the much larger ship. The others were still getting themselves ready, promising to arrive soon, not nearly as anxious as Kitty was to be under way.

While she walked slowly from stern to bow, inspecting the ship, she sensed Weddington scrutinizing her as he followed. Wishing Priscilla had kept her mouth tightly sealed regarding the kiss, Kitty wondered if Weddington suspected it was his kiss she'd described to his sister and her friend and not Farthingham's. Although she imagined no reason existed for him to suspect that he alone had kissed her passionately, she'd prefer for him not to realize that she'd spent a good deal of time reflecting on his mastery of seduction.

"What do you think, my sweet? Impressed?" Farthingham asked, as they reached the bow and came to a stop.

She darted a glance at Weddington, who stood with his hands behind his back, his gaze focused intently on her, almost as though he held his breath in anticipation of her answer. "It's lovely," she finally admitted.

Weddington acknowledged her statement with a barely discernable bowing of his head, while Farthingham took her arm with such excitement that she would have thought he was the one responsible for the magnificence of the vessel. "Let me show you belowdecks. That is where you'll find the true beauty of this yacht."

"If Weddington doesn't mind," she said.

"Of course, I don't mind," Weddington said. "Make yourselves at home. Once we shove off, we'll be serving tea to the ladies on the deck."

Tea for the ladies—as though ladies were incapable of doing anything more while on board than sit and sip. It was a commonly held belief that Kitty's lingering headache was no doubt causing her to resent.

Tugging on her arm, Farthingham left her with no choice except to leave Weddington standing where he was, gazing after them as Farthingham escorted her down the dark wooden stairs into the main saloon. Intricately carved paneling greeted her, along with rich burgundy velvet-covered chairs and sofas. Exquisite tables and collections of tiny porcelain and marble figurines decorated the room.

"Are you even more impressed now?" Farthingham asked.

"I was quite impressed before. Everything is so beautiful." And rivaled her father's yacht in magnificence. Because they traveled on the water to such a great degree, he'd had the interior of *The Lone Star* designed with comfort, convenience, and appreciation in mind so that it was a pleasure to live on board. Kitty thought the same could be said of *The Fair Lady*.

"The library is through that passageway, and on the other side is a room where guests sleep. But through here"—he took her hand and led the way—"is where the master sleeps."

Although much smaller than the bedchamber she was using at Drummond Manor, the room was not that much different. A four-poster bed dominated the room, its comforter the same as the one that covered the bed she'd slept in for a few hours the previous night.

"I thought we might use the yacht for a wedding trip," Farthingham said quietly.

An image of her and him nestled within that bed jumped into her mind, and just as quickly he slipped away and Weddington replaced him. She felt the heat suffuse her face. She and Farthingham would share a bed. Of course, they would. She would find it most pleasant and enjoyable. "Weddington might have a thing or two to say about that," she said.

"Not really, since the yacht is ours."

Kitty turned to stare at him as though he'd lost his mind. "What?"

"It's ours," he repeated. "Weddington is giving it to us as a wedding present."

Now she was certain that he'd lost his mind. "Nicky, you can't accept—"

"Of course I can, my sweet. Actually, I must accept. It's an insult to the bearer of the gift to do otherwise."

"But it's too . . . it's too . . . magnificent a gift."

"Of course, it is. That's the very reason I wanted you to have it.

What's more, he's arranging with his solicitor to have a certain amount set aside each year for ten years to go toward its upkeep—which can be quite costly, I can assure you."

She shook her head emphatically. She was quite aware of the expense involved in keeping a yacht seaworthy. "Why is he doing this?"

"Because he is a friend who wishes to see us happy." He cupped her cheek. "Why aren't you joyous?"

"It's too grand a gift."

He laughed. "My sweet, Weddington can well afford to give this yacht away tenfold. It means nothing to him."

"Nicky, simply because someone possesses something in abundance doesn't mean that he no longer values it. It's like children. If you have one, then another, your love for the first doesn't diminish, and you don't love the second any less than you did the first. Abundance doesn't always cause value to lessen."

He moved his hand aside and furrowed his brow. "I thought you would be pleased. I want you to have it. If I could purchase it for you myself, I would without hesitation. But I can't. Not even the settlement your father agreed to will ever allow me to purchase something of this grandeur."

Now it was she who cradled his cheek. "Nicky, you're what I want, what I need. Not things. Not yachts, not jewelry, not gowns."

"Because you've always had them, you've not learned what it is to miss them. But you will, my sweet. You will. Be gracious. Accept Weddington's gift, if only because it will please me for you to do so."

She so wanted to please him, but she couldn't help but believe that not only the yacht but ten years of upkeep were far too generous of Weddington. She didn't trust the gift, feared it more closely resembled a Trojan horse. What would Weddington gain by giving it to them?

She forced herself to smile. "May I have time to think about it?"

He grinned broadly as though he'd already won the argument. "Of course, my sweet. But don't take too long. I was serious about our using it for a wedding trip."

Nodding, she walked out of the room and headed for the stairway that would return her to the deck. A few months ago, she'd been so sure of her course, and now she suddenly felt as though she'd somehow managed to become lost in a fog. Weddington's generosity. Farthingham's willingness to accept it. She was no longer sure what to make of any of it or her feelings toward either man.

As soon as Lady Priscilla, Lady Anne, and Freddie had arrived, Weddington had ordered that they cast off and be on their way. Since he'd confessed to being terrified of the sea, Kitty was surprised by his eagerness to be under way, and yet at the same time, she fully understood it. She'd never been one to put off unpleasant tasks. Better to get the unpleasantness over with as soon as possible, so she could move on to pleasanter endeavors without guilt.

Yet watching Weddington at the wheel, she couldn't help but believe that he was determined to control the sea—or at least his destiny—as much as possible. He stood with his feet spread for balance, his hands gripping the wheel, his gaze trained ahead of him, man battling the elements.

He had his crew, who saw to the sails and watched the sea as well, but she had no doubt that Weddington was at the helm, completely in charge. Not a figurehead, playing at commanding—as her father was prone to do from time to time—but the absolute commander, in charge of the ship, the men, the guests, the course. She thought if it were possible, he would have commanded the wind, the swells . . . the manner in which the sunlight glinted off the water.

Farthingham and Freddie had gone to the bow—for a clearer view—while Kitty, Lady Anne, and Lady Priscilla sat in wicker chairs at a wicker table, politely sipping tea that a servant had delivered from belowdecks. So terribly civilized.

Kitty was well aware that a lady's place on the yacht was relegated to one of pleasure only—simple enjoyment. All the ladies, including her, were dressed for afternoon tea with their tight dresses and their fancy, wide-brimmed hats. They could quite successfully disembark and walk through Hyde Park without anyone being the wiser about where they'd spent the afternoon.

And even now, aboard the ship, no one would know how she'd spent her time watching Weddington instead of thinking about her betrothed. She couldn't quite get over how she'd spoken in his defense last night at the bathhouse when Lady Priscilla had mentioned how much more fun Farthingham was.

Kitty couldn't deny that Farthingham was the one who made them laugh and smile; nor could she deny that he was the one who generally possessed such scathingly brilliant notions for having fun— yet Weddington somehow appeared to be the one who made the fun available. Accepting ridiculous wagers so that people had an opportunity to take sides and be able to place more emphasis on, take more interest in, an event than it rightly deserved, thus making it more enjoyable for all involved, participant and spectator alike. He made his residence, his yacht, his opera box, his carriage, his coach available for anyone who asked. With complete unselfishness. Never demanded or apparently expected anything in return.

And yet, he'd tried to take her away from Farthingham. To steal her away, actually. With daring, forbidden caresses and slow, sensual kisses. He'd left no doubt in her mind that he wanted her. Had tormented her constantly with that knowledge. And yet, had she not continually placed herself within his reach?

He was the one who held his hands behind his back so he wouldn't touch her. He was the one who appeared to be a perfect gentleman, while she knew a part of him was a corrupting rogue. Knew his true nature because she'd certainly allowed him to tempt and corrupt her. She hadn't put up much of a fight either, nor had she ever bothered to protest except *after* the fact.

Men were beasts. It was a woman's place to keep them in line, to give them no opportunity for misbehavior.

And yet for all her contradictory actions with regard to him, he seemed to hold no ill will toward her. He was gifting her with his yacht, for pity's sake. She hardly knew what to make of him or his generosity.

She certainly couldn't understand why Lady Priscilla didn't consider Weddington handsome. Ruggedly so. Strong-jawed. Bronzed by the sun. He could appear at home in the fanciest parlor or on the stormiest sea. Kitty couldn't determine why she found him so incredibly attractive. Yet if she were honest with herself, she had to admit that something about him did draw her to him, did force her gaze to wander over to him.

He'd removed his jacket and cravat, loosened the buttons at his throat, rolled up his sleeves. The wind billowed his shirt, revealing glimpses of his chest—as bronzed as his face, and she wondered if he would dispense with his shirt or perhaps even his clothes entirely if no ladies were presently on board. She thought he possessed a bit of barbarism. As though he'd reluctantly donned the mantle of civilization because he'd realized it would serve him better than running wild.

She recognized that she should make her way to the bow so she could be nearer to Farthingham, and yet, here she was casting sly glances at Weddington, grateful Lady Priscilla and Lady Anne were too busy gossiping and occasionally lapsing into silence with a bit of a green tinge to their faces whenever they hit rougher waters. Drinking a good deal of wine the night before a venture on the sea was not a wise course of action.

But then she was beginning to wonder if she'd recognize a wise course if she happened upon it. She'd always considered herself smart for latching on to Farthingham, and yet doubts were suddenly beginning to plague her. Not because she didn't love him, but because she was beginning to fear that she might not love him enough. She'd always felt safe because he didn't tempt her, but she'd never truly given any thought to crawling into bed with him, couldn't imagine him touching her as Weddington had. And yet, she wanted his touch, would welcome it. She'd kiss the dew from his flesh. With her lips, she'd capture the droplets as they slowly rolled—

"Miss Robertson?"

She jerked her gaze from Weddington's throat, glistening with moisture, to his gaze, intense, speculative, and challenging, not certain when the fantasy in her mind had shifted away from Farthingham and on to Weddington.

"I was wondering if I might bother you for a moment and have you hold the wheel," he said.

"Richard, women don't sail ships," Lady Anne said.

"I believe Miss Robertson is fully capable of handling it for a short time."

Kitty nodded. "Yes, certainly I can do that."

She rose to her feet, a little unsteadily after sitting for so long, grabbed the railing, reestablished her sea legs, and made her way to where he stood. He moved his right hand away from the wheel, while still holding it steady with his left, the muscles on his forearm bunching and tightening with the additional strain.

"If you'll grab that spoke," he ordered.

She wrapped her hand around the wood, surprised that it seemed as though she could feel the soul of the ship tingling through her fingers. He took a step back, and she moved in so she was trapped between him and the wheel.

"Place your other hand on the spoke near mine," he ordered. "I won't release it until I know you have control."

Nodding, swallowing hard, she placed her hand near his. What a contrast. His large, dark hand beside her pale, fragile-looking one. The muscles bulging in his thick wrist, his dark coarse hair stirred by the breeze. While her delicate wrist was covered with the long sleeve of her dress.

"Are you ready for me to release my hold?" he asked quietly.

"You won't go far will you?"

"I shan't go anywhere at all."

She glanced over her shoulder. "Why did you need me to take the wheel then?"

His mouth shifted into a slow, easy grin. "I don't recall implying that I was in need of anything . . . but if that's how my request was interpreted, I am not bothered in the least."

His eyes held a kindness, and she wondered why she'd failed to notice it before. He possessed a generosity, somehow always managing to ensure that those around them had their needs, wants, desires satisfied.

"Perhaps you shouldn't release your final hold," she said.

"I can reestablish it quickly enough," he assured her. "Gaze ahead, concentrate on the sea, on where you wish to take the ship, feel the wind billowing her sails . . ."

His voice was as mesmerizing as all that surrounded her. She lost herself in his commands, lost herself in the ship, in its motions, in the feel of it beneath her feet. Always before she'd been a passenger, an observer . . . but from this vantage point she was beginning to feel an entirely different appreciation for all that was involved in taking people out on to the sea.

She'd traveled extensively with her father, but he had a captain, a pilot, a navigator, a crew that saw to all their comforts, all their safety . . . and she suddenly realized with startling clarity that a man who was terrified of the sea would not leave the command of it in someone else's hands. He no doubt inspected the ship, knew every inch of her, knew her strengths, corrected her weaknesses . . . he'd never put at risk himself or others.

Even as the thought took root and held, she quickly glanced down at her left hand, only to find it alone on the spoke of the wheel. She didn't know when he'd relinquished absolute control into her keeping. Her heart pounding with a sense of accomplishment she'd never before experienced, she looked back out to sea.

"Well done, Miss Robertson," he said quietly behind her. "Well done."

And in that moment, for the first time since she'd met him, she felt unexplainably, remarkably safe.

Chapter 16

Kitty couldn't sleep. She'd lain in bed, staring at the shadows, trying to make sense of her feelings. She'd never been more confused in her entire life. She'd always been so certain of the road she traveled, of what she wanted in life, what she expected of herself and others, what her behavior should consist of—and the thoughts rumbling through her mind were contrary to everything she'd ever hoped to attain.

She'd called for her maid and gotten dressed simply because she couldn't stand to be isolated in her room any longer. She needed to roam, and she certainly hadn't wanted to be caught by anyone in her nightclothes. For some reason, she thought they would be a large sign proclaiming her wanton thoughts.

She'd chosen a simple dress that required no corset or bindings. If fate were kind, she wouldn't cross paths with anyone except servants. Surely this time of night—a little past midnight—no one would be up and about. Since Lady Anne had not come for her, she was fairly certain they had no plans for any excursions to the bathhouse that night. She was halfway tempted to go there by herself, but she decided that action would be the height of rudeness—to ask the servants to prepare the building for her personal indulgence.

Instead she wandered through the shadow-filled hallways, the gaslights low and flickering. She was passing one dark corridor when she glanced down it and saw light creeping out along the floor—no doubt seeping out from beneath a closed door.

She'd only taken two steps toward it, when the door suddenly clicked open, the light from the room illuminating the footman standing nearby, a man she hadn't noticed as she stood some distance away.

"Oh, no, I hadn't wanted—" *to go in.* With frustration, she didn't complete her thought aloud, because she'd realized that since he'd opened the door he'd committed her to going through it whether she'd wished to or not. She could only hope that the lights had been burning by mistake, that no one was actually inside the room, although she thought it highly unlikely that she'd find the place deserted. Why else would the footman be standing within reach of the door so attentively?

"Thank you." She forced herself to smile as she strolled casually by him and into the room—a study, an office. Weddington's office. She had no doubt it was his because he was sitting behind a massive mahogany desk, while a gentleman sat in a chair before him. Immediately both men came to their feet.

"Miss Robertson," the duke said.

"Please, forgive me. I couldn't sleep. When I looked in the hallway, the footman mistook my destination—"

"Where was your destination?" Weddington asked. "Perhaps I can help you locate it."

She shook her head. "I didn't really have one."

"Then please sit for a few moments, and I shall accompany you on your journey. I would hate for you to get lost in this rambling structure. Allow me to introduce Mr. Alexander. He oversees a good part of the estate here. We're about to finish up, then you shall have my undivided attention."

She didn't want his attention—undivided or otherwise—but she couldn't very well reject his offer with one of his employees standing in the room. She was well aware that a man of his rank had to maintain certain appearances. "Thank you, Your Grace."

She selected a chair off to the side that would not require she look at him. She heard, more than saw, both gentlemen take their seats, heard the low rumble of their voices as they continued with whatever matter of business they'd been discussing before she'd interrupted.

This room was a man's domain, and she could well imagine every duke before the present one conducting his business here. Plotting, planning, conquering, controlling. It had a strong presence, a commanding presence, and she wondered if the room seeped into its owner or if the owner seeped into the room.

Slowly she slid her gaze toward the desk and decided the owner seeped his way into the room. He left no doubt that he was the one in charge. Even when Mr. Alexander was speaking and Weddington was listening, it was evident who was master. Shifting in the chair, she found herself mesmerized by the way Weddington gave Mr. Alexander his absolute attention.

She and her family had spent some time at Farthingham's estate, but she'd never seen him address any managers or workers. He'd gone about his business of entertaining her as though the estate managed itself. While she knew that was not the case, she'd never really given any thought to exactly how much work was involved in overseeing the family's properties.

Weddington and Mr. Alexander came to their feet. "Thank you, Mr. Alexander. I appreciate your agreeing to meet with me at such a late hour."

"I serve at your pleasure, Your Grace." The man turned toward her. "Good night, Miss Robertson."

"Good night, Mr. Alexander."

The man left the room, and Kitty came to her feet. "An odd time to hold a meeting," she said.

"Business must be managed, Miss Robertson. I had to choose between giving up my time with my guests this afternoon or sacrificing a few hours' sleep. I chose the latter."

She nodded. "My father does that as well. He says the day doesn't contain enough hours. He's always put his family first."

"A commendable trait." He walked around his desk, his hands behind his back. "Shall we continue on with your late-night excursion?"

Only she didn't want to be in the shadowy hallways where she couldn't clearly see his face. "Farthingham said you're giving us *The Fair Lady* as a wedding gift."

"I am."

"Why?"

"Because I was led to believe that you enjoyed yachting, and after watching you on the sea this afternoon, I know that assessment to be true."

"But you offered it to him before this afternoon."

"An offer would signify an opportunity for refusal. It was not an offer, but a gift."

"Given before you saw me on the yacht."

He shrugged. "I've known Farthingham for many years. I trust his ability to judge accurately the truth of a situation."

"I don't understand why you gave it to us."

He shook his head. "I fail to understand what it is that you don't understand."

"What do you think you gain by giving us your yacht?"

He angled his head as though truly baffled. "It is a gift, Miss Robertson. It comes with no strings attached, no expectations on my part."

"It's too grand a gift."

"But it pleases me to give it to you."

"But it belongs to you."

"And now it is yours."

She didn't know how to explain the sense she'd had on the ship that it was as much a part of him as he was of it. "I simply had the impression that you cared a great deal for the ship."

"I care more about your happiness. Farthingham is unlikely to invest in a yacht when he has more pressing expenditures to address."

"I can live without a yacht."

"You could, but you don't have to." He tilted his head toward the door. "Shall we begin the walk before you determine that you are angry at me for my generosity?"

"Too late. I'm already angry at you."

He smiled slightly. "I know. That is something else about you that I fail to comprehend—how it is that I can never do anything that doesn't make you angry."

She spun on her heel and walked to the door. He barely beat her to it, opened it for her, and followed her through. The hallway echoed the clicking of their passing footsteps. He walked beside her, his hands still clasped behind his back, and she thought of the time in the garden when he'd confessed that he'd take her in his arms if he released his hold on his hands.

"It would make me happy if you wouldn't give us the yacht as a gift."

He had the audacity to laugh, the deep rumble echoing off the walls and circling around her. "You're very clever," he finally said when his laughter stopped. "Now I must weigh your happiness and determine which action will make you the happiest despite your protests to the contrary."

"I don't want Farthingham beholden to you."

"He's already beholden to me."

His response came quickly, darkly, as though something sinister was hidden behind the words.

"Are you referring to the forfeit that you won because of the tennis match?"

"Yes."

But the answer sounded hollow, unconvincing. She couldn't quite determine why she felt as she did. "Is he in your debt for something besides the forfeit?"

"No."

That answer rang more true. What a strange conversation—as though questions and answers weren't truly related. "He thinks very highly of you," she said.

"And I think highly of him."

"You claim to be good friends, and yet before this Season, he'd never introduced me to you."

"Perhaps he feared you'd cast him aside in favor of me."

About the time she began to like him, he revealed his arrogant streak. "I hardly think that is the case since I've never given him the slightest cause to doubt my affection."

"Then perhaps we've never been introduced because while Farthingham plays, I see to the management of my estates."

She was beginning to realize that was probably more likely to be the case. "And yet this Season, I can hardly take a step without running into you."

"I see no great mystery there. I have been forthright regarding my intentions toward you. You should not be surprised that I have rearranged my daily schedule, my entire life so that I might spend a few moments in your company."

Abruptly she stopped walking and turned on him. "I love Farthingham."

"I know you do."

"I will be a good and faithful wife."

"I doubt that not for a second. I am a great believer in loyalty. Ironically, it is an aspect of your character that I greatly admire and that makes me care for you much more than I should." He cradled her face with one hand and slowly stroked her cheek with his thumb, his eyes holding hers. "Is there any chance at all that you would reconsider marrying Farthingham if I were to tell you that I have fallen madly in love with you?"

Her heart slammed against her ribs, and she began to tremble. He hadn't said he loved her, only that he would tell her he did. She stepped back, beyond his touch, beyond his warmth, beyond his reach. He was a man who didn't enjoy losing, and he had yet to understand that he had no hope of winning her.

"I beg you, please, give up your quest of obtaining me."

"I can't."

She was totally unprepared for the speed with which he moved, clamping his arms around her, drawing her into his embrace, blanketing her mouth with his.

His kiss was demanding, insistent, so reminiscent of the one he'd bestowed upon her in the garden that she feared the journey he might again be leading her toward even as her body urged her to follow.

She once again felt as though she were on the deck of his yacht, swaying with the tide of emotions over which she had no control. He had the power to take her under as easily as he could lift her above the swells. Even as she longed to reach the heights to which he could carry her, she feared the depths to which she must plunge.

To hear his taunting reminder that Farthingham would never make her body respond in this manner, would never bring her pleasure of this magnitude. She was torn between weeping and rejoicing. Weeping for the loss of what only Weddington could give her. Rejoicing because she would never have to fight temptation again once she was beyond his reach.

Filled with sorrow for the exact reason. She would never again experience these incredible sensations. Because she knew in her heart that Weddington was correct. Farthingham would never heat her body to this magnitude, his mouth would never threaten to devour her, his body would never press hers as close, as firm, as hard against his.

She'd never responded to Farthingham's nearness as she did to Weddington's. With Weddington, she was caught in the midst of the storm, sensations swirling around her and through her over which she had no control. Her resolve to resist the tempest was weakening with each sweep of his tongue, each caress of his hands.

Drowning, she was drowning. And God help her, she wasn't certain she wished to be rescued.

Pushing against his chest, she broke free of his kiss and staggered back. His eyes held a desperation that she feared mirrored hers.

"I would do anything for you," he rasped.

With a tiny whimper, she tore down the hallway, never looking back, because she knew what she would see.

A man standing in the shadowy hallway who made her fear herself.

Chapter 17

With a heavy heart, Nicholas Glenville stared out at the dawning sky. He'd go down to breakfast shortly, but for the moment he merely contemplated the horizon and his future.

Red sky at morning, sailors take warning.

Wasn't that how the ancient mariner's saying went? A day that began with a red sky was a prelude to stormy weather. How appropriate, considering all the storms currently housed within Drummond Manor.

He'd been heading to his bedchamber, shortly after midnight, having left Freddie in the billiard room to continue practicing his shots—the man was atrocious at the game—when Nicholas had passed a hallway and noticed a couple in the shadows. Then their voices had reached him: Weddington and Kitty.

He'd heard Weddington's declaration of love. Damnation. He wasn't surprised that Weddington had become enamored of Kitty, but he was surprised the man would admit his feelings for her and admit them to himself, for that matter. Love controlled a man. Years earlier Nicholas had proven that unfortunate fact by falling in love with someone of whom his family would never approve. And Weddington was not a man who liked to be controlled.

Although if Kitty's initial reaction to the man's kiss had been any indication, Nicholas suspected that she might have feelings for Weddington as well. It had taken her an inordinate amount of time to push Weddington away.

Pressing his forearm against the casing and leaning closer to the window as though that small act would help him bring the horizon into better view and allow him to see what lay beyond it, he tried to remember what Weddington had told him during previous conversations.

That Kitty feared the man.

Yes, that's what he'd said.

Ah, dear God. He bowed his head and closed his eyes. Not the man. She feared the passion he stirred to life within her, the passion Weddington had warned Nicholas she possessed, the passion she'd never revealed to him, the passion he'd thought she lacked. The passion she'd displayed in the hallway last night.

She possessed such a passion for life that he'd always assumed she needed no other. His assumption no doubt had been a way for him to convince himself that marriage to him would not harm her.

She'd felt safe with him, she'd told him so countless times. Safe. And he'd never thought to question, "Safe from what, my sweet?"

He raised his head. What exactly had transpired behind the hedges in Harrington's garden? He'd known that Weddington had distracted her, removed her from the path. He'd assumed a kiss or two had been delivered. Had the man delivered more?

Kitty had been frightfully upset, overwrought. Yet she'd stood on the yacht yesterday afternoon, Weddington at her back, her hands on the wheel . . . she'd looked truly magnificent, and at that moment, he'd thought that even he could fall in love with her.

No, she didn't fear Weddington. She feared herself. He understood those fears only too well, to fear giving in to passion's siren . . .

The jagged lightning in the far distance snagged his attention. *Sailors take warning.*

After spying Weddington and Kitty last night, he was in a mood to tempt fate.

He turned from the window and headed for the door. Now all that remained to be seen was if he had the courage and the fortitude to release Kitty into Weddington's keeping. More importantly, he needed to discover if Weddington had the courage and fortitude to help him achieve that end.

"You can't be serious?"

Kitty stared at Freddie, unable to believe the words he'd just uttered. She'd purposely delayed coming down to breakfast, hoping to avoid another encounter with Weddington. It appeared she'd avoided *everyone* as well, except Freddie, who merely shrugged before moving his food from one side of his plate to another.

"Freddie!"

"I know, I know. It's madness. I told them both that, but they insisted. You know how Farthingham and Weddington are once they've decided something. You might as well be talking to a stone wall for all the good it will do you to try to persuade them to see things your way."

"How long ago did they leave?"

"Close to an hour now, I'd say."

She sank onto a chair at the table, near Freddie. "But you have only to look outside to know that this isn't a day to go sailing."

"You don't have to convince me."

And it was far too late to convince Farthingham if he'd already been gone for an hour. She pressed her fingertips against each temple, striving to stop the headache threatening to arrive as fiercely as the storm that hovered on the horizon. "What was he thinking?"

Freddie tapped the tines of his fork against his plate, an irritating clicking that made her want to scream.

"I suppose he was thinking that he wanted to try out Weddington's smaller sailboat. And Weddington is always an accommodating host."

"A careless host if he takes a guest out on the sea with a storm coming in."

"You mustn't worry so. I know the sky looks bleak in the distance, but that doesn't mean a storm will arrive here. Besides, I'm certain they meant to do little more than take the boat out for a short time. They'll be back before you know it."

Only they weren't.

Kitty stood in the hallway outside her bedchamber, staring through the pristine windows at the churning sea, barely visible in the distance. Black clouds had rolled in, and with them a heavy rain, darkness, and screaming winds. She'd crossed her forearms over her chest and was constantly rubbing her upper arms, seeking comfort as her dread increased with each passing moment.

Hearing footsteps, she spun around, only to have disappointment wash through her as harsh as the torrent of rain.

Freddie, appearing as worried as she, gave her what was obviously a forced smile. "No sign of them?"

"No." She turned back to the storm. "They should have returned long before now, don't you think?"

"Without a doubt. I went down to the harbor, but I saw no more ships coming in."

"Damn them!" She stomped her foot, squeezed her arms, and fought not to double over from the agony of worry. "Why aren't they back?"

"Maybe they took refuge elsewhere once the storm came up."

"But what if they didn't, Freddie?" She glanced at him. "Weddington is so damned competitive that I don't think he'd retreat before a storm. And Farthingham would probably make some stupid wager that they could survive it."

Freddie smiled softly. "Yes, Farthingham probably would."

She shook her head in frustration. "I can't simply stand here doing nothing. What if the boat has wrecked? What if they've washed up onshore? Cold and miserable? Or worse yet, hurt?" She pivoted about and headed for the stairs. "I'm going to get lanterns and go down to the shore."

"I'll accompany you."

He did more than accompany her. He decided that a search party of more than two was needed. Waiting impatiently on the terrace while he gathered several servants and lanterns, she couldn't help but feel that each passing moment lessened their chances for locating Weddington and Farthingham. It didn't help calm her mind to realize that she seemed as worried about Weddington's safety as she was Farthingham's.

She told herself that it was simply because she valued all life. Weddington certainly had never done anything to deserve a ghastly end, but part of her concern stemmed from knowing Weddington feared the sea . . . and she simply didn't want it to claim him. She thought that his demise during a storm would be the height of unfairness. Not that losing Farthingham to the storm would be any fairer.

Her thoughts were all jumbled, as scattered as the dried leaves before the storm. An umbrella was of no use, because the rain pelted from all sides. Her hooded cloak wasn't much better, although it did manage to offer a bit of protection when it wasn't twisting in the swirling wind that threatened to pick her up and haul her to the sea.

Freddie finally returned to her side. "Perhaps you should stay here, inside. Farthingham will never forgive me if you should take ill while searching for him."

She shook her head, the futility of the situation almost overwhelming her. "No, I'm going, with or without you. I have to feel like I'm at least doing something."

"Very well then. You and I shall walk south, the servants to the east and west, and hopefully someone will have a bit of luck."

Considering the severity of this storm, she thought it likely that they'd need more than a bit of luck. She was terrified that they'd need a miracle.

* * *

She was cold, wet, chilled to the bone. Her eyes ached from staring at the dark sea and into the black of night with only the faint light from the lantern Freddie had given her earlier to provide any sort of hope.

"Nicky! Richard!" The gusting winds captured her words and threw them back at her. She wondered when she'd stopped calling out for Weddington and had begun to yell for Richard as though he were more likely to answer to one name more than the other. "Nicky! Richard!"

At one point, she'd thought she'd caught sight of a sailboat, and her heart had soared, but it had quickly disappeared, and she hadn't seen it since. When she'd called out to Freddie, rushed over to him, and pointed to the sea, trying to get him to see what she had, he'd simply shaken his head and suggested it was no more than wishful thinking on her part.

She'd wanted to smack him. When had he become such a pessimistic creature?

Although she could hardly blame him as she wended her way around the rocks, illuminating nooks and crannies with the lantern, ducking each time the surf crashed against the shore. Her own optimism was dwindling. If they hadn't found them by morning, she'd gather the crew and take *The Fair Lady* out herself. After all, the yacht was close to being hers, and she was desperately hoping that the possibility existed that maybe the men had shown a little sense and taken refuge on one of the nearby Isles of Scilly if they'd been too far out to return to this shore.

She didn't know how far they'd planned to travel or in which direction they'd intended to sail. Madness. It was sheer madness, and when she found them she was going to knock some common sense into their uncommon heads—

A shadow that didn't belong! A shape! Long, lean, stretched out on the shore.

The light from her lantern wavered. She heard a sound that wasn't the screaming of the wind. Beneath it all. Lower. Vaguely familiar. Retching.

"Freddie! Here! Freddie!"

She scrambled over the rocks, the lantern swinging, the light dancing around as though caught up in some eerie, frenzied waltz. As she neared, the glow from the lantern cast a halo around the man, but he remained dark. Dark hair. Black hair. Plastered to his head—as she'd seen it once before.

Not blond. Not Nicky.

She dropped to her knees. He was up on his elbows, gasping, sputtering, coughing, his head bent, his body jerking. "Richard?"

He continued to cough, no doubt needing to bring up all the water he might have swallowed. She set the lantern down, removed her cloak, and draped it over him. "Richard, where's Nicky?"

He shook his head. He didn't know. Of course, he didn't know. They'd arrived at shore separated no doubt. She'd been silly to ask, but she had to find him, find him quickly. She reached for the lantern—

"Are you daft, woman?" Freddie asked as he knelt on the other side of Weddington, snatched up her cloak, and tossed it to her. "Put your cloak back on, before you catch your death."

Under the circumstances, she thought it was the most absurd thing he could have said, as he whipped off his coat and placed it over the man trembling before them.

"We have to find Nicky," she told him, grabbing the lantern, preparing to rise.

"No," Weddington rasped, wrapping his frigid fingers around her wrist.

He was watching her, his bleak eyes captured in the glow of the lantern. He shook his head as though he had neither the strength nor will to do so. "Won't find him."

"I certainly won't find him if I don't look for him," she said, trying to be patient with him after what he'd endured, but desperate to get on her way so she could locate Nicky.

He tightened his hold on her. "Not . . . here."

"I know he's not here, that's the reason I need to search for him."

He shook his head, his eyes imploring her to listen with more than her ears to what he was trying to convey. "You won't find him. He's not here."

The words when repeated with such deadly calm sent a fissure of fear through her. She jerked her gaze over to Freddie, who was staring out at the churning waters, as though that was where they needed to search. She lowered her gaze to Weddington. "Perhaps you're mistaken."

"No," Weddington insisted, with strength of conviction in his voice. "I'm sorry."

Horrified with the implication of his words, she could do little more than stare at him.

"Your Grace, what happened?" Freddie asked.

His gaze holding hers, Weddington replied, "Boat sank. I swam to shore."

"And Farthingham?" Freddie asked.

Weddington's eyes never left her as he shook his head.

"You're wrong!" she yelled. Grabbing the lantern, she lunged to her feet. "Help me search for him, Freddie. He has to be here. He has to be!"

Somewhere nearby. Dear, funny, laughing Nicky.

Staggering like a drunk, she held the lantern aloft, cursing its ineffectualness at illuminating the area. He could be at the water's edge, shaking like Weddington had been. Cold, miserable, spewing out the sea that he'd swallowed. But she refused to believe that he hadn't made it to shore. That the sea had claimed him.

She'd doubted her feelings toward him, but now they rang with crystal clarity. She didn't want to lose him. Didn't want him dead. Didn't want him drowned. She wanted him in her life.

Oh, God, oh, God, oh, God.

Tears blurred her vision, dread shadowed every staggered step. She searched, and searched, and searched, with tears washing down her face, mingling with the pouring rain. With each passing moment, the ache in her chest intensified, her throat closed into a tightened knot as though someone were cutting off her air. She couldn't swallow, she couldn't breathe, she couldn't see him.

Nicky couldn't be gone. He simply could *not* be gone.

Who would keep her safe?

She needed him, wanted him.

"Nicky!"

She shrugged Freddie off when he tried to stop her, when he told her it was no use to continue, that no one else was to be found. She refused to believe, refused to give up.

"Nicky!" She screamed for him until her voice was hoarse and raw. She combed the shoreline until her arm trembled from fatigue and could no longer hold the lantern high, until she couldn't take another step. Releasing a keening wail, she collapsed into a pitiful heap of despair.

Nicky! Nicky was gone.

It was never easy to lose someone. Richard knew that, and yet he'd been completely unprepared for the depth of Kitty's anguish.

He'd refused to make his way back to the manor as Montague had recommended, had refused to do anything more than follow behind Kitty and try to dissuade her from continuing in the fruitless search.

Now he knelt beside her and draped Freddie's coat over her quaking shoulders, wrapped it around her, and drew her up against him. "I'm sorry, Kitty. I'm so sorry."

"Damn you!" she cried. With her balled fists, she began pummeling his chest.

He held her more tightly, lessening the intensity of the deserved blows. His back was an agony of knotted and spasming muscles. Awkwardly, he rocked her as much for himself as for her. "Shh, Kitty, shh," he crooned near her ear. "He wouldn't want you to mourn like this."

Wretched, heartrending sobs erupted from deep within her as she collapsed against him. Holding her close, he looked over her head at Montague, who was crouched near them. From the deep lines on his face and the worry in his eyes, it was obvious that Kitty's despair was more than even Farthingham's friend had anticipated.

"What should we do?" Montague asked.

"Take her home, strive to comfort her as much as possible."

Montague bobbed his head like a ship on the sea. "We brought some of the servants. I didn't think to let them know we'd found you. They're bound still to be around. I'll fetch one to carry her—"

"I'll carry her."

"You have to be exhausted—"

"I'll carry her. I'll need your assistance in getting to my feet." He turned his attention to Kitty. The wind had died down, and the rain had dwindled into a light patter. He'd not believed his luck when the storm had come up as quickly and furiously as it had. He'd hoped for a bit of rough weather to erase the evidence of what he'd done, and instead he'd been blessed with a squall.

"Kitty? I need to take you home."

She dropped her head back, and even with the dampness of the weather, he could still make out her tears, glistening in her eyes. "Tell me there's a chance—"

"There's none. He's gone."

"Why?"

He pulled her back into the nook of his shoulder. How could he explain that? How could he give her reasons that would only cause her to experience more pain?

"We need to get you both home," Montague said. "It's doing none of us any good to stay out here."

Nodding, Richard wound his arms more closely around his precious bundle. With Montague's help, he managed to get to his feet, holding Kitty near. Her sobs had subsided, but he could still feel the tremors traveling through her.

As he walked toward Drummond Manor, he'd not expected to feel so cruel, had not anticipated the guilt that would bombard him. He'd been convinced that his actions were best for her, that taking Farthingham out on the sailboat would result in a satisfactory resolution of his dilemma.

Now doubts spawned, and he couldn't help but wonder if he might have acted hastily, if a closer inspection of the options might have revealed a way to accomplish his goals without causing her such profound grief.

Chapter 18

Kitty's maid wrapped her in blankets that had been warmed by the fireplace, while Lady Anne poured wine down her raw throat, and Lady Priscilla continually replaced damp linen handkerchiefs with dry ones. But none of their comfort served to make her feel any better, nothing served to make her feel less cold.

The ladies had sat on her bed, one on either side of her, weeping and bemoaning fate's cruelty. Kitty had found some comfort in their shared grief, but not enough. When her eyelids had grown heavy from too much wine, the ladies had left her to sleep, but sleep eluded her.

Nicky's absence was a sharp pain in her heart. She didn't want to be alone, and instinctually, she knew neither Lady Anne nor Lady Priscilla could give her what she wanted, what she so desperately needed. Nor could Freddie.

Ironically, she didn't want to receive deep, abiding comfort, but she had a strong need to provide it, to provide it to poor Weddington, whose own grief and misery had given way to hers on the shore and inside the manor. Who'd comforted him? Who'd rubbed his back and held his hands and plied him full of numbing drink?

He'd carried her back here, seen to her comfort, made certain she was looked after before he'd given any thought to his own needs—and she was certain they were many. Her last memory of him was standing at the foot of her bed, concern clearly etched within the lines of his face, profound sadness reflected in his eyes, a tightening around his mouth from the strain of what he'd been forced to endure.

He'd survived.

And no doubt felt guilty for having done so, for having failed his friend and, in so doing, failed her. In a voice rough with emotion, he'd apologized numerous times on the trek back to the manor. Upon their arrival, he'd refused to relinquish her into anyone else's keeping until he'd placed her gently on the bed—with a low moan.

She'd paid little attention to it then, lost in her own grief, her own emotional turmoil that was almost a physical agony. She'd not given any thought to what he was truly suffering. He'd been battered about on the sea, made his way to shore. Dear Lord, he'd probably had no business at all carting her about. She should have been the one to see after his needs.

Slipping out from beneath the covers, she snatched her wrapper from the foot of the bed and drew it around herself. She was surprised by how cold she felt, as though with Nicky's death all warmth had seeped right out of her, and she feared it might never return. She wasn't certain if it was all the wine she'd swallowed or all the tears she'd shed that now made her mind lethargic, barely able to form coherent thoughts or engage in deductive reasoning.

She felt as though she walked through a fog as she went into the hallway and down the stairs. Somewhere in the hazy corners of her mind, she noticed that the flooring was cold beneath her feet and realized that she should return to her room for shoes, but the effort didn't seem to justify the result. Strange how her mind could be sharp with her need to find Weddington and exceedingly dull about every other aspect surrounding her.

She caught sight of the butler, moving through the entryway, obviously on his way to complete some task. "Excuse me. Do you know where I might find the duke?"

"Yes, miss. He had us prepare the bathing house for him. I'm fairly certain that he's still there."

The bathing house. Of course. Its swirling warmth would be heavenly. She thanked the butler as he opened the front door for her. Again, she had a sense of knowing that what she was doing would be perceived as improper, but she also knew servants risked losing their positions if they didn't keep to themselves all the comings and goings that they witnessed.

Besides, at that moment, her reputation was the very last thing she was worried over. As far as she was concerned, it could go to hell in a handbasket. Nicky was gone. She seemed unable to silence the resounding echo of his loss.

The ground and grass were damp beneath her bare soles. The air carried the scent of rain residue, a portion of it the fragrance of life. The water would nourish the plants, but even the thriving vegetation wouldn't replace the life that the storm had stolen.

And she did feel as though Nicky had been stolen from her. Taken unawares, without a chance to say good-bye, without the opportunity to gaze on him one last time. Earlier yesterday evening, to have been going to bed and to have waved him off with a carelessly delivered "I'll see you tomorrow," as though tomorrow were guaranteed.

Dear Lord, she thought she might never again watch someone leave without questioning whether or not he would return. She'd never had anyone she cared so deeply about die. The sense of loss was overwhelming, as though a huge gaping hole that could never be filled had been dug into her heart. And even as she thought this, she realized that she would fill it with memories, and perhaps in time, as the pain lessened, the emptiness wouldn't echo with such hollowness.

Reaching the bathhouse, she hesitated for only a heartbeat before ascending the steps, pressing on the latch, and pushing open the door. A mist of warmth enveloped her and drew her inside, the door banging shut behind her.

Only one gaslight flickered. Its light faded into shadows, as though its only purpose was to reveal the darkness, not what lay within it. She couldn't help but feel as though she were in some sort of strange place where she was not truly herself, and her thoughts were warped by grief.

And then she saw him. On the far side of the pool, ensconced in shadows. Perfectly still. His gaze honed in on her, watchful, steady, dark. As dark as the storm that had rolled in from the sea.

Slowly she descended the stairs until her toes were near enough to the water that one more step would place her within the bath. She sat on a rough-hewn step, only then giving in to the true depth of her sorrow. To have done so before would have prevented her from reaching her destination, and she had so dearly wanted to be here, to ask of him one more time if all hope was lost.

"Is there any chance—"

"None whatsoever." His voice echoing around her, he cut her off before she could complete her question, as though he had no wish even to consider the remotest possibility that Nicky had survived. Not to consider the possibility had to mean that he'd witnessed his death. Why hadn't he done for Nicky what he'd graciously done for his father—brought him to shore?

It was so difficult to mourn without absolute proof. With tears filling her eyes, she wrapped her arms around herself, squeezing tightly. She'd thought to comfort him, and instead, she again felt the overwhelming need for comfort.

"I keep thinking that he's going to suddenly appear, looking like a drowned cat, but with that lovely smile he has that seems to say the whole world is to be enjoyed—and he'll tell us it was all a prank."

Weddington glided toward her, the water barely rippling with his movements. "I know it's difficult to think that you'll never see him again, but I truly believe that he'll be rewarded with happiness." He released a strangled groan as though whatever pain he'd been holding at bay needed a momentary respite from captivity, and suddenly he was near enough to take her hands. "My sentiment is incredibly trite, my words inadequate. I don't possess the eloquence you so desperately need right now." He trailed his fingers along the side of her face. "I do know that he wouldn't want you to mourn."

Tears rolled over onto her cheeks. "How can I not when I loved him?" She shook her head, the words spilling forth before she could stop them. "Why him and not you?"

"Because I'm a stronger swimmer."

"Oh, God." A sob tore from her throat. "I'm sorry. I'm so sorry." She buried her face in her hands. "I didn't want you to die. I didn't want either of you to die."

"I know," he rasped, taking her in his arms.

She could feel such strength, such comfort, and she was also aware now of the tiny shivers running through him, shivers she was certain had nothing to do with cold, and everything to do with what he'd endured before—at the sea's mercy. They'd both lost: she her betrothed, he his friend. Her heart told her that hers was the greater loss—if loss of such magnitude could be measured at all. But she couldn't begin to imagine—didn't want to contemplate—how awful it had been for him to know he couldn't rescue Nicky.

Once again her chest tightened, her stomach knotted, and tears flourished. Why, why, why did fate have to be so malicious? Why did these two men have to be so stubborn as to not return to shore at the first hint of foul weather?

She wanted to strike out at them both, but only one was here. Forever, only one remained, only one would be available to her. And while he might have been her last choice for comfort, he was suddenly her only choice. All the inner turmoil and struggles that she'd been battling deep within herself—to love one man, yet desire another—were inconsequential.

Unfaithfulness could no longer apply. The knowledge should have been liberating. Instead, it was devastating.

She wound her arms around Weddington's neck, eased her body

closer to his, felt the billowing of her nightclothes as the water eased over her bare calves, knees, thighs as she sank farther down. She wanted comfort, wanted to celebrate life, wanted to fill this damned overwhelming emptiness that threatened to consume her.

Wanted the hurt to cease, wanted everything she couldn't have. She felt as though the storm hadn't withdrawn, but had simply moved inside of her, turbulent, unyielding, threatening to destroy her.

She was vaguely aware of the water rising higher, over her hips, traveling up to her waist, caressing the underside of her breasts. She wrapped her legs around Weddington's middle as he pressed his hot mouth against her throat. Gratitude swamped her because she could feel, because the chill that had descended on her earlier in the afternoon was dissipating with his nearness, with his touch.

"Hold tight," he ordered in a hoarse voice.

Then it was no longer the water skimming along her flesh, but his hands, beneath her nightclothes, along her legs, up over her bottom, carrying her nightclothes, up, up, up, until he'd lifted them over her head. Raising her arms, she felt the last of her clothing pulled away, heard the slap of damp cloth against dry stone as he tossed her garment aside.

And then she was swirling in the heart of the storm.

Richard wanted to devour every inch of her. Greedily, he ran his lips and his tongue over her throat, along her collarbone, relishing the sweet taste of her flesh, allowing it to replace the bitter saltiness that had filled his mouth only hours before, gagging him, threatening to take his life.

He'd been forced to shove the terror back into the farthest recesses of his mind, had been determined to ignore it, not to let it paralyze or conquer him. Only here, in the privacy of the bathhouse, surrounded by warm water, silence, and solitude, had he dared lower his defenses, had he been willing to acknowledge the fears that had ridden with him on the waves.

He'd yet to reconcile them, had not completely faced them, when she'd appeared suddenly like a wraith in his lonely world. He needed her as he'd never needed anyone, needed her sweetness, her innocence, her bravery, her determination, her competitiveness.

A thousand times during the late afternoon and early evening, he'd imagined her beside him, urging him on, demanding he not give in to defeat. He'd heard her voice, imagined her touch, but none of the imaginings were as satisfying as the reality.

She was within his arms, against his rock-hard body, her bare legs wrapped around his waist, her heated flesh melting against his. He was surprised the water surrounding them didn't boil as ferociously as his blood.

Dear God, but he wanted to forget . . . wanted to forget this afternoon, this evening . . . his wrestling with his conscience, his struggles in the sea, his desperation to reach land. He wanted to forget all that had come before this moment, forget everything except for the woman in his arms, the woman rubbing her body against his with fierce abandon as though she, too, wished to forget the past, wished only to experience the intensity of the present and the glory of life that continued to flow through them.

He slid his hands beneath her bottom and lifted her higher, until he had easier access to the sweet mounds of her breasts. He ran his tongue over the lily-white skin, circled the pink nipple, until he closed his mouth over the taut pearl and suckled gently. With a low moan and a digging of her fingers into his shoulders, she pressed the apex between her legs against his stomach.

He trailed his mouth over the curve of one breast, dipped his tongue into the valley between, and gave the same careful attention to her other breast, kissing, tasting, sucking, relishing the fact that he was alive to do so.

A part of him realized that it was madness to be here with her like this, that a civilized gentleman would have sent her on her way—or at the very least would have never approached her, but would have stayed at the far side of the bath. But the sea had beaten civilization out of him, had sent the gentleman within him into hiding until all that remained was the crude, uncivilized part of him that refused to be defeated.

He wanted Kitty, had wanted her from the first moment he'd set eyes on her. He'd wanted her in London, he'd wanted her here. He wanted to possess her as none ever had, touch her, hold her, carry her to the pinnacle of pleasure as he had once before—only this time he wanted to share the journey with her.

He didn't recall making a conscious effort to reach the stairway. He only knew he was there, and that she was still wrapped around him. He climbed them effortlessly, water sluicing off their bodies.

Then he was laying her down on the bundle of blankets he'd brought from the manor that he'd intended to use to dry himself. They were not as thick, not as soft as a mattress, but they would serve him better than the bare stone floor.

Here within the tiny alcove that led to the changing room, shadows lurked and light fled. He couldn't see her clearly, but it mattered not, for she was emblazoned on his mind: each detail, every curve, line, and tiny freckle. He wedged himself between her thighs as though he belonged there, and with one powerful thrust he drove himself into the heat of her sanctuary, into the blessed relief of affirmation that he still drew breath.

Kitty gasped, not certain if it was from the sharp pain that quickly passed or the wonder of Richard's fullness stretching her, filling her, completing her. And then all thoughts vanished. Instinctively she lifted her hips, welcomed the deeper nestling of Richard's body against hers, the slow rocking of his hips against hers, the arching of her body, the silent crying out for release. She heard tiny moans, little cries, barely recognizing the sounds as coming from her while his deeper groans echoed around her.

Bodies damp from the pool they'd recently left soon became damp with desire. Flesh warmed by the bath was heated by yearning. She felt incredible sensations spiraling through her. She felt as though her entire body was curling around his even as it tightened, even as she writhed against him.

They became a tangle of limbs, stroking, caressing, kneading, striving to touch all at once. He began to pump his body into hers, deeper, faster, harder . . . carrying her higher and higher and higher until she was suspended on the horizon—

Her scream echoed around them as he catapulted her over the edge into ecstasy. His guttural groan and last driving thrust began before her scream silenced, and she found herself tightening her legs around him, holding him closer.

Her body curled in on itself even as it seemed to flow away from her. Her harsh panting breaths matched his. His arms were shaking with his effort to keep his weight off her.

She skimmed her fingers over his back, along his shoulders. Then the tears that had begun earlier and stopped began again. For what she'd lost. For what she'd gained. For what should have never happened within this bathhouse.

For the guilt that swamped her. Her betrothed was only hours drowned, and here she was, lying beneath his friend, relishing the comfort of his body nestled within hers.

Disgust and shame flooded her.

What had she been thinking? She'd not been thinking at all. She'd only been feeling. Incredible sensations. For a while, no sorrow existed.

And now too much rushed in.

He pressed a kiss to her temple, her cheek, her jaw, and when he moved for her mouth, she turned her head to the side, averting the kiss he wished to bestow.

He lifted himself slightly, to look down on her more clearly she thought, but it was impossible to see plainly in the shadows. A reprieve from sight for which she was most grateful.

"Please, get off me," she whispered.

With his thumbs, he rubbed her jaw. "Kitty—"

"Please get off," she demanded.

Ever so slowly, he eased back. She was torn between the devastating sense of loss as his body left hers and the overwhelming knowledge that they should have never been joined to begin with. She didn't want to remember her screams, or her cries, or her exploring hands. Grabbing a blanket, she scrambled back, striving to cover herself, to reestablish the propriety that she should have never lost.

"I want to go home," she said, her voice low.

"I'll help you get dressed, walk you back to the house—"

"No!" She shook her head frantically. "Home. Where my parents are. In London. Now."

"Right this moment?"

Pressing a balled fist against her mouth, she nodded her head briskly. "Yes, I need them. I need them now. Right now."

"All right. I'll make the arrangements. Immediately."

"Farthingham's family—"

"Freddie left earlier to deliver the sad news. He preferred to do it in person."

"I should have gone with him."

"You weren't in any condition to travel."

And she was in even worse condition now. She'd not only lost Nicky, but she'd lost her virginity, her self-respect. She thought she might never be able to look at herself in the mirror again. And she definitely never again wanted to set sights on Weddington.

Chapter 19

Managing five estates at various locations throughout England might have been a daunting task for some men, but Richard had always welcomed and relished the challenge. This area of his life placed him at the helm completely and absolutely—as did his numerous business ventures. He sullied his hands with none of it, but his keen mind gave him the ability to lay out strategy and to issue orders as naturally as he breathed.

As he sat at the desk in his study at his London residence, with ledgers and reports spread before him like offerings before a god, he found his distraction unsettling. He could barely grasp a coherent thought that might help him to put into place a brilliant plan.

It had been nearly a month since Kitty had wept in his arms at the loss of Farthingham, a month since he'd awakened all the servants and set them to the task of returning to London. Anne and Lady Priscilla had also been ready to return. They'd all traveled back in his coach, quiet and solemn, as befitting the death of a dear friend.

Lady Priscilla's penchant for gossip had assured that all of London would know before a week had passed that Farthingham had drowned at sea, and that his younger brother would acquire the titles. Titles few knew Farthingham had never wanted, had found burdensome and oppressive.

Richard had tried to pay Kitty a call, but she was in seclusion, mourning, not accepting visitors. He couldn't determine how best to proceed. While he respected the mourning period, she was not a widow, and he hoped she had no plans to mourn an entire year. Although if forced to wait twelve months before pressing his suit, he would.

Farthingham was gone. She had turned to Richard with her loss, and he'd turned to her for comfort as well, although he was certain she'd not fully comprehended his reasons or his needs. How close he'd come to death. His terror of the sea had not diminished that fateful night. If at all possible, it had intensified. They'd taken comfort a bit farther than he'd planned, but he had no regrets. He had every intention of marrying her . . . and if he had to seduce her again to achieve that end, then he would.

He would willingly do anything for her. As the actions he'd taken during the storm proved.

The door to his study quietly clicked open, and the butler entered. "A lady has come to call, Your Grace." He presented the tray.

Richard read the name on the card, and his heart pounded with joy. He'd not had to go to her after all. She'd come to him. He nodded and came to his feet. "Show her in immediately."

He fought not to be overly optimistic, not to unjustly hope that any reservations she might have had regarding his intentions had evaporated. He moved around his desk, wanting nothing between them, anxious to greet her.

Then she entered the room, a shadow of the vibrant woman she'd once been. He'd always considered her delicate, but now she possessed a frailty that startled him. She'd indeed taken the loss of Farthingham hard, much harder than he'd expected she would.

"Miss Robertson."

"Your Grace."

She failed to meet his gaze, seeming to focus instead on a pearl button on his black waistcoat.

"Would you like to sit?" he offered.

"Yes, thank you."

She settled into the nearest chair, the one closest to the door as though she expected to have to make a hasty retreat. He forced himself to sit opposite her when he desperately wanted to kneel before her and ask her what he could do to ease her pain, to return her gorgeous smile to her lovely face. "Would you care for some refreshment?"

With her gaze lowered, she replied, "No thank you. I'm feeling a bit queasy from the journey here. I need a moment to steady myself."

He watched as she closed her eyes and licked her lips. Her skin had no color, but more closely resembled the chalky bluffs at Dover.

"Perhaps a walk, a bit of fresh air would serve you better than this stuffy old room," he suggested.

Opening her eyes, she nodded as though it took all her strength to do so. "Yes, thank you."

He stood, extended his hand, and felt the slight tremors in hers as she placed it within his and rose to her feet. He led her across the room and through the French doors, onto the terrace, then beyond it to the perfectly manicured gardens. She shifted her hand to his forearm, but he was left with the distinct impression that it was only because her mourning had reduced her to a weakened state that forced her to accept his assistance. She would have preferred not to have touched him at all.

He damned Farthingham for his lack of insight, for not recognizing how she would suffer at his loss.

"Have you been eating?" Richard asked.

She shook her head slightly. "These days my stomach is in revolt."

"Are you sleeping?"

"Do I look as though I'm sleeping?" she responded tartly.

Her spark, albeit small, caused him to smile. "No. You look as though you have journeyed through hell."

She stopped walking, faced him, held his gaze for only a heartbeat before tears pooled, and she glanced away. "I'm with child."

Richard's gaze darted from her eyes to her narrow waist. "Are you quite certain?"

"I have absolutely no doubt."

Unadulterated joy shot through him like a strong wind into the billowing sails. Possessiveness so powerful as to almost bring him to his knees took hold. This remarkable woman whom he'd sought to win was now his . . . by default.

Joy abandoned him. She'd come to him not out of desire but out of need. She needed his name, and it was obvious studying her that she was not at all pleased with that necessity. "I shall make arrangements for us to marry, with haste."

He thought it impossible for her to grow any paler, but she did. She pressed her lips into a tight line.

"That is the reason for your coming here, is it not?" he asked.

She nodded slightly, color rising in her cheeks. "I'd feared you would make this moment difficult." She shook her head, swallowed. "You cannot fathom how very much I did not want this."

And she seemed incapable of fathoming how very much he did. How could two people with such incredible passion evident between them be at such cross-purposes?

"On the contrary. You have made your true feelings regarding me perfectly clear. I cannot, for the life of me, determine why it is you find me so reprehensible."

She released a brittle bark of laughter. "Can you not?" She punched her finger into his chest. "My betrothed is drowned at sea, and you took advantage—"

"I sought to comfort—"

"—and before that you used every opportunity to your advantage, seeking me out, attempting to seduce me—"

"Attempting? I had but to touch you, and you were clay within my hands, your passion to be shaped to match my desires. Argue all you want that you had to endure my touch at the opera, but not in Harrington's garden. You had but to whisper no once, and I would have ceased my attentions, you had but to take one step back, and I would not have followed."

"I cannot begin to express how much I loathe you."

She spun on her heel. Reaching out he grabbed her arm, turning her about to face him. Fire was in her eyes now. He much preferred it to tears. But his anger was as livid as hers, his hurt cut just as deeply. "Now it is my turn to be perfectly clear. I will not have a wife who denies me. If I take you as my duchess, when it is but you and I, you may curse me into perdition as much as you want. But you will not show that side of our marriage to the servants, to my mother, or to my sister. You will play the role of faithful wife."

She angled that perfect chin of hers. "For my child, I can even feign happiness." Yet she looked to be brimming with sorrow. "I have no desire for my parents to know that I go into this union out of obligation."

"Then we are of a like mind on that matter at least."

She nodded. "I suppose we are."

"Good. I'll call on your father this evening to properly ask for his permission to take you as my wife."

"I'll let him know."

The words had all been delivered with heated emotions, but lacked caring. Not at all how he'd planned to ask her to become his wife. Not at all how he'd hoped she'd accept.

He walked her to her carriage, thinking that he'd seen funeral processions that exhibited more joy.

It wasn't until she was settled into the carriage that he finally spoke again. "It need not be bleak between us, Kitty. I can make you happy."

She gave him a sad smile. "I think only Farthingham had the power to accomplish that."

"You still miss him then?"

"I shall miss him until the day I die."

His heart slammed against his ribs almost as loudly as the door's closing. Signaling for the driver to drive on, he stepped back and stared after the retreating carriage.

He cursed himself, cursed Farthingham, and for good measure, cursed Montague as well. Farthingham's death had only served to free Farthingham while trapping everyone else in hell.

Kitty sat in the parlor playing her third game of checkers with Emily in less than twenty minutes. Her mother was reading in a chair nearby.

Weddington and her father were in the study. What could be taking so long? Weddington was probably making all sorts of demands. He had the advantage. Her parents would try to protect her and the child, and they'd give away the farm to Weddington to achieve that end. He could ask for any amount, any consideration, any holdings. He could manipulate them as he'd manipulated her.

If only she hadn't gone to the bathhouse. He hadn't managed to fill the emptiness inside her. He'd only caused it to increase, because now guilt ate at her daily. Though not yet married, she'd been unfaithful. She'd given in to lust, desire, and her body's yearnings. She'd succumbed to animalistic urgings. And now she'd be trapped in a marriage she didn't want.

His harsh words kept playing through her mind like the worst lines in a play: *I'll not have a wife who denies me.*

Yet how could she give him again what she'd given him before? She could still hear her screams of ecstasy echoing through the bathhouse, could still recall the splendor of his touch. When she should have been consumed by grief, she'd been consumed with passion.

She'd never forgive herself for what had transpired, never forgive him. Her hell would be living with a man who would constantly serve to remind her of her failings.

"I wonder what your father and the duke are discussing," her mother said.

Ignoring her mother's question, Kitty moved a checker that Emily had been patiently waiting for. Kitty couldn't keep her thoughts on the game, and Emily was well on her way to trouncing her once again.

"Maybe the duke wants to marry Kitty now that Farthingham is dead," Emily speculated, then quickly jumped two of Kitty's pieces.

Kitty's stomach jumped right along with her sister's movements over the pieces. Honestly, Emily was too often too bright. Out of the corner of her eye, Kitty saw her mother furrow her brow.

"Why ever would you think that, Emily?"

Emily shrugged her narrow shoulders. "I thought maybe he fell in love with her the night he took her to the opera. He never took his eyes off her when he was watching her walk down the stairs, never stopped looking at her even after she greeted him."

"What's this?" Her mother scooted up slightly. "When did Weddington take you to the opera?"

Kitty slid another checker into place. "At the beginning of the Season. He and Farthingham had made a wager, Farthingham lost." She watched as Emily jumped another piece and removed it from the board.

"You never mentioned—"

"It wasn't important. Besides, we were chaperoned. The duke's sister was there."

"I see."

Only she knew her mother didn't see at all.

"It was really nothing, Mother."

"I thought he looked sad when he arrived tonight," Emily said.

"We're all sad," Kitty said. "Farthingham's gone, and we miss him." Weddington had also looked incredibly handsome and confident. How would she survive marriage to a man who made her feel as he did?

She heard the footsteps and snapped her head around to see her father coming into the parlor alone. That didn't bode well for their meeting. She knew her father could be equally determined, equally forceful as Weddington. "Where's Weddington?" she asked.

"In my study. Emily, it's time for you to go to bed," her father announced.

"David, what's wrong?" her mother asked.

"Is Kitty in trouble?" Emily piped up.

"No, she's not, but your mother and I need to speak with her, and it's late enough that you should be off to bed."

Emily leaned across the table. "Will you tell me later what Papa says, let me know if I'm right about the reason that Weddington is here?"

Nodding, Kitty forced herself to smile. "Of course, I will."

While Emily said good night to her parents, Kitty rose to her feet and moved to a more comfortable chair, facing her mother, prepared to explain how she'd come to be in the dreadful situation she suddenly found herself in, not exactly certain if it could be explained.

"David, what is it?" her mother asked as soon as Emily was gone.

Her father walked to the fireplace, placed his arm on the mantel, and focused all his attention on Kitty. "Weddington asked for Kitty's hand in marriage."

Her mother looked horrified. "I thought he and Farthingham were friends."

"They were."

"Farthingham is only a month gone. What sort of man wouldn't allow a decent amount of time—"

"That's what I'm trying to find out," her father said, his gaze never once leaving Kitty.

Her mother scoffed. "I can't believe these English lords. I know American heiresses are sought after, but coming to us this quickly, while Kitty still mourns her loss is cold, uncaring, and calculating. I know our daughter will bring a good settlement to the marriage—"

"He doesn't want money," her father said.

Kitty couldn't prevent the surprise from washing over her face. "What?"

"That's sorta what I was thinking. He's determined not to take any funds from me—which leaves only one question to be answered. Do you want to marry him, Kitty?"

How was she supposed to answer that question? *Of course, I don't want to marry him* was her initial thought, but the truth was that she did *want* to marry him if only because she had no wish to bring shame on herself, her child, and the parents who had taken her in when her own mother couldn't. She conceded that different levels of want existed, and she could answer truthfully—if not with total honesty. "I'm open to the idea."

"Kitty, what on earth is going on?" her mother asked.

She darted her gaze between her mother and father, and her mouth grew dry. She wouldn't hurt them for the world, and yet here she stood on the brink of doing just that and much worse. She'd given in to her impure, lustful yearnings and engaged in impure, lustful actions that had resulted in the conception of a child. How did she announce all that without breaking their hearts? "It's difficult to explain, Mama."

"I know you're grieving over the loss of Lord Farthingham and still reeling from the unexpectedness of his death. Sweetheart, now is not the time to make a hasty decision regarding your future."

"It's not a hasty decision, Mama. I've thought it through very carefully."

"But you loved Lord Farthingham."

"I'm fairly certain she still does," a deep voice boomed into the room.

Kitty jerked her attention away from her mother to see Wedding-ton standing in the doorway. He strolled into the room as though he owned it, more importantly holding her gaze as though he owned her. In a way she supposed he did. He could demand of her what he would, and she would, in all likelihood, agree to it—for the sake of her child and her family.

"Then why offer to marry her?" her father asked, moving away from the fireplace.

"Because she carries my child."

Kitty heard her mother gasp and saw tears spring into her eyes. Her father's jaw tightened, and his hands bunched into fists at his side. Texas was only just beginning to lose its frontier edge. Wed-dington's nose wouldn't be the first her father had broken.

Through the pool of her own tears, Kitty said, "I'm so sorry, Mama."

"You've no need to apologize," Weddington said, "when the fault lies with me. I took advantage of your daughter, and I'm here to put the matter to rights."

"You goddamned son of a bitch," her father hissed. "If we were in Texas, I'd beat you to within an inch of your life. Hell, I might do it anyway simply for the satisfaction."

"If that is what is required to gain permission to marry your daughter, I'll step outside and make myself available for the pummel-ing," Weddington said.

Her mother crossed the short expanse separating her from Kitty, sat on the arm of the chair, and put her arms around Kitty in a com-forting gesture she'd made a hundred times throughout the years. "What do you want to do, Kitty?"

"I want to do what's best for my baby." *My baby.* She'd never before spoken the words aloud, and yet in doing so the reality seemed to sharpen into clarity.

Her mother hugged her. "Of course, you do."

Her father's sigh echoed through the room. "I'll contact the lawyer we use when we're in London so we can meet with yours tomorrow to begin negotiating the settlement. Took a month with Farthingham."

"It shan't take that long with me. All I want from you is your daughter. Determine what you require her yearly allowance to be, and I shall agree to it. I've already sent word to the managers of my estates. They will all be here within the next day or so to present you with an accounting of all my holdings. As will the gentleman who handles the assets of my business ventures. I shall see to obtaining a special license and making arrangements for the ceremony to take place a week from Saturday at the parish church."

"How long have you been planning this?" her father asked, suspicion laced through his voice.

"Kitty told me of her circumstance this afternoon. I am not a man who believes in wasting moments hoping that a situation will right itself."

"That's all well and good, and while all these fellas you're sending my way may be able to convince me that you're financially solvent, I'm more interested in how you personally plan to treat my daughter." When her father was angry his Texas upbringing came to the foreground.

Weddington's eyes met hers, a challenge in his, along with a commitment. "I shall treat her as though she holds my heart."

"You damn well better, because if she's not happy, I'll give you the beating you deserve."

"People will talk," her mother said. "With Farthingham gone only a month—"

"People will always talk," Weddington interjected. "But she is not a *widow*. Therefore etiquette does not dictate that she need spend a year in mourning."

"But I will," she said defiantly. "As a matter of fact, I'll mourn Farthingham for much longer than that."

She saw a spark in his eyes, as though he were welcoming the challenge of convincing her otherwise. "He is indeed a fortunate man to have earned your complete devotion."

"If he were truly fortunate, he'd still be alive."

He flinched at that, and she silently cursed herself for taking her frustrations out on him. She was in an appalling situation, and he'd not once sought to avoid his responsibilities. As a matter of fact, it seemed he was doing all he could to make the entire situation as pleasant as possible. "I'm sorry, Your Grace. I don't hold you responsible for Lord Farthingham's death."

"You're most kind, Miss Robertson."

Her mother suddenly stood. "David, will you come with me to look in on Emily?"

Her father's brow furrowed deeply. "Why do we need to check on Emily?"

Her mother sighed. "I'm sure the duke and Kitty would appreciate having a few moments alone."

"If you think I'm leaving this man with Kitty—"

"You're planning to let him marry her. Are you also planning to move in with them?"

Her father rubbed his jaw. "Did I give my permission?"

"You mentioned contacting your lawyer," her mother reminded him.

"Then I guess I did give permission." Her father looked at her. "Is this what you want, sweetheart?"

She gave him a small semblance of a smile. "The marriage or a few moments alone?"

"Both."

She rose to her feet, crossed over to him, and hugged him. "I love you, Papa."

"If you don't want this man, Kitty, we'll work something else out."

Leaning back, she held his gaze. "It's what I want."

"All right." He glared at Weddington, a thousand threats and promises delivered in silence. Then he took her mother's arm, and they left the room.

Kitty sank into the nearest chair with a sigh. "Well, that wasn't too awful."

"On the contrary, I believe I would rather face the sea than your father."

"Good. I don't want this to be too easy on you."

"Nothing involving you has ever been easy."

He knelt before her, and she resisted the urge to press herself back against the chair to avoid his nearness. Holding out his hand, he unfurled his fingers to reveal the most beautiful stone-studded ring she'd ever seen, the band so delicate she wondered how it could hold the diamond and emerald stones set within it.

"My family embraces its traditions, takes pride in its legacies. My grandfather had this ring specially designed for my grandmother, the emeralds for the shade of her eyes, the diamonds for the way her eyes sparkled whenever she saw him. He gave her another ring on the day that he took her as his wife. It nestles up against this one to signify their perfect union. I shall deliver that ring to you on the day that we exchange our marriage vows."

He slipped the ring onto her finger, and she felt the weight of it circle her heart. For a moment she couldn't breathe as the reality surrounded her, terrified her. Had Jessye been right not to marry the man who'd gotten her pregnant? Was Kitty doing the right thing by this child, or would he grow up to resent her because she'd married a man she didn't love?

Starting to shake, she withdrew her hand from his and clutched it against her stomach, surprised to discover how perfectly the ring fit. "It's lovely. Thank you."

"I know I am not your first choice in a husband, but I will be your last. We shall make the best of it."

"I've already promised to play the part well."

His mouth spread into a slow, easy smile. "And you did admirably tonight. Your parents hardly suspect that you were desperately hoping your father would carry through on his threat to thrash me to within an inch of my life."

She found herself fighting to contain her smile, because he'd guessed correctly: she had indeed been hoping that her father would deliver at least one blow. "It seems you know me well. As for my father's threats, my parents lost their first child, a son. As a result, my father has always been a bit overprotective."

"I suspect he is overprotective because you are so very precious."

He made his intent to kiss her known by cradling the side of her face with one hand while slowly moving toward her. His mouth contained no hunger, the heat held in check, the passion leashed.

It was a kiss that touched her more than any that had come before it, a kiss of apology, a kiss filled with promises.

Drawing back, he held her gaze. "Earlier I said that I knew I was not your first choice." He placed his thumb against her moist lips. "Never forget, Kitty, that you were always mine."

Chapter 20

Why was it that black ink made everything seem so permanent, unchangeable? Kitty read the announcement of her latest betrothal in *The Times*, but she found no joy, no excitement. Only a sort of odd acceptance.

And then the callers began arriving. The curious, the piqued, the intrigued. She was home to none of them, refused to receive them, while her hopes were dashed that the ceremony would be quiet and attended by only a few. English law prohibited church doors from barring entry during weddings, and she was beginning to fear people would be continually pouring through them.

Then the Duchess of Weddington and her daughter arrived, and Kitty felt it would be the height of rudeness not to receive them when they would become her relatives in a matter of days.

Wearing a black crepe dress with a plain collar, Kitty walked into the drawing room to welcome them, comforted by the fact that they also wore black.

"Oh, my dear girl," the duchess said, as she crossed the room and took Kitty's hand. "How brave you've been since Farthingham's death."

"I hardly feel brave, Your Grace."

"Still, you have been. I cannot tell you how sorry I am that I wasn't at Drummond Manor to offer comfort that fateful night. That damned sea. I don't know why Richard fancies living within sight of it. I could barely tolerate it after it took my dear Weddy, but now that it has taken your Farthingham as well, I don't know if I shall ever return there. Although now that you're to marry Richard, I may never have to. I'm moving into the dower residence in London this week, and at the end of the Season, I shall move to the dower estate. And I shall take Anne with me."

"Oh, no," Kitty said, her gaze moving from one lady to the other. "I don't wish to kick you out of your homes."

"Nonsense, dear. You are kicking me *into* my homes. I have long wanted to find solitude within my own residence, but Richard is so busy with the managing of his estates and God knows what else, that he had no time to oversee the household. Now that task shall fall to you, and I am most grateful."

Kitty was glad to know she'd made someone happy. "Will you please sit, make yourselves comfortable? Tea should arrive shortly."

The ladies took their places, Lady Anne and her mother on the sofa, Kitty in a chair across from them.

"I must admit to being quite surprised that you agreed to marry my son so soon after Farthingham's passing, but I must also acknowledge that I am most pleased that he has finally consented to take a wife."

"And Mama is most pleased that it is *you*," Lady Anne said with a kind smile.

"Oh, yes, quite," the duchess said.

Kitty forced herself to smile. Pleased, pleased, pleased. Everyone was so damned pleased, and all she could think to say was, "I'm *pleased* that he was willing to marry me."

"As well you should be, my dear girl. He is quite the catch if I do say so myself."

Kitty couldn't have been more relieved when the servant arrived with the tray of tea and biscuits. After serving her guests their tea, she sat back and took a welcome sip from her own cup.

"I hope you'll forgive me for being crass," the duchess began, "but since you are American, I did want to make certain that you understand that your first order of business is to present my son with an heir."

Kitty very nearly spewed her tea.

"Mama!" Lady Anne cried.

"I meant no offense," the duchess said, her bejeweled hand raised, "but she is American, and Americans do not always fully comprehend the necessity for an heir."

"I understand completely, Your Grace," Kitty said, surprised that Richard hadn't told his mother the exact reason that had necessitated their hasty marriage.

The duchess smiled with approval. "Splendid. I must warn you now, however, that the heirs to Weddington tend to arrive a month or so early. I had been married but eight months when Richard arrived. Eyebrows were raised, I can tell you that, but I quickly set everyone straight that it is simply the way of Weddington men to get on with business as quickly as possible."

At that, Kitty wasn't certain if the woman knew the truth of her situation or not. "Thank you. I'll keep that in mind."

"I hope that you will. There are no finer men in all of England. I truly believe that."

"Mama is a bit biased, I think," Lady Anne said.

Kitty smiled her first truly warm smile. "Yes, I think you're right."

"Have you given any thought as to what you'll wear when you marry Richard?" Lady Anne asked.

Kitty cleared her throat. "Actually I have. I have a pale lilac dress that I thought would be appropriate."

The two ladies exchanged glances that spoke volumes. They'd apparently anticipated just such a response. The duchess set her teacup aside and scooted to the edge of the sofa.

"My dear, lavender is worn when a bride wishes to signify she is mourning the loss of a relative."

"I am in mourning, Your Grace." Kitty was certain her sharp tone was responsible for the duchess's eyebrows rising.

"You are mourning a man to whom you were not married. All of London knows this. A week from Saturday, you shall marry my son. While I understand your need to honor Farthingham's memory, I beg you will reconsider your attire and not insult my son by flaunting your grief."

Lowering her gaze to her hands in her lap, Kitty wondered exactly how much this woman did know and how much she simply suspected. A delicate hand covered hers, and Kitty looked up.

The duchess smiled softly. "I realize there is hardly time to have a gown sewn. I was hoping that you might consent to wear the one I wore the day that I married Weddy. Our wedding was only the beginning of the happiest years of my life."

"It's a truly beautiful gown," Lady Anne said. "When Mama was younger, she was almost as slender as you are."

"It should require only a minimum of altering," the duchess said.

"You love your son very much," Kitty said softly.

"With all my heart. He is a good man, Miss Robertson. Sometimes good men behave quite naughtily, and I suspect, although he has not confided in me, that in this situation he might have done just that. You need not confirm or deny my suspicions as to the reasons for so hasty a wedding. But in the years to come, you will look back on the day when you exchanged vows with my son, and I should like very much that you not look back on them with regret."

Tears stinging her eyes, Kitty pressed her hands to her mouth. "I'm so afraid I'll do exactly that. Look back on my wedding with regret."

The duchess bestowed on her a sympathetic smile. "I know, my dear. I think Richard fears that as well. So we must make the best of it all the way around, mustn't we? May I send my girl over with the gown and have her see to making the alterations?"

Kitty thought that in the grand scheme of things what she wore on her wedding day was hardly worth considering, but if it would help to get her marriage off on the right foot . . .

She nodded. "Yes, please. I'll be honored to wear it."

The duchess beamed. "Splendid!"

Less than an hour after the duchess and Lady Anne had departed, Freddie Montague came to visit. Kitty hadn't seen him since he'd left to inform Farthingham's family of his death at sea. Although she'd paid her own respects to the family in the first few days following the drowning, she'd not seen Freddie at their residence.

It was comforting to be with him, walking through the garden, her arm crooked around his. In ways she couldn't quite put her finger on, he reminded her of Farthingham—the sense of playfulness perhaps. Even though presently it was absent, she knew it still resided in him. Or at least she hoped it did. She would hate for them all to spend their lives melancholy because the sea had stolen their laughter.

Although she had no brothers, she thought the way she regarded Freddie was very much the way that a sister looked to an older brother—for comfort and support. With him, she felt as she did with Farthingham: safe.

She wondered if he'd consider marrying her and raising her child as his own. Yet even as the thought crossed her mind, she knew her plans were too far gone to change now.

"I keep thinking that I'll turn a corner somewhere, and there he'll be, waiting, smiling, teasing me," she said quietly.

"I think we all tend to think that way when we lose someone who matters to us."

"Will you write a play about him?"

"Probably not. Might write one about you, though. Your life is much more interesting."

"My life would make the audience weep."

"But it needn't, Kitty."

She looked up at him and met his kind, gray eyes.

"Farthingham wouldn't want you to mourn," he said. "He'd be pleased to know that you've moved on, that Weddington offered for you, and that you accepted."

She shook her head. "Freddie, it's barely been a month."

"All the better. Life is far too short. Farthingham would be the first to tell you that. He'd not want you moping about."

She narrowed her eyes at him before quickly averting her gaze in order to deliver her lie. "I'm not moping."

"Yes, you are. Rumors abound that you're not home to anyone. I was quite delighted that you deigned to see me."

"Everyone is simply curious. They don't truly care. I feel like an exhibit in the zoo."

"All the more reason you must get out and about. Weddington will expect it."

She released a brittle laugh. "Yes, well, he may find his expectations are not mine."

"Then don't marry him."

She stopped abruptly and faced him. "I want to, and yet I don't. I feel guilty, so soon after Farthingham's death—"

He touched a gloved finger to her lips. "You mustn't. I swear to you that Farthingham would be immensely gladdened by your decision to marry. He has the utmost respect and highest regard for Weddington."

"*Had*," she corrected. "He hasn't anything anymore."

"Quite right. Sometimes I forget he's gone, and I find myself speaking as though he's still here."

She wound her arm around his again and began walking. "It's all right. I do the same thing."

"Still, although he is gone, I believe his sentiments would remain. He would be delighted beyond measure that you are to marry Weddington."

"You don't think it makes me appear disrespectful?"

"I don't think you should worry overmuch about what people think."

"I've spent my whole life worrying about it."

"Then it's high time you stopped."

She squeezed his arm. "Farthingham would say the same thing. I'm going to miss you, Freddie, when you leave."

"You'll have to come to America to visit sometime."

She smiled up at him. "Life's ironies. I'm American and will make England my home. You're English and will make America yours. When do you leave?"

"Not for a few more weeks."

"Will you come to the wedding?"

Now, he was the one who smiled. "Weddington's given me no choice. He's asked me to stand as his best man."

Again, she stopped, only this time it was to stare at him. "I would have thought he would have asked . . ." Her voice trailed off. She wasn't certain whom he might have asked, but she'd thought it would have been someone with influence and power comparable to his. When she thought about it, however, she realized she knew none of his friends—other than Farthingham. She certainly hadn't thought he was close enough to Freddie to ask him. She could do little more than shake her head in astonishment. "I'm surprised."

"So I see. We're not really close, he and I, but I suspect his selecting me had more to do with his wanting you to feel comfortable during the ceremony."

Moving away from him, she dared to voice what she'd only whispered to herself at night. "I don't want this marriage, Freddie. I really don't. Why is he being so nice?"

"I suspect because he knows how you feel."

"Maybe it's guilt."

"Why would you think that?"

"It was his boat. He consented to taking it out. With his experiences on the sea, he should have known better."

"The storm deprived you of Farthingham. You mustn't think otherwise. It'll only add to your unhappiness."

"I suppose you're right." Walking back to him, she patted his arm. "I'm glad you'll be near me during the ceremony."

"As am I."

They began strolling again.

"May I ask you a question?" he asked.

"Of course," she answered.

"You'll continue yachting, won't you?"

"I haven't really thought about it."

"Don't let what happened to Farthingham detract from your joy of the sea."

"I'm afraid losing Farthingham detracts from everything in my life."

"But it needn't."

"Spoken like a man who has never lost anyone he cares about."

"Spoken like a woman who doesn't appreciate what she has."

Spinning around she glared at him. "Why is everyone trying to convince me that Weddington is so wonderful?"

"It's not my place, I know. It's simply that Farthingham—"

"Would want me to be happy," she snapped. "I know. If he wanted that, then he shouldn't have goddamned died!"

Excusing herself, she left Freddie to stare after her while she made her way to the house. For the first time since the drowning, she was consumed with rage . . . for what Farthingham's carelessness and Weddington's determination to win at all costs had wrought.

How could she ever forgive either of them?

Chapter 21

Her wedding day. Kitty could hardly believe the day had arrived or that the hour was rapidly approaching when she would leave for the church. Vows were to be exchanged at the fashionable hour of two-thirty. Afterward, her parents would have an afternoon tea for the guests, hosted at this house. Then she and Weddington would leave, and she didn't want to think much about what would happen after that.

Bittersweet memories swamped her as Nancy prepared her hair, not for Farthingham as she'd often anticipated, but for Weddington. Richard. She supposed she should begin to think of him more personally. After all, her body knew him intimately.

When Nancy was finished only a few tendrils touched the nape of her neck, the remainder caught up in a very becoming fashion that Kitty thought would indeed look lovely when wreathed with orange blossoms and covered with the Honiton lace veil.

Then Nancy helped her slip on the wedding gown. "Oh, miss, it's so beautiful," Nancy said with reverence.

It was only then that Kitty peered into the mirror. The white satin-and-lace gown had been altered perfectly for her proportions. A long train of satin and lace beaded with tiny white pearls made her appear so elegant.

"Are you ready to see your father?" Nancy asked.

Looking past her reflection in the mirror to Nancy's, Kitty tried to force her thoughts away from thoughts of Farthingham. "My father?"

"Yes, miss. He informed me that I was to send for him once you were ready. He wanted a few minutes with you before he accompanied you to the coach that the duke sent."

Kitty pressed trembling fingers to her temple. "I can barely remember everything I'm supposed to do today."

"Not to worry, miss. The duke gave me a list of instructions to follow, and he spoke to us all last night regarding what to expect today. He wants nothing to go awry."

"Of course, he doesn't," she said distractedly. He didn't like for things to interfere with his goals.

She turned away from the mirror, but couldn't turn away from her doubts. "Yes, I'm ready to see my father."

When he walked into the room, she dearly wished she wasn't wearing clothing that constrained her movements, wished she could dash across the flooring and into his arms. He wore a dark blue morning coat, and although his hair was turning silver, she thought she'd never seen a more handsome man.

Unless it was the duke.

"My God, girl," he said quietly, "aren't you beautiful?"

Tears stung her eyes. "Oh, Papa, I love you so much."

"No more than I love you, sweetheart."

"I'm so sorry."

He touched her cheek. "For what?"

"For mistakes I made." She shook her head. "This isn't exactly how I dreamed my wedding would be."

"I don't know that it's going to be so awful, Kitty. Not many brides would have a day like I think this one is going to be."

"I know." Sniffing, she blinked back her tears. "It's simply that I always thought you would be giving me over to Nicky's keeping." She shook her head. "I guess I simply miss him."

"That's understandable, girl."

She licked her lips. "You've always been so good at judging men. What's your impression of Weddington? As a man. I mean if he'd never compromised my reputation"—which she truly couldn't put completely on his shoulders since she'd gone to the bathhouse and sought him out—"if you weren't angry with him about that, what would your opinion of him be?"

"I like him. And God knows I tried not to. I was ready to skin him alive that night that he came to the house, but I think he'll take good care of you."

"You think he's a good man, then?"

Her father grinned. "You think I'd give my consent to your marrying him if I thought he was a bad man?"

"No, I guess I'm simply nervous."

"That makes two of us. Giving one of my girls away"—he shook his head—"it's not going to be easy. Years ago, you were a gift to me and your mother. Unexpected, but definitely wanted. When your mother and I would have guests over, you'd sit on the stairs, peering into the parlor. I'd always find you there, and then we'd waltz with you standing on my feet, before I carried you back up to bed and tucked you in. I'd look down on you and think how lucky I was that you were my little girl. Now you're grown-up, but you're still my little girl. Today's not going to change that." He reached into his jacket and removed a velvet box. "Here's a little something to help you remember that."

"Oh, Papa, I'll always remember." Still, she took his gift, opened the box, and felt tears sting her eyes. "Oh, Papa, it's beautiful."

He removed the diamond necklace, slipped behind her, placed it around her neck, and clasped it in place.

She turned toward the mirror. "It's perfect." She turned back to him. "And thank you for loving me."

"Sweetheart, that's always been one of the greatest pleasures of me life. Loving you, Emily, and your mother." He held out his arm. "Now, let's go see if this duke of yours can appreciate you as much as I do."

If not for Farthingham's death, if not for her delicate condition, Kitty might have thought she were living in a fairy tale. Weddington had sent an open carriage for her. White, trimmed in gold, with four matching white horses, gorgeous creatures. In her lap rested the bouquet of orchids and white roses that had been delivered to her at the duke's request.

Sitting beside her, her mother held her hand while her father and Emily sat opposite. Emily was going to lead the way into the church by tossing orange blossoms in Kitty's path. Kitty would only have four bridesmaids, friends she'd made over the years, but not anyone to whom she was especially close. Perhaps she was more like Richard than she realized.

"Will you look at the stars tomorrow night, Kitty?" Emily asked. "We'll be on the yacht."

She smiled. "Of course, I will."

"Are you certain you don't mind us going to the Riviera for a while?" her mother asked.

"Of course not. I'll be very busy adjusting to married life. When you return, I'll have you over for dinner."

"We wouldn't leave if we thought you needed us, but often newly married couples can use some time alone."

Which was the very last thing she wanted with Weddington. Still, she smiled at mother. "I'll be fine."

People were lining the streets, and as the carriage drew nearer to the church, she saw crowds swarming about. She knew people had an interest in seeing the participants of a fashionable wedding dressed in their finery. She was suddenly very glad that the duchess had suggested—rather insisted—that she dress in splendor for the occasion.

She glanced up at the sky. It was gloriously sunny, and she hoped that Freddie was right, that Nicky was looking down on her and smiling. Although it hurt, she smiled in fond remembrance of him and prepared to step out of the carriage.

Her gaze swept the crowd. Blond hair. A familiar smile. Gone in the blink of an eye.

Her heart stopped.

She frantically searched the crowds again.

"Kitty?" Her mother said from behind her. "Everyone's waiting, dear. We need to get into the church."

"I thought I saw Nicky." She allowed the footman to help her down, and immediately walked with purpose toward the crowd in the churchyard, her gaze darting between people as she wended her way between the throng, ignoring the hands touching her, pulling on her.

"Kitty!" her mother called after her.

But she'd seen him. She was certain she'd seen him. His blond curling hair—

"Kitty!" her father demanded. "Let me through here."

She'd seen him. There!

She rushed forward—

Only it wasn't Nicky.

It was a man as tall as he was, as blond as he was . . . but the features were all wrong.

"Kitty." Her father took her arm and turned her. "Whatever is the matter with you?"

She looked up into her father's face, imploring him to understand. "I thought I saw Nicky."

"Sweetheart, he's dead."

She nodded. "I know. I just . . . he had his smile." She looked back to the man she'd thought was Nicky . . . only he didn't have Nicky's smile. How could she have mistaken him?

"We need to get into the church," her father said.

"Yes, of course." She glanced around once more, hesitant to leave, when the recognition had been so strong. She'd seen him, she was certain of it. But she couldn't have. She knew that. Her head knew that. Her heart . . . she'd been looking with her heart . . . at the sky, the crowds . . .

She repeated that litany as her father led her toward the church, parting the crowds like a man accustomed to having his way. Over and over she repeated that only her heart had seen him, but the repetition couldn't convince her that her eyes hadn't seen him as well.

The guilt was making her see someone who no longer existed, the guilt because she'd turned to Richard so soon. The guilt because she was getting married to another man.

As she walked up the steps, she smiled in reassurance at her mother who was standing by the door.

"Kitty, are you all right?" her mother asked.

"Yes, I'm fine. Mama, I could have sworn I saw Nicky."

"It was probably your heart seeing him."

"Yes, yes, I'm sure you're right."

But even as she said the words, she wasn't convinced that she believed them.

Standing before the altar, Richard would have patted himself on the back for exercising unbelievable restraint in not removing his watch from his waistcoat pocket and verifying the time. He was fairly certain that he'd been waiting for the arrival of his bride much longer than he should have been. And judging by the tittering of those in the pews and the many people who continually darted quick glances over their shoulders, he wasn't the only one thinking that it was taking an inordinate amount of time for Kitty to appear.

"She'll be here any moment now," Montague said quietly.

"I should hope so. We have a schedule to keep."

"Everyone will understand if you're a moment or two late in slicing the wedding cake."

Richard refrained from commenting. He'd asked Montague to stand as his best man, so Kitty might feel more at ease. He didn't know how he could do much more for the woman than he'd already done to earn her favor. Yet she still seemed reluctant to grant it. He hoped she hadn't changed her mind completely. They had a child to think of. His child. A possible heir.

He would have preferred to have turned her heart toward him before giving her a child, so he could be secure in her affections, and she could be certain of his. With or without a child, he would have married her.

But he was plagued with doubts that without a child, she might not have ever married him.

However, doubts could be erased with actions. He could woo her more ardently from that moment on. And it would be his pleasure to do so, and hopefully a bit easier. After all, he no longer had the shadow of Farthingham hanging over him.

The soft music that had been filtering from the organ suddenly hit a resounding chord, as the "Wedding March" began, and he finally had hope that the blasted waiting was about to end. He shifted slightly and watched as Emily littered the floor with orange blossoms, then four ladies whom Richard vaguely recognized strolled down the aisle. Friends of Kitty with very respected fathers no doubt. They probably moved about in his circle, but he'd never paid them any attention.

Exactly as now, he hardly noticed them at all, taking their places off to the side, because Kitty had come into view, and he thought his gaze had never before fallen on a woman as beautiful as she. He'd feared she'd arrive in black crepe simply to remind him that she'd not gotten over her loss of Farthingham. And here she was in pure white, strolling gracefully beneath the archway of orange blossoms. He could not have been more pleased that she'd gone to such lengths for this moment.

Then she was standing before him. He'd hoped by now that some of the color might have returned to her face, but even through the veil, he saw she was incredibly pale. She offered him a small semblance of a smile, and he gave her a brusque nod.

The bishop's voice rang out, "Who giveth this woman to be married to this man?"

"I do," David Robertson said as he placed Kitty's hand within the bishop's, and he, in turn, relinquished it into Richard's keeping.

He was surprised by how badly she was trembling, almost as badly as she'd been the morning he'd taken her from the sea or when he'd held her during the storm. Nervousness, of course, was the culprit. She had to stand before all these people, most of whom were probably strangers. His mother was too ensconced in Society. He doubted an empty seat remained anywhere.

The bishop asked Kitty to repeat her vows. Richard became distressingly aware of the silence that followed and the bishop striving to look as though he were not waiting for a response.

"Kitty," Richard urged quietly, barely moving his lips.

The bishop cleared his throat. Montague cleared his throat. Richard thought he heard one of the ladies standing beside Kitty clear her throat, so for good measure he cleared his.

"Kitty," Montague hissed. "Your vows. Repeat your vows. Farthingham—"

"I saw him," she whispered.

Everything within Richard stilled. "Pardon?"

Kitty flinched, and Richard cursed as his voice echoed around him. Her gaze wandered over his face, and he wondered if she saw the guilt there, suspected what he'd done.

"Yes, please," the bishop said. "You'll need to repeat your vows a bit more loudly so we might all hear them."

She looked to the bishop then. "I'm sorry. Will you say them again?"

The bishop repeated the vows, and Richard held his breath while she said them, every word. The remainder of the ceremony could not have happened quickly enough.

Richard repeated his vows. They knelt on the cushions and bowed their heads to receive the blessing. The bishop's voice echoed with the most beautiful words Richard had ever heard.

"Those whom God hath joined together let no man put asunder."

Richard breathed a sigh of relief. He'd done it! She was his! And now no one could take her from him. Not even Farthingham.

As Richard escorted her out of the church, it dawned on Kitty that she was married, and she wondered if she was obligated to uphold vows she could barely remember speaking. As they went down the steps, into the sunshine, she glanced around the waiting crowds who were cheering and applauding. So many people. Anyone could hide within them.

Richard helped her into the carriage, then joined her. Only this time, instead of sitting opposite her as he'd always done in the past, he sat beside her.

"What about my parents and Emily?" she asked.

"They'll follow in another carriage. Smile, Duchess, and wave. You're as close to being royalty as many of these people will ever see."

She did as he commanded, smiling and waving, remembering her promise never to let anyone know that by his side wasn't where she wanted to be. The carriage started off, and she couldn't have been more grateful. She would have a few hours at her parents' home, then she and Richard would return to his London residence. She didn't want to contemplate what would happen then.

"What did you mean in the church when you said you saw Farthingham?" he asked quietly, once the crowds had dissipated and no further need for smiling or waving existed.

Suddenly feeling silly, she shook her head. "I thought I saw him."

"Where?"

"In the crowds, outside the church. There were so many people. I looked around as I was getting ready to get out of the carriage, and I thought I saw him."

"You do realize that you can't have seen him."

"I know. I simply thought . . . what if he survived?"

"He didn't."

"How can you be so sure?"

"I was there."

She studied his face. "Did you actually see him drown?"

He averted his eyes, seeming to take interest in the shops they passed. "Kitty, he's gone." He turned his attention back to her. "If he were alive, if you'd truly seen him in front of the church, do you not think that he would have rushed inside and put a halt to the ceremony? Do you not think that he would have claimed you for himself?"

"Yes, yes, of course, you're right." She lowered her gaze to the ring he'd placed on her finger during the ceremony. Another perfect fit, as though it had been designed specifically for her. "Unless he thought we betrayed him."

He released a deep sigh that was rife with frustration. "And why would he think that?"

"You took him sailing when the sky promised a storm—"

"It was his idea to take the boat out."

"Was it?" she asked.

"Yes."

"But if he survived, if he were badly wounded and it took him a while to recover, and when he did, he saw our announcement so soon after his supposed drowning—"

He cut her off by cupping her cheek with his gloved hand and pressing his thumb against her lips. "I think you've been reading too many of Montague's plays."

She smiled at that, actually truly smiled. She released a tiny laugh. "You're right. You're so right. That was one of Freddie's plays. I remember now. What was it called?"

"*A Sea Change.*"

"That's right. Have you read it?"

"Yes."

"A woman's lover tried to drown her husband—"

"But the husband survived and killed the lover," he finished quickly. "I was not overly impressed with it."

"I thought it was rather good."

"Perhaps it is, if it has you seeing ghosts."

"You're right. I actually read some of it last night when I couldn't sleep. It must have been on my mind. I found the man I thought was Nicky, but he didn't look anything like him when I got near enough to see him clearly."

"I'm glad that matter's settled satisfactorily. Now tell me why you couldn't sleep? Anticipation of the day?"

"More like dread." She regretted the words as soon as she'd spoken them. "I apologize."

"No need. I prefer complete honesty when it is only you and I. I have a feeling there will be enough playacting the remainder of the time. Besides, I dreaded it as well."

"Why?"

"I feared you'd change your mind. That I would stand there like a fool, waiting for a woman who had no intention of arriving."

She found that she didn't much like the idea of him being a fool. "How long would you have waited?"

"Until I was old and gray." He cupped her face once again and lowered his mouth to hers for only a heartbeat as the carriage drew to a halt. "We're here. This shall no doubt be the most unpleasant part of the afternoon, pretending for a time that you're in love with me."

His words hit her hard. He'd done all he could to make this day as pleasant as possible, and she was grateful. She placed her hand on his arm. "I won't be pretending that I'm honored to be your wife."

He gave her a warm smile. "Thank you for that."

She could do little more than return his smile and wonder if perhaps the pretense was actually that she *didn't* love him.

Chapter 22

It was dark by the time they left the afternoon tea her parents had arranged at their home. This time Richard had a closed coach waiting to whisk them away. Kitty leaned out the window, waving good-bye until she could no longer see her family. Then she settled back into the coach, so tired she barely had the strength to notice that Richard sat beside her.

"Tired?" he asked quietly.

She laughed wearily. "Exhausted."

"We'll be home soon."

She squinted through the darkness at him. "Will your mother and Lady Anne be joining us there?"

"No. They've taken up residence at the dower house."

She nodded, not certain what else she should do. The Dowager Duchess had told her that she would move into the other residence. Kitty had hoped it wouldn't be immediately, but a day or two after the wedding, after she'd grown accustomed to her new status. Although she feared that she might never become accustomed to it.

"It only now occurred to me that I've seen very little of your London residence."

He took her hand, his thumb circling the rings on her finger. Rings he'd placed there. "Everything happened quite quickly for us, but I shall make you happy."

"I'll try to do the same for you."

"I ask no more than that."

The coach came to a halt before a grand house, and Kitty's first impression of her new home was that she hoped the staff was efficient. The coach door was immediately opened, and a gloved hand appeared inside the doorway. She slipped her hand into the waiting footman's and stepped out of the coach. She didn't know why she was suddenly more nervous than she'd been all day, why the reality of all that had transpired was coming home to roost.

"Are you ready?" Richard asked.

Taking a deep breath, she placed her hand on his waiting arm. They walked up the sweeping steps. Another footman opened the massive door, and Kitty found herself halfway hoping that she'd find Lady Anne waiting inside as she had the night they'd gone to the opera.

But the only one waiting was the butler. "I've called for the servants, Your Grace," he said immediately.

"Thank you, Watkins," Richard said.

The butler turned and as if by magic, servants began appearing, of all ages, shapes, and sizes. A considerable number, many more than her parents had ever used. My goodness, she'd been taught to manage a large household, but she thought it highly unlikely she'd remember everyone's name—

"You need not concern yourself with remembering everyone's name," Richard said.

She peered up at him. "You must have been reading my mind."

"Your eyes seemed to be growing as they came out. Mother and Anne have taken their lady's maids with them. Yours should be arriving here at any moment with her things."

She felt as though her eyes really widened then. "You mean Nancy?"

"If that's her name. I arranged her transfer to my household staff as part of the settlement. I thought you might be more comfortable if I weren't the only person you knew in the house."

"Thank you."

"You're most welcome. Allow me to introduce you to those who will be of the most service to you. They in turn will introduce the others to you over time as needed."

"I'm acquainted with how it all works. Americans aren't totally barbaric."

He grinned. "That surprises me, since your wildness was the very reason I married you."

She looked away, embarrassed to remember the reason he had married her, a result of the night when she'd behaved as anything except a lady.

"Duchess, may I present Watkins. He has been in our employ for many years."

"Watkins," she said with as much dignity as she could muster.

"Your Grace." He had a kind smile.

"Our cook, Mrs. Butler," Richard said.

"Mrs. Butler." Mrs. Butler looked as though she sampled generously of her own cooking, which Kitty took as a good sign. "I look forward to going over menus with you in the morning."

Mrs. Butler curtsied. "Thank you, Your Grace."

"The head housekeeper, Rose."

Rose's cheeks blushed to the color of her name. Kitty didn't think the woman seemed old enough to be in charge.

"Rose."

"Your Grace." She curtsied.

"It appears you manage an excellent household."

The woman's cheeks burned into a reddish hue. "Thank you, madam."

"You're most welcome."

Richard then introduced her to the remainder of the staff with little more than a grand sweeping of his hand, after which a round of curtsies, bows, and "Your Graces" followed.

"I look forward to getting to know each of you," Kitty said.

"All right now, back to your duties," Watkins ordered, and everyone scurried away as though they'd never been there.

"Was the package delivered?" Richard asked.

"Yes, sir. I had it readied as per your instructions and placed it in your library. I assigned the underfootman the task of keeping watch over it."

"Thank you, Watkins. My duchess and I will retire to the library for a while. Send word when her lady's maid has arrived and settled in."

"Yes, sir. Will there be anything else?"

"No, thank you."

Richard turned to her and extended his arm. "I thought we might relax in the library for a bit."

Now he asked, after already indicating that they'd do exactly that. "By all means, lead the way."

He escorted her past several rooms, pointed out various items, and explained their history in relation to his family. She was too tired to take notice of much of what he said. He led her into the library with its walls and walls of books, and the musty smell that she so loved next to the scent of the sea.

"Hello, Henry," Richard said.

"Evenin', Your Grace."

"Kitty, this is Henry. He serves as underfootman and keeps all the boots and shoes polished to a shine."

"Hello, Henry," she said, charmed by the smile that the boy bestowed on her. She didn't think he could have been much older than twelve. "I must confess that I've always been quite impressed with the shine on the duke's shoes. I can almost see my face in them when I glance down."

The boy's smile brightened, and he puffed out his chest. "That's 'cuz I've got good spit, and I ain't stingy with it."

Striving to bite back her laughter, she darted a look at Richard and saw him fighting to hold back his own. She thought this might have been the most relaxed moment of the evening. "That's very commendable, Henry."

"Thank you, Your Grace."

Kitty became aware of a whining, a thumping.

"Have you been keeping careful watch over my wife's gift?" Richard asked.

"Yes, sir. Been keeping it under the desk so's it wouldn't be seen 'til you was ready."

"I suppose now is as good a time as any." He indicated a chair. "If you'll sit, we'll retrieve your gift."

She hardly knew what to say. "You don't need to give me—"

"I want to."

She took a seat, watched the eagerness with which he and the boy went round behind the desk. Her husband was almost a child himself. He lifted a box that didn't have a lid. The thumping and whining increased, and her stomach began to knot. She'd never had a fondness for dogs, not since she was a child and one had snapped in her face. Cats. She loved cats. Kittens. She adored kittens. *Please, don't give me a dog.*

But he did. With expectation clearly written on his face, he set the box before her and crouched beside it. Leaning over slightly, she peered into the box.

A dog. A tiny dog. A puppy she supposed. With a reddish brown coat and a huge green ribbon tied around its neck.

"It's a spaniel," he told her.

"Yes, I can see that."

"I thought it might make you less lonely. I spend a good deal of time dealing with business interests and the estates. I haven't the time to play as . . ." His voice trailed off.

"As Farthingham did."

"Yes."

"You can hold 'er," Henry said, as he reached into the box, lifted the dog out—

"No, no," Kitty said, jumping to her feet, skirting quickly around the box.

Both man and boy stared at her as though she were insane.

"I'm sorry, I'm sorry. I'm simply not fond of dogs."

Henry looked at her as though she'd kicked the puppy. "How can you not like dogs?"

"Henry," Richard chastised sternly, "it's not your place to question the duchess."

"Sorry," Henry said, looking truly contrite.

"Why don't you let the dog sleep with you tonight?" Richard suggested.

"You gonna keep 'er, sir?"

"Of course. I like dogs. We'll dispense with the ribbon, though, I think."

Henry grinned at that. "She'll be right glad, sir."

"I'm sure she will. Off with you now."

Cradling the dog as though she were a baby, the boy walked out of the room.

"I really am sorry," she told Richard.

"As am I. Your mother mentioned your fondness for cats. Unfortunately, I failed to take into account that you might not like dogs. And I should have taken it into account considering that I'm not overly fond of cats. But I shall see about getting you some."

"No, Richard, I don't need cats. I haven't played with them in a long while, and in a few months I'll be too busy to be lonely."

"Yes, of course you will. Would you like me to pour you some wine? I have a good vintage."

"No, I'm really too tired."

"It has been a long day." He looked past her. "Yes, Watkins?"

"The duchess's lady's maid has arrived, Your Grace. I sent her on up to Her Grace's bedchamber."

"Thank you, Watkins."

Watkins quickly retreated, and Richard extended his arm toward her. "I shall escort you to your chambers."

"There's really no need."

"As you wish."

"Good night then." Grateful for his acquiescence, looking forward to some time alone, she rushed toward the door and suddenly stopped.

"Discovered there was a need, did you?" he asked, and she could have sworn she heard humor laced through his voice.

Without turning around, feeling like a complete idiot, she merely nodded. He came up beside her and extended his arm. She peered up at him and found him smiling kindly. "I'm accustomed to independence," she stated.

"I've no wish to deprive you of it."

"But all the legalities of marriage do deprive a woman of her freedom."

"They shan't within our marriage."

He walked out of the library and along a hallway until they reached the hallway entrance. He turned toward the stairs that curved up toward the next floor and led her up them. "If you have such an unfavorable view of marriage, why did you consent to marry Farthingham?"

"I liked him."

He raised a brow. "Liked. I thought you loved him."

"I did. But I also liked him."

"You *did*? So you no longer love him?"

She suddenly felt trapped. "I still do. Yes. I always will."

"I don't wish for him to be between us tonight." It was a softly purred command issued as he stopped beside a door.

"I can't simply exorcise him from my heart as though he never existed."

"Then you leave me no choice except to exorcise him for you."

His mouth came down on hers with fierce determination. All the civilized rituals and traditions of the day were flung to perdition, as though they were merely window dressing designed to disguise the true nature of what lay within. Some corner of her mind urged her to resist the invasion of his tongue, his taste, his moist heat. Not to welcome the desire that curled through her as she met his tongue and wrapped her arms around him, pressing herself against him.

With his hands still gloved, he plowed his fingers through her neatly coiffed hair, bracketing her head, angling her mouth, settling his more solidly into place. She was vaguely aware of pins escaping her hair and clinking on to the floor, more aware of his harsh breathing, the intensifying of his kiss as though he sought to consume her.

Her hair tumbled around her shoulders, along her back, as his guttural groan of triumph echoed along the hallway. He was winning this match so easily, conquering, and achieving exactly what he'd claimed he would.

He tore his mouth from hers. Opening her eyes, she saw the

barely leashed desire in his. "I shall join you shortly to say good night."

Still striving to regain her wits, she merely nodded. He spun on his heel and headed back down the stairs.

She opened the door and strolled into the bedchamber. Nancy came up out of the chair in which she'd been sitting.

"Ah, Your Grace. Are you ready for me to help prepare you for your wedding night?"

Perhaps it was her unfamiliar surroundings, the sight of Nancy—a warm smile on her familiar face, the realization that it would take little for Richard to carry through on his promise to exorcise Nicky from her heart, or the fact that she understood he intended to return and do a great deal more than say good night. Or perhaps it was simply the little puppy with the big almond eyes that she'd been unable to welcome into her arms. Or the long day, the longer night to come.

Whatever the reason, she burst into tears.

Within the library, Richard poured himself a generous amount of bourbon and finished half of it before he took his chair in front of the fireplace where no fire burned, no heat emanated. He should have taken her to Drummond Manor, where they would have had access to the bathing house and the sea. He shouldn't have given her a dog. He should have found her a cat, even though he held no affection for the furry little beasts.

Dogs were loyal to their master or mistress. As far as he could determine, cats were only loyal to themselves.

He took another long swallow, released a deep sigh, dropped his head back against the chair, and closed his eyes. The problem wasn't the dog. It was Farthingham. The manner in which she held on to his memory. Blast it all. The man had been with them at the church, while they were exchanging vows.

By God, he'd not have the man in his bed.

He released another sigh.

Loyalty and love.

He feared he might one day have to choose one over the over. And what then? Could he live with betrayal on his conscience?

Opening his eyes, he downed the remainder of his bourbon. Betraying either loyalty or love would be a form of cheating. He was not a man who cheated.

He would exorcise Farthingham from her heart. He would do so with his skills and his devotion, not by being disloyal to Farthingham.

She need never know the truth about Farthingham or his death. The truth would accomplish nothing, except to bruise her heart.

And he loved her too much to risk that outcome, would do anything to ensure her happiness. He could only hope that in time, she would come to love him. And to that end, he would apply himself diligently.

He rose from the chair. She was preparing herself for him. It was time he went about preparing himself. He would sway her heart, and he would do it without revealing Farthingham's secrets.

Chapter 23

Kitty awoke to a featherlike touch along her chin that trailed up to circle her ear, followed by a gentle nibbling of her lobe and warm breath wafting over her neck. She opened her eyes. It was still night. The room was dimly lit by the gaslight she'd left on so she wouldn't fall asleep while waiting for her husband. Seemingly she had done so anyway.

Raised up on an elbow, he was stretched out alongside her, enticing her out of lethargy with slow, light caresses. He smiled down on her, a smile of amusement and contentment. Although she was certain he wouldn't appreciate her description, she thought it was a very sweet smile.

"I'm sorry," she said.

"For what?"

"For falling asleep while I was waiting for you."

"Kitty, you must learn to stop apologizing to me. There is very little you would do that would require an apology to me." With his finger, he outlined her face. "You cannot imagine how often I've thought about having you in my bed."

She swallowed hard, her breath backing up in her lungs, as his finger journeyed along her throat and down to the first button of her nightgown. With little more than a quick flick, the button was free of its constraint, and he moved on to the next one, the next one, the next one . . . his gaze never straying from the slight parting of the material.

And with each button's release, it seemed her inhibitions escaped the restraints she'd placed on them. Although the blankets were bunched at his waist, and she had no memory of his slipping in beside her, she knew he wore no clothing. Her mouth grew dry with the thought of where all this was leading and how desperately she sought the journey.

With the last button freed, he slid his heated gaze up to hers for a mere heartbeat before turning his attention back to the task at hand. He snagged the corner of the opening and slowly peeled back the cloth, one side, then the other, his breathing growing harsher. She thought perhaps she should have felt a need to cover herself, yet she'd been revealed to him before, and she was mesmerized by the reverence with which he gazed on her, as though he'd never seen anything quite as humbling.

He cradled one breast, his eyes fluttered closed, long lashes resting on his cheeks, and he lowered his head.

The first gentle tug almost had her coming off the bed for the sensations he sent surging through her, as though they'd been previously corralled and suddenly unleashed. A tiny whimper escaped as she rolled toward him and threaded her fingers through his hair. Now that she was married, she'd expected the fire to abate, had thought marriage would somehow calm the storm that always seemed to swirl around her whenever he touched her, whenever he kissed her.

But there was no abatement. Instead it seemed as though with the exchange of vows, her body welcomed the pleasures that marriage would bring. And she could not deny that the pleasures were many, already mounting, spiraling, climbing to new heights as his breathing grew harsher and he greedily kissed her breasts, nipples, the valley between, her collarbone, her throat, her neck . . . her.

The kiss was deep, powerful, hungry. Lips locked as though forever joined, body to soul, soul to heart. As though this night, their bodies would exchange vows as permanent as those they'd spoken earlier.

Without unlatching his mouth, he shifted and slid his arms beneath her, around her, pulling them both up into a sitting position. His mouth sojourned along her throat while his hands pulled her gown off her shoulders until it pooled around her hips. He kissed the top of her shoulder, the back of her shoulder, the curve at the side of her neck, a breast, a rib, her stomach, her hip. Working the gown past her hips, thighs, calves, feet. He tossed it aside and skimmed his hands up the length of her legs and back down. Then his mouth was following the paths his hands had forged, first one side, then the other.

She watched in amazement as the muscles in his back bunched and tightened with his movements. She skimmed her hands over the firmness of his back, desperate to give, afraid to give, not certain what was acceptable and what was wanton.

How did a lady not behave as a whore when she desired all that he was offering?

He returned his mouth to hers, and in the process eased her back down on the bed until her head touched the pillow. She could hardly think from the sensations building within her. Flesh to flesh, hip to hip, chest to breasts. His hands and lips roamed over her entire body, from forehead to toes, from heel to nape, turning her for easier access for each spot he wished to torment.

And it was torment. Sweet, sweet torment. Hot and blissful. Decadent and pure. How could it be the best and worst of all things? How did he manage to make her yearn for his every touch?

Then he was nestled between her thighs, easing himself inside her, withdrawing only to return with a more forceful push, again and again until her body drew him all in and closed tightly around him.

Raising himself over her, he began to rock against her, each movement increasing the pleasure, increasing the pressure and the tension until she was writhing beneath him and screaming out for release.

Glorious release that arrived with a myriad of colorful stars behind her lowered eyelids, and the arching of her back, and a final cry that was almost drowned out by his deep groan of satisfaction as he drove into her one last time.

Panting and with weary limbs that she thought she might never again move, she lay beneath him, staring at his bent head, the dampness on his shoulders, aware of the trembling in his arms as he fought to keep his weight off her, and his short gasps that slowly began to lengthen.

He eased off her, barely distancing himself enough so that he didn't squash her before he dropped onto his stomach beside her, his heavy arm angled across her stomach, his fingers curled possessively over her hip.

He pressed a kiss to her shoulder, and there his mouth remained. Only after she recognized that his breathing had evened out, did she realize that he'd fallen asleep.

She stared at the length of him sprawled beside her, the manner in which the dew, caught by the lamplight, glistened over his back and buttocks, much as the sea and sun had that first morning she'd spotted him. She didn't like admitting that she still considered him magnificent. That experiencing the full measure of his power satisfied her even as it left her clamoring for more.

He looked near to death. If his warm breath wasn't skimming along her arm, she might have thought he was indeed dead. She wondered if she could lure him out of his lethargy as he'd lured her. And even as the thought took hold, she shoved it away.

A lady shouldn't be wanton, screaming like a savage. Here she was contemplating waking him when she had no idea how she'd face him once he was awake.

Richard awoke to the musky scent of sex filling his nostrils, Kitty's screams still echoing in his ears, and his body so sated that he thought he might never again move. And he might have followed his first inclination had he not gradually come to realize that no other warmth existed beyond his. He was alone in the bed.

His heart thundering, he bolted upright and twisted around. His heart quieted as he caught sight of Kitty's profile. She sat curled, her feet tucked beneath her, in one of two chairs positioned before the fireplace. She was again wearing her nightgown. A pity that. Although in retrospect, he'd enjoyed removing it the first time. He'd enjoy removing it the second, although he thought he might move with a bit more speed the next go-round.

He snatched up his silken robe from the foot of the bed where he'd discarded it earlier, before he'd slipped beneath the covers to be with her. He'd watched her for long moments before he'd finally undertaken the joyous task of waking her.

As he belted his robe, he walked toward her, his bare feet making no sound over the thick carpets. If she'd heard him get out of bed or was aware of his approach, she gave no indication. As he neared, he saw the last thing he'd expected, the very last thing he'd wanted to see: tears dampening her cheeks. Based on her heartbreakingly sad expression, he knew they weren't tears of joy or jubilation, but rather disappointment, perhaps regret.

With a despairing heart and the realization that perhaps he'd been arrogant to believe he could bring her happiness, he knelt before her. "Kitty?"

Without looking at him, she shook her head. "You can't fathom how much I didn't want this."

He thought his heart might shrivel into nothing. "So you've said before."

With imploring eyes flooding with fresh tears, she looked at him and rasped, "I'm exactly like my mother, and I tried so hard not to be."

She pressed a hand to her mouth, muffling her sob. Richard was having another of those moments where he felt densely slow. "Why

ever would you not want to be like her? Your mother is the most gracious, elegant—"

"No." She shook her head sadly. "Madeline Robertson is the
mother of my heart. Jessye Bainbridge is the mother of my body, and
my body"—she swallowed hard and wiped the sleeve of her nightgown beneath her nose—"my body cries out to be like hers: common
and coarse. A saloonkeeper's daughter, she relished a man's touch,
gave birth to me out of wedlock, and passed me off to the first couple
who came within sight of her. And here I am no different. When this
child is born, all of England will know we fornicated without benefit
of marriage."

"You're adopted?" It was a silly thing to take note of, to respond
to, considering all she'd revealed.

She nodded. "A bastard. Illegitimate. People of that ilk aren't well
thought of over here, are they?"

"They can't inherit," he said inanely as though that were important when he was really striving to wrap his mind around the impli-
cations that he'd taken as his wife a woman of tainted bloodlines. He
could trace his heritage back generations, recorded by births, deaths,
and yes, marriage licenses. "Did Farthingham know?"

She laughed almost hysterically and shook her head. "Of course
not. Why would I reveal my shame to him, to anyone? I'm only
telling you because the evidence of my common roots is apparent
every time you touch me. I writhe and scream as though I'm an uncivilized barbarian. My behavior is disgusting. I don't know how you
tolerate me."

He sat back on his heels, so stunned by her comment that he was
speechless. If he opened his mouth at all, he feared he might laugh.
She was sitting, curled in the chair, her arms held tightly against her,
tears on her face because she thought he found her reaction to his
touch disgusting? When in fact he relished every aspect of it.

"Kitty—" A burst of laughter escaped, and he clamped his
mouth shut.

"It's not funny."

He cleared his throat, swallowed, and cleared his throat again. "I
realize that." Another sound clearing of his throat. "Kitty, I tolerate it
because I love you, and besides—"

"No." She shook her head. "No one should have to tolerate dealing with that sort of behavior. Regardless of any affection they might
hold for that person. I've been thinking that if you were to gag me
and tie me to the bedposts, then I wouldn't thrash about, and I'd be
unable to scream."

He fought a valiant fight, but in the end the laughter won, a resounding rumble that echoed around them.

She slapped his shoulder. "Stop laughing!"

But he only laughed harder. "Oh, dear Lord, you're deadly serious."

"Yes!" She launched out of the chair and began hitting his shoulders. "Stop it! Stop it!"

He grabbed her flailing hands, twisted her about as gently as possible, always mindful of her delicate condition, until she was on her back, pinned beneath his weight, her arms held in place above her head, one of his hands wrapped around both her wrists. They breathed in tandem, each harsh breath causing her breasts and his chest to touch.

"I'm sorry, Kitty. I know I shouldn't have laughed. Your circumstance isn't funny, and I need"—he cleared his throat and swallowed back the laughter that wanted freedom—"to treat this matter with the seriousness it deserves." With his thumb, he gathered the tears that rolled along her cheeks. "That night in Farthingham's garden, you said that I terrified you. Was it because of the way you felt when I touched you?"

She nodded, then shook her head as more tears surfaced. "Not only that. You have but to look at me . . . or be in the same room with me." She shook her head more vigorously. "No, not even that. When I'm alone in my room, I think of you constantly. As you were that first morning."

Wasn't that interesting?

He trailed his finger along her jaw.

"Don't do that!" she ordered.

"Does it make you want to scream?"

"Yes!"

"Farthingham never made you want to scream, did he?"

"Of course not. Nicky was safe. He was always safe."

Speaking of barbarism, he suddenly felt like some tribal lord who'd gained a kingdom. And for the first time since the afternoon of the storm, he felt a lifting of the oppressive guilt. He'd been right all along. She did belong to him. She might not like it, she might not want to admit it, but her body knew what her heart refused to acknowledge.

"I'm not going to gag you, Kitty," he said quietly, before pressing a kiss against the sensitive spot beneath her ear. He heard her sharp intake of breath. "And I'm not going to bind you." He moved his mouth to the other side and kissed her there. Another gasp. "Do you know why?"

She shook her head.

He lifted his own and looked down on her. She'd turned her face to the side, but he could still see that she was miserable. "Look at me, Kitty."

"No."

"Kitty."

She finally looked back at him. He released his hold on her wrists, framed her face with his hands, and caressed her cheeks with his fingertips. "I'm not going to do anything that you've asked, because I so enjoy hearing you scream."

"But it's barbaric."

"Ah, yes. So it is." He kissed her chin. "Sometime I want you to tell me all the things you thought when you were alone in your room."

"No."

"Yes. Meanwhile I intend to make you scream again."

He lowered his head. She grabbed his hair and jerked his head back up. "Please don't. It's embarrassing."

"There's no shame in it. Do you have any idea how many men go through their lives with docile wives who lie beneath them out of duty and think about the latest dress patterns while their husbands are getting about their business?"

Her eyes suddenly widened. "Dress patterns. I could think about dress patterns as a distraction. Or better yet, I could recite Shakespeare within my mind. I memorized *Romeo and Juliet* when I was younger. I'll have to refresh my memory. Do you have an edition in your library?"

"Yes, but I'm not going to lend it to you. I don't want you distracted. I want you screaming and writhing and bursting with pleasure."

"Why?"

"Because I want you to enjoy having me in your bed as much as I enjoy being there."

"You don't scream."

"I grunt." A kiss on her lips. "Groan." A kiss on her throat. "Moan."

"What's it feel like for you?"

He grinned at her. "Glorious. My body burns, stretches, tightens, reaches for deliverance."

"You fell asleep afterward," she said as though to chastise him.

His grin grew. "Yes. That's how you know it's been very, very good. When I can't move if my life depended on it."

She licked her lips. "But what I feel seems so wicked."

"Nothing wrong with wicked, my darling."

"I always thought there was something wrong with it."

He began to loosen her buttons. "Well, there isn't. Most men have mistresses because they need a bit of wickedness now and then, and their wives are too busy thinking about dress patterns or reciting Shakespeare. How fortunate I am that all my needs will be met by my wife. I shall never have to stray." He lifted his gaze and held hers. "And I shall work diligently to ensure that you never feel a need to stray either."

He lowered his mouth to hers, and her fingers pressed against his scalp. The fire between them blazed as though the embers of their desire had been in need of only the tiniest spark to set it alight. He could take her here on the floor, in the chair, on the way to the bed. Drawing back, he saw the doubts cloud her eyes. He still couldn't believe the irony in that the very thing that drew them together was what had threatened to keep them apart. "Let's go back to bed."

"To sleep?"

He grinned. "To scream. Then to sleep." He stood and helped her to her feet. Holding her hand, he walked her to the bed.

"Remove your clothing," he ordered as he went about removing his much more quickly. He sat on the bed and basked in the sight of her nightgown rippling along the length of her body to the floor.

"Aren't you going to get into bed?" she asked.

"Not this time. Come sit on my lap."

"That sounds indecent."

"Only if you don't want to, and I force you. But I'll never force you, Kitty. I will, however, urge you to try."

She gnawed on her lip and furrowed her brow before moving to stand before him. Reaching out, he grabbed her hips and urged her forward. "Come on, straddle my lap, knees on the bed."

She did as he bid, her stomach to his chest, her breasts in his face.

"Mmm, lovely," he purred, before taking a pink nipple into his mouth.

She moaned, her fingers dug into his shoulders, and her head dropped back. He slid his hand between her thighs, testing her readiness. She was hot and moist. He guided her down until she enveloped him completely in her heavenly heat. He could only hope that it didn't take her long to scream because he was near to screaming himself.

"You see?" he asked. "Now I have access to all of you. Your back, your stomach, your breasts—which by the way, I greatly adore."

He thought if the light were brighter that he might see her blushing. With one hand cupped at the back of her head, he guided her mouth down to his. He gloried in her sweet sigh of capitulation. He cupped her bottom and began guiding her through the movements, and when she caught the rhythm, he turned his attention to other pleasures: skimming his fingers along her spine, her back, her sides, her stomach. Up and over. Down and around while her hands were just as frantically touching every aspect of him that she could reach. As he'd pointed out only moments before, he groaned, grunted, moaned, tensed . . .

She began to release tiny mewling sounds that rose in crescendo as her body tightened around his, and she began to piston faster and faster and faster. She cried out, and he held her tightly in place, pumping his seed into her, as his own release came swift and hard. He wrapped his arms more firmly around her and lowered himself to the bed, bringing her with him until her limp body was sprawled over his.

Right before he drifted off to sleep, it occurred to him that if they continued making love with this intensity that he'd live a very short life, but it would certainly be a glorious one.

Chapter 24

Kitty awoke to find a bit of sunshine peering through a parting in the draperies, her husband's arm across her stomach, his hand cradling her breast. He'd not drawn the draperies around the bed closed, and so she was able to see him a little clearer in the morning light.

Her husband. Gingerly she skimmed her fingers over his hair—which was in dire need of a brushing. Then she touched her palm to his bristly cheek. Lethargically he opened his eyes, and a slow smile eased over his face.

"How are you this morning, Duchess?"

"Nauseous."

His smile instantly disappeared and his brow furrowed. "You're not feeling well?"

"I usually don't in the mornings these days."

His gaze dipped down her stomach. "Ah." He lifted his eyes to hers. "What do you need?"

"Some tea and toast."

Rolling slightly, he reached up and tugged the bellpull. She made a motion to get out of bed and found his arm snaking around her and bringing her back down to the bed.

"Where do you think you're going?" he asked.

"To get dressed."

"Not yet."

There was a sharp rap on the door, and Kitty brought the blankets up to her chin. The door opened, and Nancy peered into the room. "You called for me, Your Grace?"

"Yes," Richard said. "Please bring up some tea and toast for Her Grace."

"Yes, sir."

The door closed.

"I'm not ill," Kitty told him. "I don't need to stay abed."

He gave her a devilish grin. "Oh, you need to stay abed. I'm not yet finished with you, Duchess."

"It's daylight," she whispered harshly.

"The better to see you with, my darling."

She knew her eyes had widened considerably, and she snuggled down into the bed. "You can't be serious."

He wiggled his eyebrows.

"During the day?" she asked.

"Why not?"

"You're insatiable."

Grinning, he trailed his finger along her arm. "Let's hope, shall we?"

Laughing lightly, Kitty watched him. "Is this all you think about?"

He nodded. "A good bit of the time, yes. Don't you?"

She turned her head toward the window. "How can you be so comfortable with it?"

"How can you not?"

She looked back at him. His eyes held compassion and understanding.

"I shall keep you here until you are comfortable with it," he said quietly.

"And if I never am?"

"Then I shall die well sated." He lowered his head and kissed her bare shoulder. "What do you require of me to become at ease with passion?"

"Practice, I suppose."

His head came up and grinned. "You're more comfortable with it now?"

"More so than I was last night. I feel so silly. All the things I worried over—"

"Only makes me adore you that much more."

A brisk knock on the door, and Nancy walked in with a bed tray. Richard helped Kitty sit up, placing pillows behind her back and ensuring that she was modestly covered with the blankets. Nancy set the tray over her lap. "Thank you, Nancy."

"You're welcome, Your Grace. I've had a tray brought up for His Grace as well."

Nancy retrieved it from someone standing in the hallway. Richard's tray held almost ten times as much food as Kitty's. As soon as Nancy left, they both began to eat.

"How long does your nausea last?" Richard asked.

Sipping her tea, Kitty was grateful for the way it seemed to calm her stomach. "It comes and goes throughout the morning. I've found dry toast and plain crackers help."

"Do you suffer in other ways?"

"I wouldn't call it suffering." She took a small bite of toast, watching as he ate an omelet.

He suddenly stopped. "Do the aromas from my tray bother you?" he asked.

"No."

"Good. I've never been around a woman with child. What other discomforts do you have?"

"A little soreness," she admitted.

He furrowed his brow deeply, his chewing slowed. "Where?"

She wiggled her finger over her chest.

"Your breasts?"

She rolled her eyes. "How can you simply blurt it out?"

He shook his head. "Before this day is done, I intend to make you comfortable with your body and mine."

She nearly choked on her toast. "I am comfortable with your body," she said indignantly.

"No, you are comfortable with my back and shoulders, occasionally my buttocks, but there is more to me than that."

She stared at him, fighting to hold his gaze. "You don't mean . . ."

He arched a brow and nodded.

She took another bite of toast. "What am I supposed to do with it?"

"Touch it, would be nice. Wrap your fingers around it would be better. Stroke it, caress it. Kiss it."

She stopped chewing and everything within her stilled. "Kiss?" She shook her head. "I would never"—she shook her head again— "No. I can't even imagine it."

"Not even during the time when you were alone in your room?"

"Of course not!"

"What did you think about?"

"Certainly not that." Kissing . . . it. How utterly . . . intriguing. She cursed him for planting the notion in her mind.

No, she would never do it. Never.

Still, she couldn't stop thinking about it.

Richard was in heaven. He was in hell.

Following breakfast, he'd made love to his wife once more. Then he'd gone downstairs to the bathing room and bathed. While he'd been soaking in the hot water, a marvelous idea had come to him—how best to make her comfortable with their lovemaking.

Once she was lost in the midst of their passion, she seemed quite comfortable with it. Although he enjoyed seducing her, he certainly wouldn't mind if she occasionally instigated their lovemaking.

So in an attempt to secure that end, he was now stretched out on the bed, his hands behind his head, his fingers pressing into his skull, while he'd given her leave to explore his body.

He'd promised to keep his eyes closed and his hands off her. While she had permission to touch him wherever she wanted, however she wanted.

And he was quickly discovering that his little wife was skilled at torture. She'd run her hands over his chest, his stomach, his thighs. She'd trailed her mouth over his chest, his stomach, his thighs.

With every caress, she'd deliberately avoided touching the one part of him that was standing at attention, begging to be touched. Every time her hands got near enough that he thought she would finally offer him relief, she retreated.

"This doesn't tickle?" she asked, her fingers fluttering over his quivering stomach.

"No," he ground out through clenched teeth.

She pressed her mouth against his chest, took his hardened nipple between her teeth and tugged gently. He groaned low.

She released her hold. "When you groan, you like what I'm doing?"

"Yes."

"You don't sound as though you like it."

"I do. Very much."

Her mouth and hands roamed over him with exquisite slowness. Lower. Lower. His breathing became harsh with anticipation.

Then she was gone and her lips were near his ear. "You sound as though you're in pain."

"I am in agony."

He felt a featherlike touch along the length of his shaft, and he thought he may very well come up off the bed. She wrapped her hand around him, and a shudder traveled through his body, and a groan rumbled up through his chest.

He rolled her onto her back, plunged himself into her, and welcomed immediate release.

"I wasn't finished touching you," she said plaintively.

Chuckling low, he kissed her neck. "I'm more than willing to let you touch me again."

"But everything happens far too quickly when I do."

"Only because you drove me to madness with anticipation."

"What will the servants think about us still being abed when it is close to being after noon?"

"They'll think that their duke is a very fortunate gentleman, a very fortunate gentleman indeed."

It wasn't until they'd finished eating lunch in bed that Richard had finally left Kitty alone, with a promise not to return to her bedchamber before nightfall.

Lunch in bed. It had been absolutely decadent. And fun. Richard was fun. He truly was. Teasing her, tickling her, kissing her. Spoiling her. Yes, she had to admit that he did indeed spoil her.

It hadn't taken long after he'd gone to his bedchamber for her to hear him in the hallway. It was very unfair that men did not have to wear corsets and petticoats and all the trappings that a lady did. It had been an hour, and she was still not ready to go out.

Nancy had only recently finished putting up Kitty's hair, and now she was helping her into the dress she'd chosen to wear for the day. Not black. But a pale green, because it enhanced her eyes, and she thought it might please her husband if she didn't wear mourning.

And she suddenly wished to please him very much.

When Nancy was finished with the last of the buttons, Kitty walked to the window and gazed out on the garden. She saw Richard strolling along the path, using his walking stick, the puppy bounding along beside him as though he were already a faithful friend.

"Will there be anything else, Your Grace?" Nancy asked.

"I didn't give him a gift."

"Pardon?"

Kitty shook her head. "In the rush to get married, I didn't think to purchase a wedding gift for my husband."

"I'm certain the duke wasn't expecting anything."

"I'm quite certain you're right, which is the very reason that I should have given him something. I don't even know what he might like."

"Most lords are pleased to receive an heir as soon as possible."

Kitty wondered if everyone was going to constantly make references to the duke's need for an heir. The way she and the duke had gotten along—or not gotten along—for so long, she suspected she was carrying a daughter. Somehow, she did not think he would be disappointed. He wanted no apologies from her, and yet, she suddenly felt as though she had much to apologize for.

"I think I'll join my husband in the garden."

She'd feared she'd have a difficult time finding her way to the garden, but she'd passed various servants who were only too happy to provide directions. Richard's gardens were truly beautiful with tiny ponds and small waterfalls cascading over rocks. She was amazed by some of the more elaborate displays.

As she walked the path she'd seen him on earlier, she heard the yipping of the puppy quickly followed by Richard's laughter. As she neared, the dog darted toward her.

Richard moved quickly and scooped the dog up. "Oh, no, Sea Breeze. My duchess isn't fond of dogs."

He cradled the writhing dog against his chest, seeming not to be disturbed in the least with the dog's licking of his chin.

"Sea Breeze?" she asked.

"You don't like it?"

"You can't be serious."

He held the dog out. "What would you call her then?"

She looked the puppy over. Her reddish brown coat, her large dark eyes. "Nicolette."

Richard arched a brow. "You think Nicolette is better than Sea Breeze?"

She nodded. "Yes, as a matter of fact I do."

He held the dog aloft. "Nicolette. Nicky for short, I suppose."

"Do you mind?" she asked.

"Of course not. I've told you before that I only wish for you to be happy." He grinned at her. "Your brow is furrowed. What are you thinking?"

"I'm thinking that you're in pain."

His smile dimmed. "A small price to pay."

He'd told her that he groaned with pleasure, but now she had to wonder if he'd groaned with discomfort as well. "What caused you to hurt yourself?"

"Sleeping in the bed." He shrugged. "I generally sleep on the floor."

She knew her eyes widened. "Why?"

"The hard, flat surface eases the discomfort I sometimes feel in my back."

"You have a great deal of discomfort then?"

"It's manageable. I've grown accustomed to it over the years."

"Put the dog down. It can't be comfortable for you to hold her like that when you're in pain."

"She's a bit frisky this afternoon. She'll jump on you."

"Then I'll kick her aside." Although she knew she wouldn't. She was only saying it because she wanted him to put the creature down.

"She's very much like me, Duchess. She'll only come back."

She sighed. "Then I suppose I shall have to grow to like her."

He angled his head thoughtfully. "Am I to assume then that you've grown to like me?"

Tentatively, she reached out and petted the puppy, snatching her hand back when it rolled its tongue toward her. "You have some favorable habits."

"I'm pleased you think so."

"Farthingham thought so highly of you. He was always expounding on your good virtues."

"She won't bite," Richard said quietly, as though he wished to turn the conversation away from Farthingham.

She supposed she couldn't blame him for not wanting to talk about his friend. She lifted her gaze to his. "Do you feel guilty about his death?"

"I feel guilty about much that happened that day."

"I don't blame you for his death."

"But he is still between us."

"Not as much, I think. I loved him for so long. I miss him."

"I know you do. Perhaps you should call the dog Farthingham."

"Perhaps I should, although it's hardly feminine. She seems playful like Farthingham. How do you know she won't bite me?"

"You've given her no reason not to love you, so she'll only seek to please you."

"When I was very young, a dog attacked me. He actually bit me." She touched the side of her nose. "I have a tiny scar where his teeth scraped me. I've not liked dogs since."

"I would have never known," he said. "The scar is not visible."

"But it's there," she pointed out succinctly.

"I think we often see things because we expect to see them. You know the scar is there, and so you see it. I didn't know it was there, and so I didn't. When I was a lad, I fell into a pond. I'd not yet learned to swim. I had a beautiful Irish setter. The dog closed his jaws around my shirt and pulled me out of the pond. I truly believe I would have drowned had he not."

"What happened to him?"

"He died many years ago. I was near to being a man, and I wept like a baby—where no one could see, of course."

"You do not strike me as a man who would weep."

"I have only wept twice in my life. When I lost my dog and when I lost my father. I do not love often, Kitty, nor do I love many, but when I love, I love deeply."

She nodded, not certain she wanted the conversation to follow this path. "I figured that out," she said softly.

"If you see this dog as a danger to you, she will be. She will become what you expect of her."

The challenge was there, the gauntlet tossed down. "Will you let me hold her?"

"Yes, of course."

She took the puppy in her arms, surprised by the softness and the warmth, more surprised by how the dog stilled, as though content to be where she was.

"Ah, it seems she is truly your dog, and well she knows it."

"I didn't give you a gift," she blurted. "A wedding gift. I didn't give you one."

"You married me, Kitty. That was gift enough."

Chapter 25

Kitty had always known that a good deal of married life involved corresponding for one purpose or another: to thank someone for calling, to invite someone to call. She'd not expected married life to entail gazing out the window into the garden and wondering when her husband might return.

Married a mere three days, she'd begun to think that she and Richard might seldom venture from the bedroom—which she had to admit was a notion she no longer felt uncomfortable with. The things they did quite amazed her. His patience, his tutoring, his explaining . . . she'd never thought actually to relish the marriage act. She'd certainly never expected to come to realize so soon that her body's reactions to Richard's touches were more natural than her constant retreats had been.

She tried to imagine spending as much time in bed with Farthingham, and she simply couldn't envision it. She thought he might have been quick about it—as quick as he was with his kisses on her forehead and cheek—and then they'd have gone off to play with friends. She couldn't help but believe that her marriage to Farthingham would have been so very different from her marriage to Richard.

She would have been content with Farthingham because she would have never known anything different. But now, having experienced marriage to Richard . . .

He'd been gone but a few hours, and she missed him already.

With a sigh, she turned her attention back to the task at hand. As a child, she'd been taught perfect penmanship, had mastered the eloquence of the written word, phrasing her thoughts in a way that made them almost poetical. So she didn't know why she'd put off the one letter she knew she needed to write, the one she had no desire to write.

Her usual habit was to address unpleasant tasks first so that her reward was taking on the pleasanter endeavors. But this chore she kept avoiding—writing to the woman who'd given birth to her. She was certain her parents had thought she'd welcome knowing Jessye Bainbridge, but the truth of the matter was that she would have preferred not to. She saw too much of herself in Jessye—the pale skin, the red hair, the green eyes.

Kitty wasn't tall, dark, and exotic like Madeline. She was coarse and too often reflected her roots. Her roots wouldn't have written the letter, so she took a deep breath, dipped the nub of the pen into the inkwell, and applied it to the delicate parchment that carried her husband's family's crest.

She began her letter as she did each one she wrote to the woman:

Dear Mother Jessye

She'd never liked the name. A man's name. She'd liked even less referring to her as Mother Jessye, as though she were a nun when she was anything but. Her dislike for this woman was not a part of herself that she relished, was not something she'd ever shared with anyone. It made her feel mean, ugly, and petty.

I hope you and your family are well. I've recently married— not Lord Farthingham as I'd hinted at in my previous correspondence—but the Duke of Weddington.

Kitty stared out the window. Where to go from there escaped her. Did she reveal the whole embarrassing situation, confess that she was more like Jessye than she'd ever wanted to be, or did she let sleeping dogs lie. Surely everyone would comprehend the truth of the matter when her child came only eight months after the marriage—if that. Dear God, she'd had visions of him coming earlier. A month early, and people would speculate. Earlier and eyebrows would wag because there would be no doubt.

Oh, the shame of it. She didn't want her child to know about her what she knew about the woman who'd given birth to her: that she'd not been strong enough to resist temptation. And yet she had to wonder if any woman—when pulled toward such incredible sensations— would have the power to resist.

She did not consider herself weak. Rather the temptation to give in to Richard's touch had been so overwhelming.

Had Jessye found herself in a similar situation? Not weak, but simply confronted by an overpowering attraction?

Kitty sat back in her chair. She'd never considered the circumstances of her conception from the angle of power rather than weakness. Yet the man had abandoned her mother. While the attraction might have been powerful, the man had been weak.

Unlike Richard, who'd not hesitated even a heartbeat before announcing that he would marry Kitty. How devastating it must have been for Jessye to have shared such intimacy with a man, and then to discover he was unworthy of her.

Yes, he was the unworthy one. Not her mother.

Kitty placed her hand on her stomach where her own child now grew. She'd always been obsessed with the shame of her birth and never considered the larger picture.

What might she have done had Richard not married her? She had wealth. She could support her child without a husband. Jessye had been penniless. Twenty-one years ago. Her mother had only been seventeen.

Her mother. She'd never truly thought of the woman as her mother before. Seventeen. Abandoned. Alone. Poor.

Not weak. Simply human. Wanting what was best for her child.

Oh, dear God, Kitty whispered, as tears stung her eyes, and she pressed her fingers to her mouth. How unfair she'd been. How judgmental. She'd judged her mother's actions without truly understanding them.

Moving the top piece of paper aside, she again dipped her pen into the inkwell before writing:

My dear Mother,

Of late, I've come to realize that life seldom provides us with an easy path to follow. The road contains far too many forks, and often the decision we make in determining which fork to travel is extremely difficult. I can't recall ever telling you that where I was concerned, I thought you chose well.

She scowled at the words, which were totally inadequate for expressing her feelings. How could she truly reveal her sentiments?

By honestly confessing all.

Sometime later, lost within the numerous pages of her doubts, fears, worries, and realizations of sacrifices made, she barely stirred when Watkins walked into the room.

"Your Grace?"

Distracted by her musings, she turned her head slightly. "Yes, Watkins."

"There is a gentleman from Scotland Yard who wishes a moment of your time."

"Scotland Yard?"

"Yes, madam."

"Whatever does he want?"

"I'm certain I have no idea."

Of course, he didn't. And even if he did, he was too proper to speculate. "I'll see him."

She couldn't imagine what the man could possibly want, but she didn't think it would be wise to deny him.

Inspector Alistair Boulton wasn't at all what Kitty expected in a man whose job it was to enforce the law. He had a youthful, eager face and startling blue eyes that invited trust.

"Your Grace, thank you for seeing me," he began.

"Would you care for some tea?"

"No, thank you. I fear this is not a social call."

"Then how can I help you, Inspector?"

"I was hoping you would be so kind as to answer a few questions that will help me in my investigation regarding the murder of Lord Farthingham."

Chapter 26

Kitty stared at the man as though he were quite mad. A strangled laugh escaped her mouth before she could stop it. "Murder? Do you intend to put Nature on trial?"

"No, madam. We intend to prove that *your husband* murdered
Lord Farthingham."

She felt as though the words were traveling through a tunnel filled
with wind, roaring through her mind with such velocity that she
couldn't grab on to them. "Why would he murder Lord Farthingham? What could he possibly hope to gain?"

The man gave her a pointed look, and suddenly, he didn't appear
so youthful or trustworthy. He appeared to be a man with a suspicious nature who searched for answers in places where they didn't
exist.

The room tilted as though some giant hand had lifted one end.
"Have you gone mad?"

"Are you aware that your husband was suspected of murdering
his father?"

"His father died during a storm at sea."

"Exactly. And another man dies while on the duke's boat during
a storm at sea. Coincidence? We think not. Rather we suspect a pattern of behavior that is most troublesome."

Kitty held her hands up in front of her as though that would be
enough to stop the images from bombarding her, to stop his relentless
pursuit of this ridiculous theory.

"Your Grace, I know this news is disconcerting, but please hear
me out. Your husband and his father had been overheard arguing
heatedly the morning before they last sailed. When the storm came

up, the crew was told to board a lifeboat. Your husband and his father remained on the ship . . . again arguing. Arguing in the midst of a storm. Your husband towed his father to shore, but the old duke's head had been bashed in. Your husband claimed it was the result of the storm. We are more inclined to believe your husband did the bashing."

"To gain what?"

"The dukedom. Men have been known to kill for much less."

The story was incredible. Kitty began pacing, her thoughts a jumble. "And now you think he killed Lord Farthingham?"

"Yes. We have a witness who overheard the gentlemen arguing."

"What witness?"

"I am not at liberty to say. The duke and Lord Farthingham went out on a boat that should have had four crewmen."

"They're competitive men who wanted to test their skills . . ."

"Or Weddington wished to have fewer around him who could speculate as to the reason behind Farthingham's death. The sea leaves no witnesses."

She shook her head, a throbbing between her temples. "It was an accident."

"He made a payment of six thousand pounds to Lord Farthingham's family and gave them a legal document, signed by him, indicating that he would provide them with an annual sum of six thousand pounds each year hereafter as long as he drew breath."

Her legs no longer able to support her, she sank into the chair. "He knew Lord Farthingham was in need of funds. It was no secret that it was that very need that caused Lord Farthingham to want to marry me. The duke was no doubt feeling guilty—"

"Our sentiments exactly."

Horrified by his conclusion following her words, Kitty could do little more than stare at the man. Yes, Richard was competitive, he didn't like to lose, he'd wanted Kitty, made that perfectly clear throughout the Season . . . but murder?

As his coach came to a halt in front of his London residence, Richard couldn't be happier with the direction that his marriage had taken. He'd been loath to leave Kitty that morning, but he did have business ventures that needed his attention. He couldn't very well begin to neglect all that provided a comfortable living for his family.

Although with Kitty at his side, he realized he needed little else. He so loved her passionate nature, as well as her curiosity—once she'd become comfortable with her body's reactions to his touch.

The day of the storm still haunted him, the decisions he'd made, the actions he'd taken—but the guilt was lessening. And he was beginning to hope that a day would come when all the doubts would no longer linger, when he might even be able to share with Kitty everything that had happened that day—and know that she would forgive him.

The footman opened the door, and Richard strode into the entry hallway. Watkins immediately approached as though he'd been waiting for Richard's arrival.

"Watkins, where might I find the duchess?"

"Her Grace is in the drawing room—"

"Thank you, Watkins." Richard turned—

"—with a gentleman from Scotland Yard."

Richard froze, as trepidation sliced through him. "Scotland Yard?"

"Yes, Your Grace."

"How long has he been here?"

"Close to half an hour."

Richard nodded. "Well, I'd best see to his reason for being here." Although God help him, he feared he already knew.

When he entered the drawing room, he was certain of it.

Kitty was as white as the sheets upon which they'd made love only that morning. Sitting in a chair, she looked as frail and devastated as she had the night of the storm, when Farthingham had become lost to her.

He crossed the room. "Kitty—"

She rose to her feet, horror clearly written on her face. "He said you murdered your father."

"That was never proven."

The words were wrong, so wrong. But he'd grown tired of proclaiming his innocence when so many had doubted him. But they couldn't doubt the facts. No one had ever been able to prove he murdered his father.

"He said you murdered Nicky."

And she believed him, her certainty evident in her eyes.

"What did you tell him?"

"She told me nothing, Your Grace, but others have. I'm Inspector Alistair Boulton, Scotland Yard. In my possession, I have a warrant for your arrest for the murder of Nicholas Glenville, the Marquess of Farthingham. I would ask that you accompany me peacefully."

Richard felt a sinking, as though he were once again in the midst of the storm, being battered about, terrified that the storm would once again win. He faced the man. "I am a peer of the realm, sir. It would not occur to me to behave in any manner except as a gentleman."

Richard headed toward the door.

"Richard, tell me you didn't do it," Kitty called after him.

In that moment, he lost all hope of ever holding her heart—not when she believed him capable of such a despicable act.

He strode from the room without answering and without looking back.

"This is absurd," the Dowager Duchess proclaimed. "It's Weddy's death all over again. What sort of son do people think I've brought up—to hold him accountable every time that damned sea has its way?"

"Your Grace, you must calm down."

The words were quietly spoken by Lionel Gurney, Richard's solicitor. He'd arrived at the dower house with his assistant, Mr. Lacey, a few moments earlier.

Into the silence that had followed Richard's departure, Kitty had realized the absurdity of the arrest as well. She'd listened to Inspector Boulton reveal the evidence bit by bit until he'd had her convinced.

But the evidence failed to take into account the kind of man that Richard was.

Murder Farthingham? No, she couldn't see him murdering anyone in order to gain anything.

She couldn't take back the awful words she'd carelessly tossed at him, which she knew had cut him to the quick. His stiff posture had told her that. She was grateful his back had been to her and she'd been unable to read the devastation in his face that he surely must have felt. Would he ever forgive her for doubting him? Could she ever forgive herself?

She'd called for a carriage and come to tell Richard's mother of what had transpired. The Dowager Duchess had immediately sent for Richard's solicitor, who'd only just come from meeting with Richard.

"When can we see him?" Kitty asked. She sat in a chair near the sofa where the Dowager Duchess and Lady Anne were holding hands.

"Presently, he does not wish to be visited by anyone. I'm certain you can understand. The circumstances . . . the man's pride," Mr. Gurney explained.

"Will he not see any of us?" Lady Anne asked.

"He'd rather not. His accommodations are sparse, but not terribly depressing. Still, he doesn't wish to cause you any unnecessary heartache."

The Dowager Duchess released a tiny sob. "My poor Richard."

"Mama," Lady Anne cooed. "He'll be fine. He's not guilty. Surely they'll see that."

No doubts were woven in Lady Anne's voice, and Kitty felt guilty that her voice had not carried the same conviction when she'd last spoken to Richard.

"I fear that they won't see it until he is tried before the House of Lords," Mr. Gurney stated. "Which shouldn't be too long in coming. These are unique circumstances, and everything is progressing quite quickly."

"Did Farthingham wash up onshore somewhere?" Lady Anne asked.

Kitty shuddered at the image, but she could hardly blame Lady Anne for wanting some sort of evidence.

"No. No body has been found," Mr. Gurney said.

"Then how can they accuse Richard of murder?" Lady Anne asked.

"Apparently they have witnesses who provide damaging circumstantial evidence. It would be best that we not discuss the particulars in case you are called to testify."

"Inspector Boulton told me that things were overheard," Kitty said.

"Quite so."

"I can't see that it's anything more than gossip," Kitty said.

"Indeed. Scotland Yard's reputation leaves much to be desired. They are in need of some sort of crime that will draw the nation's attention to their competence so that they might feel vindicated. What could be better than an opportunity to bring a peer to task?"

"I should think a true crime would serve them better," the Dowager Duchess said.

"You mustn't fret so. Your son will be proven innocent," Mr. Gurney assured her.

"I thought he was innocent until proven guilty," Kitty said, although she certainly hadn't expressed that belief earlier in the day, and now she was feeling quite ashamed of her reaction.

Mr. Gurney got to his feet. "You are quite right, Your Grace. He is innocent. Now, if you'll excuse me, I must begin to prepare his defense. Sir Ambrose will argue the duke's case before the House of Lords. You may rest easy. The duke has utmost confidence in the barrister's abilities."

All the ladies rose and bid the gentlemen farewell. Mr. Gurney promptly left the room, while Mr. Lacey lingered.

If Kitty were not so worried about Richard, she might have paid more attention to the man earlier when Mr. Gurney introduced him. He was quite young and very nice-looking.

"Lady Anne, if I can be of service in any way . . ." His voice trailed off as though he were embarrassed to have spoken at all and could think of nothing further to say.

"Thank you, Mr. Lacey," Lady Anne said. "I appreciate your kind concern."

With a brisk nod, he turned and strode from the room.

With a huge sigh, the Dowager Duchess dropped back on to the sofa. "I very nearly didn't survive the accusations before. They were most cruel. I fear they will be much worse this go-round."

Kitty didn't know how things could get any worse, but she feared that she'd soon find out.

Chapter 27

Richard's trial before the House of Lords came about much too quickly, much too slowly. He'd not let anyone visit him. Kitty wasn't even certain where he was being held. She'd considered having his solicitor deliver a letter to him, but she could find no words to express her sorrow over her initial reaction to the suspicions and her last words to Richard.

It was a dreary dismal day outside, a light rain falling, as though even the heavens were weeping. Kitty sat beside the Dowager Duchess and her daughter in a special section reserved for peeresses.

Any other time, as Kitty came to her feet along with everyone else in attendance, she might have been impressed as the lords paraded in, wearing white wigs and dressed in their scarlet and ermine robes. But all she could think was how utterly insane it all seemed: a nightmare from which she thought she might never awaken.

Then Richard was led in to answer the charge made against him. Oh, dear Lord, she thought her heart might break.

The Dowager Duchess squeezed Kitty's hand. "Do not weep," she whispered. "For Richard's sake, do not weep."

What Kitty wanted to do was scream. He looked as though he'd aged ten years. But he stood defiant and proud, and when asked whether he was guilty or not guilty, his voice rang out strong, "Not guilty."

He refused to sit, but rather stood within the place that had been designated for him. The Attorney-General came to his feet and opened the case for the Crown. In monotone, the man rambled on about how he intended to show that the Duke of Weddington exhibited a pattern of behavior which in the end would prove his undoing, and with the testimony of key witnesses, would prove that it was not Nature that had killed Nicholas Glenville, the Marquess of Farthingham, but rather the duke himself, who had purposely and with malicious intent taken the marquess out in a storm and killed him.

He called as his first witness, Jason Redman, Lord Farthingham's butler.

"The Duke of Weddington visited the Marquess of Farthingham at his London residence on several occasions, did he not?" the Attorney-General asked.

"Yes, sir, he did."

"Did he visit on the morning that Lord Farthingham's betrothal announcement appeared in *The Times*?"

"Yes, sir."

"Will you describe the duke's mood?"

"He was quite agitated. Furious in fact. He didn't wait for a proper announcement of his arrival to be made, but simply stormed into the drawing room, where Lord Farthingham was enjoying his morning tea. I've never had a gentleman not wait for a proper announcement to be made. I found it quite unsettling."

"You are quite certain of the morning in question?"

"Yes, sir. He was clutching *The Times* in his hand."

The Attorney-General held up a crumpled newspaper. "Was this the newspaper he had in his possession?"

"Yes, sir."

"And how did you come to have it?"

"As he was leaving, he tossed it to me and told me to get rid of it."

"But you didn't."

"No, sir. I enjoy reading the newspaper, and Lord Farthingham's financial situation was such that he'd dispensed with having a newspaper delivered sometime back, so I thought to keep the duke's newspaper and read it at my leisure."

"You need not look embarrassed, Mr. Redman. I'm certain no one faults you for wanting to keep abreast of the news. That morning, did you overhear any of the conversation between the duke and the marquess?"

"Immediately after I closed the door, I heard the duke say, 'You promised to wait until the end of the Season to announce your betrothal.'"

"So, on this particular morning, you witnessed the duke arriving in anger, clutching *The Times*, and questioning the marquess about his announcement. It seems then that the duke was not at all pleased that the marquess had formalized his intention to marry Miss Robertson. Did you overhear anything else?"

"Not on that particular morning, but on another occasion, a couple of weeks earlier, the duke visited and announced that he did not wish for the marquess to marry Miss Robertson."

"Because the duke had an interest in the lady?"

"I assumed so, yes."

"My lords!" Sir Ambrose came to his feet. "I must protest this idiocy. If any of you have set eyes upon the present Duchess of Weddington, you will know that any man who claims *not* to have an interest in her is lying. Of course, she drew the duke's attention. She is lovely, witty, and gracious. But interest in a lady does not precipitate murder. We have no body. We have no physical evidence of foul play; only conjecture and gossip. This trial is lunacy."

The murmurs rippling through the room gave Kitty hope that everyone would agree, and the trial would end before it had truly begun.

"My lords, there is a pattern here that must be addressed," the Attorney-General interjected. "Arguments, sailing, death. They can no longer be ignored. For who would be his next victim? His wife? Should she lose favor with him?"

Gasps echoed through the chamber.

The Lord High Steward calmed the room, noted Sir Ambrose's protests and nodded for the Attorney-General to proceed.

"Mr. Redman, was there anything else that led you to believe the duke had more than a *casual* interest in the lady?"

"Yes, sir. The duke and the lady walked about the garden alone one evening when Lord Farthingham was hosting a dinner party."

The servant was excused, and Kitty wanted to shriek. His story was only part of what had happened that evening. Farthingham had insisted on the walk, the wager. She couldn't believe that so much had been left unsaid. Did people truly believe she and Richard would flaunt an affair in front of Farthingham?

The Attorney-General called three witnesses in succession who testified that they'd seen her slip out into Harrington's garden during the Harringtons' ball. Less than a minute later the duke had followed her—neither of them was ever seen returning to the ballroom, and their absence was in time noted by others.

She had tried so hard to preserve her reputation, and here it was being ripped to shreds by half-truths. She was incredibly grateful that her parents weren't there to witness this travesty. They were in

France, on the Riviera. She'd not sent word to them because she'd not wanted to ruin their holiday. Thank goodness she'd followed her own counsel on that matter.

Kitty focused her attention on Richard, imploring him to look at her, but his gaze seemed transfixed on some distant corner as though he knew the outcome wouldn't be favorable and had already come to accept it. She was also fairly certain that he was experiencing a good deal of discomfort. There was a tautness to the set of his mouth, a stiffness to the way he held himself.

Then Lady Priscilla Norwood was called to testify.

With an audible gasp, Lady Anne looked at her mother and then at Kitty.

"But she is my dearest friend," Lady Anne whispered. "Why would the prosecution question her?"

Considering Lady Priscilla's propensity for gossip, Kitty could think of a dozen reasons why she might be called, none of them good.

"Lady Priscilla Norwood, you are a dear friend of the duke's sister—Lady Anne Stanbury—are you not?"

"Indeed I am, sir."

"Did you have occasion to be present at the dinner party when the duke and Miss Robertson took a walk in the garden?"

"Yes, sir. I was there."

"What can you tell us about their walk?"

Lady Priscilla shifted as though very uncomfortable. "They were supposed to take a turn about the garden, but they were gone for a very long time. Even Lord Farthingham commented on how long it was taking them to return to us."

"Did Lord Farthingham seem upset?"

"No, sir. Not that I noticed."

"Sometime later you spent several days at the duke's home in Cornwall, Drummond Manor. Who was in attendance?"

"Well, sir, I was there, of course, as you've stated. As was Mr. Frederick Montague, Lord Farthingham, Miss Robertson, the duke, and his sister."

"What did you observe while you were in their company?"

"The first afternoon, I'd lain down for a nap. When I awoke, I looked out the window and saw Miss Robertson and the duke returning to the stables. I thought nothing of it, of course. The duke is always a remarkable host. The next afternoon, we went sailing, and the duke invited Miss Robertson to stand before him at the wheel. He whispered something to her. I know not what, but she seemed inordinately pleased."

Sir Ambrose rolled his eyes and shook his head with theatrical exaggeration.

"But it was the following morning, was it not, that made you suspicious regarding Lord Farthingham's death?"

Kitty and Lady Anne exchanged confused glances. Was Lady Priscilla responsible for this travesty of justice?

"Yes, sir. You see, I awoke that morning and went in search of Mr. Montague. I was quite taken with him and wanted to see if he might teach me to play billiards, so I might have an opportunity to flirt a bit. You know how it is? Games of croquet and lawn tennis are really merely opportunities for harmless flirtation. And I thought billiards might be as well—"

"Yes, yes, you wished to flirt. But you did not have the opportunity to flirt, did you?"

"No, sir. As I was passing the billiard room, I heard loud voices. The door was slightly ajar, but there was no footman about, which is exceedingly unusual in the duke's home. He has so many servants that one never has to open a door for oneself."

Kitty saw Richard cast an almost despairing glance at Sir Ambrose as though he knew what was coming and knew it would not bode well for him, as though he desperately wished the testimony to end.

"Continue, Lady Priscilla Norwood," the Attorney-General urged.

"Must I?"

"You are on your oath to reveal what you know."

"Yes, of course. I . . . uh . . . I approached the door and heard Lord Farthingham say, 'The only way that you will ever have her is if I am dead.'"

The room erupted with gasps, murmurs, and whispers. Kitty had held her gaze on Richard, and in the single moment when Lady Priscilla had revealed Farthingham's words, she'd anxiously wanted him to look at her so she could convey that she knew he had not murdered Farthingham. But Richard never looked her way, and she could hardly blame him.

She'd rebuffed him at every turn, and still he'd pursued her. He'd taught her that there was no shame in her body's reaction to his touch.

She'd learned that her only shame resided in her doubts regarding his innocence. She knew this man, had known him from the first moment she'd set eyes on him. Kindred spirits. Soul mates. He would no more murder Farthingham to gain her than he would cheat to win a game.

Once the room was again quieted, the Attorney-General dismissed Lady Priscilla and called Mr. Frederick Montague.

Freddie looked as though he wished he were anywhere except where he was, and Kitty feared that he might not only corroborate Lady Priscilla's testimony but add further damaging statements as well.

The initial questions were of no consequence, simply establishing his friendship with the deceased, his acquaintance with the accused. And then the mood of the questions changed.

"You are a playwright, are you not?" the Attorney-General asked.

"I am."

"Tell me about your play, *A Sea Change*."

"My lords!" Sir Ambrose came to his feet. "Mr. Montague's talents as a writer have no bearing on this case."

"If you'll indulge me," the Attorney-General stated, "this particular play does. Tell us about the play, Mr. Montague."

"It is the story of man who seeks to murder his lover's husband, but in the end the husband murders the lover. It is a comedy of errors."

"Did the duke read your play?"

"He did."

"And what was his opinion of it?"

"He thought it rather dark. He said the humor did not ring true. That murder should not be taken lightly."

"On the morning of Lord Farthingham's death, you were in the billiard room of Drummond Manor, were you not?" the Attorney-General asked.

"I was."

"Why?"

Freddie jerked his head back as though completely surprised by the question. "Why *what*?"

"Why were you in the billiard room?"

"To play billiards, why else?"

His response garnered a few chuckles, and Kitty thought that amusement had quickly passed over Richard's countenance as well.

"Before breakfast?" the Attorney-General questioned.

"No, sir. Following dinner. We were in the habit of playing throughout the night, well into the dawn."

"I see." The Attorney-General cleared his throat. "That morning while you were in the billiard room—playing billiards—did Lord Farthingham have occasion to say to the Duke of Weddington that the only way he would ever have Miss Robertson was if the marquess were dead?"

All the lightheartedness seemed to seep right out of Freddie. A heavy silence filled the Chambers.

"You are on your oath, Mr. Montague," the Attorney-General stated.

Freddie nodded. "The marquess did say something along those lines, but it was not an invitation for murder."

"Why were you not invited to go sailing with the duke and Lord Farthingham?"

"Lord Farthingham wished to go sailing."

"The day before Lord Farthingham had wished to go sailing, and everyone was invited. Why were you not invited to accompany them on this particular day? Whose idea was it that only the Duke and Lord Farthingham should go?"

Silence.

"Mr. Montague?"

Freddie squeezed his eyes closed. "The duke's."

The room once again erupted with murmurs.

After everyone fell into silence, the Attorney-General asked, "Did you not find it odd that the duke would insist that you not accompany them on the boat? You were a guest, a friend. Why were you not allowed to go?"

"The duke thought it would be best if I remained behind—because of the storm, you see? He knew there would be some danger—"

"Yes!" the Attorney-General stated loudly. "The duke knew there would be danger because he knew murder would be committed."

"No!" Kitty surged to her feet.

The Attorney-General jerked back as though he'd been physically struck, and Kitty felt all eyes come to bear on her—even Richard's.

"These entire proceedings are ludicrous," Kitty announced. "You suspect my husband of murdering Lord Farthingham because of a few words spoken in anger?"

"I suspect him of a crime of passion. He wanted you so desperately that he would kill Lord Farthingham to obtain you." The Attorney-General addressed her, even though Kitty was certain it was a breach of protocol and procedure.

"He'd already succeeded in obtaining me, sir, and well he knew it. As did Lord Farthingham. The duke had no reason to kill the marquess."

"So you say, Duchess—"

"So I can prove! Which is more than I can say for any evidence you've presented today. Long before our marriage vows were spoken, I was carrying the duke's child!"

*   *   *

"Enough!" Richard yelled into the cacophony of voices echoing around him, fury shimmering off him in waves so great that he was surprised a tempest didn't begin within the hallowed halls.

"Enough, I say! My wife bared her heart, her soul, and by God, she will bare nothing more. You either take her at her word, or you take her not at all.

"I am sick unto death of this harassment of my family and our friends. As I have sworn previously and shall continue to swear until I die, as God is my witness, upon the soul of my unborn child"—the audience gasped—"I did not murder Lord Farthingham. At his request, we went sailing. We misjudged the ferocity and speed with which the storm would arrive.

"The sea took him, my Lords. There was naught I could do to prevent it. Yes, he spoke the words that Lady Priscilla revealed during her testimony. Yes, he and I argued. Yes, I fell in love with my wife long before that fateful day when Lord Farthingham was lost to her. Yes, I would do anything within my power to see her happy, to have her as my wife. But the taking of a life is not within my power. I would never consider or consent to committing murder.

"Again, I swear before God that I did not murder Lord Farthingham. If my word as a peer of the realm is not good enough, then hang me from the nearest gallows, but by God, leave my family alone! They have suffered enough as a result of conjecture and vile gossip.

"You know me, my Lords. If you truly believe me capable of such a heinous act, then find me guilty now and be done with it! Otherwise, end this farce before other reputations are ruined for naught.

"Lord Farthingham adored my wife. He would be revolted by your treatment of her. Were he to witness this spectacle of a trial, he would be ashamed of you all. As am I. You have done little more than provide fodder for the gossips. By God, I will tolerate it no more. Judge me now! Guilty or not! But demand no more of my family than you have already!"

Chapter 28

Kitty began to tremble violently following Richard's impassioned speech. To think of them hanging him. Dear God, how could she survive without him? Did he think she cared for him so little that she wouldn't do all in her power to save him?

After Richard had finished speaking, Freddie had declared as though he were standing on a stage, "Hear! Hear! If Lord Farthingham were here, I know he would announce to all that he had no truer friend than the Duke of Weddington!"

Then Sir Ambrose had stood to announce that in defense of his client, he could offer nothing more compelling than the duke's own testimony, which everyone had just heard.

Her trembling worsened as the lords answered his summons for an immediate verdict, each standing, placing his hand over his heart, and announcing:

Not guilty, upon mine honor.
Not guilty, upon mine honor.
Not guilty, upon mine honor . . .

Until each had taken his turn. A unanimous verdict. The courtroom seemed to explode, as reporters scrambled to get out with the news that the duke had been acquitted.

The Dowager Duchess quickly rose and grabbed Kitty's hand. "Follow me."

It was madness, insanity as they made their way into the hallway. Kitty wasn't certain how much longer her legs would support her, how much farther she could go without total collapse. She was still trembling, still shaking—

And then she was wrapped in the warmth of a familiar embrace.

"Oh, Kitty, I'm sorry, I'm so sorry. I shall never forgive myself for what I put you through," Richard rasped.

She wound her arms around him. "It wasn't your fault."

He moved away slightly. "Mother, are you all right?"

"Of course, dear. You must see to your wife."

"Mr. Gurney has gone to make certain a carriage will be waiting. Come with me," Richard urged, tucking Kitty in against his side.

Richard led them through the crowd, through the building, and into Parliament Square. The crowds seemed even thicker there, probably because the rain had begun to pour and umbrellas were raised. Richard took Kitty's umbrella—which she'd forgotten she was holding—opened it, and held it over her. "This way."

They'd only taken a few steps when he suddenly halted, and everyone stopped with him. Lady Priscilla stood before them, tears in her eyes.

"I'm terribly sorry, Your Grace," Lady Priscilla said.

"Prissy, how could you?" Lady Anne asked. "You were my dearest friend in all the world."

"I'd overheard Farthingham, and it was such an interesting thing for him to say in light of his death—"

"So you told people? You gossiped about personal matters within our house?"

"I meant no harm."

"What you meant and what you achieved were two different things," Richard said sternly.

"I didn't know people would add accusation and innuendo to so simple a bit of gossip. I never thought you murdered Farthingham . . ."

The conversation surrounding Kitty began to fade away. Richard had loosened his hold on her, to comfort Lady Anne, who was lamenting her friend's betrayal.

But none of it seemed important. The crowds were thick, thicker than they'd been the day of her wedding, but this time she had no doubt.

She'd seen Nicky.

She eased her way through the crowds, barely noticing the rain splashing around her. She rose on her tiptoes. There! There he was! "Nicky!"

The man turned and quickly disappeared. But it was him. She was certain of it. She began to hurry, weaving between this person and that one, pushing people aside. It seemed everyone wanted to catch a glimpse of the duke, wanted to see the lords leaving parliament.

Gasping, cursing her corset, her shoes, her clothing, her short height, she struggled to keep the man's path in her vision.

She could only tell where he was going because of the people parting before him. He was no longer visible, as though he'd suddenly shrunk. And then the crowds thinned, and she was left at the edge of the street, drenched and disappointed, her tears mingling with the rain. The man she'd followed was nowhere to be seen. Was he a ghost? A spirit? A figment of her imagination?

She was so certain she'd seen him. She felt as though she were going mad. Suddenly she was fighting to draw in every breath; buildings, conveyances, people began to circle rapidly around her.

And then the yawning void of darkness descended.

Richard had always thought that the sea terrified him. Not until he saw Kitty crumple to the ground in the rain did he truly comprehend the unrelenting grip of true terror.

He'd been trying to comfort his mother and Anne, especially. He'd been fighting not to give Lady Priscilla the harsh words she so readily deserved for spreading gossip that had brought such dire consequences upon his family—when he'd noticed that Kitty had slipped away from him.

He'd begun a frantic search, had finally spotted her rushing headlong through the crowds, and followed. He'd almost caught up with her when she'd suddenly collapsed. He'd been too far away to catch her before she'd hit the ground.

When he'd reached her, she'd been soaked, pale, and cold. He'd gathered her in his arms and carried her back to where his coach waited. She'd awoken once they were inside, her first words a whispered *I saw Nicky*.

Now he paced outside her bedchamber, while the doctor examined her. Richard tried not to think how badly she'd been shivering, how vacant her eyes had been, how lost she'd looked.

Would this nightmare that he'd brought upon them never end?

To further torment him, he couldn't erase from his mind, Kitty's words and her heartbreakingly sad smile when she'd announced her proof of his innocence.

He'd never in his life experienced such shame or such pride. Pride in her. Shame in himself.

Kitty had never wanted the world to know of her condition. Her shame at her own birth still haunted her, and he'd not been able to protect her from letting all of London know that she was with child before they were married. To save him, she'd revealed her shame.

And he was so completely unworthy of her sacrifice.

The door opened, and Richard staggered to a halt. "Well? How is she? Will she be all right? And the child? What of our child?"

The doctor held up his hand. "Your Grace, you mustn't worry yourself overmuch—"

"Not worry? She fainted, collapsed—very nearly in the street where she might have been hit by a passing carriage or hansom. Not worry? Good God, man! I can do nothing except worry."

"Working yourself up into a frenzied state will not change matters. I've spoken with the duchess and examined her. She and the babe are well—under the circumstances."

"What circumstances?" Richard demanded to know.

The doctor rolled his eyes. "Your trial, Your Grace. It has been a very difficult few weeks for your wife. She's not been eating as she should, nor sleeping well. She is exhausted. Worried. I'm certain today's spectacle only added to her trauma."

"Yes, of course. You're quite right. What can I do for her?"

"She needs much rest, nourishment, a bit of spoiling."

"I can see that she has all of that."

The doctor patted his arm. "It wouldn't hurt for you to have a bit of it yourself."

"I will," he said, even though he knew he wouldn't. He was in agony. The tension, the strain, the worry of the past few weeks had taken a toll on his back. "May I see her now?"

"Certainly, but do take care not to tire her further. I know you are probably in need of sexual release—"

"I'm not going to make love to my wife. I merely wish to look in on her."

The doctor raised his eyebrows as though he was surprised by the outburst. "Oh, yes, of course. By all means, you may see her now. She is sleeping."

Quietly Richard entered the room and walked to the foot of the bed. His wife appeared so frail, the blankets brought up to her chest, her hands folded on top, her red hair fanned out over the pillow.

He'd missed her so desperately. A thousand times he'd almost sent word for her to visit him. But he'd allowed her doubts to wound him—when what he'd actually done was almost as bad as murder.

He'd sworn to do anything to make her happy. And instead he'd made her miserable.

He'd done exactly as he'd feared. He'd risked destroying her.

* * *

Kitty awoke to the familiar feel of a warm body nestled up against her hip. Instinctively, she reached down and wove her fingers through the soft fur. "Nicolette."

"You no longer fear her," a quiet voice said.

Incredibly weary, she lifted her gaze and found her husband standing beside the bed. Slowly, she shook her head. "No, I don't."

"Henry said you'd taken to sleeping with the dog of late."

She smiled. "Not exactly. I let her sleep with me."

Richard knelt beside the bed and took her hand. "This afternoon you terrified me, Kitty."

"I thought I saw Nicky," she whispered.

He combed her hair off her brow. "I know."

"I don't understand why I keep thinking that I see him. I feel as though I'm going mad." Tears welled in her eyes. "Richard, I'm sorry. I know I hurt you—"

"No, I have hurt you far more. I have woven a tangled web, my darling, and now I find myself trapped inside it. The doctor says that you need to rest. I thought we would go to Drummond Manor. Escape the madness. I want to take you sailing. I want to share something with you—when you feel up to it."

"I'd like to go sailing."

"Then I'll make arrangements for us to leave tomorrow."

She squeezed his hand. "I'm tired, Richard."

"I know you are."

"I haven't slept well since you left. Will you sleep with me tonight?"

He said not a word, but merely removed his clothes and slipped into bed beside her. For the first time, in a very long time, she felt safe.

Kitty awoke to a strangled cry. The room was shrouded with darkness. Nicolette was no longer snuggling against her hip, and she assumed the dog had retreated to a corner of the room. Her husband, however, remained and was trembling beside her.

"Richard?"

"Help me to forget," he commanded in a hoarse voice. "Help me to forget."

And then his mouth was on hers, desperate with yearning. She wasn't certain exactly what he wished to forget: the storm, Farthingham, the trial . . . so many possibilities existed, but all that mattered to her was that he needed her.

They became a tangle of limbs as he made short work of removing her nightgown, and then he returned his mouth to hers, rubbing his body along hers, caressing her, massaging her, awakening her passions.

Her skin was on fire, her nerve endings so sensitive that each brush of his hand carried her higher toward the pinnacle of pleasure.

She stroked her hands over his shoulders, back, and buttocks. She rubbed her feet up and down his calves. She kissed his throat, his neck, his chest. She found satisfaction in his guttural groans, his harsh breathing, the tenseness in his muscles. She wanted to give back to him, wanted him to know how very much he meant to her.

She'd been terrified that the evidence was mounting against him, had feared losing him to the gallows. She thought of how much she had resisted the temptation of giving in to him, how the feelings he caused to surface within her had so frightened her.

And now she could no longer imagine living without his touch, without his presence, without him. He had told her that he'd loved her, and she couldn't recall ever saying the words back to him.

"Richard—"

He covered her mouth at the exact instant that he entered her, firm, and sure.

And all words were lost to her as the passion mounted and the sensations built. Oh, how she'd missed this. The press of his body against hers. The rocking motion, like riding on the crest of a wave, going under only to rise higher and higher . . .

He swallowed her scream, his release following so quickly after hers that she thought there was a bit of magic in it. He'd barely moved off her before she heard his first soft snore.

She snuggled against him, brought the covers up over them, and watched him sleep, wishing she had much more to give to him than she did.

She awoke at dawn to find him staring down on her, much as she'd been watching him hours earlier.

"I didn't mean to wake you last night," he said.

"Do you have nightmares often?"

"I've not had them for years. They returned when I was arrested. With my father's death, I was never arrested, but the accusations were there. I saw them in people's eyes, in the speculative way they looked at me. They all thought I murdered him, but I didn't."

She wrapped her hand around his. "I know you didn't."

"Do you?"

"Yes."

"Why?"

"If you and your father disagreed, I think you would have accepted his obstinacy as a challenge, to be met and conquered. To murder him would have been cheating. And one does not dishonor one's opponent by retreating before the decisive moment has arrived." She smiled softly. "Murder would be retreating in the most cowardly way, and you are not a coward."

He took her hand and pressed a kiss to her palm. "I wanted to save him."

"Anne told me a little of what happened. You told me that you and the crew arrived at shore. But you didn't arrive together. Why didn't you get in the smaller boat with the crew?"

"Father and I had planned to. We were loading the boat when my father suddenly said he'd forgotten something. I have no idea what. But he left, and I went after him. The pilot of our boat cut the smaller boat free."

"Leaving you to die?" The fury surged through her. "Why didn't you tell someone?"

"And have him held accountable for my father's death? A common man against a duke? He wouldn't have stood a chance. Besides, he was right to do what he did. He had his crew to think about, and my father was being reckless. As was I.

"I had only just caught up with him when the mast snapped." He closed his eyes tightly as though the memory were too painful to bear.

"And you saw it strike him?" she asked, her heart aching for him.

"Only after he shoved me out of the way so it might not strike me." He opened his eyes. "Had I not gone after him, had I boarded the smaller boat as he'd commanded me to do—my disobedience cost him his life."

"No," she whispered. "No. You were in a storm—"

"And I could not control it. Yes, I know. My mother told me that a thousand times. I could not control the storm. I could not control the sea. I could not control my father. And so I've tried to control everything else. Including you and your happiness. How many tears did you shed yesterday? And even now, look at you. You still weep. Farthingham tried to warn me, but I would not listen. I thought I was oh so wise. And I have recently discovered that I am naught but a fool."

"You're no fool, Richard."

"I wanted to save Farthingham," he said.

"I know."

"I wanted to save you. My heart broke when you announced to the Attorney-General that you were with child before we wed. I know you wanted no one to know there had been any intimacy between us before vows were exchanged. I know the shame you endured revealing all—"

"No, no. The only shame I would have known was if they'd sent you to the gallows when I could have stopped it. I would have told them anything."

"Even a lie."

She ducked her head as more tears pooled. "It was only a very small lie."

"You were not carrying my child the day Farthingham died."

"I could have been. That night in Harrington's garden, I could have become with child then."

"No, you couldn't have," he said. "I only brought you pleasure with my—"

She quickly pressed her hand to his mouth. "I would not have said no had you wished to go farther. It's only because you're a gentleman that I remained chaste for as long as I did."

"A gentleman? Where you are concerned, I have always been anything except a gentleman. I fear once we return to Drummond Manor, you will discover that I am a despicable scoundrel."

They'd arrived at Drummond Manor three days earlier. Although Kitty felt fully recovered from her ordeal of chasing a ghost through the rain, Richard had insisted that she continue to rest. He served her huge platters of food that a giant wouldn't be able to finish. He brought her tea and biscuits and flowers. He read to her. He saw to all her needs as though they had no servants about to look after her.

And then today they'd finally gone sailing. Their destination was the Isles of Scilly. Richard had ordered that the yacht be moored near an island that appeared deserted, and he alone had rowed her to shore, hauled the boat onto the sand, and secured it before helping her disembark.

"Why did you bring me here?" she asked, glancing around. He'd not brought food, so she couldn't imagine that they were going to have a picnic. Although the way he'd been spoiling her lately, he might have set things up in the middle of the night so that he might surprise her now.

"I wanted to share something with you." He pointed toward the foliage. "Do you see those two tall trees there, the one that's marked with a bit of white cloth twisting in the breeze?"

"Yes," she answered, smiling. So her suspicions were correct. He'd already been there and was planning some sort of surprise.

"Walk between them, and keep going. You'll know when to stop."

She glanced over at him. "You're not coming with me?"

"No, but I'll be waiting here when you're ready."

She released a self-conscious nervous laugh. "What is it?"

"Something I think you've been searching for. It's time you found it."

Baffled, she shook her head. "Richard—"

"Go on," he urged.

She couldn't imagine what it would be, and he was almost morbidly serious. Still, she hiked up her skirts and trudged to the trees. She could hear birds twittering and an occasional movement in the brush. She glanced over her shoulder. "Is it safe to go in here alone?"

"Yes."

"I won't get hurt?"

"I'm hoping you won't, but I fear that you might."

"Then why—"

"Because it's for the best. Trust that I would never intentionally harm you."

Trust. It was a game then. A test. Designed to show that she did indeed trust him. How could he doubt it after all she'd done to save him from the gallows? Perhaps he needed more. Perhaps he needed proof that she did trust him. That she would follow blindly wherever he led. That she would leave Nicky behind. That she would stop seeing his ghost wherever she turned.

Trepidation caused her heart to pound and each breath to feel as though it were a struggle. With a nod, she turned and marched with purpose along the path that barely seemed a path at all, although she thought it might have contained evidence that someone had passed this way before her. Richard wouldn't harm her, she was certain of that. Her breathing began to ease, her heart's rhythm began to slow.

She did trust him. She realized that now. And all it had taken was walking through overgrowth, thinking of him and all he'd done for her. Never making her feel guilty about the child. Pleasuring her. Loving her. Yes, she trusted him completely. And maybe more. Maybe she—

She staggered to a stop at the sight before her. Her heart beat with an erratic rhythm. Blood rushed between her ears, drowning out the sounds of wildlife. Her breaths came in terrified pants. No, no. no. This couldn't have been what Richard had wanted her to see.

And yet she knew with all her heart that it was indeed what he'd wanted to share with her. She stared in stunned disbelief at the boulder and the man sitting on it.

And then he smiled, the wonderful smile that she'd loved for so long. "Hello, my sweet."

Chapter 29

"**N**icky?"

Pressing a trembling hand to her mouth, she took a tentative step forward. "Nicky? You're not dead." She said it as though in a fogged daze, because she was having such a difficult time believing that he stood before her.

"Not quite yet."

"I don't understand. What happened? How did you manage to survive?" And then she realized that none of it mattered. He was alive. Nicky was alive! She launched herself at him, felt the solidity of his arms going around her as he hugged her close. Her tears pooled and flowed.

"I thought you were dead."

"I know," he cooed, rocking her comfortingly against him.

She wept almost as much as she had when she'd learned he'd drowned. How could he be alive? Richard had insisted Nicky was dead, discouraged anyone from searching for him. If only they'd searched . . .

And the reason they hadn't searched dawned on her with startling clarity. If Richard found Nicky, he wouldn't have her. The motive that the police had suspected for Richard killing Nicky was more accurate than she'd realized. It was the motive he'd used not to search for Nicky.

"Damn him!" she hissed, pulling back. "Richard. Damn him. He wouldn't let us search for you. He didn't want me to find you. He didn't want me to know you were alive. Oh, God!" She spun away from Nicky, the fury rushing through her. She hurt. She wanted to double over from the pain of Richard's betrayal.

Nicky placed a comforting hand on her shoulder. "He didn't allow you to search for me because I didn't wish to be found."

Slowly she turned around and stared at him. Profound sadness touched his eyes, perhaps even regret. She'd never seen him not happy. It was as though she were looking at someone she didn't know. "I don't understand."

"It's so difficult to explain." Shaking his head, he looked to the sky. "Damn Weddington."

"He's responsible for this, for keeping you from me—"

"No, Kitty." He placed a finger against her lips and shrugged. "Well, a little I suppose. He's responsible for my facing you now. He called in his forfeit, damn him. The one I owed him. I've been cursing him to perdition ever since. But I am a man of honor . . . within reason." He released a self-deprecating laugh. "Although I doubt you'll believe that once I've explained everything."

He indicated the boulder upon which he'd been sitting when she arrived. "Please, make yourself as comfortable as possible. The surroundings leave much to be desired, but I didn't wish to risk being seen. I realized the foolhardiness of that endeavor the day you married Weddington."

"You *were* there," she said, stunned. She hadn't been going insane. He'd been standing in the crowds near the church, probably near a man similar in height, similar in coloring. To blend in, so that if she spotted him, she might mistake one fellow for the other.

His face blushing red, he wore the difficult-to-meet-your-eyes expression of a man who had much to hide and little he wished to reveal. "I wanted to see you, to see that you were happy. You were radiant until you spotted me."

"Why didn't you let me know you were alive? We could have stopped the wedding—" Only she couldn't have stopped it, she realized. She was already carrying Richard's child.

Little wonder Nicky hadn't wanted to show himself, was even now hesitant to be seen. He must have known then about her delicate condition. And even if he hadn't, what must he have thought to see her traipsing up the aisle so soon after his supposed drowning? She couldn't imagine the pain she'd caused him with her betrayal. The embarrassment. The humiliation. "Oh, Nicky, I am so sorry."

"My sweet, you have nothing for which to apologize, I assure you. It's all my doing. Please, sit so I might explain. It's a rather lengthy story."

She sat on the boulder. Joining her, he took her hand, removed her glove, and threaded his fingers through hers. Palm to palm. It was the first time they'd ever touched so intimately. She was surprised to discover that she experienced none of the spark of warmth, tingling, awareness that she did each time Richard touched her. But then that was the very reason she'd always considered Nicky safe. Because he didn't cause the earth to tilt on its axis.

"Where to begin?" he murmured with a sigh.

"At the beginning?" she suggested.

He smiled sadly. "I think not in this case. Although you might be right. Perhaps I'll start at the beginning, skip the middle, and rush right to the end."

"You're putting off telling me," she pointed out.

"Yes, because I fear it will alter your opinion of me, and perhaps not for the better. But there is no hope for it, I suppose, except to face the possibility." He released a deeper sigh. "I never wanted the responsibilities that came as a result of my being born first."

He tilted his head from side to side, as though pondering how best to explain. "I suppose I didn't really mind being a marquess. The title certainly opened doors for me that might have been closed otherwise. But I was never comfortable with the notion that I needed to marry in order to provide an heir or that I needed to marry a woman of wealth in order to provide the much-needed fortune that my family lacked."

She squeezed his hand for reassurance. "I always sensed that you were uncomfortable with the money that would come to you through marriage to me."

"I was very uncomfortable with our situation and for many more reasons than simply that. I adore you, my sweet, but I've never loved you as you deserve to be loved."

She felt as though he'd closed his fist around her heart and squeezed it painfully until it could no longer beat.

"Weddington saw that from the very beginning. He urged me to be honest with you, to explain the ways of my heart, to release you, but I had those blasted responsibilities, you see. I *had* to marry. I *had* to marry a woman of wealth. Why not marry a woman I adored, even if I knew I'd never love her?"

With his confession, tears stung her eyes. He said Richard had known. She remembered Richard asking her how she'd feel if Nicky loved another. And she'd laughed, so certain of Nicky's affections for her. She dared to whisper, "Do you love someone else?"

If at all possible, his eyes filled with more sorrow. "Yes, I do. Very much."

"Will you marry her now?"

"Marriage is not an option for us. It never will be. But the more I saw of you and Weddington together, the more I came to realize that marriage shouldn't be an option for you and me either. And so, I devised an elaborate scheme to fake my own death."

Blinking, she stared at him. "Why didn't you simply tell me how you felt? I would have been hurt, but I would have hurt no more than I do now. I—"

"Because much more was at stake."

"So you put me through hell?" She lunged to her feet and faced him. "Do you have any idea how I mourned losing you?"

"Yes, Weddington told me. He even urged me to reconsider. To allow myself to be found washed up onshore. But I'm selfish, Kitty. I was free of the constraints of my title, and I didn't want to be shackled again."

"Your family—"

"Must never learn that I'm alive."

Spinning away from him, she began to pace. This was insanity. Unkind. Cruel even. She'd loved this man, thought he'd loved her. She faced him abruptly. "How can you cause them to suffer like this?"

"Because they would never approve of the life I wish to live. I don't think they could accept what I need in order to be happy. If I were unable to live up to the expectations of the title, I would bring them shame. It's better for their unhappiness to involve mourning my death rather than mourning my life."

"I can't believe you think they'd prefer that you were dead."

He shrugged. "For many years my wants have battled my obligations. *You* were the compromise. Someone with whom I thought I could be happy while still carrying through on my responsibilities."

"I was the compromise," she said quietly, testing the words, finding that she didn't much like them.

"Yes. As I said, I adore you. Weddington loves you."

Weddington had a damned strange way of showing his love. Not trusting her with the truth, allowing her to suffer.

"He agreed to this scheme to fake your death?"

"Reluctantly, but eventually, yes. It was the only way I'd give you up, you see? And he desperately wanted you to be happy. He truly believed you wouldn't be happy with me, and in all honesty, Kitty, I have to admit that I think he may have been quite right."

"Why didn't he simply tell me that you loved someone else?"

And then she remembered that he'd done just that—during their first meeting in her garden, and she hadn't believed him. She'd laughed at his absurd suggestion.

"Because he is a good friend. And years ago, when I confided in him, told him of the conflict within me, my fear of disappointing my family, bringing shame to my title, he swore to me that he'd never breathe a word of my confession to anyone. He's been true to that promise and been a much better friend to me than I've ever been to him."

"They arrested him."

"I know."

"They arrested him for murdering you, and you were alive!"

"Had he been found guilty, I would have revealed myself."

"How damned considerate!" She was shaking with anger that she didn't know where to put. Into his face was the only logical place. "You were standing in the crowds outside Parliament as well."

"Yes. How you always spot me, I haven't a clue."

He said it as though it were a joke. "We were in hell, Nicky. He, his mother, his sister, all of us. I loved him. Doubted him. Thought he'd killed you in order to have me. My God, do you have any idea how much I hurt him with my suspicions?"

"I know, and I'm terribly sorry. It was never my intention to hurt anyone. I knew you would mourn, but I also knew Weddington was near to offer comfort. It was indeed a tangled web, and I know discovering the deception is painful, but you must believe me when I say it is all for the best."

She scoffed in disbelief. "You hurt so many people."

"I am well aware of that fact. But I hurt them so much less than I might have. I draw comfort from that knowledge."

She shook her head. "The storm. How did you know you'd survive it?"

"Because I was never in it."

Oh, she wanted to hit him, to plow her fist into that fine patrician nose of his. "Richard was in the storm."

"Yes, but he wasn't supposed to be. I woke up that morning, saw the red sky, and thought if a storm did blow in, we'd take advantage of it. We took the boat out, making certain everyone saw us together. Once the sky began to darken, we sailed around to an isolated cove. A bit of smuggling, I suppose. His ancestry at its best. I disembarked. He took the boat back out. We'd hoped the storm would wait to hit, that he could get safely to shore under cover of darkness and pretend to have battled the storm. But storms aren't predictable. He'd only just begun to sink the boat when it hit."

"This is the most reckless, idiotic thing I've ever heard in my entire life!"

"I wanted freedom!"

"And you almost cost him his!"

"Which is the very reason I refrained from coming forward the instant he was arrested. To have risked so much, then to lose it all because of a moment of fear"—he clenched his fist—"I wasn't willing to chance it. Not until I knew for certain it was the only option."

She'd sacrificed her reputation because of his unwillingness to face his obligations. He'd risked lives, hurt hearts. How could she have ever thought she wanted to marry a man who'd do such things? And Richard had been an accomplice, which angered and hurt her as well.

"I don't understand how you think this deception will work," she stated incredulously, still unable to believe he'd schemed all this simply to avoid his duties. "I've spotted you. Others are bound to recognize you. You can't live your life in a hole."

He looked rather embarrassed. "I don't intend to. I'm going to America . . . with Freddie."

"Freddie? He knows you're alive?"

He nodded. "He was in on the plans. He'd performed on the stage for a while, you see. He gave Weddington a few tips on how to act convincingly while pretending or delivering a falsehood."

"Richard never actually said you'd drowned," she said with wonder. "He told me that you were gone."

"He's an exceedingly honorable man."

"Which is more than I can say for you."

He flinched. "Quite right."

She shook her head. "I can't believe there wasn't another way to acquire what you wanted."

"Perhaps there was, and I was merely too cowardly or too selfish to go that route."

"I thought we were so well suited," she said quietly. "I don't know if I can ever forgive you for putting me through this."

"You see, Kitty? It would have been far better to have always thought me dead. You should have purposely lost the tennis match, my sweet. And you would have never known the truth of my deception."

"And Richard's. And Freddie's. You weren't alone in it, Nicky."

"You mustn't blame them. They weren't responsible for the plan."

"But they helped you carry it out. Richard I can understand. He wanted to marry me. But Freddie? What in the world did he gain?"

"Not losing me."

With complete bewilderment, she shook her head. "That's ridiculous. He wouldn't have lost you. I like Freddie. He would have always been welcomed in our home."

"Kitty . . ." He hesitated, sighed. "Kitty, Freddie is the one I love."

She stared at him, trying to make sense of his words.

"You *love* Freddie?" she questioned in a whisper.

"Yes. And he loves me."

Surely he was not implying what she thought he was. "As a friend?"

"As much more." He held her gaze, and it was apparent to her that it was the hardest thing he'd ever done—to not look away from her shock and possible revulsion.

"But what of the attentions he gave Lady Priscilla?"

"Playacting, my sweet."

Tears stinging her eyes, she wrapped her arms tightly around herself and slowly sank to the ground, her knees unable to support her. Nicky rushed forward, and she held up her hands. "No, don't touch me."

He crouched before her, tears in his eyes. "Do you see now that I really did my family a kindness? How could I *not* marry when my family was in such dire need of funds? How *could* I marry when my heart belonged to another? My brother now holds the title. He will marry an heiress. My family is spared any embarrassment or pain that might have come about should my true feelings ever be discovered.

"Nor would I have been able to bear them turning away from me—as Freddie's family turned from him. You loved me, Kitty. And yet here you are, weeping, not wanting me to touch you, probably wishing you didn't know all that you now know. I'm the same man I always was. Only now you view me differently. Few people can accept different. I was most fortunate that Weddington was the sort of friend who accepted the truth of who I am without judgment."

"He risked everything, Nicky."

"I am well aware of that, Kitty. We set into motion events that were terribly difficult to stop. We hurt people, we hurt you. And in a way, I suppose, we hurt each other. Weddington was right that we shouldn't have kept our plans from you. He sought to be loyal to me, while striving to love you and keep you happy. In the end, he felt he had to choose, and he chose you, knowing that once you learned the truth, he might lose you. He didn't feel he'd gained you honestly, and he was weary of the deception."

"What will you do in America?"

He offered her a small smile, probably pleased that she still cared enough for him to wonder what he might do. "Freddie and I hope to settle in New York. They have excellent theaters there. We'll write plays together. I shall change my name and hope we never acquire worldwide acclaim that might cause anyone to recognize me and undo all that we've worked so hard to accomplish."

"You have everything planned out."

"I've dreamed of this for so very long, Kitty, but I never dared hope that I'd actually be able to achieve the happiness that always eluded me just beyond the horizon. Now all that stops me is you."

"Me?"

"I revealed all without asking for a promise in return. You could go to my family and tell them the truth."

She shook her head. "It's not my place, Nicky."

She realized that Richard must have felt the same. That it wasn't his place to reveal the truth about Farthingham. Not even to her.

"I thank you for that sentiment," he said quietly.

"What if the storm hadn't come in?"

"Freddie would have moved to America. I would never have seen him again. I would have married you, and we might have been content. But we deserve more than contentment in life, I think."

"I simply don't understand how you could love Freddie in that way."

"I don't understand either. When Weddington and I were young men, we would go to brothels together. He would stay all night, which I doubt he'll appreciate me telling you. I, on the other hand, was ready to leave as soon as I'd looked the selection over. I can't explain it. I don't expect you to understand, but when I'm with Freddie I'm happy. No pretense, no playacting. With Freddie I am always exactly who I truly am."

More tears surfaced in her eyes.

"It's not a sad thing, Kitty. Most people search their entire lives for what I have with Freddie. They die never having found it."

She shook her head. "I wasn't thinking that it was sad. I was thinking that's how I feel with Richard." Reaching out, she took his hand and leaned toward him. "Nicky, there are things about me that I never told you. Secrets. Dark secrets that I always kept buried deep within me. But I told Richard. I told him everything. At the time, I felt as though it was the most natural thing in all the world."

He squeezed her hand, and she realized that holding his hand felt natural as well. But not in the same way it did with Richard. Never as it did with Richard.

"I still care about you, Nicky. I don't know if I understand every-thing you've told me. But I do still love you. You were my first love."

"But not your last I hope."

Rather than answer him, she glanced around. "It's getting dark."

"Yes, I should walk you back to shore."

He helped her to her feet.

"How will you get off the island?" she asked.

"Freddie's waiting with a boat, hidden away where you can't see him, but I can find him."

"Will you write me from time to time?"

"Of course, my sweet. Look for letters from Nicholas Farthing."

They walked back to the shore, hand in hand. There was comfort in his nearness, just as there had always been, the comfort of a friend, not a lover. It was only now that she was beginning to understand what Richard had been trying to tell her, to show her all along. Being with Nicky was very much what she suspected it would be like to be with one's brother.

Then she spotted Richard, standing at the water's edge, gazing out to sea. Preparing to face the murky, choppy waters that terrified him. The unforgiving sea that had taken his father from him, that had injured him in ways few people realized, twisting his back until he was in agony, torturing his mind with doubt, with the inability to accept that there was nothing he could have done to prevent his father's death.

He'd faced it time and again. When he swam at dawn, when he took his yachts out onto the water. For Farthingham, he'd faced it at its worst, with the tempest roaring down on him. He'd done it out of friendship and loyalty to Nicky, out of desire for her. And perhaps more than desire. For his love of her and his wish to see her happy, regardless of the cost to himself.

He couldn't have known when he embraced Nicky's plan that Kitty would become pregnant with his child, couldn't have known for certain that she would be the prize, or that storms would still have to be faced.

"I've been so unfair to him, Nicky. I held him responsible for your death."

"I know."

"He's always terrified me."

"He's a good man, Kitty. The very best I could have in a friend."

"I understand that now. But he makes me feel things. He stirs to life these strong physical urges that frighten me."

Nicky smiled sadly. "Those urges are natural, Kitty. They're wonderful, actually, to be savored. Not everyone has the fortune to meet someone who can make them as powerful as they have the potential to become."

"I'm going to miss you."

"Only for a short while, my sweet. Then you'll be too busy with all the children I'm certain Weddington would like to bestow on you."

"Be happy, Nicky."

Nicky leaned toward her and placed a kiss on her forehead. "I would wish you the same, Kitty, but I know Weddington well, and I have no doubt he will see to it that you're happy. The man likes to control everything, including happiness. So there is no need for me to wish for you to find it. I suspect it's there already if you only look."

Tears stung her eyes as she hugged him tightly, one last time, a man she now realized she'd hardly known. He'd brought smiles, laughter, and a safe harbor into her life, and she'd thought it enough.

There was comfort in a safe harbor, but more excitement in the storm.

She left Nicky there and walked across the sand, leaving her footsteps behind until she reached Richard.

He turned his head slightly and looked down on her as though he were almost surprised that she'd returned to his side. "Did you find what you were searching for?"

"Yes, I believe I did. I wish there was a way to go home without traveling on the sea."

"There isn't."

"But the sea terrifies you."

"Not as much as the possibility of never possessing your heart. Are you leaving it here in Farthingham's keeping?"

Reaching up, she cradled his face. "Oh, Richard, how can you know so much about what I need to be happy and not know that I love you?"

With a groan, he drew her to him and kissed her, hard, thoroughly, passionately. Then he moved his mouth to her throat. "I was so afraid, Kitty. So afraid when you found out what we'd done that I'd lose all hope of ever truly having you as mine." He braced his hands on either side of her face and held her gaze. "I wanted to tell you that night. When I saw your pain. In the bathhouse, I thought if I could only make you forget it"—he shook his head—"I would do anything for you. You have but to ask."

"Will you make me scream?"

He laughed. "Every night if you wish."

"Oh, Richard, I never would have been happy with Nicky." She was as guilty as he for the tangled web that had been woven. "I realized it the night before the storm. I'd made the decision in the early hours before dawn to tell Nicky that I couldn't marry him."

"Why?"

"Because I'd come to realize that I loved you."

He brought her back up against him, and she felt the shudder ripple through him. "Doubts have plagued me for so long that you were mine only because Farthingham was not yours."

"I promise you'll never again doubt my love."

"Will you be happy with me?"

Standing up on tiptoe, she wound her arms around his neck and right before she kissed him, she whispered. "I already am."

Epilogue

The package was delivered to Kitty in the drawing room. A sense of gladness filled her as she opened it, removed the letter, and began reading.

My dearest Kitty,

It is difficult to believe that five years have passed. I know I have been negligent in writing, and I beg your forgiveness for my inconsiderateness. As Weddington can attest, I'm often more inconsiderate than I am considerate.

Be that as it may, at long last here is the letter I promised.

I must confess that I love New York, far better than I ever did England. Those with old money, Knickerbockers they're called, are as pompous as our aristocracy, and I enjoy them. Freddie and I have been welcomed into the fold—quite an accomplishment from what I gather.

But then everyone in New York seeks to welcome us. We are quite the toast of the town. Our play has turned into a smashing success, much to our utter astonishment. Our secret remains safe. People believe us to be only writing partners, and we've come to accept that there are very few people who will ever truly know us.

Give my best to Weddington and to those sons of yours. I saw the announcements of their births in The Times. *Yes, we actually receive it here, late, but better than not at all.*

You and Weddington must come visit us sometime. I can find no one here who will wager with me as eagerly as Wed-

dington did. But then again, neither have I found a truer friend.

Freddie sends his best. We've enclosed a little gift for you—our latest play. We hope you'll enjoy it.

Take care, my sweet. You're never far from my heart.

Nicky

Kitty pressed the letter against her breast. *Oh, Nicky.* How she missed him.

She pulled the play out of the box, curled up in her chair and, with a laugh, began to read.

Invitation to Seduction
Written by Frederick Montague
and Nicholas Farthing
Act 1

Scene 1: The Cornish coast. A man stands on the shore. Enter a lovely young woman . . .

Richard heard his wife's laughter long before he entered the drawing room. He'd left his sons, ages four and two, under the close supervision of their nanny to play with the latest batch of spaniel puppies.

"Now that is a sound I enjoy hearing, second only to your screams," Richard announced as he approached.

She snapped up her head, wiped tears from her cheeks, and smiled at him with boundless love in her eyes. Her affections toward him always humbled him. When he'd sought her love, he'd not realized how very much she had to give.

"I received a letter from Farthingham." She shook her head. "I suppose I shouldn't call him that."

"No, you shouldn't," he said, as he sat in the chair beside her. "What mischief is he up to?"

"Success apparently. He and Freddie have written a successful play. It's quite good. You'll have to read it."

"I suppose I shall at that."

She set the papers aside, rose to her feet, sat on his lap, and wound her arms around his neck. "He wants us to come visit."

"That is a long journey on the sea, but we shall go if you like."

"Would it terrify you to go?"

"Only if in the going, I risked losing you."

"You shall never lose me. I love you, Richard. I love you more each day. It terrifies me sometimes, to love you so much, and to think that I might have never loved you at all."

"There was little chance of that happening, my darling. I told you shortly after we met that I was not a man who easily gave up when he determined that he wanted something, and I wanted you."

"I'm ever so glad you did."

Bringing her lips nearer to his, he whispered, "As am I."